CELEBRANT

SON OF NO MAN SERIES

BOOK 2

SON OF NO MAN SERIES
Celebrant
BOOK 2

D. LAMBERT

Celebrant
Son of No Man Series Book 2
Copyright © 2021-2024 D. Lambert. All rights reserved.

Published By: 4 Horsemen Publications, Inc.

4 Horsemen Publications, Inc.
PO Box 417
Sylva, NC 28779
4horsemenpublications.com
info@4horsemenpublications.com

Cover and Typesetting by Valerie Willis
Editor Amanda Miller

All rights to the work within are reserved to the author and publisher. No part of this publication may be reproduced, stored in a retrieval system, or transmitted in any form or by any means, electronic, mechanical, photocopying, recording, scanning, or otherwise, except as permitted under Section 107 or 108 of the 1976 International Copyright Act, without prior written permission except in brief quotations embodied in critical articles and reviews. Please contact either the Publisher or Author to gain permission.

All characters, organizations, and events portrayed in this novel are either products of the author's imagination or are used fictitiously.

All brands, quotes, and cited work respectfully belongs to the original rights holders and bear no affiliation to the authors or publisher.

Library of Congress Control Number: 2021948920

Paperback ISBN: 978-1-64450-404-8
Hardcover ISBN: 978-1-64450-503-8
Audio ISBN: 978-1-64450-402-4
E-Book ISBN: 978-1-64450-403-1

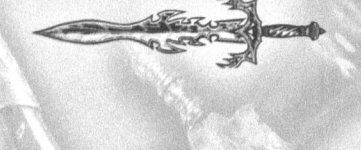

To my sister Rachel,
for inspiring my love of writing

Table of Contents

Chapter 1	1
Chapter 2	21
Chapter 3	36
Chapter 4	52
Chapter 5	71
Chapter 6	82
Chapter 7	103
Chapter 8	120
Chapter 9	136
Chapter 10	153
Chapter 11	171
Chapter 12	195
Chapter 13	207
Chapter 14	218
Chapter 15	228
Chapter 16	245
Sneak Peek of Northlander	257
Chapter 1	259
Glossary	263
Author Bio	269
Book Club Questions	271

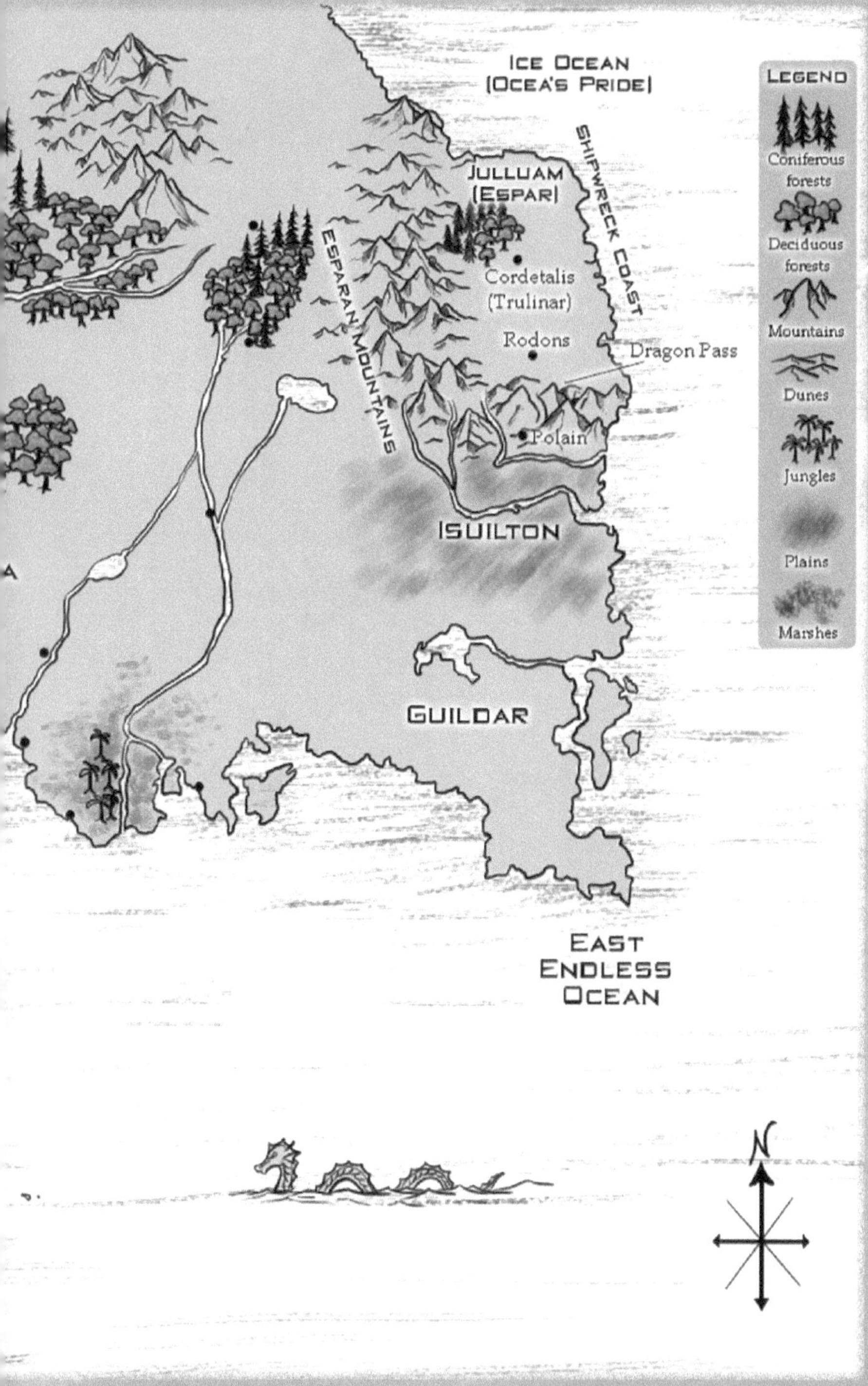

Ice Ocean (Ocea's Pride)

Shipwreck Coast

Julluam (Espar)

- Cordetalis (Trulinar)
- Rodons
- Dragon Pass
- Polain

Esparan Mountains

Isuilton

Guildar

East Endless Ocean

Legend

- Coniferous forests
- Deciduous forests
- Mountains
- Dunes
- Jungles
- Plains
- Marshes

"The fires of the soul burn brightest under conflict."

- Loni Firedancer,
Celebrant of Inac

Chapter 1

"Good idea," Darak said behind Tohmas. "Your arm will get weak if you don't use it regularly. I usually recommend things that are a little less fragile. Be a shame to break it."

Tohmas placed the glass orb he had been fiddling with atop his folded, green tunic on the large table. Master Kitable had warned breaking the sphere would defend against hostile magic and warn Kitable about the attack. Cutter Darak was right; he did not want to break it prematurely.

Tohmas' shoulder panged as the cutter tightened the bandage, having replaced the moss bandages with fresh ones. The arrow wound bled surprisingly little, but he had a bruise from his arm to the middle of his back because of it.

"I had noticed it was slow," he said. Truthfully, his left arm screamed in pain if he moved it. He found it hard to grip a weapon and could not lift anything beyond his dagger. His natural tendency was for his left hand, but he had trained to use his right to better fit in among the Esparan. He hated to think he would have to rely on it, knowing his left was faster, stronger, and less expected.

"Three days since you got shot in the back, and you're surprised that your shoulder hurts? You've not been sparring, have you?" the cutter demanded, interrupting the prince in a way few dared. The cutter glared at Carsh, who was perched on a nearby chair back. Tohmas' prime protector fiddled with a knife, weaving it over his fingers, much like Tohmas had the orb. "Did you spar? Prime Protector, your duty is to defend this stubborn oaf, even from himself!"

Carsh gave a sharp-toothed grin that looked demonic in the light of the lamp hanging from the central post. The small candle atop Inac's altar flickered behind him, heightening the sinister look.

Rydans were not known for holding back. Darak may not have realized it, but Tohmas' upbringing among the Rydans was the main reason he hid the discomfort of his wound. But he saw no reason to explain that.

"I have to be fit when we meet Northlanders, Darak," he answered. "For the moment, that means I am behaving myself. To a point, of course."

"To a point?" The bandage now secure around the prince's entire shoulder, Cutter Darak pulled a pot from his pocket and applied an ointment on Tohmas' exposed back.

"Yes, Darak, to a point. Are you quite finished?"

"You have a rather impressive number of scars that—"

"My scars are fine. They have not grieved me yet, and I do not expect them to grieve me in the future." Despite the continued administrations, Tohmas stood.

"Alright, alright," Cutter Darak said in surrender, not tall enough to reach Tohmas' scarred shoulders without Tohmas being seated. He presented a handful of pills to the prince, but Tohmas shook his head.

"I promise to recover without your herbs. I will not upset your reputation, I assure you." When he crossed his arms, the statement was final. The cutter replaced the pills into one of his voluptuous pockets then adjusted his collar where the pressed flower denoting his service to the God Pari was pinned.

"As you wish, my Prince," Darak said with an undisguised roll of his eyes. He shoved his tools unceremoniously into various pockets as he added, "If you want to improve the use of your arm—"

Carsh leaped from his seat, toppling the chair behind him and drawing a second knife instantly. Tohmas joined him, forgetting about his wound and drawing his sword. Fiery agony shot from his neck to his fingers. He swapped his sword to his right hand, ready despite the pain to deal with whatever Carsh had detected.

Nothing happened.

Chapter 1

Darak cleared his throat into the ensuing silence. "I was going to suggest a coin," he said awkwardly. "It will keep your fingers from getting tired and make you look important at the same time. Or do Rydans have an aversion to coins? Don't tell me I offended him!"

Tohmas' eyes were on Carsh, who was poised like a mountain cat about to pounce.

"*Flya*," the Rydan hissed.

He'd sensed nearby magic, Tohmas translated. There was a caster nearby, but while Carsh would consider it a threat, Tohmas was less concerned. Most wizards he knew were allies or at least claimed to be.

Tohmas straightened slowly, letting his sword lower.

"No offense," he told the cutter. "Good night, Darak."

"Good night, my Prince." With another bow of his head, Cutter Darak left, followed by his old dog, Stitches, carrying a bone Carsh had tossed her.

As the cutter left, a protector stuck his head through the tent flap. "Prime Protector Severin for you," he said.

Explains Carsh's reaction.

The bodyguard waited for Tohmas' reply. Despite the wizard's known allegiance to Prince Sol, Tohmas' uncle and ally, Tohmas contemplated refusing. His life in the Outlands, where casters were considered manipulative killers, had made it difficult to get past an inherent distrust of them. He hardly knew Master Clarin, as the Prime Protector of Solta was commonly known, and was not convinced that the master wizard merited his rank as Prince Sol's top defender.

Besides, Master Kitable also despised Clarin, and Kitable was as Esparan as could be. Although Kitable was known for hating people in general, particularly other wizards, he had also confided that Clarin had once tried to sneak into Kitable's personal vardo. As Clarin was now politely requesting entrance into Tohmas' tent, he must have learned from the event.

Master Clarin had probably traveled by Relocation from Prince Sol's besieged city facing the Northlander hoards, and he was likely needed back on the front. Waiting could leave Prince Sol at risk. Tohmas did not want to arrive to his uncle's rescue too late.

"Fine. Let him in," Tohmas said. He forced himself to put away his sword.

Carsh did not. He kept two daggers on hand, one long for stabbing and one short for throwing.

Master Clarin did not have to duck through the entrance of the canvas tent, being nearly two heads shorter than Tohmas. Dressed smartly in red and black boasting of Prince Sol's patronage, the balding man had spectacles perched on his nose and a girth under his belt. Tohmas doubted the man knew how to smile, his premature wrinkles deepest around his perpetual expression of confused annoyance.

Carsh snarled at him, and Clarin visibly flinched back. Not only was the Rydan Prince Tohmas' last defense, he also had a reputation as the deadliest man in Tohmas' service. Further, Carsh had an absolute hatred for wizards that even Master Kitable had failed to mollify.

"Relax," Tohmas told his prime protector. "We are among allies." He did not use the word "friends." But Tohmas' Princedom of Galanth needed Solta if they wanted to stop the invasion of Northlanders. Tonight, Solta was represented by Clarin.

Every movement amplified by hesitation, Carsh slowly sat on another chair, leaving his felled one on the ground. His eyes never left Clarin.

Clarin ostensibly avoided the stare of the Rydan and looked at Tohmas. His mouth dropped open, and he blurted, "You were shot?"

Tohmas smothered a smile. *Not precisely correct etiquette,* he mused.

"I am fine, thank you, Master Clarin. What can I do for you? Since you have sent yourself quite the distance to seek me out, I presume it is important." Leaving the orb and the blood-stained tunic— he had soaked through his shirt—on the table, he opened one of the many storage chests that lined the walls of his tent. Their bases thick with the mud of the last four princedoms he had marched his men through, they worked well to keep out the draft coming off the nearby river. His cot stood between two chests for the same reasons, a heap of furs piled on it. Nights were chillier in the far north, even summer nights.

He threw a new tunic over his head. The wounded shoulder took effort to maneuver into the sleeve, but he managed it without assistance.

"I..." The wizard forced words past the lump in his throat as Tohmas sat at the table and rested a hand on the orb. "I am to welcome you to Solta. We have been expecting you. My prince eagerly awaits your arrival in BellRoost. "

Chapter 1

Master Clarin's eyes stayed on the enchanted orb. Tohmas wondered what he saw in it.

"*Yadder, yadder*," Carsh grumbled.

"I do hope you have more to say than that," Tohmas said to translate the Rydan's dismissal. "I don't consider a welcome urgent. In fact, I could have done without it. But since you are here, would you like a drink, Master Clarin?" Tohmas indicated the seat closest to the door. He might as well make the most of the situation.

The invitation stunned the wizard to silence for another moment before he stuttered, "I am honored."

Carsh stared at Tohmas, his expression frustrated. Tohmas lifted his good hand to his prime protector in request.

Realization dawned on the Rydan's face, and he tossed Tohmas the wineskin from the table. Tohmas filled two cups with the wildwater Carsh had been rationing through the march, knowing full well the Esparan wizard had never tasted anything like it. Nowhere in Espar made the drink, and the Rydans hoarded their shares.

Clarin accepted the cup, his wide stare scanning the room. "Is Master Kitable not joining us, Prince Tohmas?" he asked as he took a seat on the edge of his chair, unable to relax under Carsh's critical stare.

"He has been busy of late. I can call him, but I would rather not disturb him."

"No, it's nothing important. I would like to meet with him later, but I do not want to interrupt anything."

"Then what actually brings you all the way out to the edges of your princedom, Master Clarin?" Tohmas asked, downing his drink in a single swallow. Carsh, showing an unprecedented gesture of acceptance, took a swig from the wineskin. The prime protector's green eyes never left Clarin, and neither hand put down the knife they held, but he drank.

He was goading the wizard into trying the wildwater.

"DoomDragon," Clarin said, eyeing the tar-like contents of the cup. Visibly steeling his nerves, he swallowed the contents in one gulp as they had.

The rest of his answer was lost entirely. It was hard to say if he would cough or throw up first; he retched then swallowed hard. Although he resisted, he coughed harshly. Tears came to his eyes.

"What, by the hells, was that?"

Celebrant

Without turning, Tohmas extended a hand, and Carsh passed him the wineskin again. He retrieved Clarin's emptied cup.

"Rydan wildwater," Tohmas explained with a polite smile, ignoring Clarin's continuing hacking. "One shot makes your head swim, and two makes you go blind. More?"

Clarin shook his hands and head avidly.

"Gods, no! Do you..."

Tohmas grabbed a different wineskin from the chest behind him and tossed it over. "Water."

Yanking out the stopper, Clarin poured the water down his throat between spurting coughs. It would help in the long run, but it was too late to completely rid himself of the taste or the effect of the wildwater.

"DoomDragon?" Tohmas prompted once Clarin stopped gulping the water. "You were saying something about DoomDragon and his Northlanders?"

Clarin blinked hard. His slurred words confirmed the wildwater had hit his head already. "He is coming for you. Split the forces outside of BellRoost. Is marching half this way," he choked out.

"All of Espar knows we marched north from Galanth to meet him. If he didn't know I was coming, I would be disappointed."

"But to split his men? To come after..." Clarin squinted with the effort of thinking. "You do not seem upset, Prince Tohmas. I came to warn you, but..." He trailed off, unable to finish the sentence as he got distracted by his cup. He attempted to pick it up, grabbing at the air to the left of it then to the right.

"I suspected he would try to catch us before we reach BellRoost. Anything else?" The man did not have his wits about him; this was an excellent opportunity to see what the wizard knew.

"You knew?" Clarin snapped, his eyes wide as he looked up.

"I knew it was a possibility." Tohmas went back to the chest he left open and retrieved a rolled parchment. "I can handle it," he told Clarin as he spread the map before the wizard. "Where are they?"

Clarin concentrated on the map as if willing it to hold still long enough for him to recognize a landmark. At length, his finger landed on DancingIce River and followed it down to the city of BellRoost, where Prince Sol had set his most recent northern border. With effort, he tapped his finger down hard as if to pin the map to the table.

Chapter 1

"BellRoost?"

"Well, they *were* there. They left this morning, heading east. Master Kitable should give you specif...an idea. My Scrying...my magic...it doesn›t always...it›s limited.»

Tohmas leaned over the map, running his mind along the river then to the east. "Leaving things this late, they'll be running for Barrow Hills."

Clarin sat bolt upright. "You know about the Hills?" He snapped his mouth shut with the next breath and flushed, although it was hard to say if it was embarrassment or regret.

"I do try to learn what I can about territories I am crossing, Master Clarin. Barrow Hills was identified as a good holding site as well as an ideal ambush location."

Sitting back carefully, Clarin pouted. His eyes rocked as if he were on a ship in rough seas. His words lilted similarly. "You should get there before DoomDragon. It should be easy enough from your current pah...po...from where you are now. You're outnumbered badly. A strong spot could—"

"I do not need lectures on warfare, Master Clarin. I appreciate what the Hills offer. I had expected DoomDragon and his Northlanders to be closer along by now, that is all," Tohmas said, his voice cool.

"He probably hasn't got...I mean, doesn't know that you are aware of his app... his...him coming. He won't expect you to be all that hurried. We need you alive when you reach BellRoost. Did that make *any* sense?»

"Is that all, Master Clarin? What about the casters, the Northlander Circle?"

Clarin shrugged and nearly tipped over. "Nothing seen for quite a bit. But DoomDragon—"

"I know where he is, and I know what I am going to do about it, wizard. If there is nothing else for you to add..."

Clarin slowly leaned forward, his brow pulled low. "Unless you can convince your hermit wizard to come out..."

"I will not press him needlessly," Tohmas refused.

"...then there is nothing left...else, I mean...I guess. I..."

Tohmas scooped up the wizard under the arms, a little surprised he could touch the man without magic intervening. But Clarin was known to be Kitable's lesser. Nothing stopped him from easing Master Clarin to the exit.

"Thank you, Master Clarin. Tell Prince Sol I will be seeing him soon."

He handed the wizard off to the protectors outside.

With the map still on the table, Tohmas and Carsh sat in silence until Carsh finally settled back and put away one of his knives. Clarin must have officially departed.

"*Stye ged?*" Carsh asked.

"*Ohnennohn*," Tohmas replied in Rydan, happy to speak his native tongue. "If DoomDragon can find me in Gaidol to arrange an ambush, he knows where we are. If both of us are running for the Hills, I don't know who will get there first. I just hope Kitable managed to hide what he's doing."

His adopted brother grinned wickedly.

He looked at the map again, drawing the line to Barrow Hills in his mind. Clarin was right; the Hills were a good holding position. By calling up the companions, the reserves of each city, Tohmas had assembled all the Fyrds of Galanth. He had also invited freemen to join with every stop along their march, bringing the total of his forces to just over four thousand men.

But he had less than a quarter of DoomDragon's forces. He could use a defensive position like Barrow Hills.

DoomDragon of the Northlands was smart enough to predict the plan. Tohmas had every intention of using that to his advantage.

Was Clarin expecting him to heed the advice blindly? Tohmas was no stranger to war, but the Esparans did not know that. Neither did DoomDragon and his Northlanders.

"I'll get them to drag," Tohmas decided. They had marched swiftly through all the other princedoms, but it was time to slow down. The tricky part would be making it look like they were still moving at pace. If DoomDragon realized Tohmas was letting him get ahead, he would be suspicious.

A good prince did not always use soldiers for everything.

Lance Carraway nearly hit his head as he passed through the small door of the BackAlley pub. The entrance had once been topped by an ornate arch, but a fight or siege years ago had smashed the top of the frame,

Chapter 1

leaving it short. Instead of replacing the arching shape of engraved dragons and horses, the owner had simply dropped a board across it. Entering now made a normal man feel like he was crawling between battlements. The unfriendly exterior deterred most visitors.

After going down the three steps and through the broken doorway, Lance drew stares with every step he took into the quiet room. He avoided the eyes of the other occupants, not wanting to recognize anyone and be forced into a conversation. From behind his bar, Gavin opened his mouth, likely to comment on the blue and white tabard Lance wore to identify himself as a Guardsman of Gaidol. Before a word escaped, he snapped his mouth shut. With a nod of acceptance, he indicated one of the alcoves, and Lance found his way to the concealed seat. Guardsmen who wanted to keep their reputations were never seen talking to Gavin and certainly not while in uniform. Lance was flattered the older veteran was trying to protect him.

The back of the BackAlley pub extended under the arches of a bridge that had been decommissioned when the river was drained to make room for the growing capital, SwordWood. Three small alcoves expanded the room, and thanks to the grungy curtains over the openings, provided privacy.

Left in peace, Lance took a seat in his alcove.

He had one night before he was to return to the city he had been assigned. One night to sort his mind through the changes. Some part of him thought he should take a longer road to Varidee and try to meet up with at least one of his brothers, but he did not have the heart for it. He feared what they would say. By now, they already knew what had happened to the eldest Carraway brother at the hands of one of the younger ones.

He had not decided on a course by the time the curtain to the alcove was drawn aside, and a familiar voice said, "You look like a man who needs a drink."

Lance sat upright sharply. "Gods above, Father! How did I not...?" He trailed off. The stairs behind his father were full; all eight of his brothers now occupied the stairwell that led to the upper floor of the BackAlley pub.

Gavin waved from the bar, grinning.

Celebrant

Lance's father sat at the table, wearing a serious expression. He placed a mug between them. "Most guardsmen, especially a high guardsman, would notice when the barkeep sends a runner upstairs as soon as they walk in," Hiron Carraway said. "We've been here two days, thinking you'd show up before heading out. Good thing I was right." He pushed the drink to Lance and reached for his own as if in demonstration. There, he waited.

Had Lance wanted all nine men gone, he could refuse the mug. Hiron had always made it clear that any son of his had the choice.

Despite fearing what they would say, not knowing was worse. Lance grabbed the mug and swallowed a large mouthful of dark ale. He had come into the BackAlley because he thought his family too distant. They were exactly the company he needed.

"I am a man in need of sharing a drink," he admitted.

The brothers released their collective breath. The alcove was too small, so they rearranged the tables nearby to provide enough seating for all ten Carraway family members.

"We'll put it back, Gavin," Hiron called at the barkeeper's sour expression.

"Whatever you say, Hiron," Gavin shouted back, and the curious stares of the other occupants of BackAlley abruptly turned away. Lance's father's name was still known.

Once the family had settled, Hiron asked, "So, is it true? You armed the city?"

The memories of WaterBranch were mostly pleasant. Lance had made good friends during his mission there.

"Armed and trained them. I had no other support, so I had to make some. Good people. They're running the city now."

Hiron's face fell slightly. "He sent you in alone?"

Lance's father did not need to specify who "he" was. Lance had gone to WaterBranch on Prince Dorakon's orders, the same man to whom Lance had sworn his life to more than a decade before. In this house of ears, Lance thought it wise to avoid saying the name aloud.

"Yes, alone, to kill High Guardsman Vont," Lance said. He swallowed more of the ale, finding it more bitter than usual. He was not the only one of the brothers to wear a dark frown at Baran Carraway's assumed name. "Father, Baran had made a pact with Trulin," Lance

 # CHAPTER 1

explained. The mention of the enemy princedom to the north made all the brothers sit straighter. "Baran promised them the port city in return for help taking SwordWood from Prince Dorakon. He brought together mercenaries and Truller riders and was building boats to carry them up the river to SwordWood. I had to stop him, Father. I tried talking to him, but he—"

Hiron raised his hand, and Lance stopped cold.

"Baran stopped being a son in this family the moment he betrayed his oath to Prince Dorakon," the patriarch of the family said.

It did not feel so simple to Lance, but he tried to believe his father's words. A sinking feeling crept deeper inside him.

"Then I may yet stop being a son in this family," Lance replied bleakly.

He dared not meet his father's eyes and instead stared at the mug he had been given. The wood nearest the handle had been worn to smoothness, but more than one overenthusiastic patron had gouged dents into the far lip, exposing the raw, light grain. A crest had once been etched in the side, but it had long since faded, too indistinct to be recognized.

Hiron Carraway had spent his life ingraining his sons with the meaning of loyalty. For them to survive, there could be no doubt of their devotion to the land of Gaidol and its prince. Lance had meant his oath to Prince Dorakon, but now he felt it slipping away.

"Lance?" his father prompted.

Again, Lance did not say the name. "He treats us like traitors no matter what we do. I have spent every moment of my life trying to show him that he needs not fear or hate us, but nothing changes. I slew my own brother at his order, and yet he showed no remorse, no gratitude. He did not even mention it! As if he had sent me to simply fetch his horse, not stop a rebel guardsman from overthrowing him. He chose me because I was Baran's brother, damn it. Because no matter what happened between us, he would win. Because, in the end, he didn't trust either of us."

Lance dragged his eyes up. While his brothers stood with mouths agape at his confessions, Hiron sat calmly. Lance had seen his father lose his temper only once over the course of his life. Today was not an exception. "He trusts you, Lance. He would not have placed you as a high guardsman if he did not," his father said, his long moustache bristling.

Celebrant

Among the remaining nine sons, four were guardsmen. Only Lance had achieved the rank of high guardsman.

Lance laughed, and it was as bitter as the ale. His secrets broke free of their bindings.

He leaned over the table and spoke between gritted teeth to keep from shouting. "You know why he did that? Because it was the fastest way to get me out of SwordWood when he figured out that his daughter wants to spend her life with me instead of him."

Silence landed as sudden as a horse's kick. Lance finished the mug of ale vindictively as he waited for what his father, the man who had always preached obedience and propriety, could possibly say calmly in answer.

Hiron said nothing for a long, callous moment. The brothers exchanged glances, ready to let someone else comment first. To lay an unapproved hand on the prince's daughter was treason and punishable by starvation. If Hiron thought betraying one's oath was cause enough to disown Baran, Lance thought himself at least equally as damned.

But instead of anger, his brothers slowly started to smile. One by one, smirks cut through their surprise. Suggestive grins were passed around until Lance's youngest brother, Anrive, burst out laughing and declared, "Here I was thinking you'd never marry!"

The insanity of it struck Lance, and he too had to smile. The Carraway sons had spent their lives walking the perfect line of loyalty to Gaidol. He had been assigned as one of Lady Valia's personal guardsmen for years when the single most unpredictable thing had happened: he fell in love with her. All the training in the world could not have prepared Lance for the woman Valia had become.

But there was no hope for them. Lance could not win Dorakon's approval, no matter what he did. Valia might one day marry a high guardsman, but it would never be Lance.

With a sad shake of his head, Lance joined his brothers as, one by one, they chuckled. Even Hiron was smiling when he prompted Lance, "Do I dare ask if he has the right to peg you to a starvation post, Lance?"

The chuckles faded in anticipation.

"I would never sully her reputation," Lance said, and several of his brothers gave groans of disappointment. They hushed when Hiron glared over his shoulder. "I would go my entire life without laying a

 # Chapter 1

hand on her if it meant keeping her safe, I swear." He sobered his voice. "But it's there, Father. And since it's there, I need to be somewhere else."

"Varidee?" Hiron suggested. It was where Dorakon expected him to go. It was his village to command.

Lance shook his head. Too much had happened. In dealing with Prince Tohmas of Galanth, Prince Dorakon had showed his true nature once more. Lance knew his heart was no longer under the command of the Prince of Gaidol at all.

For the first time in his life, Lance did not care who heard him. "Did you know that to win a bet he made with the Prince of Galanth, he allowed a band of Rydans to enter Gaidol? He hired them to harass the Galanth forces, just so Prince Tohmas would break his oath. It was a peaceful crossing! The Rydans murdered an entire village and framed the visiting prince for it. All for a bet! Hundreds of people died because he could not play fair." Lance let his words settle for moment before adding, "I can't stay in Gaidol, Father. I can't see the difference between myself and Baran right now. Maybe you'll only have eight sons by the end of this evening."

Again, silence settled. His brothers stared at him, the admissions shaking them visibly.

"Demon shit," Hiron said. His voice was as even as ever, but the curse startled Lance to attention. Hiron frowned and demanded, "You planning on taking over Gaidol, are you?"

Lance baulked, feeling pale. "Of course not!"

"Then tell your prince that you and your guardsmen will follow the Prince of Galanth on loan. Go burn off that doubt, make sure you don't fall on any swords, and come home. Simple."

Lance stared through his father, trying to place himself at the side of the Prince of Galanth. Northlanders were invading Espar. There would be battles enough to keep his head—and his heart—busy.

He let himself smile slightly but had to shake his head. "He will never agree."

Hiron shrugged. "I've still got friends in SwordWood. I'll let him think it's his idea. In the meantime..." he pivoted his head to count his sons, "we are going to travel."

"Travel?" Anrive echoed, his voice a groan.

Celebrant

Hiron's expression was stern, and Lance knew he was not the only one of his brothers to suddenly feel uncomfortable. Only once before, when a guardsman had suggested Lance's mother still harbored plans to take back Gaidol in her family's name, had Lance heard this tone in his father's voice. Lance had been too young to remember what happened to the guardsman who dared question the loyalty of the Carraway family, but it made most of his brothers flinch when it came up in conversation.

"Do you think I failed to notice the spies following us?" Hiron asked. He gave each son a firm glare. "Or the assassins who took positions near you each when Baran broke his oath? I will not have anyone threatening this family." His gaze ended on Lance. "Lance, do what you have to. We will be here for you when you get back, that I swear."

"And may the gods have mercy on any who tries to keep you from us," Anrive added. By the nods around him, he spoke for every one of the brothers. "Go get them, big brother."

Lance surveyed them, grateful. He was the second youngest among them, yet they considered him an equal. An oath was sacred among them. And Lance finally had a way around breaking his.

The family finished their drinks in companionable chatter, their levity letting Gavin come by with additional drinks. Once the night was spent, they put the tables back. Lance saw his family out with a hug to each of them, and the Carraways dispersed into the warm evening.

In the morning, Lance heeded a summons from Prince Dorakon and presented himself in the grand hall. He was unsurprised to be given an order to return to the Prince of Galanth and fight in Gaidol's name against the invading Northlanders. He tried not to show how much the orders pleased him.

Lance and his guardsmen packed quickly and were ready to ride before the heat of the day had faded. His hundred guardsmen with him, Lance mounted his stallion, Bolt, and led the march from SwordWood.

For a moment, his heart was uncertain. He could not seek Valia out. He could not even say farewell. But

as they reached the final gate leading from the capital city, Lance spotted Lady Valia Lodaton among the crowd.

She stood alone, although he did not know how she had snuck away from her personal guardsmen. Never one for fancy jewelry, a plain traveler's cloak masked her expensive dress and left her looking plain.

Chapter 1

He met her sky blue eyes, and something snapped again in him. Lance heard the warning of the starvation post and, for a moment, didn't care. When she ran to him, Lance, with a muttered curse, dismounted. Wrapping his arms around her, Lance kissed her for all he was worth.

"When I come back," he whispered as they pulled apart, "I swear I *will* marry you."

Valia nodded mutely under a single tear and, pulling away gently, squeezed his hand. When her hand withdrew, a string of river pearls was left behind. She calmly turned away, fading into the streets like one more shopper delayed by the marching soldiers.

Lance mounted Bolt once more, making sure no one saw the pearls clenched in his hand. He didn't have to look; he knew she had just gifted him half of the chain of pearls he had brought her from WaterBranch. She had kept the other half.

When they cleared the walls, he fixed his sights on the northwest horizon and kicked Bolt into a run.

They had a great deal of ground to make up.

"Go away," the vendor snapped. Loni's fury flared. But knowing her temper could hinder her, especially when dealing with merchants, she bit back her instinctive reply. The cobbler had a dried flower hanging from his vardo window to mark his traveling home as blessed by the Earth God, Pari. Faithful men were more difficult to frighten with promises of damnation from another deity, so she saved her bombardment for a more susceptible soul and instead smiled sweetly.

"I am an honest man," he warned before she could speak. "I have no time for whores like you. Go away!"

"I only asked to buy those shoes," she said, fighting to keep her voice even. Her desire to snap at the man, or snap his neck, was powerful. "I did not ask for your soul. I can pay."

"I don't want your money! Dirty money gotten by sinful means!" he retorted, whisking the shoes under the waggon counter.

She had spent too many nights being called sinful by ignorant men. The scar on her hand and her promise to the Goddess of Fire meant nothing to them, but the power of the Goddess coursed through her veins now.

She lost her hold on her temper.

"Sinful? I am a Celebrant of Inac, blessed enough to be traveling with the Champion's army, and you dare call me sinful? The Bitch Goddess might answer your insult!" She seethed, gripping the knife strapped to her belt.

He shied away. "I have been warned."

"Not enough if you still stand in my way! How dare you—"

She stopped involuntarily. The rage that had been rising vanished. Like a slap to the face, her fury was gone.

In the vacancy, Loni found herself feeling pity for the man. He had been warned, no doubt, by his celebrant. It was not his fault he did not know better.

"Never mind," she said with a sigh, pulling a silver shard coin from her pouch. "Here, for your children. I will not bother you again."

She left him, making her slow way through the rows of the merchants. Tradition named the mixed gathering "Fixer City," recognizing its reputation as fixing anything from weapons and armor to clothes and pots. One's carnal needs could also be "fixed" in Fixer City, making its variety of offerings as extensive as a city's. This city, however, moved in the shadow of the marching army.

Loni felt more at home in Fixer City than anywhere before and yet was being ostracized. That had to change. The Goddess had brought her to Fixer City and the army marching north to face Northlanders, but Inac had been silent since. Now, her Goddess had spoken through an abrupt yank on her leash. The meaning eluded her.

She came back to herself sitting on a log by her campfire with two of her girls, Satrina and Cali, holding her. Their darkly painted eyes and bright lips mirrored hers, advertising their profession for onlookers. Each wore a thicker dress than Loni, but Loni's was brilliant red and orange where theirs were drab. Jewelry, most of which was shined copper, decorated Loni prominently. Each of her girls wore a single copper token, given from Loni's collections to mark their membership in her gathering. Inac's church customarily gave members candles, but Loni boasted her gifts were more permanent.

 # Chapter 1

"Are you alright, Celebrant?" Satrina inquired as Loni's eyes finally focused on the faded red dress she had given the girl. It had been pushing the limits of indecency on Loni's frame but fit the smaller girl well.

Cali echoed the worry, "You came in blind! I thought you were going to walk right through the fire! You terrified us!"

Loni laid a hand softly on the girls' knees. "Another fit, I fear. I went to get some shoes and ended up doing the Goddess's will instead. I fear my feet go bare for another day."

The girls offered their worn footwear, but Loni declined. She had lost her shoes that morning as a gift to one just like these two, and she did not regret it. Shoes were a luxury that inspired feelings of self-worth in those who seldom had such wealth.

"It seems," she said, "that Celebrant Barga has been preaching against us again."

Both girls frowned. Satrina, twelve years old, rested her head on Loni's bare shoulder. "Oh, that is so unfair! Why does she hate us so?"

"She does not hate us," Loni corrected softly as she ran a hand over the girl's head to smooth the short blonde locks into behaving. Before Loni's arrival, one of Satrina's clients had cut the girl's glorious long hair into a soldier's short style. For mooncycles, Satrina had been shunned by all other clients, forcing her to accept only his patronage.

The offending soldier was probably being worked to death as a slave by now. Loni had seen to it. It was hard to meet quotas when limping on a maimed knee.

"No," Loni said. "What Celebrant Barga fears is balance. She has unbalanced of the four gods in the Temple waggons to her advantage. She doesn't want that to change. That means keeping the poor poor and the powerful powerful." Loni glanced to Cali. "Did you..."

"We gifted the emerald to Barga this afternoon," she confirmed. "Varthon is quite the actor. He made sure to ask the gem be divided among the four Temple waggons, of course."

"Which we know Barga will never do. I will prepare the notes to..." Loni's eyes went to the fire, and she paused, seeing a vision in the smoke. A girl, long blond hair twisted into dreads, stood in the fires. She was tiny but mature and dressed in hide rags. The smoke played across her eyes as if they were made of flames.

Loni blinked, and the vision solidified into a person.

Seeing the attention on her, the woman stepped around the fire and met Loni's stare squarely. "We be lookin' fo' da man wid mustache," she said in broken, heavily-accented Esparan.

"Man with a mustache?" Loni echoed. She chuckled and shook her head. Her single loose curl bobbed, free from the other strands tangled atop her head. "Dear girl, do you have any idea how many men have mustaches in this army?"

"'Ee be wearin' bloo enn white, naw green."

Loni narrowed her eyes on the girl. Easing herself away from Cali and Satrina, Loni stood cautiously.

The woman carried several obvious knives, most bone-handled short blades with chipped edges.

"Where are you from, child?"

With never-failing confidence despite Loni's scrutiny, the girl replied, "Sowd."

"Really, really, far south, I presume. You're Rydan," Loni realized.

The girl did not so much as flinched at being identified.

Satrina and Cali stood to join Loni. "I wasn't sure they even had women!" Satrina said. "I'd seen a few Rydan men in Galanth, but never this far north and never a woman! Never..."

Loni spotted another woman standing just behind the Rydan. Despite her complete change in attire, she recognized her as Melody, a mute girl once part of Loni's gathering. She had vanished after Prince Tohmas hired her for a night. Loni had not questioned the event, knowing Prince Tohmas was the Champion of Inac and believing he would never do anything that was not the will of the Goddess.

"Melody," Loni called, opening her arms to the woman in welcome. "Where have you been, child? But you cannot tell me, can you? Is this your friend? You bring us..."

The smaller Rydan stepped between them as if to shield Melody. Loni let her arms lower. The newcomer was hardly more than a girl, but she held herself with assurance and did not disguise the knives tucked into her hide skirt. Melody wore hide clothing to match that of the stranger. She equally wore knives like she knew how to use them.

Melody waved her arms and, to Loni's surprise, called her companion over. The words, muddled and slurred, were decidedly not Esparan.

 # CHAPTER 1

Loni was surprised. "You speak? We thought you mute!"

"Sha naw aik Esparan," the girl said.

"Yours needs work too." Loni ran her eyes over the pair. Melody was an easy choice; she was beautiful and, in her torn hide clothes, had the allure of the foreign as well. The smaller girl was considerably plainer, but some men weren't picky. "Why don't you stay with us? I can offer you work, shelter, food—"

The girl made a face and stepped back in unquestionable refusal.

"Then go on. I warn you; I know every man in Fixer City and most of the soldiers in Prince Tohmas' army. If you want to find someone in particular, I am your best hope."

They were young and alone. They needed help surviving in the Esparan society even if they did not recognize it.

The girl glared but did not step back up. Loni thumped into her seat. "I will send the letters," she said to Cali and Satrina, putting the two interlopers from her mind and addressing the topic at hand. "There might be four Galanth celebrants now, but they are not balanced, not like the celebrants think and—"

"Ya be fightin' from ya bed," the little Rydan said, surprising Loni. She had not thought they were listening.

Loni smiled widely. "I fight most of my wars from the bed. This woman won't let me near her bed."

The girl shrugged, her smile menacing. "Den fight from 'er 'usband's bed."

"She's a Celebrant of Pari. She doesn't have a husband."

"But she has Celebrant Glorian," Cali interrupted.

Loni spun to Cali, her thoughts flying. "He sleeps with her? The Celebrant of Ocea and the Celebrant of Pari? Glorian should be married or celibate!"

Cali gave her a wicked grin that suited the sparkle in her pale eyes. "I saw the two of them go down when I was serving a client. Let me tell you: even the way they make love tells you who is the mistress of that pairing. I almost feel sorry for that pathetic newt of a man."

Loni bounced in her seat in excitement. "Could you be made to feel sorry for him? He will suspect me, but maybe someone else could give him the chance to be the master!"

Celebrant

"Of course, I could. I could have Celebrant Glorian licking the paint from my toenails if that's what you want, assuming he does not have a thing for larger women. Do you think it will help get Barga off our backs?"

"Oh yes. Getting Glorian on his back will get him off our backs too,» Loni purred, gripping Cali›s arm.

She looked back at the Rydan girl. She still stood beside Melody, her bearings calm but expectant.

It was a fair trade—one idea for another.

"The man you're looking for is Lance Carraway. I make no promises; he is Gaidolon and probably stayed in Gaidol when we crossed the border. If he's around, you'll find him in the main forces, probably near Prince Tohmas' tent."

The girl nodded precisely once and left, Melody trailing behind her. In their wake, the smoke twisted into a taller plume.

"Does Celebrant Sedgan have someone too? Could we try the same for him or Celebrant Calanor?" Satrina asked, her petite expression pensive.

Loni shook her head, her eyes on where the Rydan women had vanished. "Calanor remains a mystery I cannot solve, and Sedgan is mine. Do not fret; we will have our places soon enough."

Faithful, Satrina laid her head on Loni's shoulder once more. "I'm so glad you came, Loni," she said as she closed her eyes.

Chapter 2

"You're stalling," Prime Guardian Vallant said flatly as he joined Tohmas on his watch at the north end of the camped army. After the long march, setting camp was well practiced. Tohmas had no role to play. Even the prime guardian, Tohmas' direct representative in organizing the army, had delegated his duties to others.

The rolling slopes of Barrows Hills stretched out from the edge of camp and became rough at the horizon, where the sparse trees ended and grass inclines took over. Among the browned grasses, Tohmas saw no sign of life, and he felt almost alone for a moment. But to fully enjoy the effect, he would have to ignore Carsh, who never left his side except to sleep, and the other protectors, who formed a small crowd around him.

"Why do you say that?" Tohmas asked.

Vallant scratch his beard as if looking for something needing to be dislodged. "Fifteen of the protectors' horses have come up lame. Three herdsmen from the baggage train insist their animals broke free and have been chasing goats, cows, and chickens all over the road. Fixer City has a pandemic of missing wheels for the waggons, and someone or something broke open the gate of the corral two nights back. The stragglers are only now catching up. Plus you've been drunk at least twice."

"Have not," Tohmas replied, leaning against his horse, Honest Justice. The shadows of the setting sun stretched over the hills before him, casting the rolling slopes in fire red.

"Then why did you claim to have a hangover and start the march late?" Vallant asked with a sigh. "I'm supposed to be organizing this damn march for you, and even I can't figure out how, or why, you did this, but I'm sure it was you. We could have made it into Barrows Hills tonight. We used to do a double march every second day, but you've not pushed the fyrds once since Gaidol."

"I don't want to push them. And I don't want to camp in Barrows Hills right now."

"Are you going to tell any of us why?"

"I will at midnight."

"I'd argue, but you'd just ignore me," Vallant said with a frown as he leaned back against his own horse. "The scouts have already been through the Hills, you realize. They didn't find anything. DoomDragon's still days beyond—"

"*Rida*," Carsh interrupted from his place shadowing Tohmas. "*Risen way.*"

Translating the Rydan to mean "from the east," Tohmas glanced over his shoulder. He had been expecting riders, but not from the east.

Sure enough, a man wearing the white shoulder rope of a companion arrived on a pony as Tohmas turned fully. The token he handed Tohmas identified the man as part of the Fyrd of Barmore, which was on rearguard. While Tohmas pocketed the leather disc, the messenger breathlessly reported, "A force of close to a hundred Gaidolons is riding toward us."

There were many reasons for a hundred Gaidolons to be advancing toward Galanth's men, and only one of them was good. Prince Dorakon had not been pleased with Tohmas' departure from Gaidol. But if Dorakon wanted to make a point, he would need more men. A hundred men, regardless of their Trulin-bred warhorses, were hardly a problem for an army of forty-five hundred.

"Is the lead rider on a black horse?" Tohmas asked.

In the dusk, the man's expression was hard to read as he stuttered, "I don't know, my Prince. They had the blue and white of Gaidol though."

Had a Rydan been reporting, the lead horse and rider would have been identified down to the tattoo on the rider's chest, but these were Esparan. It had been a mistake to ask the question.

 ## Chapter 2

Satisfied, Tohmas handed the messenger his token, designating him to carry a message for Tohmas. "Invite the riders in and have them set camp west of the Fyrd of Sedinham. Send Lance to me immediately." The messenger blinked in confusion. "Lance will be the man with the black horse at the lead. Just ask for their high guardsman." The messenger nodded stiffly, turned his pony, and kicked the tired beast into a trot.

Lance's men might be exhausted, but it was necessary. Either they were fit enough to keep up tonight, or they would be left behind. Tonight's camp was not meant to last till morning.

Vallant's jaw clenched as if to cut off a complaint. He looked ready to spit, but instead he swallowed and resumed scratching his grizzled beard.

"Tired of getting overruled?" Tohmas asked as he resumed his watch of the hills.

"Tired of being wrong," Vallant replied, making Tohmas smile.

Tohmas had still not seen what he was waiting for by the time a man on a sweaty black horse rode up. The protectors, recognizing the high guardsman, let Lance pass. The light had all but left the camp with the sun's setting, making it hard for Tohmas to see how big Lance's grin was, but he suspected it was huge.

The high guardsman dismounted, and there was no tremble in his legs this time. Doubtless, he had ridden hard, but he and the horse were robust enough to manage it.

"Welcome, High Guardsman Carraway," Tohmas said, nodding his head in acknowledgment. He did not move his sore shoulder from Honest Justice's flank. "What brings you so rapidly back into our company?"

Lance presented Tohmas with a folded vellum sheet. With it came a leather token marked with the shark of Prince Dorakon of Gaidol.

"Hell of a messenger boy," grumbled Vallant, and Tohmas pretended he hadn't heard, not wanting to give Vallant any excuse to draw a blade. They had spent nine days with Lance Carraway during the crossing of Gaidol, but Vallant had never come to like, let alone trust, the high guardsman.

"Prince Dorakon had a slight change of heart," Lance explained.

Someone brought forward a torch in the fading light, and Tohmas quickly read the letter. He folded it and placed it into Honest Justice's saddle bag for later.

"You are joining us."

"If you will have us, good Prince. We would be honored to fight with you against the Northlander invaders."

There was probably a very good reason for this, but he was certain it was not the incursion of Northlanders. In all their dealings, Prince Dorakon had been unconcerned by DoomDragon's approach; it was unlikely the prince would assign nearly a hundred riders and their horses to the cause. Lance seemed to be withholding further explanations deliberately, and Tohmas decided not to press his prospective friend.

"You and your men are most welcome. You will remain sworn to Prince Dorakon during your stay?"

Lance hesitated. It took a moment for him to either collect his thoughts or his courage, then he stood straight and replied confidently, "We swore our lives to Gaidol, and it is Gaidol we will always serve."

"Would you be willing to take command of the other Gaidolons who joined us? None have yet been sworn in, and I think most of them would be happier to keep to their previous loyalties. Some will change, I am certain, but if you would be willing to be their guardian, I would be grateful."

Lance's face brightened despite the gloom. He bowed then grinned with the same smile that had once greeted Tohmas' midnight ride to Gaidol's capital. "Gladly."

"High Guardsman Carraway, you are now in charge of the Fyrd of Arrow," Tohmas declared. "I expect you to attend all my conferences as a Guardian of Galanth and follow my orders until you are recalled by Prince Dorakon. Is this acceptable?"

The high guardsman nodded but added with a raised eyebrow, "Fyrd of Arrow? Why 'Arrow'? Because you were shot in Gaidol?"

Tohmas shrugged. The wound under his left shoulder blade throbbed.

"Without an actual city to name them after, I let them pick a name," he admitted. "I will send a runner out to you with all the information as soon as I can. The only thing I need to know right now is how fast your men can be ready to march."

 # Chapter 2

"Less than a quarter of a candle from a complete sleep. When you need us to move, we will move. They are all good men; I'll vouch for that."

"Then get them as much rest as you can, High Guardsman. They are going to need it where we are going."

Lance bowed, then mounted his horse, Bolt. The warhorse was soon trotting back to the far side of the camp, Carsh's lusting eyes following the magnificent steed.

Tohmas' attention went back to the west. He pointedly ignored the way Prime Guardian Vallant's head shook in disapproval.

Not long after Lance rode away, taking his fine warhorse with him, Carsh felt the approach of magic. At the tingle in the air, he drew his second knife, but he could not locate the source of the powers sliding across the area. Tohmas tensed, recognizing the second blade as a warning but unable to sense the magic as Carsh did.

The terrible feeling of dirty air dissipated. Once it was gone, Carsh acknowledged Tohmas' curiosity and explained, "*Flya touch.*" Without waiting to see what his brother said, Carsh muttered a prayer against magic. He wanted to pull his holy symbol, but retrieving the firebug amber would force him to put away one of his knives, and he wanted both available should the caster try something.

"Flyer or wizard?" Tohmas asked.

Carsh shook his head. All magic felt equally wrong. His whole life, he had been told magic came from evil flyers that inhabited the swamps of the Outlands and that his duty was to destroy those foul casters. Traveling with Tohmas through Espar and meeting non-hostile casters had frustratingly muddied the concept. He could accept that not all casters were as evil as flyers, but he could not tell the difference between these "good" Esparan wizards and the demon-cursed flyers.

"Riders," Vallant warned, and Carsh followed the prime guardian's squinting stare out into the hills. In the deep shadows under the navy sky, Carsh made out the silhouettes of several people on Esparan horses.

Tohmas pushed off Honest Justice. "Kit!" he bellowed.

After a pause, a faint voice shouted back, "What now?" There was no mistaking the wizard's disparaging voice.

Celebrant

As the riders advanced, Tohmas gave the order to let them through the camp defenses. Accompanied by his team of weary protectors, Master Kitable presented himself to Tohmas.

Everything the small group of men had was a shade of dirty brown, and their faces were drawn. The wizard sat with a travelling cloak draped over his normal green robes, and a deep hood shaded his eyes from the torchlight. Despite the way the caster sat straight on his horse, Kitable felt tired to Carsh. Far fewer spells were hovering around the man than normal. The Rydan cocked his head warily.

"Master Kitable, ride with me to my tent, please. The rest of you are free to get cleaned up and take some rest," Tohmas commanded. He must have detected something was amiss as well.

The dismissed protectors rode resignedly away as Tohmas led the others to his large, green tent. Entering without protectors, Tohmas and Carsh were the only people present when Kitable finally pulled off his hood.

His head was wrapped with a rough bandage, and his face was as pale as a spirit's. He had allowed his beard to grow, obscuring his normally well-maintained whiskers and making him look ragged. Even his eyes were outlined by deep, dark circles, and his cheeks looked thin. Alone with the prince and his prime protector, Kitable's posture sank. He seemed about to fall before Tohmas steadied him.

"Demons, Kitable! What happened?" Tohmas asked. "Last I saw you, you were cheerily returning to your work digging tunnels!"

The wizard lowered himself into a chair with Tohmas' aid and hoarsely replied, "It's not as bad as it looks. Just enervation."

Carsh carefully leaned away. He did not know the word, but it sounded bad.

Tohmas removed his hands from Kitable's shoulders, raising an eyebrow. "Enervation?" Tohmas tilted his head toward Carsh and, understanding, Carsh retrieved the waterskin from a nearby chest. He also pulled a cup, thinking the wizard better able to handle the smaller vessel. Tohmas filled the cup with water and offered it to Kitable.

Speaking stole away the wizard's breath, forcing him to pause between words. It took a surprisingly long time for him to compose himself.

Chapter 2

"Enervation, meaning a loss of strength," the wizard muttered into his cup after a few sips of water. "It is essentially exhaustion. Magic twists it though, makes it more than just sore muscles and a tired mind. It...it feels like you've run races all day while trying to solve the meaning of life. It occurs whenever a wizard pushes his body beyond reasonable bounds."

With Kitable sitting and quietly sipping his water, Tohmas pulled out a second chair and sat across from him. Carsh flipped his knives over his knuckles in contemplation and chose a chair back to perch on.

"And why would you do that, Kitable?" Tohmas asked.

The wizard's eyes shut like a dizzy man's attempt at re-centering himself. "After fending off DoomDragon's casters at the ambush, I was a little winded but nothing serious. But almost as soon as I got back to Barrow Hills, they showed up. Three days early."

Tohmas' voice dropped to a growl. "Three days? Master Clarin said—"

"I was not using Master Clarin's reports, my Prince," Kitable interrupted. "I Scryed on them directly to track their progress. I knew them to be still three days away when they appeared on our doorstep. The men handled it better than I did; they got everything underground and hid. I finished the digging myself, but with keeping us hidden from their Scrys and making the tunnels large enough, I pushed myself harder than I normally would. The result," the wizard finished with a gesture to his mildly trembling body, "you see now."

The wizard had once claimed he considered Tohmas' family his own. Carsh had promised to test that assertion, but now he had the evidence before him. Kitable had pushed himself to his very limit to follow Tohmas' orders.

A wizard, not a flyer.

This was not the creature he had been trained to slay. This was no flyer. Carsh put away one of his two blades. He sought a wine waterskin and refilled the wizard's cup. He could have used wildwater, but Carsh worried the Esparan caster would not appreciate the hard liquor.

And Carsh, for the first time in the four mooncycles he had known Kitable, did not want to harm the caster.

Tired as he was, Kitable noted the change to his drink, and, looking vaguely surprised, he gratefully swallowed the wine. Nothing seemed to offer any relief for his shaking muscles. Every breath was strained.

Celebrant

"Is it done?" Tohmas finally asked.

The wizard closed his eyes once more and nodded. "The protectors can show you the entrance. DoomDragon and his army have camped exactly where we hoped. Everything is ready."

The wizard swayed and toppled out of the chair. Tohmas caught him as the empty cup clattered onto the ground.

He was still breathing as Tohmas laid him on the ground gently and called for a cutter.

"*Styl ged*?" Carsh asked once the runner had left them alone, the unconscious wizard at their feet.

"*Ohnennohn*," Tohmas agreed.

Everything was ready. They had to go on.

It was time to start the war for real.

After far too long, the Galanth forces, led by Prince Tohmas, reached Barrow Hills.

Seria Phasoa watched the marching army from a distance, using spells to spy on them and hide her presence. She reviewed the instructions from Master Terant, Seria's master in the magic arts, often. A single mistaken word would foul the magic and lead to early discovery. If either Master Terant or DoomDragon believed she had been responsible for betraying their masked place in the Barrow Hills awaiting the Galanth army, her life would be forfeit.

Since the enemy had set foot in the contested Princedom of Solta, Seria had been disappointed by the disorganized, slow advance. Prince Tohmas, despite rumors of skill and guile, was lining himself up to walk into their trap obliviously. She saw no sign of magic or of Master Kitable.

The Northlanders stayed in their camp, Seria's tiny canvas tent buried among them. The Northlanders planned to wait for morning. Would the foolish Esparan prince continue his march blindly or set up for fighting through the Hills? Either way, Prince Tohmas had already cornered himself. If he turned from the Hills, DoomDragon's men were well positioned to raid his rearguard every step of his retreat. A journey around the Hills would equally doom the rag-tag band of Esparans, opening them to harassment through their run for BellRoost.

Chapter 2

After their mooncycle-long trek to the north to join Prince Sol's fading defenders at BellRoost, it was going to be a quick end for the would-be reinforcements.

The only real concern was Master Kitable, which was Seria's purpose. Come morning, if the army decided to brave Barrow Hills, Seria would have to keep the Galanth wizard at bay. If they decided to flee, then she would have to make her own attack against the master wizard. It was vital, especially to Master Terant, that Kitable not survive. Now that he had engaged himself in the battle, they had to finish him.

She dropped her Scrys as night fell, content that she had seen all she needed. She would have to be quick and creative if she was to avoid being outmatched. Putting aside the vellum from Master Terant, determined to not disappoint her master, Seria chose her spells cautiously.

The first chore was the Rejuvenation spell. Seria coaxed her breathing to slow then focused on the magic and drew it in. Word by word, she built the spell that would replenish her energy, setting her up for continuous casting the rest of the night. She gave herself a full day and a half of extra stamina and released the spell from her mind.

The energy coursed through her, and her heart sped with the sensation. Despite having done a full day of travel and two bouts of spell casting, Seria tingled with vigor. Outside, night fell, but she felt no pull of sleep. Instead, she turned her attention to the list of spells she had prepared and set about bringing them to life around her. The Rejuvenation spell would take its toll later. But so long as Master Kitable was dead first, she did not care.

After she completed the list, Seria sat for a few moments more, physically weighed down by the powers around her but no more tired than she had been at the beginning of the evening. The spells flitted around her, tethered by anchors invisible to the un-enchanted eye but feeling like twisting serpents against her skin. She waited, taking stock once more before letting out a final, ecstatic breath. The caress of magic in the area held her close.

Just as she started wondering what to do with her excess energy, Seria felt a tingle from the magic. A ward outside her tent had been tripped. Seria was only one of many Esparan men and women among DoomDragon's forces, but she set her tent among the Northlanders, preferring isolation for working magic. The Northlanders feared and avoided her. Who would be sneaking behind her tent?

Seria activated one of her hovering spells—a Scry. Once the spell had taken form in front of her, she sent the magic out the tent flap, content to let it do the work for her.

Her altered vision adjusted to the dark of the pre-dawn light, the nearest fires a dozen paces away. A handful of Northlanders sat at the fires, either coming off watch or starting their morning early. As she watched, one of the closest Northlanders sent an unconcerned glance at the tents where other warriors lay sleeping. The potent spells of the Northlander Circle, the combined strength of which dwarfed Seria's powers, were hiding the entire with an illusion, and they all knew it. Tonight, they were safe.

Nearby, tethered horses stood at attention, their ears perked in curiosity.

She tracked down the ward and found the break in the magic where someone had passed.

The shadow of a man moved from one tent to another on the outskirts of the campfire light. Three more shadows followed, and in the dim light of the fire, Seria caught a glimpse of green—Galanth green—on one of the tabards.

Dropping her Scry, Seria launched into another spell without pause. If she was wrong, DoomDragon and Master Terant would be drawing lots for her head, but she knew she was not mistaken.

The alarm she gave did not use words, for most of the Northlanders would not have heeded her Esparan. Instead, the noise was that of a horn sounding, amplified a hundred fold and delivered into every tent across the field.

Her next spell placed a protective shield over her as she rushed outside.

Chaos had taken hold during the moments she had readied herself. When she emerged from the tent, she found herself in the midst of armed men, both Northlander and Esparan. The warning had forced the attackers out of the darkness and into a fight.

A stray arrow glanced off her shield. A group of four Galanth men, each prominently wearing their green tabards, ducked behind a tent when she turned on them. She could not target them directly as they

 # CHAPTER 2

were out of her sight, but she conjured a Fire Dart where she assumed they would be. A cry of pain answered.

Her first priority was getting to DoomDragon to better protect him from magical assaults. Thanks to the Rejuvenation spell, she was able to sprint the entire distance between her tent and his. As Seria ran, she tossed spells at any man wearing a green tabard, but she dared not stay to assess how effective she was being. Fewer men were answering the alarm call than she had expected. Some tents appeared to be entirely empty. But the Galanth had the advantage, and they made full use of it to badly bloody the Northlander forces.

Reaching the large hide and whale bone tent of the Northlander leader, Seria found Darknim DoomDragon standing outside, the lowered ax at his side soaked in blood. All Galanth enemies had been chased from the area already.

Where most old men shrank and stooped, Darknim DoomDragon towered. His thick, white whiskers formed a cowl around his head where his dragon scale hood would normally lie; he must have been caught by surprise and not had time to don his pelts or scales. His ax—a monstrous black, double-bladed weapon detailed to resemble a rearing dragon—was held in a one-handed grip easily. The weight of the weapon would make any other man sag.

"Woman," DoomDragon called, his voice heavy in the Esparan language but without accent, "they escape there. Manifest your spells if you can."

He pointed with his ax to a western hill.

Seria activated Dragon Sight to see through the gloom and found the shapes of men crawling along the hill DoomDragon had indicated. She did not know how the Northlander leader had spotted the shifting shadows along the hill, especially as his eyes were at least five decades older than hers, but there was no denying the enemy's retreat led to the hill.

Most interestingly, if the Esparans were fleeing to the west, they were doing so without crossing the space between the camp and the hill. Seria saw them appearing halfway along the rise, but none between there and the camp.

Tunnels, she realized. With no magic at work, they were using tunnels to escape unopposed. *Or so they think.*

Thanks to DoomDragon's keen eyes, the enemy was now at her mercy. She would not let them escape.

With her feet planted, Seria activated a hovering Fire Blast. She released it, and the fur-draped Northlander Hunters around her, each two heads taller than her, took several steps back from the shockwave.

She turned to smile at DoomDragon.

"That," she said, "is what I can do."

The fire would burn those on the surface, and the shock blast would seal the tunnels below. She had trapped the enemy.

Sitting on his bored waggon horse, Kitable regarded the movement of shadows with tired eyes. For candles on end, nothing happened in the Northlander camp that was nestled between the hills below him.

He waited.

Just as the eastern sky lightened with dawn, a horn sounded, and activity exploded over the camp. Still, Kitable waited. Two casters had confronted him before, and their possible involvement worried him. The spells that hid the enemy's forces, deceiving him into believing they were still far from Barrow Hills, had been incredibly potent. Kitable was the only one able to stand between that power and the soldiers of Galanth.

As men started arriving back through the tunnel at a run, Kitable's enchanted vision showed him only occasional bursts of magic within the camp. A caster was among the Northlanders, but whoever they were, they did not seem to be casting anything more than weak spells that ended before he could even consider a counter.

But when Kitable saw the cloud-like, red aura of a fire creation spell, he knew he would have to get involved. He had not had time to cast hovering spells, for he had not known which to cast and did not have the energy to cover them all. A full cast was the only option.

This, he thought with a wince, *is going to hurt.*

Kitable finished his spell a flicker after the Fire Blast was set loose and, with a gesture of his weary arms, threw the Force Wall at the ball of flame. Sure enough, the fire was deflected wide and struck the next hill over.

 # Chapter 2

With his concentration lost and his body failing, the wizard was grateful for the protector who came forward to lead his horse. The last thing he thought before falling unconscious was, *I hope they all got out.*

Tohmas emerged from the cover of the tunnel with Carsh right behind him. The rest of the protectors were assembled in broken groups, but every last one of them was grinning. Tohmas leaped onto his horse and tucked away his weapons, not even giving the handler time to make an offer of assistance.

"By the Flame, that was fun!" he called.

Carsh bared his teeth in approving grin. "*Troo stard.*"

Bashuran, Carsh's horse, stomped his foot in objection at having been left out, but a slap to the horse's flank startled him into calmness and allowed Carsh to mount.

"A true start," Tohmas agreed. In the Outlands, it was believed that wars ended the way they began. Tonight, they had appeared among the enemy during the night and snuck a blade into every sleeping man they could. Things had started off well.

"Even if only every second Galanth killed one Northlander..." a protector muttered as they stared down between the hills that had hidden the tunnels.

Another protector finished the thought. "That puts us down to... what? Four thousand of us and...ten...or twenty thousand of them? They left half in BellRoost so—"

"We will have to wait until morning to see the results," Tohmas interrupted. "I have no intention of being anywhere near here by then!"

Surrounded by a scattering of chuckles, Tohmas turned his horse to the west.

He felt the eyes of the protectors on him, their stares critical. They had sparred before, but this marked their first true battle at his side. Some were watching him for signs of strain as if worried killing upset him. Others tried to peer through his enthusiasm to see if it concealed hesitation or self-doubt. Battle could change a person. They wanted to know how it would affect him.

Celebrant

But none of them realized Tohmas had spent the last ten years fighting for survival among the warring Rydan clans. He had led Rydan raiders and annihilated cities. He had been the destroyer of the Second and Third Clans. With his Chief's support, Tohmas had conquered all of the Outlands.

There would be no change. This was already who he was.

Somewhere in the north, a powerful rumble shook the ground, and fire flashed along the crest of a nearby hill. It crashed into the earth one hill over, missing the tunnels and the men who were finishing their escape. Even Honest Justice shied from the explosion.

Tendrils of fire blasted across the dark hilltop and left a large, black patch where grass had once grown. The disturbed, blasted dirt fell like hail stones but were too small to harm. Tohmas blinked to clear the brightness from his vision.

"I bet that would have hurt," Tohmas said. He got nervous laughter from the protectors.

He surveyed the group, counting and thinking. They had been the last ones through the tunnels deliberately; Tohmas needed to make sure his fighters were clear before he lit the fires.

"Time to go," he called, kicking Honest Justice on. Light grew in the enemy's camp well beyond that of the dawning sun.

"Is that…smoke? In the camp. There's…fire?" a protector asked.

"Inac's Flame in action," Tohmas confirmed. "Swords can cut an enemy down. Fire can burn a city." He avoided mention of the saying's origin. Quoting Rydan lore may upset them.

The protector nodded solemnly. "Smart."

Tohmas proudly grinned. "It's been a good night."

He brought Honest Justice into a canter. They needed to make their head start count.

When the Fire Blast went wide and crashed into the wrong hill, DoomDragon only snorted and shrugged at Seria's outrage. That it had taken another wizard to defeat her did not seem to matter to him.

Chapter 2

She activated Spell Sight and searched for the magic auras that came with wizards and their pre-casted hovering spells but found nothing. *Kitable's hiding*! she thought with a hiss. She had missed him.

And now her spells were diminished. She did not think she had enough to go after him as she planned, having used so much magic defending herself and other Northlanders in her rush to DoomDragon's side. To hunt Kitable now would be deadly.

She cursed profusely as DoomDragon began reorganizing his troops. In the pre-dawn, they broke camp and made ready to pursue.

"We will catch them easily," she declared once DoomDragon's Hunters had left to see to their men. "He cannot march straight!"

The huge Northlander leader fixed her with a curious, half-amused expression from under his thick, white eyebrows. His words were firm like a patient father. "That was a ploy. Tohmas fooled us into thinking his stop outside the Barrow Hills was accidental, when in fact he had already readied the place against us. I do not expect to catch him, wizard. He will be much faster now."

Seria opened her mouth to argue but could not fault his logic. Tohmas' march *had* been faster before reaching Solta. It was likely he would resume his previous pace now that he was pursued. The Prince of Galanth also had a lead thanks to the ambush. Further, they had Master Kitable to aid them.

The thought made her pout.

She would have to report to Master Terant. Her master was strict at the best times, and he was going to be furious that the opportunity to be rid of Kitable had been missed so soon.

DoomDragon dismissed Seria with a wave of his hand, and she plodded away. She had reached the flap of her tent by the time the scent of fire reached her nostrils. In the bare-dawn, she saw the plumes of smoke.

It would take much more time to stop the fires and repair the damage.

"Damn you," she cursed. "Damn you, you demon."

Chapter 3

In the shadows of the trees lining DancingIce River, there was no reprieve from the bugs. No wind pierced the thick forest, leaving the air stagnant, and the insects thrived. A small candle with scented smoke burned at the center of the meeting table in Tohmas' tent, doing its best to discourage the biting flies. More than one of the nine guardians Tohmas had summoned to the meeting were wrinkling their noses, but Tohmas thought that probably because Carsh had coated himself with bear fat imbued with cedar oil against the bugs. In the warm air of the midsummer, the result was pungent.

Diplomatically avoiding any mention of the stench of the prime protector, Guardian Tantian asked, "Could perhaps Master Kitable conceal us?"

Tohmas shook his head. "I fear he is far too busy at the moment. Use your own eyes. Do not count on a wizard to tell you where to find the enemy." At the seat farther from the door, he glanced at each guardian in turn. He was pleased they met his stare readily.

When his eyes reached Guardian Rusk, the man twitched his upper lip and scowled. He had lost his right eye during the ambush of DoomDragon's camp and wore a band of cloth over it. Someone had drawn a picture of an eye on the bandage, although it had little resemblance to the guardian's other eye. "The land becomes marshy. We cannot continue west," the guardian warned. His forces were leading the way, and he had already become bitter at the terrain's sogginess.

 # Chapter 3

"So, we go north," Tohmas decided.

"DancingIce River," the one-eyed guardian said flatly.

"We cross."

"We cannot make a bridge fast enough for the waggons—"

"We make a light bridge, enough for the men only," Tohmas said, then paused. Was he asking too much of them?

His adopted father had been thorough, determined that Tohmas could pass as a proper Esparan. Rydans never bothered with bridges—their horses could swim the waters of all but the most raging rivers—but his lessons with Chief Tamv had detailed assembly of simple Esparan bridges. He suspected Northlanders would be like Rydans, although he wondered if they had much experience with swimming considering their cold homeland. DoomDragon was not travelling with the supplies to make a bridge; Tohmas had seen that when he raided the camp. The Northlander had probably never needed one, and that was to Tohmas' advantage.

"We make the bridge. The waggons stay in the shallows as the men cross," Tohmas continued. "They lead a trail to Craos Woods then double back, let loose the bridge, and cross back downstream before the night is done. The waggons meet us and take refuge with us in the woods along the river."

"Why by night?" the next guardian asked. "We cannot move as quickly in the dark, and we—"

The argument was not worth hearing out. "DoomDragon has casters, but they look for us during the day. So, we move by night. No lamps, no torches."

"It will be slow," Prime Guardian Vallant cautioned him. The large man, made larger by his leather armor, sat with his hands on the table. The guardians nodded in agreement.

"It will be fast enough. If he cannot decide which way we went, he will have to send more than one group of scouts. DoomDragon cannot afford to guess; he needs all his men to be within reach of each other when we meet," Tohmas insisted, glad no one had mounted an argument over the bridge idea.

"We remain by the river. If he finds us—" Guardian Rusk warned, apparently the most outspoken of Tohmas' skeptics.

"If he finds us, he will still have to get his men to us. Come tomorrow night, we move upstream again. We stick to the river as long as we can and see how long it takes him to determine which way we have gone."

There was, for one blessed moment, silence at the table. Then Guardian Tantian, his hand on his nose, asked again, "Could Master Kitable not block the casters??"

"Put simply, no, guardian, no he cannot. Remember that they deceived us. If not for having people in Barrow Hills when they did not expect, we would never have known about the forces camped there. We would have marched right into them, into their trap."

Prime Guardian Vallant sat forward in his chair and folded his hands. "Now for the bloody details."

The sun had begun its westerly descent by the time the wide tracks of the Galanth army led to the river. Called by his Hunters, Darknim DoomDragon stood on the muddy bank of DancingIce River, feeling only the barest hint of fatigue in the warm dusk. Tohmas was gaining ground, he was disappointed to realize. The prince had moved his forces overnight.

But it was more complicated than that. Prince Tohmas had erected a full, perfectly normal camp and then, once darkness fell, quietly broke camp and marched his men again. Fires had burned all night unattended to further the ploy. The watching eyes, both the natural ones of his Hunters and the magic ones of the Northlander Circle, had not seen the deception.

The prince had gained a half-day on the Northlanders, but it came with a toll—the Esparans were being worn out. They would slow. Darknim's men, on the other hand, could hold their steady march. Decades of battle and a nomadic life had prepared them well.

Now he had reached the river and was forced to congratulate his opponent once more. Prince Tohmas had crossed the river overnight, a feat itself, and put another obstacle in Darknim's path. It would take time to organize a crossing, and in that window, Tohmas Galanth would continue his flight.

 # Chapter 3

Tohmas Galanth. Darknim frowned at the name. He knew little about this prince, except that he had taken up the challenge of dealing with Darknim's Northlanders when others had refused to for a decade. Tohmas was of the line of Zayban Galanth, but his ties to his family were weak. Everyone knew he had a Rydan prime protector and friend, although none knew how they had met. Darknim had seen the two men fight side by side, and their skills had surprised him. And now Tohmas Galanth marched his men like he knew what he was doing. It was astonishing how much a boy raised in peace knew about the strategy of war.

Elder Tril, his eyes bright against the wolf pelt over his shoulders, arrived silently beside Darknim. Unlike many of the other Circle members whose eyes changed to match those of their animal spirit Aspects, Tril's wolf eyes differed very little from a normal Northlander's. It made him the most inconspicuous of the Circle members, sometimes resulting in embarrassing apologies from those who had failed to recognize the younger man as an elder until he smiled and revealed his fangs.

Darknim rose from his crouch and turned. "You have learned patience in your age, Elder," he said.

Tril's smile showed his long, canine teeth. "I can only hope to have as much patience, or age, as you one day, DoomDragon." The smile quickly sobered as the elder reported, "There is no change. Master Terant anchored our spells on the home of Master Kitable. We cannot drift away and have no way to know where the spell is. Master Kitable has not entered his vardo either, so we have taken no direct action against him."

Letting out a long, annoyed sigh, Darknim glanced across the wide river. He could not figure out how Tohmas had so quickly built the bridge that had taken the waggons across the fifty-pace span of the river. It must have been Esparan ingenuity; the Northlander Circle would have spotted magic overnight.

His eyes were drawn to the horizon, where the rocky slopes nearest the river broke into thick forest.

"If Seria could come to the Earth Lodge..." Tril suggested.

Darknim shook his head. "Sadly, the child granted herself energy temporarily and is now paying the price. We cannot wake her until her spells wear off at midnight. I have sent the Hunters to the far side of the river. They will bring word."

Celebrant

The Circle elder did not move as Darknim crouched in the sand again by the water. Tohmas had chosen a narrow stretch with a beach on one side. It had been a good place for Darknim to launch the Hunters in their boats.

The elder and DoomDragon waited as the sun touched down onto the horizon. A boat bearing a pair of Hunters returned as the river reflected the red sunset. As soon as the boat landed, a Hunter presented Darknim with a fist-sized stone.

"Both ways," the Hunter said.

The stone he held had lain flat, but the scuffing of tracks showed movement in two directions.

Just when he had been intending on closing the gap between him and his opponent, Darknim had to halt at the river. Prince Tohmas had marched his men to the woods, the tracks said, but then come back to the river?

"Search again," Darknim said. "Hunters, find them."

The reporting Hunter had his friend pull up the boat and left in a jog that could pursue caribou for leagues. He was quickly joined by others. They all knew it was too late; by the time the Hunters found the Esparan forces and reported back to him, the lead would be too great to correct in a single day. The only thing faster would be magic but, thanks to her selfish spells, the spoiled Esparan caster was unavailable.

To the rest of his men, Darknim commanded, "Set camp." He pulled his ax and tensed his grip along the shaft in concentration, feeling the cold metal under his hand focus his mind. Heat wanted to rise in his anger, but he saw no need for it. He forced it down.

Horns rang out over the army, prompting Northlander and Esparan alike to set the campfires and basic defenses.

"We can be a conduit when she wakes," Elder Tril offered.

Darknim nodded in acceptance. "I will have a Hunter watch Seria and bring her to me as soon as she awakens. We will come to the Circle. You will find our quarry."

Prince Tohmas would not be given the chance to escape again. There were many deaths DoomDragon needed to repay.

Chapter 3

Having a Temple waggon during the march allowed Celebrant Sedgan to sleep overnight, but the midday service for the Goddess Inac was sorely unattended as the army sought slumber instead of worship. He could not blame them for wanting to be ready for the next overnight march.

The change of night to day did not disrupt the Temple waggons enough for the four Celebrants of Galanth to skip their quartercycle meeting. Tasked with maintaining religious observations during the march, they would allow nothing to interrupt their routine.

Sedgan brought a spare coat when he went to meet the other three Celebrants of Galanth, knowing the Temple waggon of Wind was always chilly. Thankfully, they had come to the north in summer, and the wind was not too brisk. Once the sun set, however, the air cooled quickly.

The Temple waggon of Totho, God of Wind, was built of pale birch and carved at regular intervals with Totho's stars. Where Sedgan would have expected a painting, the builders had instead created full-thickness carvings which opened the waggon to the wind at any angle. The lamps within were low and shuttered against the passing breezes.

The privacy of the meeting was lost with the half-open walls, but Celebrant Calanor still sent his acolytes out. Once the door shut, the four of the celebrants sat at the divided table.

First to arrive, Sedgan took his place at the west corner of the table. Celebrant Glorian Dew took his place at the east. The bookish man hunched in his seat, his spectacles magnifying his already huge, glassy stare. The pattern of Ocea's holy waters had worn out along Glorian's sleeves, leaving the symbols incomplete, but the blue of the robes made clear the man's chosen deity. Sedgan felt something amiss with the man, but Celebrant Barga Earthsworn's arrival prevented him from investigating. Tent-like, brown robes ballooning around her, Barga stomped into the waggon and thumped into the chair at the south corner of the table, making it flex dangerously under her weight. Calanor, who had been hovering by his diamond-decked altar in the north corner of the Temple waggon, joined them by taking the north seat and completed the quartet.

They should have been discussing the toll the overnight marching was having on the army, but Sedgan could not concentrate. Instead,

Celebrant

Sedgan's mind kept drifting back to an anonymous letter and the accusation written on it.

Finally, when he could no longer bear listening to the Celebrant of Ocea talk about a nervous mother-to-be Sedgan had requested he see, Sedgan interrupted.

"Did you get an offering from a young man, Earth?"

Jumping in her seat, Barga's wide face fell. There was such as long pause, Sedgan feared she had forgotten she had been asked a question.

"I had heard as much," Calanor said into the silence, his voice a strong whisper from behind his scarf. "A gem, I understand, which was to be gifted to all four gods equally."

Barga's mouth seemed to form the word "how," but no sound emerged.

"Did you know of this, Water?" Sedgan pressed. He looked to Glorian, thinking he had found the source of the man's unease.

This time the pause was expected, but the reply was not. "I had received warning to that effect, yes," Glorian stammered. Barga fixed her glare on him, and Glorian shrank back into his pearl-bedecked robes. "I do not know the source. It could have been a ploy."

"Except for your reaction, Earth, I would have believed that," Sedgan said. "Had you feigned ignorance right away, you may have gotten away with it."

Barga's scowl darkened under the lamps. "Do not lecture me, Fire! How many of your rubies were gifts? You have a greater collection than any of us!"

"Those were gifts to Inac, not to the four gods. You are sworn to divide gifts that are presented to you, or had you forgotten?"

"He did not specifically say it was for the Four."

"People do tend to forget to make these things clear," Glorian supported, sitting straight and adjusting his spectacles consciously. "Perhaps he commissioned the letters belatedly to clarify since he felt he had not done a proper job of it earlier."

"Excuses," Sedgan grumbled. He looked at the Celebrant of Totho for support but gave up the moment he saw Calanor's disinterested, blank stare. Under his cream and grey scarf, Calanor was the most reserved of the four Celebrants of Galanth. The Goddess Inac

Chapter 3

herself would show up before Calanor so much as spoke a harsh word to someone.

"Fine," Sedgan said with a dejected shake of his head. "Since the gem is to be divided, I expect a quarter of its value delivered to my acolytes by tomorrow. Beyond that, I will forget the misunderstanding."

It was untrue; he was not going to forget the lie in the slightest, but he could at least pretend he was not going to keep it in mind the next time someone from Barga's gathering requested his aid. He would have to be more cautious dealing with the temple of Earth.

And Water, he reminded himself. As always, Water and Earth stood against him, and he was defeated.

The celebrants turned their attention to the difficulties of the march and the strain that had fallen onto the Healing waggons after Tohmas' night attack against the Northlanders. The topic kept them from discussing the woman in red who had set up a home in Fixer City masquerading as a Celebrant of Inac.

For that, Sedgan was grateful. He did not know what to say about Loni anyway.

With Master Kitable still too enervated to do anything about the Scrys that might find them, Tohmas carried on with the overnight marches and set camp in the woods at first light, despite the bugs. The army fell asleep rapidly, except for the unfortunates who had to keep watch.

Tohmas slept in short bursts and kept a close watch on Kitable, whom he had placed in one of the Healing waggons under a false name. Kitable's customary seclusion rendered him conveniently anonymous to the majority of the population.

Tohmas visited all the Healing waggons in turn, making general inquiries to disguise the checks on Kitable. The wounded seemed to appreciate the interest he feigned in their progress.

Just over fifty soldiers had been wounded during their raid against DoomDragon. Nearly a hundred more were dead. Considering how outnumbered they were, Tohmas had been satisfied with the price they paid for killing several hundred of their enemies.

During one of his visits, he had to reconsider.

He was in the waggon of Healing Mother Vera when the last of the night raid's fatalities occurred. The man had taken a dagger under his ribs during the raid, but his friends had carried him through the tunnels to safety. Despite the best efforts of the cutters, the dark-faced blacksmith took his last breath around midday.

Tohmas stood at the bottom of Ciene Arvanon's sleeping mat. He had not given the blacksmith much thought since meeting him in Clandac at the beginning of the march. Seeing the first man to join his march die brought much of the world down on Tohmas' shoulders. In every way save one, he had killed Ciene.

The weight did not stay. Unlike some of the younger men to join Tohmas' march, Ciene had known exactly what awaited in Solta. He had chosen war. He wore the blue rope of a warden now; Guardian Faron of the Fyrd of Rest clearly thought highly of the level-headed blacksmith.

Tohmas wanted a knucklebone, a Rydan tradition that carried the soul of the respected person. But he could not think of a way to justify the desire to the healer who had been called over to confirm the death. Instead, Tohmas looked to what the hand was holding.

When Tohmas took the unlit prayer candle, no one objected. With the candle clutched in his hand, Tohmas sought Guardian Faron and asked for Companion Sabian Arvanon.

The midday sun was descending among the trees by the time Tohmas located the unlit fire-pit. Although he should have been sleeping, Sabian crouched among a crowd of other boys, showing off his skills by spinning a knife across his knuckles. Had they been in a city, Tohmas would have expected to see a hat out collecting coins.

Everything stopped when the boys spotted the prince and his shadowing protectors. Despite his surprise, Sabian caught the knife handily and slipped it away. He had his brother's fair hair and leather-tanned skin but was much shorter than the broad blacksmith. Lanky in youth, Sabian looked almost Rydan.

Words were unnecessary. The moment the boy saw Tohmas, he understood.

"Demons..." Sabian's eyes brimmed with tears as he sank onto a nearby log seat and covered his face with his hands. "Ciene..."

A look from Tohmas dismissed the other boys. The protectors kept a respectful distance as Tohmas joined Sabian on the log.

Chapter 3

Others would have given comfort, but no one had ever comforted Tohmas when he grieved lost friends. Tohmas did not know what to say. If the boy was to survive, he would have to deal with death.

"He was the first to join me. I felt I should honor that," Tohmas said.

The boy rubbed away each tear as it fell, denying the perceived weakness. He had locked his jaw.

Tohmas lifted the candle. "He was a follower of Inac?" he speculated.

Sabian nodded stiffly. His beard was thin and patchy in immaturity. "Always was, with his forge. She should have protected him better."

Tohmas smiled at the accusation; similar words had crossed his lips when war had been new. Tohmas had been fighting for a decade, despite what the Esparans believed, and he knew better than to blame gods for what men did.

"Maybe, but I do not believe his devotion to her has gone unnoticed. Hard to accept, I know. You have to get used to it."

Red-streaked eyes glared at him from under Sabian's mat of blond hair. "Used to it? Is that how you deal? Get used to it? He joined because of you!"

Tohmas' grip on the candle tightened, but he had nothing to say. It was true.

"You should not have come to Vait," the boy declared as he stood, staring down at the prince as if the momentary height would give him the advantage. "If you had not come…"

"Ciene would be alive," Tohmas finished the thought. There was no point in denying his guilt; he would be lying to himself and Sabian both.

"He would be alive!" the boy repeated with venom. "My brother! How can you even pretend to understand! You have no family, so what do you care? He was my only family! You—"

In his anger, Sabian reached for his knife.

Before the protectors could move, Tohmas swept off of the log, caught the boy's wrist, and twisted his arm. The next move would have used the boy's own knife, with his hand still on the handle, to cut into the spine and kill him. Tohmas had performed the maneuver a hundred times and knew it well, but this time he caught himself.

The last time he had caught a wrist like this, he had killed someone in reflex. He had learned not to be so careless.

Celebrant

Pinning the knife flat against the boy's back, Tohmas warned in a low voice, "Never pull a knife in anger, Sabian. I guarantee you will get yourself killed."

Whether from the pain or the momentary struggle, much of the fury had faded from the boy's face by the time Tohmas let go of his wrist.

Grief remained.

"You—"

"You can blame me if you want, Sabian," Tohmas interrupted. "Most people would. But if you want to deal with your brother's death, find a way to honor him. Take some part of him with you and turn to it when you feel his ghost near. Use that pain."

Although Tohmas would have liked to keep the candle for himself, Sabian needed the presence of his brother far more. He placed the candle on the log.

The red-eyed glare abated as Tohmas left the campfire. War was hard. Men dealt with it or died. The advice was more than anyone had ever given Tohmas.

Tohmas left the grieving brother with his tears and returned to his tent.

Carsh slept just inside Tohmas' tent, doing his part to keep the camp small. The Rydan partially opened one eye upon Tohmas' arrival. With a grunt, he rolled over on his cot.

There was no actual blood shared between them, but fifteen years of sharing a father and a war made Carsh Tohmas' brother as much as Sabian's blood tied him to Ciene. No one outside the Outlands knew them as brothers, and he was forbidden from telling them. They did not even know Tohmas spoke the language.

After checking that no one was within earshot, Tohmas spoke in Rydan. "Brother, don't die."

"I won't," Carsh muttered into the furs lining the cot.

"Another dead?" Loni snapped. "Another one from the Gathering of Fire?" Sitting at the vardo counter of a Fixer City distillery, she scowled at the cutter beside her, knowing the crime wasn't his but not caring. In anticipation of another overnight march, Fixer City, the unofficial

 # Chapter 3

merchant and supply train following the Galanth army, was quiet. Loni had been forced to goad her unwittingly helpful cutter out of bed to get a drink into him. After enough time catering to him, she knew he was most reliable when he was drunk.

"Yep," the cutter said. "Had his candle right there too. Prince Tohmas saw him personally, but the guy was just a warden, so I don't know—"

"The Champion of Fire," Loni said, picking up the sieve in anticipation, "sees even more than even I! He knows what's happening! I was right to be suspicious."

The drunken cutter shrugged again and swallowed the rest of his ale. "What is it then?" he asked himself. "One earth to four waters, two winds and...uh...twelve..."

"Thirteen from the Fire's Gathering," Loni corrected. "Only one earth, while the rest of us die. Barga's hands are blood-soaked this time, and the prince sees it! I knew he would."

The cutter stared at her, his expression curious. Loni stopped, smiled sweetly, and emptied the pitcher of ale into his cup through the sieve. She did not have to be too subtle, for he was already far gone. She popped open one of her many rings and dumped the contents into the mug.

"Never you mind. The jug's empty, so we can go as soon as you finish that cup," she cooed.

He was unconscious shortly.

When she left him on the counter, Loni took the pills from the cutter's pouch. The server would take him back to the Temple waggon as directed. Anyone who had seen him with her would politely ignore the cutter's indiscretion. She had what she needed.

Seria was in her nightgown when she came before Darknim. His Hunters had taken him literall when he said to bring her to him immediately after she woke, for they had not even allowed her to change out of her shimmer-thin garment. She was lucky she was not Northlander; Northlanders did not use sleeping clothes. She could have been brought to him completely nude.

She was a good-looking Esparan, if young for him. He would not have minded.

Seria's hair was unattended, and her eyes carried sleep in them when she glared up at him.

"I must go to Arcott," Darknim informed her. "Call your master if you must, but I need to go now."

The Esparan woman's pale eyes narrowed. "He does not like being awoken."

Darknim stepped forward. He was wearing his full dragon scale shirt and carried the dragon shaped ax over his back. Atop the armor, his bog-iron pendant hung dangling in her view as he warned, "This is important, wizard. Get me there."

Seria tracked the swinging sword-shaped pendant for a moment, then, with teeth gritted, nodded.

When she sat down, the girl's hair was long enough to cushion her seat and her thin garb fell tight against her body. Darknim dismissed his Hunters once the pale shine of magic started to swirl in the tent. After a long conjure, Seria spoke in a clear voice. "My apologies for the interruption, Master Terant, but DoomDragon insists on going to Arcott tonight." Seria cocked her head to listen to the reply that only she could hear. "Yes, I can provide an anchor."

Her eyes closed as more magic manifested around her. Darknim stepped back warily, but his eyes did not leave the slight woman on the floor. She was not casting that he could see, but there was still a cloud of blue and purple swirling around her.

A blue and black clad man, tall and thin, appeared directly behind Seria. His bright cerulean eyes landed on her tangled hair and slight coverings and disapproval flashed across the master wizard's face. The harsh glare then snapped onto Darknim.

"What cause have you to disturb us so late at night?" Master Terant Palnon demanded.

Seeing the master wizard in his typical embossed robes and innumerable gold or silver magic trinkets made Darknim doubt he had woken Terant at all.

"My business is with our patron," Darknim replied evenly. "Take me to him. Now."

Chapter 3

With a bow of his head in concession, Master Terant muttered a few words and wrapped Darknim in powerful magic. DoomDragon tensed, feeling as if the blue and purple light that appeared would squeeze the air from him. But as soon as he recognized the unpleasant sensation, he was elsewhere, and the magic was fading. Darknim was impressed. Seria was only a short time away from being named a master wizard, yet she could not even cast the Relocation spell that would move two people.

Travelling by magic left Darknim disoriented. He had to follow the wizard through six rooms before finally recognizing the corridors of the Manor of Arcott. Bothering Terant in the middle of the night was an effective way to convince him to be direct, it seemed. He took him to Prince Marfaie immediately.

Prince Marfaie sat on his whale and caribou bone throne in a uselessly large and empty hall. He had been hastily woken and wore a robe over his bedclothes. For a rare moment, Darknim saw his patron without jewels and gold. The prince looked stronger for it as far as Darknim was concerned.

The prince's face had been worn by the winter winds of the north, leaving his skin as tough as hide and as dark as stone. Five tattoos, each the same bear claw slash, crossed his face, two from the left and three from the right. His lower arms, usually covered but tonight bare, wore black writing and symbols Darknim did not understand but thought arcane. The tattoos on the face were meant to impress the men of the sword—his soldiers. The writing on his arms marked him as an authority for the men of the wand.

Feeling cowed by neither symbol of power, Darknim demanded, "Tell me about this new prince. You told me many things about the others, but this man is strange to me."

Had he made a similar demand of Terant, Darknim would have been chastised a dozen times before being given an answer, but Prince Marfaie only smirked under his crisscrossed tattoos. "Prince Tohmas? Not much to tell you. He is a grandson of Zayban and the son of Habal, who died this spring. Beyond that, the man has manipulated every prince or pauper who has met him and driven them all to attack you. He is young and rash and bloodthirsty."

"He is not rash," Darknim corrected. "He has been well-controlled and clever. These are not traits I expect from the sons of Zayban."

"Prince Sol is cornered and making mistakes. The other two show their colors through their inaction. But their hearts were turned to stone long ago, DoomDragon. Do not expect mercy from them." The prince scowled, his wrinkles forming deep crevices over his brow.

"I expect no mercy from any son of Zayban, be they this new prince or older ones. I need to know more about him, my Prince."

"He is of the line of Zayban," the prince said with a sigh. "He continues the oppression his father established. He is here only in search of conquest and glory. I do not want him to find either."

Darknim shook his head and frowned. "I will not give them to him," he promised.

As the silence lingered, he realized that was the extent of the information to be had. The Prince of Galanth was new to his title. There was not much known about him yet.

On a whim, Darknim asked, "What happened to his father? How did Prince Habal die?"

Prince Marfaie scoffed. "A son of Zayban? Is it not evident? Tohmas slew him, of course. It has been hidden from the people of Galanth, covered up to ensure Tohmas inherits smoothly. Ask your precious Circle if you want. The ruthlessness of Zayban transcends generations."

Now that it was spoken, it seemed evident. No cruelty the sons of Zayban demonstrated would ever surprise Darknim, not after the history he had learned in Tanble. Prince Tohmas was no different.

But the Esparans had illusions about their society that had to be maintained. How was it they followed a man who had slain his father and taken power by murder?

"Is that why you came, Darknim?" the prince grumbled from his throne. "You woke us all so you could hear me say things you already knew?"

Darknim jerked his finger toward the wizard. "I have reached an impasse. I need Terant."

The reply was swift and from two sources. "You have your own wizard!" both men said.

Darknim shook his head. "Seria was sleeping, and I could not wake her until now. I find her magic unreliable. I cannot afford mistakes. Or do you want Galanth to reinforce Prince Sol's defense of BellRoost? I

Chapter 3

could let them meet, but then the others might start thinking in terms of unions, and I would see—"

"Take Master Terant," Prince Marfaie interrupted. Without turning, Darknim could tell his back was the target of a dark look from the master wizard. "If you cannot handle this on your own, Darknim, I give you leave to use the wizard. Might I know why you are so unable to finish this without such powerful magical aid?"

The double-edged question rolled off Darknim. He had been given a task, and he would achieve it. However he did that was success.

"Prince Tohmas marches by night and is avoiding my Circle by hiding in the woods. He has either moved east or west along DancingIce River. I want to see where my enemy hides. Your magic is the best way."

The prince frowned deeply, and shadows covered his face. "He will have moved toward Sol. If he—"

"If he is as rash and bloodthirsty as you think, he may have moved east so he could attack me from behind. He has already claimed too many lives with his trickery. I will not have my men paying the cost of a repetition," Darknim said.

The Esparan prince sat in silence until, at length, he waved in vague agreement. Darknim left the hall with the wizard. Together they travelled to the Circle of the Raven, and together, they sought their prey.

Chapter 4

Since the wards that guarded his personal vardo would have made it dangerous for even the magic-sensitive Carsh to venture into, Kitable understood why he woke in a Healing waggon.

When Healing Mother Gracie checked on him, it became clear little was known about him and his condition. The healing mother admitted she did not know his name or why he had arrived unconscious. She insisted on having the acolytes help him wash and shave; his hand was still too unstable to manage it alone.

Despite how unsteadily Kitable walked, the healing mother seemed to know she could not stop him as he left the waggon. Telling himself he was just weak after too much time spent in bed, he sought out Prince Tohmas. He needed to shake the enervation quickly, but he felt slow and groggy. Heading into the rows of tents confused Kitable further. He had thought it dusk by the light through the windows of the waggon, but it was dawn. The army had camped in the woods around a large river, making the usually predictable pattern of fyrds and their defenses twisted and hard to navigate. The Healing waggons had been spread among the forces instead of clustered around the Temple waggons, dumping Kitable into the heart of the Fyrd of Rest. He had to find a guardian's tent and ask the ranking officer for directions to the prince. They did one better and found him a protector. The bodyguard led him to a green tent that was being erected.

Dawn, and they are setting camp?

Chapter 4

The prince's tent wrapped around a series of trunks as there was no space large enough for the entire structure. Given leave by the protectors, Kitable entered the malformed tent to find Prince Tohmas at prayers before his personal altar to Inac. Prime Protector Carsh sat with his feet on the table, chewing on an apple.

Tohmas rose swiftly, his smile broad. "You're up! Excellent!"

Kitable mutely nodded as he found his way to a chair. To Kitable's amazement, Carsh offered him a piece of the apple he was munching. Kitable declined. Healing Mother Gracie had insisted he eat something before leaving, and the ration of sweet bread and cheese was still sitting in his stomach. The smell of cedar that strangely coated the prime protector mixed with the sour smoke from the yellow candle on the table and made his breakfast shift uneasily.

He was also too amazed by the Rydan's good humor to trust anything Carsh offered.

Kitable sat to give his weary legs a chance to rest, and the Rydan took his feet from the table. "How long have I been asleep?"

"Just over two days," Tohmas replied. He filled a cup from a wineskin as he spoke.

"Every time I come in here, you try to get me drunk," Kitable grumbled, but he gratefully took the wine, waving off the flies from above the cup. With the muddy bank not far, the buzz of insects was loud. There were spells that could help, but Kitable did not have the energy for them. Instead, he shifted his seat a little closer to the scented candle.

"It implies trust, Master Kitable," Tohmas mildly pointed out. "I only offer drink to men I would drink with." True to his word, he sat across from the wizard with his own cup. The bare sincerity of the remark stunned Kitable into a silence that lasted until the prince cracked a smile, swatted a fly, and added, "And you can tell how much I like you based on what I offer."

Kitable looked in the cup. "What does wine mean?"

"It means I know you dislike heavy ale but think you worth more than plain water."

To his right, the prime protector took a swig from his own wineskin and grinned at Kitable with his sharp teeth.

Kitable cocked an eyebrow. "Not wildwater?"

Celebrant

Tohmas laughed harshly, and the Rydan grinned wider. "Wildwater without warning is a prank. Wildwater with warning is offered to those who appreciate it. That, or I *do* want the person drunk." Tohmas followed swiftly with, "How are you feeling?"

"Still shaky," Kitable surprised himself by answering. To anyone else, he would have lied. When there were wizards near, Kitable had to maintain appearances. He would be able to handle several spells, but he was in no shape for dueling. A few days more would see him recovered so long as he was not required to push it before then.

"This happen often?"

Kitable smiled to hear the query. "No. I was forced to cast excessively to keep the men hidden after DoomDragon arrived early while also moving a great deal of earth magically. It tired me. Full casting a Force Wall to deflect that Fire Blast took another huge amount of energy, which is why I fell unconscious. If I can just get some more rest, I will be fine." The shadows over their faces at his words made his stomach sink. "Where are we, anyway? Where is DoomDragon?" The only thing he was certain of was the pressing need for him and his magic, and that worried him.

"We're camped on the bank of DancingIce River to the southwest of the last location you remember. DoomDragon is to the east of us and probably very annoyed by now. We have been keeping out of sight since your collapse, but we will be making another run toward BellRoost when night falls after the men have had some sleep."

"Any sign of his wizards?" Kitable pressed. "Have they not tried anything in my absence? Two days is a long time to wait when our forces are in such close proximity."

Tohmas shrugged and refilled both cups. Kitable did not remember drinking his, but it was empty. "We have kept to the forest and moved only at night. They cannot—"

"Trees are not an obstacle for a caster with an anchor," Kitable protested, "nor is night a difficulty with the right spells. Are you certain they have not spotted you?" Kitable looked at the Rydan for assistance.

The prime protector nodded. "Tey naw be passin' near."

Kitable looked at Tohmas for an explanation of the explanation.

 # Chapter 4

"They do not appear to be passing magic near enough for him to sense at all. Even the rearguard has seen nothing of the Northlanders yet. I'm hoping they haven't decided which way we went."

Kitable's head throbbed in anticipation, but he dragged himself through the thoughts anyway.

"That we have not yet been assaulted by magic supports that theory, my Prince, but I blocked a Fire Blast. That is no trifling spell. A wizard capable of that certainly has enough power to set an anchor and follow it." He glanced at Carsh again, but the Rydan did not move from his place. "Maybe they know about Carsh and are avoiding getting close enough? Or... or..." Kitable's head pulsed in pain, interrupting his thoughts. He leaned back with a hand on his temples to settle the pain and squeezed his eyes shut. The final conclusion came quickly. "Or they don't have an anchor. Maybe we got lucky. Maybe they are excellent at creation but can't hold an alteration."

He heard Tohmas chuckle but did not open his eyes to look. "A specialist? Those exist?" the prince asked.

Kitable did not waste his energy by nodding. "Some people have a predilection for certain types of magic or at least study one more than others. Focus too much on one domain or element, and one may find it more difficult to use the others. They are rare but..."

In the middle of his explanation, Kitable sensed a tingle of magic drift into the tent through the ceiling, just close enough for him to feel. He sat bolt upright, grateful to see Carsh jump to his feet and draw his second knife.

"*Flya touch! Tey wak!*" the Rydan exclaimed. Carsh's eyes narrowed, but the magic did not take solid form, giving him no valid target for his knives.

Kitable froze, waiting for the spell to manifest enough to determine the appropriate counter. The timid fragment of magic could be only an anchor. Depending on the skill of the caster, what was attached to the anchor might be as harmless as a Scry, but a truly powerful wizard could put something more devastating down the anchor if they had reason to.

Mentally, Kitable checked himself over. He had not cast any spells that morning and was, for a rare moment, without any hovering spells. He still had a few tricks in the form of enchanted objects—the crystal that hung around his neck was enchanted to be hidden from all but the most penetrating of investigations—but he probably looked innocuous enough.

When he looked back to Tohmas, the prince had Kitable's glass sphere—enchanted and left to him as a defense—out and was rolling it around on the table gently. Should a threat appear, Tohmas had been instructed to smash the sphere and release the magic within it. It would work nicely to ruin the anchor.

The magic thickened slightly, then held. Suspecting a Scry, Kitable did not let the silence in the tent linger. An ability to sense magic was uncommon, particularly among non-wizards, and there was no reason the caster would recognize Kitable. The observer did not necessarily know the tent was aware of them.

"Attacking DoomDragon straight on is suicide. I cannot condone it." He quickly downed the rest of the wine, hoping it would help calm his nerves. He was uncommonly vulnerable and wished it was not so obvious.

Tohmas caught on to the bluff at once. His posture slouched, and his attention wandered like a bored apprentice. Even the careless, clumsy way he handled the cup implied a complete lack of grace.

"Do not argue with me, you lout," the prince grumbled with a drunken slur. "I want them turned around and ready to face the brute when he shows his sorry face." Carsh smirked at the comment, but Kitable could not tell if the Rydan knew it was ruse or not.

"We will show him the might of Galanth!" Tohmas insisted as he slammed his dagger into the wooden table, then left it there as he rose to his feet. The glass orb had silently disappeared from view, but Kitable did not doubt it was still on hand. "I want him dead before we reach BellRoost, so I can show my demon-kissing uncle how war is meant to be fought! I'm not going to wait another ten years to chase the rats from our lands! The sooner, the better! I do not fear any mongrel dressed in rotting furs and dulled antlers. Let him…"

As Tohmas continued to boast of his prowess and mock the Northlanders' ineptitude, Kitable focused his attention on the push of magic above them. Like a slight breeze, it descended behind him and touched down on a chest against the tent wall. It was too weak to be a threat, but he kept a hand on one of his trinkets, ready to activate a powerful multi-way shield if something unpleasant came down the anchor.

 # CHAPTER 4

The moment the spell was in place on the chest, the tense feeling of magic vanished. The caster was gone.

Kitable leaped to his feet, his movement stopping Tohmas' diatribe mid-sentence. A string of words drew in magic, and another string wove it into Spell Sight, allowing him to see the aura of the spell on the chest. With Carsh at his back and Tohmas calmly peering over his shoulder, Kitable examined the cloud-like aura of purple. A thin tendril reached through the roof.

Kitable released a breath and lowered back into his seat. "A Binding. I guess they didn't have an anchor after all, for that seems to be what they just created, the lazy bastards."

As soon as he knew it was clear, Tohmas called, "Runnah!"

"Who...?" Kitable wondered.

A protector hurdled through the tent flap, his hand out to catch the leather token that Tohmas threw at him to assign him as a messenger.

"Get the men up and moving. Now. We march to the fields and then west. Guardians to me."

The protector left at a sprint.

When the prince faced him, Kitable anticipated his question and said, "Yes, they know where you are. They are using that chest to track you. They could, if they were clever, find a way to define something directly, but apparently, they have not been that creative yet. Instead, they are using for an anchor 'the chest I have enchanted with this binding.'"

"You can break the binding?

"Easily. I believe they are counting on it not being noticed, which also implies that they do not know Carsh can sense magic. I think it is safe to say they did not recognize me, my Prince, or they would not have been so careless."

"Or kind," the Rydan added.

Despite himself, Kitable had to nod in agreement.

Tohmas appeared to be baffled.

"I am wearing no hovering spells," Kitable explained. "Right now, I make a tempting target." A flash of worry crossed Tohmas' face, but the prince seemed to dismiss it in the next blink. Kitable chose to be complimented by Tohmas' confidence in him.

 # Celebrant

"We need to get to BellRoost," Tohmas said. "I need Sol to help me. Master Kitable, are you able to send a message and tell him where we are?"

Kitable leaned back in his chair and nodded through his headache. There was little doubt he was going to be fatigued again tonight, but he had been through worse. A few Sending spells would be easy enough.

Maybe then he would get to rest until they reached BellRoost.

Stacked stones formed an unlit and uneven passageway down from the hide flap entrance of the Earth Lodge. In the company of the shorter wizard, only Darknim had to stoop to avoid the ceiling of the tunnel. By the time they reached the door, they were more than a stride underground, a short height of circling stones lifting the dirt-covered ceiling over them. Having bashed his ax handle into the top of the doorframe more than once, Darknim carried the weapon at his side as he left the dawning hills where he had camped the Northlander forces and descended into the hut below. Master Terant followed him down.

The Circle were ready for them, torches mounted and lit on the wall of their burrow. It was not unexpected. One of the greatest abilities of the Circle of the Raven was divination.

The lodge was two dozen paces wide and cold despite the torches. At the center, the frozen pool had been allowed to take whatever shape it preferred. This time it resembled a spread bearskin. The seven Elders of the Circle sat on their respective pelt seats around the pool, the furs or feathers representing their Aspects draped over their shoulders. None of the smoke or warmth of the flames along the walls passed the elders, leaving the core area frigid. A mist drifted over the surface of the pool, and tiny lights flickered under the fog like trapped firebugs.

Darknim DoomDragon placed his ax by the entrance then moved to the edge of the ice. Unarmed, he faced the Voice of the Raven, Elder Ela, across the pool. The old woman was so frail, she stooped under the weight of her robe of snowy owl feathers, but her face was carved with laugh lines, and her eyes were sweet as they gazed, wide with hazy sight, at Darknim. Elder Tril sat to her left, his head tucked low against his white wolf pelt.

 # Chapter 4

"We are graced by your presence, DoomDragon," Ela said. "Welcome, and welcome Master Terant."

Ela had more strength to her voice than usual, and a glance around the room explained why. "You are Linking. We have intruded," Darknim said.

The images flickering in the frozen pool ahead of him formed a pattern, and Darknim through he heard distant, broken whispers through the mist. That he made out the shape of wooden structures in the ice surprised him.

Ela gave a hoot of laughter. "You sense the Linking? Perhaps our DoomDragon has come into his *visaln* at last."

Darknim shook his head. "The floor takes on a purple glow to my eyes when you are Linking. That, and you all blink in unison."

Around the pool, although their eyes were still on the ice, all the Circle members smiled. Many of their mouths showed the fangs of their Aspects.

"You will yet grow this gift, your *visaln*," Elder Ela confided in a croak. "You see."

The ability to see magic was not new to Darknim; he had seen the pale lights of magic since childhood. He thought perhaps the colors were getting brighter over time, but it was slow. At over sixty years of age, Darknim did not think he had sufficient years remaining for the magical skill to become useful.

Interrupting the conversation, Master Terant stepped up to the pool's edge. "He requests my use of your Circle." His voice terse, he glowered as if wanting to scold them for ignoring him.

The images in the pool slowly faded from view, and the various animal stares of the elders lifted to regard the Esparan wizard.

"I know, wizard," Ela replied in Northlander. Darknim hid his smile. Ela was the Seat of Thought in the Circle of the Raven. She had likely slipped through Master Terant's defenses and looked into his mind, but Terant did not seem to realize it. Terant's beaded bracelet would translate Ela's Northlander words, but the magical assistance did not reveal the meaning behind the words.

"As always, we act in service to DoomDragon," the voices of the Circle joined to confirm.

Celebrant

Under the stares of the Circle of the Raven, Master Terant squared his shoulders and knelt by the pool. He glanced up as if checking they were still watching then launched into a spell, weaving together tendrils of multicolored lights.

A long thread of white and yellow, like a brilliant hot flame, trickled from Terant's fingers into the pool. The magic in the room deepened, dimming the torches and allowing figures to appear in the ice more clearly. Darknim stepped away and leaned against the cavern walls, ready for a long wait. He watched blurred movement in the pool but could not make out the features of the people in the ice. He heard mumbled voices as the Scry progressed, Esparan words delivered in a half-shout, but they were too distant for him to understand.

He was unsurprised that Terant found the army with ease despite how the task had confounded the Circle. The Circle had never been meant to find men; their duty was to protect the Northlanders. They could lessen a windstorm, provide fire for heat when no other source would hold, make sheltering caverns out of shear rock, and moderate the worst of the feuds among the families, but searching for a strange man in unknown territory was not within their powers.

They were learning, of that there was no doubt, but their new skills limited them. They had accepted Terant's lessons on tracking, but the new approach to magic bound them too tightly to their target to see anything beyond Kitable's vardo. If they did not use the binding to the vardo, they were lost among unfamiliar landmarks and limited by what they could spot from above, which Prince Tohmas seemed to have predicted and hidden himself from.

Terant cast once more, and a purple thread of magic entered the pool. Something flashed in the ice then faded. The images snapped out of sight.

The casters, including the Circle, faced him. Darknim left his leaning position to stand tall before them.

"Prince Tohmas is located to the west along the river," Elder Ela informed Darknim. "He is camped but a day and a half's journey from your men, DoomDragon. He has hidden himself among the trees."

"Trees are not an obstacle. Your Circle relies too much on vision," Terant said, his expression a sneer.

 # Chapter 4

"They have been casting for more years than you have breathed, wizard. Do not criticize them lightly," Darknim warned. The Circle of the Raven was the source of his title. Diminishing them would only weaken the Northlanders.

After a moment of irate silence, Terant stood and said, "I have put a binding spell on a chest in the prince's tent, so your Circle should be able to track that as they do Kitable's vardo. They ought to be able to hear their plans and location from there. When I have a moment, perhaps I will show them how to drift from an anchor without severing the Scry, but I am not in a good enough mood this morning. Goodbye, DoomDragon."

Terant pivoted sharply and stalked from the hut, into the cold light of morning. Darknim assumed he would soon use magic to Relocate himself and wondered why the man had not done it from the hut. Stones and dirt were not obstacles for a caster such as Terant. Was there something he wanted kept from the Circle?

Darknim let him go; he had questions to ask the Circle.

But as he took up the place Master Terant and vacated, Ela pre-empted him. "There was strangeness to that vision," Ela muttered into her feathers so softly that Darknim was unsure how he heard the words at all.

"What strangeness?"

"We shall show you. Accept the Linking."

Darknim closed his eyes to hide the distracting purple flashes around him. He trusted the elders enough not to be frightened by their spells, but the whispers hissing in his mind made his temples hurt. He had to concentrate to hear any specific voice, and when someone spoke to him through the Link, he could not ignore it.

His chest felt lighter; the weight of his bog iron pendant had vanished.

Watch, DoomDragon, and you will see what we saw, a voice said in his mind. By the growl it in, it had been Tril.

When Darknim opened his eyes, the figures in the ice were clear. The view was of a tent without a top; no, he was within the tent, hovering near the ceiling. Darknim recognized the Prince of Galanth and his prime protector from his previous encounter with them, but he did not know the third man who sat at the table. Voices, speaking Esparan that the Circle would struggle to understand, resonated among whispered thoughts and words of the Linking Circle.

"Attacking DoomDragon straight on is suicide," the unidentified man said. "I cannot condone it." The voice sounded distinctly southern and the man himself was strongly Esparan. The prince, who made a loud comment before slamming his dagger into the table and getting up to pace, boasted an even stronger Esparan heritage with his larger size and sun-yellow hair. His colors, worn in everything from his tunic to his riding boots, were green and silver.

With Prince Tohmas ranted like a child throwing a tantrum, Darknim frowned. They had crossed blades before and the fact that Prince Tohmas had survived the encounter had won him Darknim's respect, but Darknim felt he should reconsider if the Prince of Galanth was this spoiled child. Perhaps the other man at the table truly commanded the forces. Was the prince merely being used? How could this pacing, irritating boy be the one who had countered Darknim's plans for Barrow Hills?

The more Darknim watched, the more the discrepancy weight on him. Prince Tohmas moved wrong. In the Scry, the prince had no smoothness to his gait or gestures. Darknim had seen Prince Tohmas fight with precision, balance, and ingenuity. Who was this tottering idiot?

Abruptly, the vision was over. Darknim saw only the ice.

"Again," he said aloud. "I want to see the others."

It began again, but this time, Darknim studied the man in the chair instead of the prince. He could tell little about the Esparan, except that he was not a military man. It seemed unlikely the prince would share a drink with anyone not of high rank, yet there was no rank rope on the man's shoulder. He seemed to be paying attention to the prince, yet his eyes were slightly unfocussed as if he was lost in thought.

That one has powers, the Circle warned. *We thought him a wizard, but Terant did not acknowledge him.*

"A wizard?" Darknim asked through the Linking. His head shook in answer to his own question.

Not like the Esparan we work with, for he does not have magic manifested around him. His power is in things, DoomDragon. He wears tools of magic, not active spells.

Chapter 4

He sounds familiar, he heard through the Linking, *but I cannot place him.*

A representative of the wizard? A friend of the prince? Not a soldier, so another rich boy with magic trinkets? The man was older, but he was not dressed as well as the others.

The Scry ended once more, and the man at the table had not spoken another word. Darknim did not have to ask for the vision to be repeated; the Circle knew. This time, his eyes went to the last man in the room.

The man looked, at first, very Esparan, but he was lean and his features thin. He was also dressed differently; his attire was mostly hides without fur, and he wore dried grasses around his wrists. The man's sandy hair was rough, and an earring of bone hung from his right ear. The blades in each of hand matched the dozens of blades on his belt and double baldric. His bare feet, also a rarity among Esparans, were planted firmly.

Darknim had met the man before when he tried to end the war by slaying Prince Tohmas. No one seemed to know much about Prime Protector Carsh, except that he was Rydan and an expert with his blades. Darknim had seen the prince and his prime protector working together in combat with great skill. To kill Tohmas, Darknim would do well to separate them.

It was not until the Rydan glanced directly up at the Scry that Darknim understood what the prime protector was so tensely guarding against.

He sees us, a voice of the Circle whispered, sharing Darknim's realization.

Impossible, someone else answered.

This one has sensed us. The Esparan wizard was wrong to pass so close. If he knew, all they heard was false, the first voice said.

"Tohmas plays the fool to make us believe he is incompetent," Darknim agreed. "The plan for facing us is a ploy. They will run for BellRoost. We will let them meet the rest of our forces and crush them against the walls of the city."

He felt the Circle's agreement just before the whispers were cut off and the frozen pool went black.

Celebrant

Darknim blinked to regain his vision. The barely discernable purple line passed directly in front of him now. The Linking to him had been dropped.

Gathering his ax, he headed back to break camp. Elder Tril came with him to lead the way to Prince Tohmas' forces now that they had found them. Speed was vital. He had to trap them before they made their run to BellRoost.

Lance's fatigue fully manifested when they stopped the second overnight march at dawn and set up camp. Once the camp was set, the men of the Fyrd of Arrow were freed from their duties and sent to bed. Lance did one final check of the area before deciding on sleep. A handful of men remained awake outside his tent, but they would probably soon find their own rest. After two nights, they all needed it, and at that moment, Lance was too tired to care. He ducked into his tent.

Recognizing abruptly that his tent was not empty, Lance scrambled out. He did not even have time to figure out who the intruder was.

The men outside, guardsmen who had followed him from Gaidol, broke into raucous laughter. Only one kept a straight face, an ex-mason by the name of Wadley. Wadley did his best to look offended as he asked, "You don't like our present?" The mason held his quivering lip until the girl stuck her head out of Lance's tent, at which point he joined his fellow guardsmen in laughter.

Lance did not share their mirth; he knew the girl they had let into his tent.

The Rydan slunk out and stood tall in the cool evening air, her hide wrapping covering only the most essential areas and leaving her with gooseflesh. She had at least put aside her knife, but Lance was not fooled. *Where is her companion?*

Lance gripped his sword's hilt in readiness. The guardsmen's laughter faded.

"What, by the hells, are you doing here?"

The girl—young enough to be his daughter if Lance had married young—reached out with open hands. "Naw 'ome," she said.

 # Chapter 4

"No...no home?" Lance dropped his ready stance and let his hand fall with a sigh. "You don't have a home to go back to."

"You *know* her?" Wadley exclaimed, his eyes wide. The other guardsmen dropped their jaws in shock.

"She tried to kill me. I had a chance, but I didn't kill her."

"Ya be goh man," the girl said.

"I'm not sure I am," Lance replied. "Look, girl, you don't belong here. Northlanders are two feet off our arses, and it's going to be tight to reach BellRoost. They've got nothing against you. Why don't you—"

"Naw 'ome!" she snapped. She stepped forward in emphasis, and he backed away. His hand went for his sword again, but he resisted the urge to draw it. Seeing him skitter away from a child was scaring the guardsmen enough.

"Fine, alright," he soothed. "I get it. You don't have a home. You probably don't have anyone else left either. What do you expect me to do about it?"

She looked at him with huge eyes and a lost expression.

"Oh demons," Lance cursed.

"I think she's got you figured," Wadley called brightly.

She was tiny, alone, and foreign. Without help, she wouldn't have a chance. And what did a Rydan know about living with the Esparans? Who would fairly trade with her even if she did figure out how to speak Esparan? At least she seemed to understand the language well enough.

"Can you cook or something?" Lance asked.

She nodded, her smile broad as she recognized his defeat. With a wave, she called over her friend, who had been hiding behind other tents. The guardsmen fell silent, but Lance could not tell if it was because they had so clearly missed spotting her or because she was the most attractive woman any of them had ever seen.

Lance was more concerned with the extra knives the woman had collected. He remembered them having only one each, but as the taller woman joined the first, she handed over three knives, including one set tied together by a lanyard. All of the knives were bone-handled and flint-bladed.

"Your names?" Lance asked as the women stored their weapons. Lance missed where the smaller girl put at least one of hers.

"Sori," the small spokeswoman said.

Celebrant

"Tanuka," the taller woman offered.

One of the guardsmen cleared his throat, the cheeriness gone at the sight of weapons. "Lance, do you need—"

"Boys," Lance interrupted, "meet Sori and Tanuka."

"Who are they?" asked Carthy, the most levelheaded of the lot of them. He was holding his eating knife at his knee, just in case.

"They're Rydans who are, in exchange for somewhere to sleep and food to eat, going to cook for us."

Lance got a nod of acceptance from Sori, but the silence from the guardsmen was long.

"They any good at mending?" Wadley asked into the gap. Lance shot him a glare, and the guardsman shrugged. "Tore a hole through my glove this morning."

Sori retrieved a bag from beside the tent and proudly pulled out a bone needle and thick thread.

Wadley smiled. "At least they're useful."

The knot in Lance's chest slowly released. The women seemed friendly and willing to work to earn their keep. Sori's expression remained factual, but Tanuka's was flirtatious.

"You all get to know each other," Lance said, pointing the two groups at each other. "Boys, they are to be treated fairly in all things, or I will personally lop heads. Got it?"

"Yeah, yeah." Wadley waved his hand as if to knock the threats from their path. The others nodded.

"I'm going to ask someone a few questions," Lance said. He glanced at the young women. Hoping to keep them out of trouble, he added, "Please have some food ready when I get back."

Sori made her way to the cooking fire and shouldered the current cook out of the way. Lance felt her eyes on him as he left.

As Kitable settled onto the floor of his vardo, he reached out his senses to the magic that surrounded and protected him. He had only cast two hovering spells—poor substitutions for his usually extensive repertoire—but the spells wrought into the walls of his travelling home finally made him feel safe.

Chapter 4

He needed rest. Casting the simple defenses had drained him further. Unconsciousness due to enervation provided no relief, not like a proper sleep would have. He would send the message Tohmas requested then sleep the rest of the way to BellRoost. In his vardo, he could let the horses do the walking for him, Colt driving them.

Sitting on the floor, Kitable crafted an anchor.

He had no energy to cast a Scry and guide the anchor visually. But so long as he defined the target to the magic's satisfaction, that would be irrelevant. Magic did not recognize names, those were a human creation. And from magic's unique view, all timelines were just as likely to have happened or be about to happen. The only thing consistent was the present, as it stood, at this very moment. Kitable had to find someone he could describe accurately in this instance, else would be thrown into either a reflection or a divination, and that was not what he needed.

Wizards knew the danger of being targeted by description. It was common place to vary their appearance from day to day and remain undefinable. Kitable changed everything from his shoes to his trinkets, including identifying marks such as the burns on his left arm and his scarred back. The only consistent item he wore was the heavily enchanted crystal around his neck, which could cast a Relocation spell to send him back to his home in Wayburn. The item, which was concealed from every spell he could conceive, was activated by mixing the crystal with blood. It was a secret he revealed to no one.

He needed to find someone who was not as careful.

Clarin was a potential target, but the wizard likely had defenses in addition to a varying appearance, making him a poor choice for an anchor. No wizard dared let unknown magic enter the area they occupied anyway.

Kitable smiled feebly. He had done that just that morning. Enervated as he had been, there had been no choice.

Prince Sol was a second possible target, but Clarin would have defended his prince. Kitable had no way to predict or counter all the possible combinations of spells. He needed someone undefended.

A protector would suffice. And, to his advantage, only Protectors of Solta wore a red and black rope over their shoulder.

Kitable breathed deeply and used the sharp exhale to mentally push aside all extraneous thoughts. In the stillness, he reached his mind to the source of magic. In his thoughts, he saw the source as a wall of churning colors on the far side of a deep chasm. The art of pulling magic in was much like leaning over a steep riverbank, trying to get a single cup of water without either losing the cup or falling in. The bigger the cup he tried to fill, the higher the chance of disaster. But the spell was not difficult, and the powers he required were easy to snatch up. He ensured he had more than enough. The burn of any leftover magic was a casting consequence he was accustomed to. Much of his life had been devoted to fine-tuning the draw of powers to take only what he needed, so reducing the pain of the burn. Usually, he was flawless in execution, but today was different. Today, he chose to draw extra magic in case he failed to control it tightly. Insufficient magic would cause the spell to fail, and he did not have the strength to try again.

Kitable collected the magic he needed, first wind, then binding. Weaving the two elements through the domain of alteration and creation, he spoke aloud his message, collected the words, and bound the message to the anchor. He attached a final binding to it, wanting to know when the message was delivered. Done, he released the spell.

A dull fire ached in his muscles as he relaxed his shoulders and blinked repeatedly to regain his vision. The extra magic burned through him, dissipating now that the spell was complete.

Satisfied the message would soon be in BellRoost, Kitable crawled into his bed to sleep off the Spell Burn.

He had only just drifted off when the magic bound to him ended. The unexpected sensation jarred him back into awareness.

A spell had been dropped. His message had been prematurely disrupted.

Kitable rose, put his sandals on, and went in search of Tohmas. He found the prince riding beside High Guardsman Lance Carraway among the ranks.

"So, what am I supposed to do with them?" the high guardsman was asking.

"Don't get them pregnant," Tohmas replied. Kitable's weary mind could not even begin to sort through the topic they were discussing.

"No chance of that. And if I have to explain to you how that sort of thing works..."

Chapter 4

Chuckling, Tohmas glanced at Kitable and gave him invitation to speak with a nod. Lance shook his head and left as Kitable stepped closer.

"Problem," Kitable said. "The message was stopped. Worse, I think it may have been intercepted, meaning they may know what you are planning, my Prince. They will be ready for you."

"They?"

Kitable rubbed his forehead in frustration, hating his answer. "Good chance it was the Northlander casters. I lost the spell shortly after it left me, long before it reached BellRoost," he admitted.

For a moment as short as the flicker of a candle, the son of Habal did not speak, his eyes distant in thought. "North then," he decided.

Kitable checked the surroundings, but only Carsh was within earshot. "I thought you were avoiding the north because of the river. There is no space between the walls and the bridge."

"We will send the fighters north across the river and hit the Northlanders at Basalt bridge. When they are planted, the rest of the men can move in from the east. That will catch DoomDragon's fighters in a pinch. If we can get Sol to push through his north gate, we could clear enough room for the waggons to get through. It requires more fineness than the southern route, but we can do it."

"So, I need to get a message to Prince Sol without the enemy knowing and tell him to help us at the north gate?"

"If you can, Kit."

The silence lingered as Kitable walked beside the warhorses in thought. His energy was failing rapidly. He did not do well on so little sleep and so much casting. His legs were having trouble keeping up with the strolling horse, and every step came with a twinge because of the Spell Burn. More casting would leave more burn.

"If there is a prob—" Tohmas began.

"I can do it, but it will not be easy."

Tohmas raised an eyebrow. "I thought communication was relatively simple."

"Most messages are aerial—sent through the air. The enemy casters are watching for that, so I have to send it another route, which means guiding it myself. I will need a Scry."

"And that means?"

 # CELEBRANT

"A Scry is essentially taking one's consciousness for a walk without the body. After the spell, I am going to be a bit of a useless stump for a while. You can still call me if—"

"We will manage until we get to BellRoost," Tohmas said, taking his turn interrupting. "I want Sol ready to help us."

"Very well. I will start immediately." Kitable's feet dragged on the way back to his vardo.

Chapter 5

In the newest Earth Lodge in the heart of DoomDragon's army, Tril took his turn maintaining the vision in the ice pool. The day had been long. Although they had finally located the enemy, night forced the army to halt. The Circle built the Earth Lodge quickly these days, so practiced were they in digging the half-structure and doming stones over it. The pool at the center of the dugout hut was the shape of a bird in flight with asymmetrical wings and a small vulture-like head. He thought the shape apt; the Circle had linked through the pool, giving Tril a bird's-eye view of a vardo.

The spells keeping the water frozen misted Tril's breath, but his thick fur coat kept him warm. He was more concerned about his headache from holding the spell for so long. Although the Circle supported him, it was his focus that kept the connection open.

Tril was bound to the wood of the empty vardo with only his Aspect, his wolf skin, between him and the far enemy camp. It felt useless. In the ice, the vardo moved along, its contents swinging, but there was no one within.

"Where is he?" Master Terant grumbled from his place beside the pool. The Esparan's voice always lowered as his annoyance increased. It was coming out as a deep husk now.

"The man sat there for some time and cast, Esparan," a Circle member—Tril did not know which—replied.

"Seria caught his message and stopped it. Are you certain it was Kitable?"

"We saw a man sleep in the vardo," the same elder said. "We called you so you could confirm it was the man you sought."

"Where is he?" Terant mumbled.

There would have been another protest, Tril was certain, but the Esparan wizard stopped before another word escaped him. In the frozen pool at Tril's feet, the waggon door opened, and someone entered. After replacing the spells over the door, the newcomer settled onto the floor of the vardo, crossed his legs, and closed his eyes.

"Kitable..." Terant whispered, the word a curse.

"It is the same man who sat with the prince this morning. You did not recognize him then?" the Circle member asked.

"He is hardly ever seen, Northlander. I did not know his face, and he wore no spells then! There is no doubt now; no one else would enter that vardo with such impunity. That is Kitable. We have a target at last."

Tril sensed motion nearby, but he dared not turn his head, lest he disrupt his concentration. The vardo had remained unchanged and unoccupied for so long, Tril no longer found its hanging tools, candles, and stacked wood-bound books interesting. Instead, he brought his eyes to the most dangerous man in Espar.

Kitable would have been considered slight had he been a Northlander but was of medium size for an Esparan. He had shaven recently. Tril cocked his head in thought. He looked familiar, but not in this place or with these clothes. In his mind, Tril put a beard on the man in the pool and immediately recognized him.

Dressed in a tattered coat and wide-brimmed hat, this same man had confronted Tril and Ela during Darknim's assassination attempt against Tohmas earlier that season. Without the filth and rags, Kitable looked fresher, but there were heavy bags under his closed eyes. Although he sat with purpose, Tril saw the fatigue in the man's posture.

Tril focused on the magic that Kitable was manifesting. He would not be able to understand the spell—the casting was too different from Circle magic—but he thought to memorize it. Perhaps later analysis would provide insight.

"You will not anchor him? Are we to lose sight of him once more?" one of the elders asked the brooding Esparan wizard.

Chapter 5

Tril knew the answer; if they moved any closer than the surrounding wards that hid their presence from the wizard, Kitable would be aware of them. In addition, the wizard was protected and would likely shrug off any binding. Kitable had cast fast enough to hurt Ela during their last confrontation. Tril did not want to give him the chance to try again.

"Now that I know him, I can seek him out. He will be visible tomorrow when they reach BellRoost. I will get him then. I have much to prepare." Terant's voice distanced as he headed out. The sound of footsteps faded down to the entrance.

You can release it, Tril, the Circle told him, and Tril let the vision fade from his sight. Just before he disconnected, Tril saw Kitable glance up. Tril's consciousness was gone before the Esparan could give his location more than a brief look.

Tril's eyes slowly managed to focus on the cold stone of the Earth Lodge walls, and he found many of the Circle staring at him.

Did Kitable see? someone wondered. Tril, like the rest of the Circle, shook his head. No, Kitable had not seen. Their presence remained invisible.

We wait, someone else thought, and in a torrent of thoughts, the rest of the Circle agreed.

It took Kitable longer than normal to settle into a comfortable position in the waggon, and he caught himself losing concentration more than once. Every jostle reminded him that he had not slept. He had to deliberately focus his thoughts.

His first message had been intercepted. Were DoomDragon's casters watching for another attempt? He had to assume so. The magical defenses of the vardo would keep them out, but as soon as his mind left the waggon, Kitable would be exposed. There was little the enemy could do to his detached conscious save dispel it back to his body, but the threat of failure unnerved him. Tohmas wanted the message delivered. Kitable could not allow the spell to be detected.

The wards around him were stable and strong yet did not assuage Kitable's paranoia. The back of his neck prickled, a primal feeling of being watched, but he could find no source despite extensive searches.

Finally, he gave up looking and moved on to the Scry and the many spells that would hide it.

Reaching out mentally, Kitable drew in the magic he needed. Once he held sufficient wind and light in his mind, he selected the domain of alteration and layered it atop his elements. Kitable crafted the Scry onto his eyes and ears with words recited from memory. The spell set together as precise as a jeweler's masterpiece.

He sent his mind through the floor and into the fields where the army marched parallel to the river. He knew that the vardo was moving steadily along with the army but could only feel motion if he concentrated on the body he was leaving behind. Around him, detached senses masked the real sensation of the floor under him and the sounds of the creaking wheels.

He found the river and drifted along it, losing track of time.

Knowing the enemy would be watching, Kitable studied the sky, trying to sense the tingle of nearby magic. Coming across none, he caught the pull of the river in his mind and rushed his Scry downstream faster than any man or animal could run. He traversed leagues in mere flickers, the sights and sounds of the river a blur of instants.

In his haste, Kitable almost missed the bridge, but the long shadow attracted his attention and interrupted his careful watch of the sky. He let his consciousness drift onto the bank and took refuge beneath the bridge for a moment to get his bearings.

Despite its name, Basalt Bridge was made of primarily granite on the surface, so heavy that it required three sets of piles to hold its long arches. Most of the stonework was grey and lichen-crusted along the piles, the deck, and into the abutments, but a hint of white stone peeked out at the bases of the pilings and along the main span. Unlike even the finest marble, the seamless white stone had no grain, and so provided no anchor for lichen or moss.

Kitable had never experimented with wizard stone, but he knew enough to recognize it. It had to be old to be buried under the granite construction that lined the bridge, but when a wizard of that strength graced these lands, Kitable did not know.

He lingered for a while longer, feeling magic pass over the area more than once. Under the bridge, he was sheltered from mundane Scrys, although if someone was looking for auras of magic specifically,

Chapter 5

he would be discovered. Kitable suspected the spells above him were Sendings—basic communications—but he could not be certain without activating Spell Sight, and he did not want to add unnecessary power to his hiding place. Instead, Kitable waited. Once there was a long pause in the passing of magic, Kitable slunk the Scry out.

It took Kitable beyond nightfall to find his way through a series of grates and drains into BellRoost. Navigating the city was even harder, for there was no large manor to target. Kitable was forced to wander until he found a Soltan guard leaving his post and followed the man to his barracks. Under the cover of roofs, Kitable layered Spell Sight onto his Scry and saw the defenses Clarin had erected around various doorways.

He thought it ironic that *he* would be the one to cut through them.

Alteration was easiest. Channeling a newly crafted spell down his Scry, Kitable bent the wards and slipped through them toward the most concentrated area of magic.

Instead of finding Clarin, Kitable found Prince Sol asleep on a large cot, two protectors on duty at the enchanted doorway. Clarin had invested the most magic in protecting the prince.

Kitable quietly cast alterations to open the way through several more wards. He did not break the spells, not wanting to alarm Clarin, but adjusted them to make a gap. Once his Scry entered the prince's room, Kitable had to figure out how to wake the man. It was comforting to see the three-way shield Clarin had put up around his prince during his evident absence—at least it gave the impression Clarin was competent—but it prevented Kitable's simple spell from touching the prince.

From his vardo far away, Kitable cast a tiny auditory spell and sent it along the Binding that held his mind in BellRoost. When it arrived, it activated into the sound of a whistle, low but firm.

Sol started from his sleep as if he had been shaken, a blade in hand instantly.

Kitable released the message he had prepared and sent it along the Scry.

"Prince Sol," he heard his own voice say, "Prince Tohmas requested I give you notice of his plans to approach BellRoost on the morning of the fourteenth by the north gate. We request your assistance in gaining access to the gate. You can expect us early on the morning of the fourteenth, no later than noon. Your reinforcements have arrived."

It was late; the morning that Kitable identified was only candles away. The Soltan forces would have to scramble.

He pulled his consciousness back along the Scry slowly and watched the room with the confused prince be replaced by drains, river, forest, and at last, his vardo. When Kitable next looked out, it was through his own eyes.

His head pounded, and his clothes were stained by sweat. Maintaining even such a simple spell for so long had taken its toll, and he was again shaking. He struggled to keep his eyes open.

He could not sleep, for Kitable would need spells for the fighting, and he did not have enough ready.

Roughly swallowing some food and water, Kitable resumed casting. He tethered spells to make himself a significant threat to the enemy then dragged himself up to the door of his vardo.

Dawn had arrived, and the waggons were moving west once more at a pace that suggested they were being pressed. Behind him, the Fyrd of Rest did their duty in protecting the straggling waggons as they advanced toward what he hoped was a way into BellRoost.

Kitable grabbed his spare waggon horse, saluted his driver in passing, and rode ahead to find his patron, hoping he had enough energy to control the spells he had bound to himself.

Breaking camp was habit now; Sabian could do it in his sleep and thought perhaps this morning he had. He remembered nothing of getting up, donning his basic padded armor and green tabard, or strapping on his sword.

His sword...how odd that was. He had not been given a sword when he joined, but when Ciene died, the sword had passed to him. It belonged in the hands of a warden, not a lowly companion like him. Sabian did not even know how to use it. One of Ciene's friends had shown him how to tie it on—he owned no scabbard—but it continued to hang heavily on his hip, threatening to trip him. Like much of the trappings of the camp, the presence of the sword felt perpetually wrong.

 ## Chapter 5

Around Sabian, the Fyrd of Rest readied themselves, tossing their packs into the heaping waggons and falling back to join their individual squads. Those small groups of five were then lined up with their blocks, sour-faced wardens at the head. It looked very organized, at least for the moment. If previous battles were any indication, the organization would not last beyond contact with the enemy.

Following the death of Ciene and the others in the raid of Barrow Hills, the squads had been reorganized. Whenever Sabian saw the warden who had taken Ciene's place, he felt a stab of anger. No one should have been allowed to stand in Ciene's place. Who was that man, to have lived when Ciene died? Why did the gods favor him over Sabian's brother?

Someone must have noticed his anger, for Sabian had been reassigned to Warden Nisser, an old warden from the borders of Galanth. Sabian now marched with four strangers as his squad.

"Watch it, Sabe," growled a low voice, and Sabian glowered up at Torbi as the sailor caught the backswing of the pack Sabian lobbed over his shoulder. A pot came all too close to striking Ciene's friend on the temple, but the older man ducked it expertly. Sabian had once heard Dabon tease Torbi about his reflexes; Torbi said he was light on his feet because the waters he traveled forced him to develop keen balance. Dabon claimed it was because the first woman Torbi married had liked to slap and Torbi was used to dodging.

Without answering Torbi, Sabian marched to the waggon and threw his pack aboard. He was heading away when Torbi stood in his path, his fishing lure earring dangling from his left ear. The sailor had managed to get a boiled leather armor cuirass from somewhere, although how he had found one to fit his broad shoulders, Sabian did not know. Over top of the armor, the green tabard of Galanth was ragged on the edges. The purple stains reminded Sabian about the Barrow Hills ambush. Nothing got bloodstains out of the green cloth.

He could have gone around, but Sabian refused to. "Move," he said, crossing his arms. "I have to get to the squad."

Torbi lifted a white candle. "You forgot this."

The unused candle was a short, white taper. Gold lines prominently formed the symbol of the Goddess Inac on the front and back.

Snapping up Ciene's candle, Sabian turned for the waggon. He was certain he had put it in the pack. Now he would have to find...

Torbi caught him, pulled the candle from his grip, and tucked it into Sabian's belt pouch. "Don't put anything in that pack that you need to get back, Sabe."

Sabian pulled sharply away, feeling his face flush. "Don't mother me, Torbi. It's just a candle. One night, I'll need a light, and it'll get burned up. So what? Wax and wick and—"

"We miss him too, but that's no reason to be getting careless with important things."

Sabian's voice caught. He swallowed hard against the lump in his throat. "My brother's dead, you idiot. Maybe I will be too at the end of all this! And what difference would it make?"

Torbi stepped forward, suddenly looming over Sabian. Sabian tried to step back but bumped into the pack waggon and slipped in the mud of the tracks. Torbi caught him, lifting him by the collar of his padded shirt. He was face to face with the man, in full line of fire of the stinking breath of the sailor-turned-soldier.

"Difference?" Torbi growled. "Dead men sure don't make a difference. You can only ever make a difference when you're alive, kid. So smarten up. Dabon and I will be watching out for you, and if you go getting reckless, you might get us all killed. What difference do you think that would make?"

Sabian pulled uselessly on Torbi's grip, but it was as useless as attempting to unlock a pit hound's jaw. "I don't need you looking out for me. Just because Ciene told you to doesn't mean—"

Torbi released him, and Sabian fell against the waggon. When it lurched forward, moving on to collect more packs, he staggered to keep his footing. Falling into the mud would get him mercilessly ridiculed by his new squad. Better that they have someone else to tease.

"You think we do it for Ciene?" Torbi asked, his voice briefly raised in humor. "Kid, I changed your diapers when you were a babe. I don't need Ciene telling me to look out for you. I do it because I've put effort into getting you to this age alive, and I don't want my fine work to be for nothing. Keep your wits about you today, and don't go looking for a sword to fall on." Torbi's murky blue eyes flashed to the sword on

 # Chapter 5

Sabian's hip. "You've got a good head on you, kid. Don't forget to goddamn use it."

The sailor pivoted and headed back toward the extinguished campfires. Dabon joined him there, the former warden casting a brief look back at Sabian. He had been required to leave his sword in Vait since it technically belonged to the Prince of Clandac and had armed himself with a mace. Most members of the block had shields rigged from wood and mental banding, but Dabon carried an iron shield. For them, it was a basic tool. For Dabon, the shield was a weapon.

Sabian put his left hand on a knife hilt. He had six on him, from short throwing knives to a single long knife originally meant as a sticker for pigs. The throwing knives were too valuable to leave in his pack; he padded his pockets by gambling in knife-throwing games. There was always someone in Fixer City who didn't know how good Sabian's aim was and could be convinced into a match.

But knives were not weapons for battle. A sword and shield were proper. *If only I knew half as much as Dabon did or even as much as Torbi or…*

Swearing, Sabian joined his squad, his sword whacking the side of his leg with each step. A bruise had formed for it to bang into, and Sabian fought not to limp. None of the four other members of his squad met his eyes, although a couple glanced at his sword. Should he survive, he would end up defending the valuable weapon from thieves among these men. He shrugged to himself.

First, he would have to survive, and that seemed unlikely. The Fyrd of Rest was assigned to the rearguard and were one of only two positions guaranteed combat with Northlanders. While others cheered the idea of locking blades or axes with the stinking, fur-clad invaders, Sabian had no heart for it. Before Barrow Hills, he had a reason to fight but had since forgotten it. It no longer mattered.

If he did survive, and his allies wanted his sword, they were welcome to it.

As the order was given to head out, Sabian cursed the sword, the Northlanders, the coming rains, cursed whichever ax or dagger had taken Ciene from him.

Head bowed, he trudged into battle.

Celebrant

Dawn broke over a dark sky. Summer rain had come after not falling in nearly a mooncycle, and the cooler damp gave the men some respite from the baking heat. The army had camped just outside the tree line of the river. At the first sign of dawn, Darknim spotted BellRoost ahead of them and knew the extra push had been worthwhile.

Prince Tohmas, with his army now breaking camp, had to be between Darknim and BellRoost. He was within reach. The Circle said the prince had taken refuge in the forest beyond the walls, just far enough out that the Northlander forces set by the gates of BellRoost would be unable to reach them without opening themselves for retaliation. It was hard to tell if the prince was still hiding or readying himself for battle, but battle would come this day regardless.

As the morning dawned and the Northlander forces moved onto the road to BellRoost, Seria received word from Master Terant and the Circle—they were ready.

"I will draw Kitable out," Seria explained as she walked alongside Darknim, taking two steps for each of his one. "The Circle will follow me, and when there is an opening, he will die."

Darknim thought it sounded rather simplified but only shrugged. If Kitable was left unchecked, he could wreak havoc. Darknim preferred the wizard dead.

Despite the smell of rain, he was predicting a good day. It had been too long since he bloodied his ax.

Darknim at their head, the Northlanders picked up their pace. It was not long before the first of the Hunters reported the position of their quarry still concealed by the river.

Had the Prince of Galanth intended to take the south gate of BellRoost, he would have left his hiding place to make his run by now. The Northlander forces were not difficult to spot on the road; Tohmas must know where they were. Prince Tohmas could not make it to the south gate without getting pinned between three forces now.

The plan had changed.

"Woman," Darknim called, "he will be trying the north gate. That is where you will find your foe. I give you leave."

 # Chapter 5

Seria's fine brow wrinkled in confusion. "Kitable's message said he was coming from the south!"

"Must have changed his mind."

With a nod, she dashed away. He spotted her eager grin.

Darknim set his sights on the trees where he knew Tohmas had stopped and brought a hand to the pendant that weighed heavily around his neck. A promise lay in the pendant—a promise to avenge a slight and clear the world of the family of a tyrant. There were days the burden of the memory was a physical pressure on his chest under the pendant. Today, the simple sword and circle ornament felt cold.

Releasing his grip on the pendant, Darknim broke into a run, his dragon-wing ax in hand. If he did not hurry, he would miss out completely.

The rains began as he charged the city.

Chapter 6

Tohmas sent the first assault across the bridge, High Guardsman Carraway leading it in the misting rain. Tohmas had been tempted to cross the river himself, to be in the thick of things when the Galanth forces hit the Northlanders at the north gate, but he was too much a tempting target, particularly for Scrys. He dared not give away the approach. While Tohmas sat on the chest pulled from his tent and left on the side of the road, two fyrds totaling nearly thirteen hundred men crossed Basalt Bridge to the north of BellRoost and cut into the Northlander blockade.

Hearing the rain-muffled horns announcing the official engagement, Tohmas gave the chest a pat and mounted Honest Justice. He waited a few heartbeats—just enough to let the Fyrds of Arrow engage the forces on the bridge—before trotting his horse out to stand with the remaining forces.

He had remained with the waggons and the other fyrds on the city side of the river, knowing DoomDragon's army was closing in behind them. It had been impossible to cross everyone over again so quickly, and he was counting on getting his men up to the bridge on this side.

Leaving the shelter of the trees, Tohmas lead his men out into the farmlands nearest BellRoost at a run, aiming for the gap between the city's walls and the bridged river. Had they been ready for him, a bare dozen Northlanders could have held the space, but their attention was drawn north to Lance and his men. In quick time, the Northlanders

 # Chapter 6

on the bridge were pushed back and lost their footing as they were forced into the trampled mud beside the stone bridge. Under the press of Tohmas' forces, the Northlanders fell back to the west. Galanth took the corner of the city and, with it, the north gate.

Once in the fighting, he quickly became soaked but did not know if it was sweat or the drizzling rain. His shoulder ached, the almost-healed arrow wound too fresh to be ignored. Despite the wound, Tohmas made sure he was contributing as much as any of his protectors. With each swing of his sword, he beat back the invaders to secure the road into the city.

Esparan blades cut through Northlander furs and leather armor, opening their tanned skin to flesh and bone. But the wounded men roared back into battle and made their way through the mud to challenge Tohmas and his protectors again and again. Only a dead Northlander gave up.

The horns kept him informed of the progress. As Tohmas adjusted his shield to block a sling stone about to take his head off, one of the guardians sounded a "met-up" call. The Fyrds of Arrow and Traiton were no longer separated by Northlanders but had come together at the bridge and wall. The Fyrd of Rest answered with their horn, confirming the start of their run to BellRoost with the waggons and Fixer City. Tohmas himself blew the horn that announced that they were holding the path clear as he arrived on Basalt Bridge and led a charge along the line, keeping the Northlanders from coming back over the bridge. The mounted protectors succeeded in breaking the charge of the Northlanders, and the Galanth forces moved to the far bank.

The north gates of BellRoost were theirs. Behind them, the waggons skidded along wet paving stones to get into the city before Northlanders, led by DoomDragon himself, caught them.

It took Clarin a full candle to figure out what was going on. The prince had evidently decided something required immediate action and left his sleeping quarters. Every time Clarin thought he had caught up with his patron, Prince Sol moved elsewhere. All Clarin could determine was that something was happening and it involved fighting.

Celebrant

When he finally found Prince Sol, Clarin was surprised. In his armor, surrounded by protectors, Prince Sol was giving orders from the command post near the center of BellRoost.

"...north gate, all of them, quickly!" Sol finished his order. The messenger took off at a run, nearly careening into Clarin in his haste. The runner muttered an insincere apology but did not slow in his sprint toward the north defenses.

"Kitable contacted me," Prince Sol explained before Clarin could ask.

Clarin's open mouth dropped open, his heart leaping into his throat. "How? If he can target you for a message—"

"I do not care how, Clarin," the prince interrupted. "Tohmas is coming, now, and we need to get him inside. I need you at the north gate with me."

The only thing Clarin could stutter was, "Of course."

If the Galanth wizard could target Clarin's prince for messages, he could target him for other things too, including attacks. The thought unnerved Clarin. He promised to figure out how Kitable had squeezed through the shields. He hoped it was only possible because Kitable had been targeting a harmless spell, but he doubted it. The Galanth wizard was just too powerful.

Clarin did not have time to dwell on it. He cast spells, most of them hovering spells tied to himself, as he followed Prince Sol into the emptied streets of BellRoost. The city had been a village once but had been built up in layered circles as it grew beyond its borders. Walls had not been needed then; the defenses constructed were new, built in anticipation of the Northlanders.

Now, all Prince Sol's forces called the city home. In their diminished state, they only filled half of the homes.

As he walked down the deserted streets, Clarin realized that BellRoost, despite having the status of a city on the map, was already dead. Even if the Northlanders were completely defeated by morning, there were too few original citizens to repopulate. Some might return from the capital, Narsol, when it was safe, but it would take a generation to replace what had been lost.

Taking up their official duties in the city turned fort, the protectors marched behind Prince Sol and Clarin through the ill-planned streets of the doomed city. When he had first been given the rank of prime

Chapter 6

protector, Clarin had tried to take a role in commanding the protectors, but it had quickly become apparent that he lacked a prerequisite: he was not a warrior. It was not that they disliked him, but rather that he was not worth their notice.

Feeling the many blank stares on his back, Clarin walked a little more briskly.

The gate was, like most of the walls around BellRoost, a recent construction of ash wood spikes. Flimsy ladders led to the ramparts, which were thin strips of wood just wide enough for two men to pass. Clarin did not trust the construction, knowing it had been quickly assembled by desperate men three years ago and put under a lot of strain since.

A horn sounded beyond the walls, and the first clash of battle followed.

Once at the gate, Prince Sol immediately climbed the ladder and took a lookout's position. Clarin scrambled to set up a series of shields to defend the prince against arrows, stones, and even magic but did not climb the ladder himself. Clarin had no desire to see actual combat, finding it unnecessarily brutal. Instead, he was content to wait for a sign of magical involvement as indication that he was required. If there was none, then the protectors and the fyrd on duty at the gate could deal with the actual fighting.

But I am fated to be involved, Clarin thought with a sigh. After examining the bridge and road beyond the walls, Prince Sol brought his horn to his mouth and announced that his men were joining the fray. The gates opened, and the Soltan companions and wardens charged out in support of the Galanth soldiers.

Clarin watched, feeling sick. He begrudgingly followed Prince Sol to the gate, hoping the Northlanders would not reach so far. He did not want to use his spells. He had no interest in killing anyone.

Wave after wave, the Northlanders tried to win back the bridge. Tohmas set his protectors against them, keeping the men on foot in strong lines to repel the charges while the riders swept in from the side to beat down stragglers. They had just fended off one such assault when, in the process of chasing down a handful of stubborn Northlanders, a flash of green sparked beside Tohmas. The enemy he had been facing fell back, instantly dead.

"Daem'd wizard," Tohmas muttered, searching from atop Honest Justice for the wizard he knew had joined the battle.

Before he could figure out where Kitable was, Carsh give a war cry, announcing a worthy opponent. Knowing Esparans of any kind were no challenge to Carsh, and certainly not worth drawing attention to, Tohmas spun in his saddle to find his brother instead.

Carsh's horse, Bashuran, barreled down the far side of the arching bridge, churning through the latest Northlander charge with blood-soaked hooves. The Rydan launched himself from his perch on the horse's back and into the mass of Northlander warriors. His target, as near as Tohmas could tell, was a woman.

Whoever she was, she collapsed under the assault and disappeared beneath the crowd of Northlanders, Carsh on top her. A horde of Gaidolons, Lance among them, flooded into the surrounding area on Carsh's heels to beat back the enemy.

The woman had to be a caster. Anyone else would be beneath Carsh's notice.

Kitable arrived at Tohmas' side as Tohmas decided Carsh was fine on his own. If he needed assistance, Carsh would whistle.

"The way into BellRoost is clear," Kitable reported, turning his skittering waggon horse to face BellRoost. "The waggons are moving through already. I thought you may want a hand."

"I knew that from the horns," Tohmas replied. "Let's be honest: Vallant sent you." Kitable grimaced. "Fine by me. I lost him and half the protectors shortly after taking the bridge. Some of them probably hold the east line. Clumsy, I know." Nearby, the protectors were making known their presence, but the chaos prevented them from properly securing the area. A pair of Northlander warriors lunged through the lines, knocked aside the nearest protector, and sprang at Tohmas.

Tohmas gave Honest Justice leave to kick and swung down with his blade as the first warrior came within reach. The old arrow wound lanced pain down Tohmas' side, but he kept his blade and repeated the swing despite the throb from his shoulder. The stitches pulled, and the warmth of blood seeped against his shoulder.

 # Chapter 6

He had only knocked the first enemy away when the wizard said a word, and both Northlanders fell back under a wave of shimmering air.

"BellRoost," Kitable interrupted pointedly. "Please get inside BellRoost, my Prince." Another word whispered in a foreign language repeated the blast that swept over the attackers. Tohmas found himself without anyone to hit; both Northlanders had been thrown off the bridge.

Tohmas checked on Carsh, who was standing up and brushing himself off. Beyond him, Lance and his Fyrd of Arrow had formed defensive lines at the end of the bridge. Granite railings funneled the enemy into the narrowed space over the long crossing.

Although Tohmas could see bodies around Carsh, none appeared to be female. Carsh had been burned; two first-sized blistering patches of red, one on either side of his sternum, steamed in the cold air. They sat above the tattoo on his chest—a lucky thing for a Rydan who relied on his tattoo as identification.

"*Daem'd Flya!*" the Rydan declared then whistled for Bashuran. He was on the horse's back in a single stride. He rejoined Tohmas. "*Gawn.*" The burns were not enough of a concern to mention.

At the least, Kitable had learned to recognize the Rydan word "*flya.*" The wizard straightened.

With Kitable keeping targets away from him, Tohmas grudgingly made his way toward the city gates, followed by the protectors. Nearer the gate, fighters in Solta's black and red tabards joined his green-clad Galanth. Waggons rattled into the city as fast as the worried horses and mules could run without knocking themselves over. By now, DoomDragon's forces at the south gate were probably on their way up to harass the supply waggons and Fixer City, but the Fyrd of Rest announced it was holding them off. As another horn sounded the "halfway" signal, Tohmas paused beside the opened gate into BellRoost to give the waggons room. Kitable hesitantly joined him there. He opened his mouth to comment, then suddenly stopped.

The wizard pitched himself off his horse and rolled out from under the hooves. His robe now streaked with dirt and pebbles, Kitable rose instantly, his hands out to his sides and his eyes, scintillating in waving colors, searching in every direction. Carsh's cringe told Tohmas magic had been involved. Where another man might have cursed, Kitable went still, tension in every muscle.

The wizard spun, shouted, and waved his hand. A moment later, he was back in his previous position, ready. The pause lasted only a heartbeat; Kitable spun and gestured again, deflecting something Tohmas could not see. Tohmas looked to Carsh, but the Rydan shrugged. The powers were moving too quickly. Carsh could do nothing to stop them. Tohmas fruitlessly searched for any sign of a wizard.

Whatever Kitable sought refused to reveal itself as a fourth, then a fifth, invisible force assaulted the wizard. Each defensive spell made Kitable's posture slouch a little bit more.

He was shaking, Tohmas abruptly realized. He was becoming enervated.

"Enough," Tohmas decided aloud. The first of the green coats were coming up behind the waggons. Only the Fyrd of Rest was left to get in.

He dropped from his horse, moved to Kitable's side, and ordered, "Protectors, cage me!"

The protectors formed a tight circle around him, their backs to him and their shields facing out. Tohmas threw an arm over Kitable and ducked the wizard down.

"Lift shields!" Tohmas shouted and the shields lifted as if to intercept arrows, a second row of protectors replacing the lower shields. They shuffled in closer, the two circles of protectors closing together until a roof of shields had been erected over Tohmas and Kitable.

More than once, Kitable had talked about spells using line of sight. Without being able to see the target, the desired recipient of the spell had to be described in a manner that could not be confused with any other. Kitable had insisted that he kept himself "undefinable," so the spells being aimed at him were using line of sight. If there was no way to see him, there was no way to hit him.

Or so Tohmas hoped. He had no idea what effect, if any, a wall of physical shields would have on a spell. At least the shields blocked the rain, which had become heavier.

Keeping their heads low, Tohmas ordered the protectors to move into the city.

After being eerily silent, Kitable suddenly grimaced. Tohmas' heart quickened. Carsh shouted a warning.

 # Chapter 6

Before Tohmas could decide on an action, Kitable spoke another nonsensical word. A flash of blinding white light shot out, forcing Tohmas to release the wizard and cover his eyes. There was a second flash, one of blue, and Tohmas rocked back several steps under the force of it. Above him, the cage of shields cracked as protectors were knocked from their feet.

Tohmas stumbled into the center of the circle.

He had allowed Kitable to cast spells on him before, always without feeling so much as a tingle of power on him. He wasn't trained like Carsh—magic was undetectable to Tohmas—yet he felt he had stepped into a waterfall of power.

Like falling ash, the powers pouring down on him singed his skin wherever it touched. Tohmas was brought to his knees under the pressure, covering his head but knowing his arms would not protect him from the powers of flyers. With his pained eyes closed, he waited for death.

But the rain of power flashed through him and into the ground without intensifying or harming him. In an instant, the spell was gone, and Tohmas was blinking his spotty eyes to clear them. When at last he could see, Carsh was crouched at his side and Kitable lay prone nearby. Rain fell evenly over them.

The protectors scrambled to their feet, quickly circled Tohmas, and lifted their shields once move, providing shelter and protection.

A glance was all Carsh needed to know Tohmas was unharmed. The prime protector stood, his knives ready to keep any Northlanders from following them in their withdrawal. In Carsh's hands, even the wet grips did not slip.

No time to question their good fortune, Tohmas scooped up Kitable and ran for the city, the circle of protectors around him and his brother guarding his back.

Each Circle member tracked movements individually within the Linking, making the view of the battle outside of BellRoost a series of confusing and upsetting distractions.

Celebrant

Before the Circle, Tril had been a hunter. He was accustomed to killing for the sake of food, but he felt nauseated to see the death wrought in the ice pool between them. The feeling intensified when things went wrong on the bridge, and the Esparans found their way behind the Northlanders. Tril wondered if he was going to keep his breakfast down.

His emotions, as hard as they were to isolate among the intense reactions of the other Circle members, were mostly disgust and disapproval. More than once, he saw the face of someone he knew and was reminded that his friends were dying below him in a haze of rain and violence, and he, watching silently, was doing nothing.

He had been a moderate hunter but was no warrior.

Desperate to bring his attention to something else, Tril turned his eyes to Master Terant, standing at the edge of the frozen pool. The magic that the Esparan had readied hovered around them like a tethered giant, huge and deadly. Only a word was required to set loose the monster, and Tril, for the first time, feared the Circle would fail to contain it.

The casting of the spell had come at a great cost. Terant had not stopped his heavy breathing since arriving, and while they waited, the man leaned on the wall, mildly trembling. It would take another burst of control to release the spell, and Tril wondered what would be left of the man.

In the scene below, Seria was attacked, but not with magic. The grass bracelets identified Prince Tohmas' Rydan prime protector.

It was not an accidental passing of enemies; without hesitation, the prime protector charged his horse through the Northlanders, leaped from his horse, and tackled Seria. Blades out, he pounced, but her defenses proved stronger and the knives were deflected. Seeing his attacks were failing, the prime protector lifted Seria and her shields into the air. Seria's hands wrapped around her attacker, pressing against his chest, and a visible flash of magic scorched into his skin. If the pain of the burn bothered the protector, he did not show it. When he slammed Seria into the wet ground, causing her head to be jarred even with the magic shields, it was well controlled.

Carsh was about to slam her down for a second time when Seria disappeared. Her shield could protect her from the cut of blades, but the impact would kill her if she did not escape.

 # Chapter 6

The elders did not have time to mourn the disruption of their plans. The instant Seria vanished, a sweep of magic cleared the rise of the bridge.

The Circle followed the spell back and found their target sitting on a horse among the fighting, talking to the Galanth prince. He wore a simple robe of green with no coat against the rain.

Kitable, the Circle recognized.

Terant moved like an old man to the edge of the pool and knelt to aim his spell.

Before Terant could release his tethered calamity, new powers became visible in the pool. Confusion filtered through the Circle. A series of multicolored, flickering balls were attacking Kitable, but none of them knew who was responsible.

Kitable pitched off his horse and rolled out of view. A moment later, he was standing again, using small, green spells to deflect the other balls of magic that Tril knew would only be visible with enchanted sight.

Even Terant does not know who casts now, Elder Ela told the Circle. *The woman wizard has fled. This is not their doing. Perhaps their other ally?*

It took another moment for Terant to decide on a course of action. By then, a group of soldiers had surrounded the enemy and were blocking the Circle's view with their shields.

"Where?" Master Terant grumbled. "He was at the center..."

In the chaos, Tril searched for the yellow-haired wizard, but the rain had become heavier and obscured his view. Too many green-and-silver-clad men rushed around with their shields lifted, hiding the prince and the wizard. Then, although Terant had not yet cast, another spell flashed in the pool's view of the battle.

Two spells collided. The first, cast from above and behind the circle of soldiers protecting the Galanth wizard, manifested as billowing red and white magic. The second, cast afterward but moving twice as fast, was just as multicolored but set in a sphere around the protectors. The resulting clash knocked men from their feet and showed a glimpse of a yellow-haired man ducked among the shields.

Tril did not know what word Terant used, but it was none he had ever heard before. The moment the colors that flowed from Terant in a cascade touched the frozen pool, the vision physically shook. Tril focused on maintaining the Linking to the frozen pool.

Celebrant

Using the Circle's Scry to transport the spell across the distance, flashing colors descended from the sky like a meteor shower. The maelstrom of magic landed directly on the man who stood at the center of the shields and was brushing off a bloodied shoulder that bore a black rank rope.

Terant had not struck Kitable. Tril's shock nearly broke the Linking. After he had re-established his focus, he shared the realization with the rest of the Circle and felt them groan. A moment later, they pulled back. The vision faded until they were looking at the white surface of the ice.

While the elders were conscious, their breathing came roughly, and many of the wrinkled brows were shining with sweat. Elder Vel's fox skin was singed, and several owl feathers lay in Elder Ela's lap, testifying to the strain they and their Aspects had endured. Master Terant, who was apart from them and not defended by the powers of the Circle, lay unconscious, his body a tangled mess with one leg on the frozen pool.

The Linking dropped, for none of them had the energy to maintain it. For a moment, Tril sat in awe of the power that allowed a single man to create a spell so large that all seven Circle members strained to contain it.

Ela smiled weakly at Tril from across the blank pool.

"So much power, and yet now he lies vulnerable," she whispered.

Tril's awe changed to pity. Without the assistance of the Circle, Master Terant would die. Worse still, they would only see to the man's recovery because it was DoomDragon's wish, not because they cared for him.

"We struck Prince Tohmas, not Kitable," Vel said, her voice a weak grate of disappointment. She patted her fox skin to stop the smoldering. "He did not fall." Despite the magic that poured onto him, the prince had simply risen from the assault and run for the city. Even if they had failed to kill Kitable, Prince Tohmas would have been a good accidental casualty to offer to DoomDragon.

"Terant's spell was meant to strike a wizard," Tril explained, rising from his seat on unsteady legs. "Prince Tohmas had no magic of his own and so was unharmed."

"We will wait," Elder Ela said into the silence that followed, "and see what the Esparan says when he awakens. Our DoomDragon will continue his quest, no doubt."

 # Chapter 6

Those who were able to nodded. The rest sat mutely, staring.

The least negatively affected, Tril saw to the fallen Esparan wizard. He felt carefully for defenses before throwing a fur from one of the seats over the breathing, but otherwise still, form. He wrapped up the Esparan and slung him over a shoulder to take him to the warmth of the camp above.

"I hope his aim improves," was the last thing he added before leaving the silent, tired room into the summer showers.

The sword, stuck in a mud-crusted Northlander's chest, slipped from Sabian's hand. The Northlander collapsed backward, but to follow would drag Sabian off his feet. As the dying enemy fell, he swung one final time. Sabian brought his left arm up sharply, and the ax bit into the wood of his shield. The pressure of the blow tossed Sabian back, and he lost the fight to keep his feet. He stumbled into the mud.

The tread of waggons had come first, softening the ground, then the passage of feet. The Fyrd of Rest numbered into the hundreds, and every boot had walked along this road, churning the dirt path into a slurry. Finally, blood coated the ground, turning packed dirt into brick-color mud.

Into that mud, Sabian fell. He did not rise.

He ached everywhere. His legs trembled from the constant adjustments in the treacherous terrain, and he could feel the squish of mud between his toes despite his solid, leather boots. His hands were numb but shook when he tried to force them into action. He could not understand how he could sweat so much when he was shivering. His skin felt chilled by the drizzling mist around him, but he was sweltering under his tabard and padded armor. His lungs burned, and his vision blurred with sweat. His heart felt like it was trying to break out of his chest.

He had no intention of rising.

Barrow Hills had been different. Then, the Galanth moved slowly between enemies, dealing individual, careful blows. Ciene had been there, deciding which squad would go where as they moved surreptitiously among the enemy. The greatest danger was discovery. They fought against their chuckles as, one by one, they lowered their enemy's numbers. As much as the killing had been new, it had been simple.

This time, since the first glimpse of Northlanders approaching from the east, chaos reigned. Although Sabian listened for the horn commands, he struggled to stay with his squad. The waggons went ahead, and the Fyrd of Rest was expected to hold back the invaders. The Northlanders and their allied Esparan launched into skirmishes with no fear of death.

Their numbers had broken the line.

After that, Sabian moved from blow to blow. Surrounded by furs and axes, he lost track of other Galanth in the haze. Sometimes he thought he spotted a familiar face in the mess, but too often, in the absence of a green tabard, he simply swung his sword.

And now he had no sword.

He lay back in the mud, shivering. Clashing warriors jostled around him, risking getting their feet caught on him as they sought solid footing on the boggy road. Sabian did not care. Mud sank between his limbs, a tight embrace seeking to hold him.

He had been wounded, that much he knew, but it wasn't bad. His cut arm, a scratch from an ax that had nearly taken off his head, was seeping blood into the muck. He remembered the encounter vaguely. The Northlander had been wearing fox furs, his ax made of twisted bog iron that blunted easily under strain. It had bounced off Sabian's padded armor, unable to cut even that rudimentary protection, but caught on his arm. It had probably been rusted. A rusty, muddy cut.

Reason enough to stay where he had fallen as far as he was concerned.

A man in a green tabard crashed to the ground beside Sabian, landing with his face only a hand's breadth from Sabian's own. The man's oozing skull gaped wide, his eyes glassy.

Sabian would have been sick, but he had long since thrown up everything he had eaten and could only dry heave. He rolled to his side, putting his back to the dead man.

An ax sliced into the ground beside him, digging into the mud where Sabian had been. Someone knew he lived.

He tried for a moment to push himself up, but his arms were too weak. He fell face first into the muck and did not bother to try a second time. With his back exposed to the enemy, he hoped the blow would

 ## Chapter 6

kill him quickly. Sabian prayed Torbi and Dabon wouldn't think he had been running away. He never wanted them to think Ciene's brother was a coward.

But instead of the bite of an ax, hands touched the back of his tabard. He was dragged to his feet. The Northlander who had been standing over him was being pushed back by Dabon's shield bash. When the enemy stumbled, Dabon slammed the sharpened edge of the shield into the Northlander's face. Blood spurted from a surely broken nose, and the hairy Northlander careened backward, knocking down one of its fellows as it went.

The hands on his back stabilized Sabian before releasing him.

"Told you no falling on swords," Torbi's gruff voice said behind him.

Sabian watch mutely as Dabon chased the falling Northlanders down. With the edge of his shield, he chopped down hard over the second enemy's neck. The attempts to rise stopped. Both Northlanders lay dead.

Torbi moved out from behind Sabian, completely unarmed. When a Northlander lunged at Dabon from the right, Torbi's fist met him. A second Northlander moved up from the left, and Dabon faced him. The two friends stood for a moment back to back. Dabon slammed his mace across the Northlander's gut, moving fast enough to get the sharpened tips of his mace through the hide garments and into the flesh. There was not much muscle over the abdomen, Sabian realized. Although Dabon had sliced only a finger's breadth deep, the enemy's innards cascaded out. While the enemy looked down at his intestines, Dabon smashed in his skull.

Torbi moved just as quickly. He caught the second Northlander's ax handle and, before the enemy could react, swung the blade and the Northlander over his hip. He stomped his heel into the fallen man's chest, crushing ribs, and the Northlanders suffocated quickly in blood.

Torbi squinted at Sabian in the mist. He snatched the ax from the Northlander and shoved it into Sabian's hands. The blood washed gently away in the rain.

"Focus, kid," Torbi scolded.

Finding his voice at last, Sabian shunted Torbi away. "I don't need you," he snapped. His limbs trembled as he held the ax, unable to decide if he should throw it away. He had no use for the damn weapon anyway.

Celebrant

Torbi stood directly over him, dwarfing Sabian. "I don't care," the sailor stated, emphasizing every word heavily. The stench of drying blood, spattered guts, and sweat overpowered Sabian, and he fought against retching again.

"Torbi!" Dabon called, and Torbi turned away from Sabian. Three new Northlanders were approaching Dabon. A stone, shot from a sling with enough power to concuss a man, bashed off Dabon's shield. Torbi swiftly skipped to his friend's side.

"We're meant to be following the waggons," Torbi reminded them. "That means keeping up, not getting slogged down by hairy, antler-wearing demon-kissers. Work your way west, damn it. Show us Ciene's training was worth something to you! Come on!"

The words made sense, but Sabian could not understand them. The ax felt strangely heavy as if it was made of solid stone from shaft to blade. He let it drop.

He could not hear the horns now, just the screams of Esparans and Northlanders amidst the clang of weapons on armor and the thump of blades into flesh.

Blood burned as it trickled down Sabian's frozen arm.

Movement to his right interrupted his daze. An Esparan man, wielding a bent, bloodied sword, swung at him. The blow was aimed to take Sabian at the nape of his neck, perhaps thinking to remove his head in a single swing. Torbi and Dabon were out of range, dealing with their own enemies. They did not noticed the enemy between them and Sabian.

The man, although he was Esparan, wore no tabard.

Sabian did not have time to think, and he did not believe he had time to act, but his instincts proved him wrong. His body lunged to the side as his hand found and drew a throwing knife. He needed only a flick of his wrist—easily accomplished from the skewed angle—to send the knife into the man's throat.

The expression of rage on the Esparan's face morphed to one of shock. His eyes crossed as if trying to see where the knife had gone under his chin. Without a stagger, the man fell forward, flat as a felled tree.

Sabian stood from his lunge, finding his second throwing knife already in his hand. The tremble was gone.

 # Chapter 6

Swords, maces, and shields confused and left him weak, but knives were familiar.

Show us Ciene's training was worth something to you.

Sabian assumed Torbi had meant the training undertaken with Ciene as his warden, but who had taught him to throw a knife? Who had goaded him into a dozen games, until the little brother could consistently beat his older brother? Who had been filled with pride with every game Sabian won?

The vast, chaotic world narrowed around Sabian. He heard only the battle cry of the Northlander who charged him amidst the din. His knife, thrown with the precision of a master-gambler, slipped between the Northlander's ribs and was just long enough to hit his heart. Another enemy fell face first.

Feeling his heart steady, Sabian took a deep breath. Ciene wasn't here. He wasn't coming back. But Ciene had given Sabian the tools he needed. He would survive even this.

In the brief pause that followed, Sabian heaved the Northlander over and retrieved his knife. He grabbed the hair of the dead Esparan and yanked his head up so he could dig his first blade from the corpse's throat.

Sabian glanced up, decided which direction was west, and began to fight his way toward the waggons. Torbi and Dabon were doing the same. He felt their eyes on him when they entered his narrowed world, but they did not need to come to his assistance again.

When he ran out of knives, he used the enemy's weapons.

Sabian moved from enemy to enemy, eventually becoming aware again of the pain of his wounded arm, the ache of his weary legs, and the pounding in his chest over time. His heart no longer panicked but pounded on like a drummer who had finally set his pace. Although his hands shook in exhaustion, Sabian's accuracy did not waver. Where he aimed was where the throw landed. When he had only a blunt weapon, he stunned the enemy with a throw before using his long pig sticker to kill.

At some point, he found himself among green tabards and had to stop himself. The world widened, allowing him to see not just the faces near him but also the waggons jostling their way along a city's wall. In the distance, Torbi and Dabon were corralled into their squad now that they had returned to the main body of the army.

He recognized his squad and his block but didn't understand their blank, shocked expressions.

He followed their stares and glanced down. He was covered in mud, blood, and entrails with an ax in one hand and a short, stolen bog iron dagger in the other. A handful of other knives had found their way into his belt. He did not even want to imagine what his face looked like.

"Nice throw," someone said. A wiry man, his smile made crooked by a smear of mud over his chin and thin beard, nodded to the corpse at Sabian's feet.

The Northlander lying in the mud was a brute of impressive size. He looked to have survived several skirmishes and wore as much muck and entrails as Sabian did. A huge ax had fallen with the man and now lay in the mud just beyond the Northlander's grip. The leather tether around the ax handle was decorated with teeth. Many of them looked fresh.

A knife—a short-handled iron blade Sabian had scavenged off a dead Galanth soldier—protruded from the giant Northlander's back just above the heart.

"That demon-kisser damn near took my head off," the mud-smeared Galanth man said. "I owe you a drink, friend!"

Sabian had no reply as his mind rocked back and forth, focusing on now irrelevant details then unable to focus at all.

"You children done playing?" a gruff voice shouted, and every man on the line straightened sharply. The action was so reflexive even Sabian squared up for the warden.

Warden Nisser walked with a limp that got worse the closer rain came. He wore mostly metal armor, although it was made of pounded, irregular bits tied with leather shoelaces. He had slung a chain over his shoulders and clattered when he walked. Every companion of his Block knew to pay attention when the clanging approached them.

"Good," the warden barked, squinting a scarred eye toward Sabian in criticism. In the sentience of recent battle, Sabian noticed for the first time that the warden's scar over his eye reached his ear on the opposite side. It was extremely fine and must have come from a well-crafted knife.

"We're meant to be keeping these asses off the waggons, not making ourselves a meaty bump in their road! The wall! Get yourself into the

Chapter 6

wall! Keep moving! Anyone who falls behind'll end up decorating some demon-kisser's ax with their eyeballs! I ain't going back for you, not when I can bloody well see the gates! Move it!"

Sabian briefly met the stare of the wiry man he inadvertently saved from the huge Northlander's ax.

"I wanna stand next to you, friend," the stranger said, quickly coming up to Sabian's side.

Sabian let himself smile, tight and small, before dragging his feet back the way he came to join his squad in holding back the Northlanders. Behind him, the waggons clambered on.

Tohmas had slung Kitable over a shoulder and realized his error as soon as he got through the gate—blood was leaking from his throbbing wound. He was forced to set the wizard down just inside the gates of BellRoost in a small corner that would protect them from getting trampled.

"Protector," he snapped to the first man he saw wearing Galanth colors and a green rank rope, "take Master Kitable to Healing Mother Gracie's waggon and have Cutter Darak look at him. Make sure you don't call him by name. Be quick."

Kitable was rushed off to spend another night in a Healing waggon, and Tohmas smiled weakly at the thought of the wizard's inevitable objections. Darak would know what to do. The cutter had already hidden Kitable once before.

The wizard had only just been carried away when Tohmas found himself surrounded by red-and-black-clad men bearing weapons. To Tohmas' relief, Carsh was instantly at his side, a blade in each hand.

"Welcome to BellRoost!" a man shouted, and Tohmas was faced by one of the few men who could look him in the eye without craning his neck.

Prince Sol wore black-stained leather armor but no tabard. Chain sleeves dangled down his arms and decorated the sheath of his sword. The attire was immaculate. Around him, Sol's protectors were spattered with mud and blood, their shields dented or chipped, their helmets crooked. For a moment, Tohmas thought to address one of the soldiers instead of Sol; it was clear they had more invested in the battle than the prince did.

Courtesy won out.

"Thank you, Prince Sol," Tohmas answered. "I appreciate your assistance."

The man grinned like a trout that had escaped a net as he clasped Tohmas' forearm. The force behind it hinted that he had to feel Tohmas' flesh before believing his presence.

In clasping his uncle's arm, Tohmas became acutely aware that his hands were empty; he lost his sword in the skirmish by the gate. Although he could retrieve a long knife from his belt, he had been disarmed.

Seeming to recognize his realization, Carsh tucked a knife into Tohmas' belt from behind, and Tohmas nodded gratefully.

Having failed to listen to the prince while he worried about his sword, Tohmas was about to ask the prince to repeat himself when Prime Protector Severin stepped forward. Tohmas understood immediately why Carsh had given him a blade.

The wizard looked exactly the same as he had the first day in HomeStead. There may have been a change to the specific robe, but Master Clarin was still wearing the same golden glasses, long robes, sandals, and trinkets he had been for the last mooncycle apparently.

"Well done!" Clarin said. "I am eager to speak to Master Kitable now that you have arrived. We have much planning to do if we are to rout the Northlander casters before your next—"

Tohmas held up a bloodied hand, and to his amazement, the wizard stopped, likely because of the blood spattered over his sword arm.

"I am first going to get changed and see to my soldiers and the healers." Tohmas' attention went briefly to his protectors when he commanded, "I want an account for all the waggons that got through, including Fixer City. I need a list of dead, as close as we can make it, and I need a new sword as soon as possible. Twelve stay with me; the rest of you *geddit*!" None of them hesitated despite the use of the Rydan word. They knew "*geddit*" meant "get to it" and left no room for discussion.

As they sorted themselves out, Tohmas again faced the slack-jawed wizard.

Kitable was unconscious, but Tohmas had no intention of letting anyone else know that fact if he could avoid it. "Master Kitable will

 # Chapter 6

contact you, Prime Protector Severin, when he is interested in discussing his plans. Prince Sol and I can discuss strategy shortly. I hope you can manage a few candles on your own while we get settled."

The wizard still had not closed his mouth, but Prince Sol nodded in approval and, stepping forward, began discussing combining their defenses. Tohmas allowed the man to put an arm around his shoulder and guide him toward what Tohmas presumed was their main tent or building. After only a few steps, Sol paused and withdrew his hand.

His host's hand was covered in fresh blood. Sol had touched Tohmas' weeping left shoulder.

"You are..."

"*D'aems*," Tohmas cursed. "I forgot about that."

He had only to look at a protector to hear the reply he wanted. "Cutter Darak will meet you at the main post."

He shrugged and kept walking. After a pause, Sol followed but did not restart the conversation for a long time.

By the time DoomDragon's men reached the rearguard, the first of the Esparans were making their way into BellRoost.

Darknim saw Prince Tohmas at a distance during the battle, but he was too far away to do anything about it. A handful of unlucky Northlanders were trapped and slaughtered when the north gates closed, but Darknim was not among them. The close of the gates ended the battle.

DoomDragon's Hunters arrived not long after to provide an explanation for their failure, but Darknim refused to let them dwell on the errors.

"We have them trapped. We finish this." It was his turn to deal a blow, and he intended to sack the city.

He was planning the storming of BellRoost when the woman caster arrived with a long face and an embarrassed blush.

"I take it you failed," he said.

"Master Kitable is notoriously difficult to—" Over the last two mooncycles, he had heard all of Seria's excuses. He did not care to hear them again.

Celebrant

"Can you track the Galanth now?" he asked, cutting her off.

Seria again frowned. If she continued to spend all her time with that scowl on her face, he mused, she would end up as wrinkled as Elder Ela by the end of the season.

"He left the chest behind. He knew it was the anchor. But we still have the wizard's vardo. If your Circle could learn to expand the distance of their anchors, then we need nothing more. I could—"

"You would be spotted," Darknim refused. "At least they can remain out of sight while they watch."

She had no reply.

His thoughts went back to BellRoost. There were many ways into the city, but he had to figure out the best route to...

Another thought interrupted.

"Did you say Prince Tohmas left the chest behind? What was in it?"

Caught unprepared, Seria withdrew sheepishly. "No one has touched it. They fear..."

He left without waiting for her to finish. With his Hunters trailing him, Darknim sought the chest abandoned near the tree line where the Esparan camp had been set. Amidst the debris left behind, the well-made chest stood out starkly.

After Seria confirmed no magic was present, one of DoomDragon's Hunters pried open the lid gingerly.

Inside was a single wineskin.

Darknim pulled the stopper from the skin. A dark liquid flowed thickly and smelled vile within. Although he was unwilling to swallow anything the Prince of Galanth left for him, Darknim took the wineskin to his tent and set it on the table as a reminder of his quarry.

Chapter 7

"Oh, in Pari's name," Darak exclaimed, throwing his hands in the air. "Will you just hold still?"

The Prince of Galanth shot the cutter a glare, which Darak made a point of ignoring. The prince paced away once more, traversing the room in long strides. The furniture of the room forced him to dodge two chairs and a table to make it to the fireplace. He quickly turned back, ready to make the return voyage to the window.

"You take too long," Prince Tohmas objected.

"Only because you keep moving!" Darak retorted, stalking after the prince. "Stop pacing!" He placed himself in the prince's path, cornering the man by the fire. "And stop swinging your arms! I want that shoulder still for as long as possible lest you undo all my work yet again. I thought I said no fighting!"

By the time Darak finished his tirade, the prince had lowered himself into a chair beside the fireplace across from Prince Sol, whom Darak was also ignoring. Stitches was immediately at Tohmas' knee for a pat, which the Galanth prince obliged.

With the dog keeping the prince still, Darak took to repairing the damage to the exposed shoulder.

"You never mentioned it," Prince Tohmas insisted despite his temporary compliance.

"I most certainly did! I tell you, you are going to be the death of me, Prince Tohmas. If you do not stop running all over the place, your arm is going to fall off! I swear I will not be the one sewing it back on either!" The look of shock on Prince Sol's face reminded Darak that he was out of line, and he let his voice drop. "Besides, my stitching is terrible."

It was possible Prince Sol's shock was more Prince Tohmas' doing; the Galanth prince had been forced to remove his shirt, and his unexpected scars, back and front, were visible.

Tohmas chuckled, and Darak lightly slapped him on the back of the head. "Stop that! I told you to hold still!" The scold only made the prince laugh more. Finally, under Darak's glower, Prince Tohmas calmed, and Darak was able to resume his work. He kept a wary eye on Prince Sol as he did, trying to remind himself that the Soltan prince had just as much right to reprimand him for his behavior. It still failed to cow him.

"You were shot by an arrow in Gaidol?" Prince Sol finally overcame his surprise to ask. "How?"

The Prince of Galanth replied with a shrug that elicited a string of curses from Darak despite himself. "By nightfall, you will have that story in great detail and embellishment. For our purposes here, it does not matter. I am still alive."

Darak finished bandaging his patron's shoulder faster than he thought possible and, desperate to get clear of politics, gathered up his supplies.

But his eyes fell on Prime Protector Carsh, and Darak sighed. *Not done yet.* He had seen the burns on the Rydan's chest flanking the tattoo of a snarling mountain cat. Although Carsh moved with no hint of pain, Darak suspected the wound would be grievous, being magical.

"You next," Darak told the prime protector.

The Rydan sneered and stepped away with a blade lifted in one hand. "I be—" was all the prime protector said before Prince Tohmas interrupted.

"A quick look, Carsh. If they are deep, they need treatment, and he has everything here."

With Darak's prompting, the prime protector pulled the assortment of blades and the vest from his scarred shoulders to expose the wounds. He kept a blade in hand.

Chapter 7

Like Prince Tohmas, the prime protector sported dozens of thin scars over his torso. All were well healed. Besides the burns, Carsh had come out of the recent battle unscathed.

Prince Sol's stare alternated between Prince Tohmas and the prime protector, comparing their various scars. Before any conclusion could be drawn, the Prince of Galanth donned his shirt and retook his seat.

The burns were superficial and required only a light ointment. Darak was applying the aloe and ment ointment when the door opened to the room, and a line of guardians entered. Each wore their rank rope, but the tabards alternated between Galanth and Soltan colors. There was a single blue of Gaidol among them.

"Thankfully, the burns are shallow," Darak reported to Prince Tohmas, who seemed to have more interest in the wounds than the Rydan did. "He was lucky. I would say that was—"

"Magic," a new voice offered from behind the wave of guardians.

Leaping away from Darak's administrations, the Rydan spun and threw one of his baldrics over his head. A second blade appeared in his fists, making Darak retreat.

The man arriving could be nothing except a wizard. Among the armor and tabards of the soldiers, he wore a decorated robe and a hundred gold and silver trinkets. He had a green and black rank rope. Darak knew that meant he was the Prime Protector of Solta, but he had a hard time believing the squirrely man could be considered a bodyguard of that importance.

Darak didn't understand magic and had no desire to, so he left it at that.

Prince Sol called his prime protector over, but the distance he put between Carsh and the new arrivals seemed to have little effect; the Prime Protector of Galanth stood as if ready to lunge. Deciding not to press the Rydan again, Darak packaged up the discarded bandages and tried hard not to think about politics. He folded the prime protector's discarded vest for him and placed it on the table since the Rydan seemed to have completely forgotten about the garment.

"Is everything alright, Prince Tohmas?" Prince Sol asked. "You seem—"

"Carsh dislikes wizards. Having him so uptight tends to have its effect on me as well. We mean no disrespect to Master Clarin, of course."

CELEBRANT

The Prime Protector of Solta smiled graciously. "I do not take any offense, Prince Tohmas. Magic can be a frightening thing to those who do not understand it."

Prince Tohmas' smile became slightly more genuine, but Darak felt it darken too. "Oh, he has no fear of you, Master Clarin. He simply wants to kill you."

The comment was so out of place no one was able to answer. In the silence, Darak cleared his throat, his mind turning.

Master Kitable was in Healing Mother Gracie's waggon for a second time, but no one was supposed to know about it. Darak chose his words carefully. "Everything else is in place, my Prince," he said, hoping his prince understood the meaning. "I will back on the morrow to look at your shoulder. No more fighting, please, between then and now."

With a whistle to Stitches, Darak left before hearing more things he wanted to forget.

Once the healer was gone, the group of Soltan and Galanth, with one Gaidolon, settled around the table and talked about plans for holding the city. Tohmas assigned his men as he felt appropriate. His guardians took it in silence, not daring to speak out of place in front of a foreign prince. Their arrangements finally made, Prince Sol rose and declared his intent to attend the Totho's evening wind service.

"I had better go over a few more things with my men," Tohmas said. "I will join you later if I am able, but we need to get settled quickly. There is much to do."

Tohmas could tell that Sol almost argued the need for the religious service, but the good manners of a host prevented him from causing a scene. Prince Sol left into the early evening.

Tohmas waited until Carsh put away one of his two blades—Prime Protector Severin was out of range—before addressing the guardians.

"This city is not going to hold," he declared.

The guardians collectively sighed in relief.

Prime Guardian Vallant ran a hand over his face. "Gods, I am glad *you* see that."

Chapter 7

"Prince Sol wants it to," High Guard Carraway added. Lance hardly ever spoke during meetings, but now that he had fully proven Gaidol's willingness to help in battle, the guardians welcomed him as an equal. Nodding heads answered Lance's cautionary words.

"Only because he has no other choice," Tohmas answered. "If he falls back now, his next holding place is Narsol, and he cannot afford to be trapped at his capital. But if DoomDragon was able to sack Arcott, Icewalk, and Field, he knows how to get through walls. I would expect border towns to have stone walls. Why are they wooden here?"

Lance made a face that made his moustache droop. The rank beads on his brow tilted. "BellRoost was never fortified before. Solta was on good terms with the Princedom of Barlaby, and it was far enough from Lour or Trulin to be of no interest. This is the first time it has been under siege."

Vallant frowned deeply, the expression making the prime guardian look like a grumbling bear. "Shoddy defenses against veteran invaders will not help us."

"Since I am not the only one thinking that," Tohmas said, "I want everyone ready, every day, to move. That said, I do not want to give DoomDragon any advantage if I can avoid it. If the Northlanders are going to take this city, I want no city left for them to take."

"Rig the walls?" a guardian suggested.

"Undermining?" another added.

"Should we fill in the wells while we are at it?" asked a third.

"Yes," Tohmas replied. "Anything you can do to cause DoomDragon grief without making life more difficult on the current population. I want things ready to fall apart the moment we leave, but I don't want to see a single stone out of place until then. The Fyrds of Flystead and Lariton are in charge of it. Any ideas go to them. Keep me appraised."

"Prince Sol?" Lance hedged as the guardians accepted their dismissal and rose to leave.

"I will speak to him in private as soon as I can. It seemed wrong to speak of it with all the guardians here."

"Surprisingly good instincts," Lance said, and Tohmas shot him a mock hurt glare. Laughing, the Gaidolon left with the rest of the guardians.

Celebrant

Tohmas smiled in earnest once they had gone, surprised at himself. Lance Carraway, a High Guard of Gaidol, had just teased Tohmas, and Tohmas felt no need to rebuke the man. Had he found an actual friend among the Esparans?

Carsh cocked an eyebrow at Tohmas once they were alone. "Followa?"

"Maybe."

He had not yet met any Esparan he could call "Follower" under the Rydan definition of the word. His Esparan men swore oaths to him, and he to them, but it was not the same. His real Followers, left behind, were close friends. He had saved their lives, and they had saved his. Obedience between Leader and Follower had to be absolute, and that meant trust and devotion. Nowhere in Espar had Tohmas found a similar ideal. His soldiers did as he said because of the oath they had taken and the expectation of pay. There was no mention of honor or duty.

What would my Rydan Followers say if I introduce them to an Esparan Follower? Esparans were too weak to be worth the effort, according to the Rydans. But if he found someone who was strong enough, who would raise Tohmas' influence with his own power, did it matter if they were Esparan?

Tohmas pushed the thought aside. He would have been ridiculed for thinking such things. Thankfully, the men who had the right to chastise him were few, and none were present.

Carsh nodded. "Maybe," he repeated in agreement.

At least Tohmas was not alone in his thinking.

BellRoost marked the twenty-fifth village Dabon and his fellow Clandac natives had visited since joining Prince Tohmas' army. In the allied lands of the various sons of Zayban, the army had been welcomed with festivals, markets, and general excitement. The besieged town of BellRoost was strangely quiet in comparison. For the first time, Dabon had the sense they were in a place they were not wanted.

He had expected refugees, but there were few. A handful of non-combatants had remained to support the forces, much like Galanth's Fixer City, but the majority of the families had long since abandoned the city.

Chapter 7

The streets and houses, left in disrepair as their owners fled, were dust-filled and ghost-infested. Although it provided plenty of housing for the Galanth men, Dabon found it to be of little comfort.

After the raid through Barrow Hills, Dabon had been unsettled. Once, he had been a warden in Clandac, one of the local members of a fyrd permanently assigned to regulating and protecting a city's population. He had been a defender and a bringer of justice, but life in his hometown of Vait had been quiet. Joining Prince Tohmas' army with his two best friends had never been in his plan. Ciene, a blacksmith and Dabon's closest friend, had convinced him into it. Then, it had been vital to join the battle and defend Espar from the invading Northlanders.

Now, Dabon was less certain.

Following the army, they had witnessed little miracles, from minor magic at the hands of Master Wizard Kitable to dragons that obeyed the Prince of Galanth. Their awe and respect kept them in the army as they crossed into enemy territory. They had taken the oaths; they belonged to Prince Tohmas of Galanth now.

When Ciene died, so did part of Dabon's motivation. His purpose became to protect Ciene's brother, Sabian.

It was harder as they marched. Sabian grieved for days only. Dabon watched his friend's brother fall into quiet reclusiveness and was helpless to stop it. Torbi worked to bring Sabian back, but they were separated into different squads and opportunities to talk were scarce.

Initially, Dabon was grateful that Sabian's unorthodox style of using his throwing knives had won him friends. Although Dabon wondered if Sabian was distancing himself to avoid the memories of Ciene, he could not begrudge him the new camaraderie.

They had hoped to get back to sleeping overnight instead of during the day, but both squads were assigned to the wall that night as part of the Fyrd of Rest. Dabon understood it was to allow Prince Sol to strengthen his other defenses, but he sincerely missed his cot as the night stretched on. He and Torbi were posted just beside Sabian's new squad, and Dabon listened with one ear to the excited group.

At first, Dabon rolled his eyes at the various claims of great exploits bluster from boys who had not yet learned better. He focused on the grounds beyond the city's rickety wooden wall, refusing to participate.

Torbi, at Dabon's side, laughed. "I could put those boys to shame!"

Dabon shrugged. "Too grandiose for me. They're just full of battle rage." He glanced over at Sabian. He seemed to be at the heart of the boasting.

"You hear that?" one of the bragging boys asked, leaning over the wooden wall and peering down from the walkway. How he could hear anything over the sound of their voices, Dabon did not know. "Northlanders..."

Torbi crept to the wall to listen, his head down lest a sling stone or arrow target his skull. Dabon ducked low and crept toward the fool brazenly leaning over the wall to pull the stupid boy back from the edge and the threat of attack.

"I'll take them out!" the boy declared. Before Dabon could take more than a step, the boy put a hand on the rampart and jumped over.

For a flickering instant, Dabon froze in shock. Had the boy just thrown himself off the wall?

"Death to the Northlanders!" a second participant shouted and jumped as well. Two more companions made move to follow. One of the two was Sabian.

As Torbi leaped after the other man, Dabon grabbed Sabian in a bear hug and braced his legs against the wall, heaving the boy back from the edge. The rest of the companions on watch scrambled to assist, calling for the warden.

"I'll kill them!" Sabian declared, surging against Dabon with more strength than Dabon thought possible. He clamped his grip harder. "Let me loose! Let me go! We can kill them now! Kill them all!"

Torbi snatched at the other jumper, but the man pulled himself free and made the leap, leaving Torbi with only a strip of cloth in his hand. Below, a squawk of alarm proved that Northlanders had indeed been patrolling nearby. Even if the Esparans survived the fall, enemies were waiting.

From his place behind Sabian, Dabon adjusted his grip and twisted hard on Sabian's arm, but the boy did not stop. When Dabon felt the bones bend, he hesitated. He did not want to break the boy's arm, but to let him go was to see him fall to his death.

Warden Nisser solved the problem. The grizzled man arrived on the walkway with a pounce that landed squarely on Sabian and Dabon, winding Dabon despite the buffer of Sabian's body. With a quick chop,

CHAPTER 7

the warden clapped Sabian on the side of his head. The boy slumped, instantly unconscious.

As the scarred squint of the warden surveyed the scene, Dabon paused, listening. Five men had leaped down. They might survive the fall, but how to help them? He had no idea how many Northlanders there were. Opening a gate to go after the demon-cursed idiots would endanger the city.

With a grunt, the old warden untangled Sabian's unconscious body from Dabon's grip and checked for a heartbeat. Satisfied, the warden cast a dark glare toward the wall.

"Nothing we can do for the rest," he said, confirming Dabon's fear. He picked another companion at random and tossed him a token. "Run your chicken legs out and get me the guardian." The runner disappeared at a sprint. Addressing the on-looking companions, the warden demanded, "Anyone else feeling suicidal? Anyone?" Wide, startled expressions were the only answer. "Good. Then get back to your posts. I don't want to hear so much as a word from anyone unless it's a report of enemy attack!"

The companions dispersed without a whisper.

"You two," Nisser demanded, staring hard at Dabon and Torbi. Dabon winced. Nisser had enough battle experience for two men, but his strength was like a charging bull. Dabon hated the thought of getting in the warden's way. "You know him?"

"Yes, warden," Dabon replied.

"Then pick him up and come with me."

Tohmas was instantly awake. Even while he slept, he knew he was at war once more. He was alert and standing beside his bed as soon as he heard his name. He snatched his sword from its place propped beside the bed and held it at the ready, unsheathed but lowered. His right hand held his dagger.

The reflex to be awake and armed promptly had saved his life quite a few times.

It took an additional moment to recognize the room he had selected in BellRoost. Sol had offered a large, luxurious house, but Tohmas took a small servant bedroom as his sleeping area to be easily accessible to the protectors. The tiny bed barely held his weight, particularly when he wore his padded leather shirt to sleep.

He thought himself better off than Carsh, who had slept on the floor by the door, wrapped in a fur. His cot had ripped in the most recent unpacking, and the prime protector refused to fix or replace it. The ground was a familiar bed anyway.

Carsh was on his feet just as fast as Tohmas, expecting an attack. He narrowly avoided tripping the protector who entered.

Not an immediate threat. Putting away his weapons, he accepted a token from the Fyrd of Rest.

"Five men on watch jumped off the wall into enemy hands. An additional one was stopped and is being held. Guardian Faron says magic must be involved, claiming the men were otherwise sound of mind until tonight," the protector reported. Standing firmly, Protector Nardon waited for a reply.

Magic? Tohmas could counter attacks, but magic was beyond him. If six men could be affected, what about sixty? His time in BellRoost would be short if the spell went uncontested.

"I want to see this held man," Tohmas commanded.

"He's in the kitchen."

Tohmas followed Nardon out, joining the three other protectors on duty outside his door. The kitchen had been stripped down to a table and a few chairs for the protectors, although crumbs and peels on the table hinted they had emptied the cupboards. The huge baking fireplace stood cold, wood piled beside the hearth.

Standing inside the opposite door, Guardian Faron directed two companions to place an unconscious third onto the table. To Tohmas' surprise, he recognized the two companions as Ciene's friends from Vait and greeted them by name. The unconscious one was Sabian.

"We need Master Kitable," Guardian Faron said immediately.

Tohmas only had enough time to open his mouth before robes burst through the main door. Carsh snarled, a second knife coming to bear as he sank into a strong fighting stance.

Obviously having sprinted, Master Clarin panted words out between breaths. "I tell you…there was no magic…involved. Your men are just stupid!"

Chapter 7

"My men are not stupid, wizard," the guardian snapped. "No man throws himself off a wall deliberately without some kind of..."

As the argument seemed likely to go on for a long while, Tohmas ignored it.

"Companion Gain," he asked Dabon, "what happened?"

"Five men jumped off the west wall into enemy hands," the former warden explained. He poked the unconscious boy on the table. "Sabian here was the only one we were able to stop. They seemed to think they were going to take out DoomDragon's army alone. He resisted restraint to the point of doing himself harm, which is why he is now unconscious."

"Was anyone else involved?"

"Warden Nisser was there too, my Prince. Besides the five lost men, no others that we know."

Having heard all he needed to justify dismissing the Soltan wizard, Tohmas stepped between the guardian and Master Clarin, grabbed a handful of the wizard's robes at the shoulder, and turned the man for the exit. "Thank you for your assistance, Master Clarin, but this is obviously a Galanth problem and will be dealt with by Galanth forces. Good night, Master Clarin."

The dismissal stopped Clarin's blathering cold. The wizard's defenses, whatever they were, were less formidable than Kitable's; Tohmas was able to shove the man out the door. He felt no need to close the door. If Clarin acted against Prince Tohmas' orders, he would face the protectors.

Clarin left huffing, probably to report to Prince Sol.

With the Soltan man gone, Tohmas returned to Carsh. "*Neetin'*?" he asked, nodding his head to Sabian.

Carsh stepped up to the unconscious companion, then shook his head. There was no magic on Sabian that Carsh could detect.

Tohmas needed a second opinion.

"Alright. You three wait here and keep him," Tohmas indicated Sabian, "out of trouble. Someone light me a fire. I will deal with the rest."

There was nothing physically wrong with Prince Tohmas when he walked into Healing Mother Gracie's waggon. Kitable suspected the prince would never step into a Healing waggon and request treatment for himself without being close to death anyway. His cutter, a stout man called Darak, seemed to recognize it as well.

"Shoulder bugging you?" the cutter called loudly enough to draw attention. "You've been overdoing it again! Can't help it, I suppose. I'll take a look." The cutter swept his eyes over the mat-covered floor of the Healing waggon and paused where Kitable sat against a wall. "Over here," he said, leading the prince over.

It wasn't subtle. Darak had to move two stools over and push aside another injured man to make space beside Kitable. Darak's dog, Stitches, didn't recognize the attempt at discretion and lay next to Kitable, her drool-covered chin on his lap.

For the first time in Kitable's memory, the Prince of Galanth did not mutter a single complaint as the cutter made a show of removing and replacing his shoulder bandage.

"How you feeling, Kit?" the prince asked softly, without looking over.

Kitable matched the soft tone. "Much better. This time, I had the sense to knock myself out with pre-casted magic, so the enervation is not as bad. I will be on my feet by morning and in full form within a few days." He paused. "Why? You need something?"

"I have five men who jumped off a wall. Their guardian is crying magic, but Carsh cannot sense anything. You able to look into it, or should I seek religious assistance?"

Darak's hands paused at the word "religious," and the man's bushy brow furrowed. Officially, Darak had the preserved flower of Pari pinned to his collar—one could not be a cutter without being an acolyte of the God of Earth—but Kitable noticed that the cutter tended to take the early shift with the wounded, avoiding the formal morning services. He seemed to be a modest man when it came to religion.

But Tohmas wasn't referring to Pari, Kitable assumed. Although it was a close-kept secret, Tohmas knew Celebrant Loni was an untouchable—able to dispel all magic she came into contact with. The woman herself was unaware, but she was usually happy to assist the prince with anything. It was a crude means of dispelling magic, but it would work.

Kitable had no desire to invite the Celebrant of Inac anywhere near him. The idea made his stomach turn sour, and he shifted in his seat.

Stitches grumbled and leaned into his lap.

 # Chapter 7

"No," Kitable insisted, gently directing the dog's head away. Drool caught on his hand. "I can handle it. It's probably not magic anyway."

"Why do you not suspect a spell?"

Master Kitable sat up from the wall slowly, wiping his hand on his leg.

He drew a long breath and was pleased he could do it without shuttering. His body ached, and his muscles shook sometimes, but his mind was clear enough. "Firstly, mind magic is incredibly complicated. I've yet to meet a wizard capable of what you describe. Thought is considered an element, but actually manipulating it is more intricate than any of the basic elements. It seems to be impossible to summon thoughts since that implies creation, which is a separate domain. Alteration also tends to overlap with creation and destruction, though no one knows if a wizard can make an illusionary thought at all. Domains get all messed up when dealing with thought magic."

The prince nodded contemplatively although Kitable doubted he fully understood. "Secondly," Kitable went on, "the mind is difficult to navigate. You know how tricky it is to define a person. Can you imagine describing a thought, fleeting as they are? If you cannot define it, you cannot anchor it; if you cannot anchor it, you cannot affect it. Lastly—and this is something few people realize, my Prince—thought magic, no matter how well anchored and targeted, will often break when the person falls asleep."

For a second time, Darak's hands stopped. The prince did not seem to notice through his own surprise but Darak glanced at the wizard. It was obvious who Tohmas had come to visit now.

"How?" Tohmas asked.

"If there is a wizard in the world who knows why this happens, they refuse to tell. I suspect it is the same reason that some people, at certain moments of their sleep, cannot be anchored either. Just a fact of magic." Kitable shrugged. He had researched the phenomenon, but no one had answers.

"But what of the minds stolen by wizards? Flyers can make a man stab himself, can they not? How can that be true if mind magic is so difficult?"

Perhaps he understood more than Kitable was giving him credit for.

"Those are stories about four-way alterations, not thought. Used in that way, they are dominations. A wizard can control the four basic elements—water, wind, earth, and fire—and move a body without the permission of the mind like a puppet. Thought, binding, force, and light are advanced elements, harder to manage. In some rare cases, there have been thought spells that compel someone, but as I said, it is very difficult and not used lightly."

What he did not say aloud, but hoped the prince would extrapolate, was that if someone was going to go through the effort of using thought magic, they would likely make the most of it by targeting the most powerful person they could. It was a defense Kitable kept active around Tohmas regularly.

The prince looked pensive for a moment. "How would you—?"

"I would not," Kitable interrupted. "I consider the use of domination spells the second worst torture and the use of thought domination spells the absolute worst. I will not do it."

The prince did not seem irritated at being told off. Kitable was relieved.

"So, it is possible, but very unlikely, that a wizard is playing with one of my companion's head right now?"

Kitable cocked his head. Darak started to rebandage the prince's shoulder, having nothing more to add to the healing wound.

"Now?" Kitable asked.

"One survivor, a kid called Sabian. Care to have a look?"

Kitable nodded. "I will stop by my vardo for a change of clothes then meet you." Realizing the camp had moved, he frowned. "I may be a bit as I have to locate my vardo."

The prince smiled with a shrug, which disturbed the knot Darak had been tying on the bandage. He ground out a curse then pointedly tightened the bandage and tied his knot. Tohmas chuckled.

"Soon as you are able," the prince said, rising. The surrounding wounded looked away as he scanned the room. No doubt some of their conversation had been overheard. It would be tricky to hide Kitable among the wounded again once the rumors began. The more he was among the soldiers, the more readily he was recognized.

It was a good excuse to avoid becoming enervated again, Kitable decided. It made him vulnerable.

 # CHAPTER 7

That in mind, Kitable called after Tohmas, "One thing, my Prince. Master Clarin cannot be present."

"He is an ally. You do not trust him?" The objection was half-hearted.

"I do not trust anyone, least of all wizards. Every spell I cast is my own creation. The less other wizards know about them, the better. Besides, I do not want to draw attention to myself."

"Easily done." As the prince thanked Darak for his overly tight bandage, Kitable pushed out from under the dog and rose. By the time he found his robe and donned it, Cutter Darak had brought over Healing Mother Gracie and organized his release from the Healing waggon. He even gave Kitable a helper to get him back to his vardo.

There was much to do.

The capture of a prisoner in the middle of the night outside BellRoost surprised DoomDragon. Of the five Esparans to plunge from the wall and refuse surrender, only one survived to be presented to DoomDragon. The messenger found Seria first, so it was the little caster who woke Darknim. She seemed to take great pleasure in it.

Darknim rolled off his cot and pulled a thick pelt around his waist, not bothering with any additional clothing. His iron pendant hung at the center of his chest, the one item he never removed. He thought the tiny Esparan woman might comment on his indecency, but the rearing head of the dragon on his ax was facing her, and she said nothing. Finding a seat on the cot, his ax handle propped against the bed in easy reach, DoomDragon had the prisoner brought before him. Seria slunk into the corner behind DoomDragon as if counting on his broad shoulders to shield her from view.

The prisoner was older than Darknim expected for a soldier who had rashly leaped off fortifications. Four Northlanders held the man while a fifth held a levelled spear at his throat. The Esparan either did not notice or did not care and continued, with varied curses and growls, to struggle. It took the combined force of all four Northlanders to get the man on his knees with both his arms stretched out before DoomDragon.

By the white rank rope on his bleeding shoulder, the man was a companion, the lowest of the army. The green tabard marked him as Galanth. Incredibly, he had sustained only minor scratches and bruises from his fall and the subsequent scuffle. Beyond that, there was nothing remarkable about him except the way he continued to fight and curse the Northlanders.

Darknim saw no magic on the prisoner, but his strength was unnatural. His determination, if misled, was lamentable. There were those who would praise the man for being so resolute in the face of overwhelming odds, but Darknim thought it folly. A sane man did not waste his strength trying to fight five men. A sane man waited.

"Your name, Esparan?" Darknim asked, and the Esparan paused briefly at his native language.

"I will tell you nothing, barbarian!" the companion declared, his chest puffed up and his chin held high. The spear advanced in reminder, but again, the Esparan did not notice it, and the threat was wasted.

"A simple thing, your name," Darknim said, his hands resting on his fur-wrapped lap. "You are a companion of Galanth; I can see that, but I would know your name."

"Do what you will! I will kill you, Northlander! I swear I will!"

His struggling became frantic, and the Northlanders adjusted their grips. In that moment, the Esparan ripped his arms from their holds. He lunged.

DoomDragon stood, caught the Esparan's outstretched hands easily, and pulled the attack up short. With a quick twist, he broke the companion's arm.

The Esparan did not stop. The moment Darknim released the broken arm and moved aside, the man swung it, limp though it was. The four Northlanders jumped on him, pinning him to the cot. Their weight broke the frame and dumped the entire pile of people onto the ground. To Darknim's amazement, the Esparan still managed to throw off one of the four and half-rise before the other three shoved him back down.

"Kill him," Darknim told the spear-bearer in Northlander. There was nothing to be gained here.

The Galanth man lashed out once more, perhaps able to understand the meaning of the command without knowing the words. Despite the restraint, the Hunter with the spear hesitated as if unsure he could land

 # CHAPTER 7

a death blow on the frenzied target. Instead, he flipped the spear around and slammed the butt into the Esparan's skull. Concussed, the Esparan fell still.

The technique was typical for seal hunting—stun, then kill. Bringing a thin blade to bear, the Hunter yanked the unmoving companion's head forward into a deep nod, located the gap at the base of the skull, and stabbed.

Clear fluid mixed with blood spurted from the wound then slowed. The man dropped to the floor.

For a long moment, there was silence in the tent. Darknim collected his fur wrap from the ground to keep it clear of the blood.

How could a man be so inspired? How could any man motivate soldiers so thoroughly? He had underestimated Prince Tohmas and his men too much already. How had he created such fanatics among the typically apathetic Esparan?

From her chosen corner, Seria stared at the corpse with disgust in her pale eyes.

Darknim directed his decision to her. "We take BellRoost in two days' time. Tell your master I will not be swayed from that path. We have to crush Prince Tohmas quickly to keep this from pouring over to the other princedoms. I am pushing Sol back."

Seria would have argued, for she had delivered the orders at the beginning of the season that kept him outside BellRoost, but she was too stunned by the crazed man's death to mutter a word. Darknim left, figuring he could continue his sleep in another part of the tent as the body, broken cot, and blood were removed.

Chapter 8

Tohmas sat by the low-burning fire with a coin playing off his fingers. His trip to the Healing waggon had reminded him of the cutter's advice about keeping agility in his wounded arm and shoulder. He fiddled with the copper table coin, testing the ability of the slightly slow fingers. Although the night was warm, Tohmas sat close to the fire, pleased by the heat that, thanks to the fireplace, was not accompanied by smoke blowing in his face.

His little sleeping room was too crowded, so he remained in the kitchen area. Protectors offered him a seat at the table, but he chose to sit on the hearth instead, watching the fire. Carsh hovered over him like a poised mountain cat, his blades flickering over his fingers in an uncomfortable fidget.

Sabian had awakened just after Tohmas' return. Unlike his usual morose self, the boy was eager to go after the Northlanders, for he felt they had somehow deceived his fellow companions. Had the prince allowed it, he would have rushed from the city that moment to deal out revenge. Instead, Tohmas convinced Sabian that he had a crippling, albeit dangerous, plan for the Northlanders. Sabian now sat at the table waiting for the rest of the assignment eagerly with Torbi and Dabon at his shoulders. The Guardian of the Fyrd, looking droopy-eyed but determined to supervise, stood by the door between protectors and kept watch over his charges.

 # Chapter 8

Tohmas did not detect any sign of fatigue in Kitable as the wizard arrived through the guarded doors. In fact, Kitable looked almost five years younger. The bags under his eyes were erased, his face no longer looked deathly pale, his beard was freshly trimmed, and his attire was immaculate.

"Fake," Carsh grumbled.

He was wearing an illusion, Tohmas realized. Kitable was hiding how weak he still was.

Companion Dabon updated Kitable in a low voice. The wizard nodded slowly, an action more sage than tired. On a blink, his eyes changed to show the shifting rainbow of Spell Sight. Kitable could see the presence of magic with a look now.

Standing ominously over Sabian, Kitable told the boy to empty his pockets onto the table. Sabian eyed Kitable suspiciously for a moment, but Torbi, the big sailor from Vait, said, "Master Kitable is going to help us get everything ready to go after the Northlanders. Once he says we can go, we'll get to bashing heads."

The promise of battle worked. Sabian scrambled to his feet and deposited everything he had onto the table.

"Looking for...?" Tohmas prompted, joining them at the table.

The wizard examined the items individually with his enchanted eyes. "I cannot see any auras on him," Kitable explained, checking the contents of a pouch before placing it aside. Ciene's short, white candle joined the pile next and Tohmas felt a knot briefly in his stomach. He pushed it aside with the next breath, surprised it had occurred at all. "I cannot feel any magic either, so I'm wondering if he was a target at one point, and this is just a lingering effect. Thought magic is so complicated that I would expect to find a residue on anything used as an anchor or..."

As he spoke, the wizard carefully examined each item in the pile, but nothing seemed to catch his attention until Dabon gave a sharp yelp and snatched a small box from Kitable's hands. Every protector in the room straightened sharply, hands reaching for their swords.

Dabon thrust the box toward Tohmas.

The box, made of thin wood, was the size of Tohmas' fist. At a glance, Tohmas would have guessed it to contain gambling dice or something similar, but the carving atop showed a warrior brandishing a sword. Tiny writing read "Bravery."

Celebrant

Since Kitable had not identified it as magic, Tohmas took it from Dabon and presented it to Sabian.

"What is this?"

"Bravery mix," Sabian replied. Confusion grew in Sabian's eyes as he recognized Tohmas' disapproval.

Tohmas shook the box then opened it. A brown-grey powder lay within. "Have you used this today?"

The only thing useful of the reply was the nod. Everything else was assertions of service, bravery, and prowess that Tohmas dismissed. Sabian was still professing his desire to attack the enemy when Tohmas turned away.

"Runnah!" The first protector to step forward was Protector Farnat. "I want a cutter here to knock this boy out with something other than a clap upside the head." He turned to Guardian Faron and handed him the box. Nothing Sabian said right now would be helpful. "I want to know how he got this. If someone is selling them, I want them brought to me. If he found it, I want to know where and how many there were. Collect anymore of the demon-cursed things immediately."

To his relief, when Tohmas turned around, Sabian had been pulled aside by the ex-warden from Vait. Dabon must have children, Tohmas decided. Like a patient father, he challenged Sabian to a contest of silence and stillness. Both were sitting by the fire with complete rigidity.

Apparently, the bravery mix concoction made the boy dense as well as brave.

Neither had moved by the time the cutter arrived.

Kitable let himself doze after the mystery of the companions jumping from the wall had been partially solved, but he remained with the prince in the tiny house, anticipating a reply to Tohmas' orders. As Kitable slipped into slumber on a pair of chairs, the only movements in the room were Carsh flipping a single knife in his grip and the flicker of a coin across the prince's hand. The metal caught the light of the fire and created a hypnotizing flash that looked distantly like the prince was balancing fire on his fingertips.

 # Chapter 8

Although he had eventually become accustomed to the rocking of his vardo, Kitable was not able to sleep though other disturbances. He woke the moment Guardian Faron returned. Dawn's light made its first attempts at cracking through the windows, telling Kitable that any chance at securing a proper night's sleep had passed.

The prince had returned to his seat on the hearth. The guardian spoke to Prince Tohmas' back when he declared, "We found him."

"And?"

"A peddler by the name of Dust Weaver. Not a part of Fixer City. Been living in BellRoost since the siege," Faron said. "He admits to selling the boxes to several Galanth men. He's waiting outside with Warden Nisser."

Kitable was certain the prince was well aware of the possibility that the peddler was in some way working for Northlanders. Having the Galanth men poison themselves out of service was clever, but Kitable suspected it was giving DoomDragon too much credit. But if the Northlander had been behind the scheme, then why had the Soltan men not been victims long before Tohmas' march?

"I would like to talk to him," Tohmas declared, coming to his feet slowly and facing the guardian.

Kitable rolled his eyes at the predictable reply.

The guardian had only to give a shout to bring the warden and his prisoner in. Once the peddler was in presence of the protectors and the prince, the warden was dismissed. The grousing man limped away, eyeing the peddler over his shoulder.

Dust Weaver was a man of middle height and dressed in bright colors that had Kitable blinking in amazement. The clothes themselves had come from a dozen sources, and they matched in neither color, style, nor size. A bright red, pointed beard and moustache stuck out under Dust's prominent nose, making him look goat-like. He entered with flourish despite the military escort, grinning widely with a lopsided, broken smile. The man dipped into a deep bow that saw his cape and cap both brushing the ground.

His outfit had dozens of pockets and pouches, and his fingers were each ringed. Although the peddler wore a single earring like Carsh, it was a large, golden hoop that bespoke more of Lourite traditions than Rydan.

Celebrant

Carsh leaned forward, examining the intruder with a confused expression as if he smelled something unpleasant but was unable to determine the source.

Kitable's eyes narrowed on the jewelry. Although Spell Sight had long since ended, he could still detect the faint tingle of magic on the man. To his annoyance, the man had hovering spells active around him.

"*Exthaol*," Kitable said, activating an Eight-layered Dispel. The spell struck the peddler mid-bow. There was no physical force to the impact, but the stranger jumped as if he had been pushed.

"Oi Rather rude welcome, I must say! You could have warned me!"

Kitable frowned and leaned back in his chair. He whispered the word that would renew his Spell Sight and examined the intruder. Having been dispelled, the stranger had no spells on him now. The Eight-layered Dispel had a lingering effect on enchanted items, disabling the man entirely. Kitable intended to have the man gone or stripped of all belongings before it wore off. "No one wears spells in the presence of my prince save me," Kitable informed the man.

"I meant no insult, good Prince. I am an apothecary first but a moderate caster. My spells were not hostile. I am..."

While the peddler continued his introduction, the hairs along the back of Kitable's neck rose. He had heard non-wizards describe the sensation of being watched—it seemed to be a primitive instinct that every living creature that had been preyed upon shared.

He was certain it was a spell.

Under the guise of taking a closer look at the intruder as he explained his wares and training as an apothecary, Kitable stood and circled Dust Weaver. He kept his vision deliberately unfocused, looking at the man, his attire, his trinkets, and most importantly, the entire rest of the room. Dust shrank under the scrutiny, but the peddler didn't dare move away.

Hidden in the embers of the fire behind the prince, Kitable found the tiny, white, smooth aura of a wind alteration. The line binding it to its target was no thicker than a spider's thread, running straight up the chimney. The passage of smoke would have easily concealed it, but its flickering light was bright under Kitable's Spell Sight. If he trusted his instincts, the binding spell was attached to a Scry.

 # Chapter 8

An anchor such as that thread, especially one that was undefended, was easy prey for a wizard with the right spells.

"What do you mean by 'apothecary'?" Prince Tohmas asked their visitor. Dust Weaver launched into a detailed description of his abilities, wares, and history as if pleased to have something other than Kitable's glowers to focus on.

One of the first thing Kitable had done once entering enemy territory was create an item enchanted with his Forced Confrontation spell. It was a spell of his own creation—one that utilized the binding of another spell to target the caster and summon them. He was particularly proud of the part which used the binding itself as an anchor for an Eight-layered Dispel complete with linger effect. Any caster successfully hit by the combination would be brought forward and utterly dispelled.

As he circled the man one final time, Kitable activated the enchanted chord on his belt and directed the Forced Confrontation spell at the binding.

The spell latched onto the thread like a wick taking a flame. Somewhere above them, the full spell came into effect, snatching the caster from their position and summoning them where Kitable had designated—by the door surrounded by protectors.

But when Kitable activated an additional spell that should have had no trouble pinning the intruder in a Force Cage, a flash of smoke appeared instead. He caught only a glimpse of the target before losing her.

What little he had seen revealed the caster to be a young woman with brilliant red hair and golden jewelry to shame the best paid dancer in Narsol's ports. She ducked into a cloud of alchemical smoke and, denied a clear target, Kitable's spell missed.

As the protectors fled the smoke and closed around the prince to defend him, Kitable activated a Wind Barrier meant to obscure areas from eavesdroppers. It had the side effect of pushing air away from it on one side. Moving the barrier swiftly away, he swept the smoke clear. Kitable realized belatedly that he had just blinded the rest of the protectors who were rushing to the prince's aid from the outer hall. It did, however, allow him to see his target.

She was a blossoming woman, graceful on her feet and quick to move, but Kitable's attention was on the magic threads she wound together in casting. Surprising him, she created a defense with a handful of words and set a physical shield against four elements around herself.

Choosing an element she had not considered, Kitable called, "*Garnita!*" The thought destruction slapped her mind and snapped her head back. Kitable followed with two more words, locking the girl's body down in a four-way alteration spell.

With the girl frozen by his spell and the protectors staring with their swords drawn, Kitable paused. He heard the end of Dust Weaver's protests; "...means no harm." The objection was muffled by the group of protectors pinning the peddler against the wall farthest from the prince.

After a final breath to steady himself, Kitable finished with "*Exano*," and the Eight-layered Dispel hit the girl in the chest. Although it released her from Kitable's alteration spell, it also destroyed her shield. She stood, magically naked, for only a breath before launching into renewed casting as if unaware of the circle of angry protectors around her. They waited, looking to Kitable for the appropriate response.

She was defenseless. A sword would do the job as well as a spell would, but Kitable no longer thought her a threat. The smoke had come from a chemical reaction, not magic, and her defenses were trivial. She was fast but did not deserve to die.

"If another word comes out of your mouth, so help me, I will Vox you permanently!" Kitable said, stepping between the girl and the protectors. "Don't you dare cast within my earshot!"

The girl's chant stopped cold. "It is just a defensive spell," she protested. "I will not be without!"

"Yes, you will. No one wears spells in the presence of my prince, girl. If you try to cast, I promise you my response will not be as magnanimous! You have been enough trouble!"

Her face flushed, she locked her jaw and fixed her glare on him. Thankfully, she said nothing further.

Scanning with Spell Sight, Kitable checked her once more for magic auras.

Like her father, the girl was dressed in layers of mismatched clothing, but unlike him, she managed to make the arrangement flattering. Golden hoop earrings complimented the beads in her hair and the golden bracelets that clinked with her every gesture. Her clothes were equally beaded, and her entire form seemed to jingle as she

Chapter 8

moved even though the only thing she carried was a canvas bag over one shoulder. All the golden jewelry was of fine enough quality to be enchanted, but they looked dull now. The linger of the Eight-layered Dispel would keep them silent.

It took another moment for Kitable to realize his audience was still present. The prime protector had three knives out in readiness, and had Kitable been more specific about the threat, he suspected the girl would have been dead the moment the spells dropped. Instead, the prime protector had positioned himself between Tohmas and the strangers. Tohmas himself was surrounded by protectors and could not even be seen through the layers of green tabards and armor.

Carsh looked to Kitable in question.

"May I introduce my daughter?" Dust Weaver's muffled voice finally said. "Prince Tohmas, this is Shimmer Weaver."

Dust Weaver, Tohmas discovered, was from everywhere and nowhere in particular. The arrival of DoomDragon early in the season had trapped the peddler in BellRoost. The rest of Tohmas' inquiries were interrupted by Dust's daughter.

Once she was contained, Tohmas escaped his surrounding protectors and assessed her. She was a tall Esparan woman, about the height of Tohmas' chest, but the most distinctive thing about her was her auburn locks. Fabulous green eyes seemed to flash when her attention was brought to him. Shimmer's face, although beautiful, was dark as she glared at Kitable.

Pity she is a caster. She looked like a dancer. Dancers were fun.

"Am I right in assuming these two are no longer a magical threat?" Tohmas asked, prompting Kitable from behind a final layer of protectors.

The master wizard stiffly nodded.

"Good. Protectors, go away," Tohmas ordered.

The protectors sheathed their weapons and filed out, each one casting a final suspicious stare at the intruders.

Tohmas chose a chair to sit on, placed his hands on his knees, and gestured for both casters to stand before him. Dust Weaver rushed over, but his daughter was slow in following his example, keeping one eye on

Kitable as if uncomfortable with the wizard at her back. Kitable came to stand at Tohmas' side, making the position easier for her.

"Now that Master Kitable has made it clear you are not a threat," Tohmas said with deliberate calm in his voice, "perhaps you two would be willing to tell me a little—"

"Master Kitable?" the woman exclaimed. Her glare vanished instantly. The venom of her green eyes morphed into awe.

"You are surrounded by green tabards, and you just got hit by an Eight-layered Dispel. Who did you think I was?" Kitable replied sharply.

The wide-eyed girl blushed heavily. "We have been in BellRoost for..." she started, but her amazement prevented the sentence from finishing. "With Prince Sol and Clarin..." she tried with no more success. "It is just such a surprise..." After enough false starts, she finally managed to get her wits about her. "I never expected to have the honor of actually meeting you, Master Kitable."

"I dare say. I don't think I have ever seen her so flustered," Dust muttered.

Tohmas laughed and shot Kitable a grin. "Congratulations, Kitable! You are famous!"

"Renowned is more like it," the peddler corrected with a smile and a bow. "I am equally pleased to make your acquaintance, Master Kitable. Well, maybe not *quite* as pleased."

"Renowned?" Tohmas asked. "I knew you to be respected, but with these two fawning over you, I'm wondering what I missed."

"Beyond renowned!" Shimmer piped up before Kitable could answer. "Master Kitable all but redefined magic nine years ago on the steps outside of Wayburn on the fifth day of—"

"You are too young to remember that!" Kitable interrupted.

"Actually, we both attended," Dust gently said with another nod of his head.

"I was nine," Shimmer informed him.

"And I suspect she understood more of it than I did!"

Under her father's compliment, Shimmer straightened further and gained enough confidence to say, "Tailoring a contingency to be applicable to every spell was brilliant! We have certainly changed basics since then, but you invented the hovering spells! An absolute genius—"

Chapter 8

Kitable waved his hand dismissively. "Enough. I just happened to be the first one to recognize the possibilities."

"Then shared it with the rest of the world," Dust added, "which in of itself is a testimony to your modesty. Shimmer, leave the poor man alone before you make a fool of yourself."

Shimmer pressed her lips together in obvious restraint and joined her father, all the while keeping her eyes on Kitable.

After clearing his throat, the peddler declared, "Good Prince, Master Kitable, we are the Weavers." The daughter matched his bow with considerably less attention and sincerity. "We are apothecaries, peddlers, and entertainers, and we stand at your service."

"You forgot 'wizards,'" Tohmas corrected.

Kitable snorted. "They are not wizards. Being a wizard implies actual training and competence. These two are dabblers at best. At worst, charlatans."

"We make no claim to be wizards," Shimmer said. "We are apothecaries and performers first and foremost."

To prevent the two of them from renewing either Shimmer's praise or Kitable's outrage, Tohmas pulled out the box and tossed it to the alchemist.

"So, you would know about this," he prompted.

The alchemist nodded eagerly, and Tohmas' suspicion faded. Proving he was the only one feeling that way, a white ball of light appeared in front of the Weavers—a Lie Light.

For the second time, the apothecary looked offended. "I only lie about my products when I fear for my life." The Lie Light confirmed the statement by remaining white. "Prince Tohmas has given me no reason to do so. I see no point in any form of deception." With another clearing of his throat, he explained, "This is one of my bravery mixes. The concoction makes a person stronger, faster, and more willing to fight. I sold a dozen shortly after you arrived."

"You do not mention that it makes them bloodthirsty and as dense as a log," Tohmas said.

The apothecary's smile remained. "I warn them all there is a dampening of one's senses, yes, but they do not care. In the thick of fighting, men tend to lose their minds regardless."

"You do not deny poisoning my soldiers then?"

"They chose what they swallow. They knew it would make them brave. It can be very useful in battle."

"But not so useful when they are on watch at the wall."

Neither entertainer so much as blinked. "They were clearly nervous," Shimmer said. "If they took more than a pinch, yes, it would make them bold enough to jump off the wall. They still bought it and took it themselves." A shy glance found Kitable but turned away quickly.

"You know about what happened then?" Tohmas pressed, and the peddlers shrugged.

"We see many people," the alchemist replied.

"We hear lots of things," his daughter added.

"Clarin," Carsh said with a snort, making the peddlers jump. Neither, it seemed, had noticed the Rydan who lurking by the fireplace. "Ya be watchin' Clarin."

They did not deny it, and Tohmas thought their honesty had more to do with the Lie Light this time.

"Master Clarin has a mixed opinion on us, so we like knowing what he is up to," Dust diplomatically said.

"If anyone is going to try to kick us out of the city, it will be him. If we keep an eye on him, we will not be caught by surprise," Shimmer said

"Why would he try to kick you out?" Tohmas asked as Kitable seemed unwilling to involve himself in the conversation.

"Because everyone knows there are wizards or 'dabblers,'" Shimmed said with another look at the Master Wizard of Galanth, "with the Northlanders that he has been unable to get rid of. People do not understand magic. If Clarin finds himself in need of someone to blame, the easy target is us."

"We make a point of staying one step ahead of things like that," Dust finished.

Tohmas put his chin in his hand, resting his elbow on the chair's armrests. The pair of apothecaries stood erect in front of him, expectant.

They admitted to being casters, but they seemed to be innocent bystanders to the war, not participants. Clarin had not chased them out. Two casters, or alchemists, might be useful.

They did not even look nervous, perhaps already suspecting the conclusion Tohmas was drawing.

 # Chapter 8

Tohmas leaned forward once his mind was made up. "First, no more bravery mixes." The apothecary shrugged in acceptance. "Second, you will collect all the bravery mixes you have sold to both Galanth and Soltan men. I do not care if you replace or repay, but I never want so much as a mention of this again."

"Not easy," Dust protested, but he followed rapidly with, "but I will certainly see that it is done."

"Third, I want a list of everything you have, and I want to know every effect it has. I presume you write?"

"Cannot be a dabbler without it," Dust said.

"Then deliver that list to one of my protectors directly. Beyond that, you are free to go."

At that, the otherwise silent guardian, Faron, who had watched the magic battles and the coming and going of the protectors without moving, became animated.

"No answer for the men who jumped off the wall, my Prince? These two were—"

Tohmas raised his hand, and Faron's objection went silent. "The men chose to buy that drug and chose to take it. I will make sure no others repeat their mistake, but as Miss Weaver pointed out, they are responsible for what they swallowed. These two are not." He put finality in his words.

With a final flamboyant bow and some shooing by Dust to get Shimmer to take her stare off Kitable, the Weavers left. Kitable followed them to the exit. He watched with his enchanted sight for a few long moments more.

There was either curiosity or consternation on the face of the wizard in addition to his suspicion as he stood in the doorway, watching the casters. Although Tohmas was certain the wizard had seen something of note, for the man's eyebrows rose briefly and he hummed to himself, Tohmas did not bother to ask what it had been. If it was important, Kitable would tell him. If it was not, Tohmas doubted he would understand the reply anyway.

Celebrant

As they left the house where the Prince of Galanth had hosted them, Shimmer kept looking back. After only a dozen paces, she stopped entirely, and Dust was not surprised to see her casting.

But *what* she casted made him lift an eyebrow.

"A Molded Shield, Shim? A bit of overkill, I must say. I cannot even cast that one!"

"I will not be undefended," Shimmer calmly said, but her excitement could not be ignored for more than a moment of false serenity. As soon as they were moving again, she grinned.

"I cannot believe we met him, Papa!" she exclaimed with a tug on his arm and a skip to her step he had not seen in years. "Did you see that? A four-way alteration! Not even targeted! Eight-layered Dispels...a Force Cage! And did you see how he used the Wind Barrier to move the smoke? It's not designed for that! But it took him only a flicker to decide on it as a counter for—"

At first, Dust walked beside her in numbed silence, but the moment he realized what was going on, he caught himself laughing. Shimmer paused.

"What?" she demanded.

"I've been waiting for this moment for years, Shim! I expected it sooner! You are infatuated with him! You have a crush, my girl!"

He expected her to deny it, but Shimmer had always been a sensible child. It took her only a blink to realize he was right.

"And why shouldn't I? He's the best wizard in the world, Papa! I dodged one of his spells too! Did you see that? Dodged it! I am such..."

Her continued ranting came as a relief even if it meant the normally sensible girl was acting like a child. Shimmer was a grown woman but, due to some mistreatment she had never fully confessed to him, had shown no interest in courting. He had been expecting her to find a boy to run off with for years.

It was the first time he had seen her so besotted, and it was his fatherly duty to keep her head a little lower lest it run off to the horizon.

"He was enervated, Shim."

His daughter stopped. "He was...?"

"You did not notice the weariness in his eyes? How about the way he leaned on the doorway as we left? Have you wondered why he had not been seen since the battle? He was enervated getting into BellRoost."

Chapter 8

As much fun as it was to see her giddy, he could not have her believing anyone, even Master Kitable, was more than mortal.

He could tell some illusions about the prowess of the Galanth wizard were already fading, but to his delight, her giddiness did not follow.

"To be expected," Shimmer said. "Master Clarin has been unable to defeat the Northlander casters for five years! It's amazing that Master Kitable was able to even get near the city, let alone within it! I would not blame him for being enervated after that, and if he can still cast that fast while enervated..."

Confident he had done his duty, Dust let her continue. She could be such a fiery person, and having her passionate once more made him happy. Still, thinking back to the man they left in the little house made him wish Shimmer had set her sights on someone a little more attainable.

First loves are meant foolish, he thought with a covered smile.

She was still grinning like a bobcat by the time they reached their vardo.

Noon was Inac's time regardless of where her gathering was. In the besieged town of BellRoost, Prince Sol had no celebrants. The presence of the four Temple waggons of Galanth was well received, giving Sedgan a large crowd when the sun was high. It was time for service.

Finally able to set a service without walking, Sedgan placed the altar in the doorway of the waggon and led the gathering through the prayers. To Sedgan's distress, the whore Loni hovered at the back in silence, distracting every one of the acolytes. Sedgan was able to keep them on task, but he was grateful when the service was over, and he could dismiss the crowd.

He wanted to chase her away but did not dare. Half of the people in the Gathering of Fire had joined because of her preaching, so he held back his more violent followers and carried on as if Loni did not exist.

The acolytes replaced the altar in the waggon then returned outside to speak to any of the gathering who remained. For a rare moment, Sedgan was alone in the waggon. It was for the best; the Blessed Flame set stop the altar, meant to be undying, had gone out yet again when they had moved the altar. It had been a constant problem during the march, specifically since the harlot Loni had joined them. Sedgan quickly set to relighting the flame, thankful there was no one to witness the failure of the lamp.

Not alone enough, he corrected when Loni stepped into the waggon wearing a sultry smile and her most recent amber dress. Her feet were bare but adorned with anklets and toe rings to match her ornate necklace, rings, and bracelets. A rag was tied around her arm as if holding a wound but was largely hidden under a black shawl. Holes in the shawl would have made it look like lacework if only it had been symmetrical.

He knew what lay under the rag on her left arm, although he suspected he was one of very few who did. The prime protector had revealed the brand on her arm to Prince Tohmas, who had in turn informed Sedgan. Since then, Sedgan had acutely noticed how careful the so-called celebrant was to keep her upper left arm covered under shawl, bandage, or sleeve.

She bore the brand of insanity, assigned to her by a court of law in the Princedom of Damoria. It was a warning that any further misbehavior would result in death. It also warned those around her that she was not to be trusted.

It should not have been concealed. Still, the prince had not insisted she reveal it, and Sedgan did not either.

"You do have a way of arranging these things," he grumbled at Loni as he carefully lit the lamp from a candle and sheltered it under a woven metal cover.

"I did not think you would want your acolytes to hear what I have to say, so my friends have come with questions for them. Like good soon-to-be-celebrants, they are helping those in need."

"I noticed the gathering was larger than normal. Come for a visit?"

"Come to give you a warning," Loni replied, and Sedgan spun to face her. He had heard stories, albeit only rumors, of her violent nature. That she dared threaten a Celebrant of Fire amazed him. Spotting the rag on her arm once more, he reminded himself that her behavior should not surprise him.

But her expression was calm under the ostentatious painted colors on her face. Rather than draw a blade or start spewing boasts, Loni stepped forward and tucked her hand into Sedgan's. She seemed sad. "Barga is deceptive," she told him.

 # Chapter 8

He snorted at the idea that secrecy was required. "We have dealt with that. I guess I now know where the anonymous letters about the emerald were—"

"Not the gem," Loni interrupted. "Yes, I set that up to let you see how she would betray you, but this is more than gems, Sedgan. This is life she plays with now."

He had never seen her so grave, and it snagged his attention. He allowed her to place something in his palm. Instead of continuing her accusations, she withdrew.

"I have worked to see the Gathering of Inac grow," Loni cryptically finished as she slipped out into the light of noon. "I will not have her kill it."

His acolytes later found him staring at the three pain pills she had deposited in his hand. They proudly told him about their conversations with the interested strangers during his absence, and he did not have the heart to correct them.

Chapter 9

The night after they arrived in BellRoost, Tohmas accepted Sol's invitation to meet again. He joined his uncle in the repurposed house acting as his central post. Sequestered from their soldiers, the two princes met with only their prime protectors on hand, putting Carsh quickly on edge in the presence of Master Clarin. The wizard stood near the door on the far side of the room as his patron paced.

The conversation did not take long to go sour, and Tohmas stood by the window in irritation. The view was of a cluttered cobble street with thin lamplight that reached through shuttered windows under the pale moon. Somewhere beyond, Tohmas pictured the rickety walls he had stationed his men on. Beyond that, Northlanders roamed.

"It has to hold," Sol said with such finality that Tohmas hesitated. He could not tell if Sol did not recognize his own delusion or if he simply did not want anyone to point it out. Due to his rank, no one had yet challenged Sol's assumptions.

But Tohmas was unwilling to let Sol keep his illusions if it meant losing Galanth men. He needed those soldiers. "BellRoost will not hold, and you know it."

The Prince of Solta spun on his heel at the end of his pace with such fervor Tohmas expected the man to fall over. His expression was that of a slighted father. "It has held for three years!"

 # CHAPTER 9

"And I have yet to discover how!" Tohmas countered. "I have never been this far north, but I thought Arcott and Field were walled cities. Yet they fell to this rabble."

"They were. They did," Sol muttered, resuming his pacing. Another quick pivot knocked his scabbard into Clarin's knees. The wizard winced, but Sol carried on obliviously.

"Then why, by Inac's Flame, has DoomDragon not yet won this war?" Tohmas asked. "Unless Northlanders have a strange aversion to wood, your walls should not hold against his forces."

Sol looked to Clarin for assistance. Ignoring his bruised knee, the wizard straightened proudly but had nothing to offer. He was even less of a soldier than Sol.

I have more advisors than I need, and Sol does not have nearly enough!

"They have held—" Sol began.

"I do not care that they have held, Sol," Tohmas interrupted. "What concerns me right now is having my men sitting in a position that is, at best, precarious. If DoomDragon's men attack in earnest, we die. I do not like it."

"Then you should not have come here, *Tohmas*," Sol answered, stopping at the end of his pace pointedly and locking stares with Tohmas. His face was flushed, but Tohmas could not tell if it was from anger or frustration.

Anger, probably. I just addressed him without his title.

Tohmas doubted Sol was aware of the challenge he was making to Tohmas' Rydan sensibilities with his direct stare. They were equals officially, but there had to be a master between them even if Sol did not realize it. Still, if Tohmas pushed the prince much further, there would only be division. Esparans did not respond well to direct confrontation. They did understand how little their blood and titles mattered.

While he could best Sol physically, Tohmas had to beat the man politically as well. That was the Esparan way.

Tohmas broke the stare first, and Carsh grunted with concern. To the Rydan, it was a sign of defeat, but Tohmas told himself it would only be victory if Sol recognized the challenge in the first place.

"Maybe you're right," Tohmas said, being cautious not to give any sign of aggression. Carsh's eyes narrowed, and he shifted forward. Defeat could not be witnessed. In true Rydan fashion, Carsh was prepared to kill those Tohmas was deferring to. Dead, they could not rule Tohmas or Carsh.

Beside the simple table, four chairs had been arranged, so Tohmas sat down. He tapped the table as he found his seat, and the Rydan backed off. Carsh knew Esparan ways were different even if he disliked them. He would, as Tohmas had commanded with his tap, wait.

"Maybe I should not have come, but I am here now. We have to make this work," Tohmas said.

It took another moment before Sol sat down as well, but by the time he did, his face had returned to a more reasonable shade.

"My men are getting along well despite the few who fell from the wall last night. I am perhaps being paranoid since our arrival started so poorly," Tohmas falsely confessed.

"BellRoost will hold," Sol asserted once more, and Clarin nodded in agreement.

"We can hold through the summer again," the Soltan prime protector added. "With the Galanth additions, maybe next year we can push them back."

Worse than no advisor, he has a bad one.

"I would like to be ready for the worst, regardless," Tohmas said. "If nothing else, it will keep my men busy until we have the opportunity to strike again. The preparations we discussed—for the wells, the houses, and the roads near the gates—should not affect your men. I can use it as an exercise if you allow."

The prince was silent as he considered the offer or perhaps searched for a lie. At length, he nodded.

"Thank you, Prince Sol," Tohmas said as he rose from his seat and bowed his head in mock complacency. It worked well to hide his frown, and he was gone before his scowl could betray him.

Carsh spoke up once they were walking outside between the buildings.

"*Blogged Esparan. Naw nye?*"

Tohmas shook his head, glad there was no one around to overhear the threat against Sol's life.

"They do not follow strength, Carsh, not in the same way at least. I will gain control differently."

Chapter 9

"'Course," Carsh replied confidently. Tohmas thought he sounded a bit disappointed.

Exhaustion dragged Kitable down as he sought Master Clarin's room. The enervation had mental and physical effects, leaving his mind groggy and his muscles worn. Even his eyes felt dry and heavy as he sized up the spells Clarin had placed over his sleeping quarters in the house Prince Sol was using.

Squaring himself up, Kitable summoned the last vestiges of his energy and set about dismantling the defenses in quick succession. The final application of a force spell threw the door open.

Clarin started so much in his seat he knocked an ink pot off his table and lost the spell he had been casting in a spark of blue light. The lack of control irritated Kitable further. Clarin had been careless, and in the hands of wizards, carelessness could be fatal. Still, surprising the wizard pleased Kitable. It was vital that the Soltan prime protector knew Kitable could do what he wanted, whenever he wanted. It was childish, and Kitable knew it. He also knew exactly when he had developed the manner of thinking and discovered its usefulness. He felt no guilt at applying it.

"Master Ki—" was all Kitable let Clarin say. The wizard did not even have time to fully rise from his chair.

"You had dabblers sitting in BellRoost, and you did not realize it?" Kitable accused, looming as best he could.

Clarin's face blanked, eyes wide as he searched for an explanation. "The Weavers?" he choked out. "They are hardly worth—"

"The girl can cast a Molded Shield!" Kitable snapped. The way Clarin's face blanched revealed how little he knew about the two performers. Kitable doubted Clarin himself could cast the spell.

"The girl? That little—"

"A better caster than her father by a hefty bit," Kitable growled. "You assumed she would be the lesser of the two, I take it. Did you even check? Unmonitored casters right under your nose?"

"I have seen their 'powers,' Master Kitable," Clarin finally interjected, pushing himself up from the chair. "Go to one of their shows, and you

Celebrant

will see for yourself. They are harmless performers and peddlers. I have more important things to worry about than—"

"And what if these dabblers happen to be allied with the powers that have kept you and your prince trapped here? Will you tell me not to worry about them? They are wanderers, probably fleeing away from crimes for all we know. Casters are dangerous. You know that as well as I do!"

"I hardly—"

"Do what you want, but do not underestimate that girl! BellRoost's survival may count on it." Kitable turned and left without waiting for the Soltan wizard's response.

Once he was back in his vardo, far from the central post, Kitable congratulated himself on finding a way to get the wizard off his back long enough for the nap he desperately needed.

Shimmer Weaver did not like being surrounded by walls. Neither she nor her father wanted to leave their rolling shop, Match and Mixer, behind for the sixth or seventh time in her life, but staying in BellRoost had become more dangerous as time went on. Getting out was already difficult. Any longer, and it would be impossible.

But the opportunity was good. The city may have largely emptied—the non-combatants long since sent away, only the army and their immediate supporters remaining—but those who were left were desperate for distractions. Shimmer and Dust's shop and shows had no competition.

Besides, even if Shimmer and Dust could escape BellRoost, fleeing would take her farther from Kitable. Now that the master wizard was in BellRoost, Shimmer refused to entertain any plans to leave. When Shimmer danced for the crowd of weary Soltan soldiers and excited Galanth men, she pretended that Kitable was watching. He probably was.

The night was eerily quiet after, amplifying her concern that battle was pending. She was grateful when, in the early dawn, she saw a woman in red walking toward the vardo's open-sided counter. A customer may help change the mood of the day. But as soon as the woman was within three paces of the counter, Shimmer involuntarily stepped back.

CHAPTER 9

Although she could see nothing out of place, a feeling of terror crept over her with every step the woman took.

Before Shimmer could decide on a course of action, the woman was in front of the vardo, smiling up at her. Tangled red hair made a nest above the woman's decorated dress and jewelry. Her face was strongly painted with deep gold over her eyes and bright crimson on her lips.

Shimmer was not new to trouble. Her and her father's tactics were subtle—coded sentences and words would warn her father.

"Welcome to the Match and Mixer," she said.

It sounded innocuous enough, but she never used "the" in front of their shop name.

A spell reached out, and Shimmer adjusted a defense to let it through. *Shim?* Dust's voice said into her head. *What's wrong?*

"Good afternoon, Shimmer," the woman in red replied.

The smile seemed sincere. The woman was relaxed. Shimmer could not tell why she felt chilled, a knot in her stomach as thick as a mooring line.

Shimmer sent out a binding to her father, allowing her to answer his Sending with one of her own.

Something is wrong with this woman! she told her father.

Aloud, Shimmer said, "Good afternoon, Celebrant Loni. How can I be of service?"

There was momentary silence in her head, letting Shimmer concentrate on the Celebrant's answer.

"You have heard of me. You are well informed." It was a compliment, but Shimmer had to force herself to bow her head and put a false smile on her face. She hoped her acting skills would be enough to keep her unease from being obvious.

Spell Sight is getting nothing, her father sent her.

I've got a knot in my stomach the size of a boulder, Papa. It's magic; it has to be!

"I have need of a scent," the celebrant said, and Shimmer tried to lighten her smile. *Perfume? All this for perfume?*

"We have dozens, Celebrant, ranging from the everyday to the extremely rare. Costs follow that range as well. What are you looking for?"

It took all Shimmer's concentration to listen to both replies at once.

"Something uncommon. Something distinctive."

141

I tried a scan, but she blocked it. Gods, I hope she didn't notice! You want an out? I can handle her if you want.

Don't you dare! Shimmer snapped to her father. He was good at handling female clients, but she wanted him to stay far away from this one.

To Loni, Shimmer said, "Let me see," and took a grateful step to one side. The feeling of terror lessened slightly as she distanced herself. Shimmer collected three clay flasks of perfume from the shelves behind her and placed them on the counter.

"The most expensive is Altio's Blossom," she introduced. "A unique smell I doubt you will find anywhere else. It comes from the west side of the Crescent Mountains, making it impossible to get for the majority of the year. Price is a silver disc." She gauged the woman's reaction for a moment, surprised the celebrant even considered the perfume. It was expensive, costing almost a cycle's pay for an average soldier. "Worth every shard if you can afford it."

In the quiet of the woman's deliberation, Shimmer thought to her father, *It's centered on her, but that's all I can tell. It's as if the air is shaking, Papa. She doesn't act like there is—*

"What about the other ones?" the celebrant interrupted.

"The Calao Flower is the second one, which comes from the coast of Nothor. It's a sweet mix, but most people find it reminds them of the ocean. Again, it is uncommon, but it costs only a single shard." Most people thought they were getting a bargain—just quarter of the cost—after hearing the much higher price for the Altio's Blossom, but Loni seemed indifferent. Shimmer pressed on. "The last one is Sweet Spray, which is a concoction done by my father. It is unique among perfumers except that it is one of our most popular scents. Costs only three copper legs."

When the woman moved up to examine the flasks, Shimmer took another step back. Normally she would have offered to give the purchaser a smell of the scents, but she felt nauseated when the celebrant approached. Shimmer could not bring herself to move closer. She also would not have normally allowed someone to pick up the item without paying for it, but she could not find the means to object.

Celebrant Loni leaned on the counter heavily and held each of the two more expensive scents in turn.

"I think I will take the Calao Flower," the celebrant finally said.

Chapter 9

Shimmer snapped up all three flasks as soon as the woman went for her purse. She replaced the refused ones carefully and wiped the Calao flower extract bottle for the celebrant. Celebrant Loni selected a wedge-shaped shard from her coin purse and offered it.

The foul feeling heightened to a tingle on her extended fingers as she reached for the coin. She stopped. Putting down the perfume with her left hand, she tucked her right behind her back.

"I cannot accept coin from a celebrant. Consider it a donation to the church of Inac." It was a lie, but it was a lie she told well.

What? her father exclaimed. He might have said it aloud, but the Wind Barrier around Match and Mixer kept his voice from escaping the confines of the vardo. *Oh, sorry*, he corrected a moment later when he realized he had sent the word to Shimmer.

I can't go near her, Papa. Sorry.

The celebrant's eyes lit at Shimmer's excuse, and a great grin settled on her ash-marked face. "How kind," Loni said sweetly. "Your generosity is well noted by the Lady of Fire, Shimmer. This will do her work well."

Since the woman expected a reply, Shimmer said, "I am glad to please the Lady."

"You are a dancer, are you not?" the celebrant asked.

Shimmer shyly smiled by habit, playing timid servant when confronted by authority. "Not like you, Celebrant," Shimmer said. She corrected herself before the celebrant could be offended. "Not as good as you." Celebrant Loni was a dancer with a different performance. She may have started the same way—moving around the fire with ribbons—but they ended in different places.

"Have you ever thought of joining the Gathering of Fire, Shimmer? You have Inac's flames in your hair. The goddess would favor you."

Shimmer painted her smile on carefully, her eyes flicking to the celebrant' locks. Shimmer's long crimson hair was partly tied back but lay loose down her back when she danced. Loni's hair remained a permanent bee's nest atop the celebrant's head, with only a single ruby red curl loose enough to sway with the movement of the head.

"I am flattered, Celebrant, but I am unworthy of the goddess' notice. I am needed here." Modesty had always worked before.

"Nonsense," the celebrant insisted, surprising Shimmer. "Everyone is worthy in the Lady's eyes. You are certainly..."

Celebrant

Need an out, Papa, Shimmer thought as the celebrant continued preaching.

The answer was immediate. Dust moved into the space just behind the curtain to allow the sounds to leave the waggon's Wind Barrier. Shimmer did not know what he chose to break, but there was a clang in the back followed by a curse that was spoken just loud enough to be heard through the curtains.

"Ah, Shimmer," Dust called in an "I-am-not-quite-panicked-but-will-be-shortly" voice that nearly made Shimmer smile. "Could you give me a hand please?"

The woman in red smiled sympathetically when Shimmer gave her a helpless shrug. After one more nod, the celebrant turned from the vardo, and Shimmer was free to sneak behind the curtain.

Her father had judged the celebrant well, Shimmer thought as she leaned against a bookcase in the vardo and let out a shaking breath. Mock ineptitude had not offended the celebrant the way a command would have.

Dust gave his daughter a few moments to catch her breath before asking, "What was that about?"

For a few breaths more, Shimmer could only shake her head and run her hands over her face. The shakiness was dissipating, but some lingered in her gut.

"That was bizarre, Papa!" Shimmer finally said. In control of her wits again, she peeked through the curtains to ensure the celebrant was gone. When the coast was clear, she stepped into the fresh air to take a few more breaths. "Everything else seemed fine. The whole time, she acted like there was nothing out of place, and yet I felt like I was suffocating! It does not..."

Her eyes drifted to where a chunk of mismatched wood now stood out against the painted counter of Match and Mixer. For a moment, she stared at the unstained wood. Her long silence convinced her father to come out into the light.

"Shim?"

"Do you remember that?" She pointed to the replaced portion of the counter.

"Sure," he said with a chuckle. "I sat over there"—he indicated the corner under the counter—"under a Full Concealment while that boy

 # Chapter 9

Anga smashed our front counter after you told him I wasn't in. I thought I'd fixed—"

"You did!" Shimmer said. "I was with you when you put up the permanent illusion to hide the repair. There is..." The realization hit her like a horse's kick, and she fell against the vardo's side in shock. "Oh goddess..." She slapped her hand over her mouth when she realized what she had said. Calling on the Goddess of Fire seemed very wrong.

With a touch, Celebrant Loni had dispelled a permanent enchantment. Shimmer had detected no magic. There could be only one explanation.

"Shimmer," her father's voice came firmly. "What is it? If I have to be hitching up the mules, I need to know."

"She is an untouchable," Shimmer choked out. "Celebrant Loni is an untouchable."

For a long moment, there was silence. When she finally regained her senses, Shimmer found Dust wearing a pensive expression and scratching his beard. He was not nearly as concerned as she was.

"Amazing. I've never met a real untouchable," he finally said.

"I have to warn Master Kitable," Shimmer declared, which won her a smile from her father.

"Good idea," he agreed. "Always nice to make friends when you're surrounded by an army. We should be fine now that we know, but Master Kitable should definitely know. Might have him come to appreciate us."

As Shimmer flipped her bag over her shoulder, slid over the counter, and dropped to the ground, Dust added, "And I will replace that illusion."

Elder Tril attached the vision to the vardo of the Galanth wizard. Kitable spent very little time in his rolling home, but this morning Tril was lucky enough to find the wizard in his vardo. Through the Linking, Tril communicated his discovery to the rest of the Circle. They collectively cast a Sending to let Master Terant know.

Hold until Terant arrives, Elder Ela requested.

Tril settled back to watch the vision in the frozen pool.

Kitable, sitting on the floor of his vardo and oblivious to the eyes hovering above him, was casting, but Tril did not understand the spell.

After a brief flare of the magic, four stones on the ground in front of the wizard went red.

Tril sat forward to better see. In the pool's image, Kitable furrowed his brow and picked up one of the stones. It was not, Tril guessed by the man's expression, the reaction he had been expecting. Tril tried again to feel the spell, but it was weak. Still, it had the feeling of Scrys about it. *Divination?*

The Galanth caster put down the stone and began casting, this time subtly. While Tril watched the wizard rise from his seat and replace his sandals, Tril felt the magic slowly forming. He tried to remember everything he saw so he could repeat it to Terant later. Knowing what Kitable was doing might help in defeating the wizard if he…

The spell finished abruptly, and Tril felt the approach of power. He leaped back in his seat, dropping the vision and shouting in alarm. He moved too late; the magic slipped through the vision, into the Earth Lodge, and dove for his chest. A flash of power rippled over him.

A moment later, Tril stood away from the frozen pool, feeling small. The Linking was gone. Some Circle member remained seated while others had stood in alarm. Elder Cark, Aspected with a white rabbit, had left her seat to hide by the wall of the Earth Lodge.

"Wha—" He checked himself, suddenly cold. For the first time in more than a decade, he was without his wolf pelt. The colors around him, from the ruddy red of Elder Vela's fox skin to the flashing green eyes of Elder Zeke's hawk, were bright. His eyes were entirely human again, he realized. The part of his mind where his wolf had sat felt distinctively empty.

Realization grew.

"He tried to summon me!" Tril exclaimed. He clutched at his uncovered shoulders. He had to use the Esparan word for "summon." There was no Northlander word for the type of magic they were facing.

Her feathered coat puffed up around her in worry, Elder Ela hooted in annoyance. "Your Aspect protected you but has been lost."

Tril thought back to the stones and Kitable's casting. "He detected the vision. The stones…I think they warned him. So, he attacked."

No physical harm had come of the attack, and the enemy was no better off for having his wolf skin but…

 # Chapter 9

Elder Ela finished the thought. "The Circle is no longer complete. We can continue our searches, but no pool can be maintained without our seventh member."

Meaningful stares were directed at Tril, who nodded solemnly. "I will seek an Aspect," he promised.

"You cannot rush such things," Cark warned, leaving the wall to join them once more around the darkened pool. Her nose twitched.

Tril shrugged his bare shoulders. "Then I must pray the gods are with us. I will continue to offer my aid to the Circle—"

"I will not have you Linking without an Aspect," Ela snapped in a surprisingly firm voice. Without the Aspect, Tril would be defenseless should another attack come.

"But what of Master Terant?" Tril asked.

Ela fell silent.

Elder Vat, his enormous form looming over the pool, grumbled like his Aspect. The man thumped down into his seat, his white bear skin folding under him. "We can watch only."

Without the Linking, the pool was inert. Without the pool, they could not funnel Master Terant's spells. Although smaller spells could be done at a distance, Terant seemed to think only the most powerful magic could defeat Kitable.

Tril nodded, at a loss. The gods had chosen him before by sending his Aspect. If his powers were still strong, he could hope to call another. It may take some time, but the Esparan wizard would just have to wait.

He felt a tickle along his forehead; Ela was with him.

"Tohmas is trapped," she gently said. "You need not hurry. Concentrate on your Aspect, Tril."

He wanted to say more, but Tril moved away. Without an Aspect, he was a just a hunter again. Only the spirit of an animal could restore his rank among the Elders of the Circle of the Raven, but that was not something he could control. How would he find another beast that would join with him? And where? Would it be a wolf again? He had never heard of an Elder renewing their Aspect, but then he had never heard of one being lost either.

Damn the Esparan caster for noticing him, and damn him for his summon that stole his Aspect.

Celebrant

Tril plodded from the Earth Lodge alone for the first time in a decade.

He would go north, he decided. He needed support, and the Elders could not provide it. It was time to go home.

His *visaln* answered the thought, bringing him visions of tundra and fractured ice along sparkling waters. He prepared a quick travel bag then trekked from the camp that day, following the vision.

Shimmer had only a vague idea where Kitable's vardo would be among the worn streets and empty houses, but she was confident in her ability to find it. The only people out in the evening were soldiers, and she caught their stares easily. When she spotted green-roped protectors milling around, Shimmer picked a particularly attentive white-roped companion and approached him.

"Lost?" he asked when she smiled at him. Nearby, his comrades watched shrewdly.

"Looking for someone," Shimmer countered. "Do you happen to know where I can find Master Kitable?"

"You're wasting your time there. Master Kitable has no patience for visitors of *any* kind."

Shimmer tossed her hair with a knowing laugh. "I will take my chances. Do you know where to find his vardo?"

The soldier shrugged. "Maybe I do. Maybe I don't."

Shimmer slid forward until he could not miss the soft scent of Altio's Blossom. "And how can I convince you to make it the former of those two?"

He would not meet her eyes. He licked his lips, swallowed, then suggested, "A kiss may help me remember."

Shimmer twirled a finger through the curls that flowed over her half-exposed shoulders. "That sounds very reasonable."

His friends laughed and encouraged him when she kissed him, but she did not care. After just long enough to get his heart rate up, she pulled away and gave the soldier a coy look. "The vardo?" she prompted.

He smirked mischievously. "Fifty paces that way." He indicated the road toward the protectors. "Look for a red waggon with two

 ## Chapter 9

horses—one black and one grey. Parked it in an open square next to a well. There's a small man tending a fire up front. It's easy to spot."

"Thank you, Companion." Shimmer winked and slipped out of the hold the soldier had wrapped around her waist. With brisk strides, she headed down the road he indicated.

"You did not give me your name!" he called.

"Not part of the bargain!" she shouted back, skipping in excitement as she made her way.

Her skin tingled when she spotted the red vardo taking up much of the plaza before her. As she approached, Shimmer sensed the magic wrapped around the waggon so tightly it seemed to be strangling it. For a long moment, she paused midstride and admired the feeling of powers winding themselves together so perfectly.

A stout man sat at the bottom of the vardo's stairs at a campfire. He wore no tabard to identify his loyalties and appeared to be burning furniture as fuel for a cooking fire, starting with a stool.

"Pardon me, Good Sir," Shimmer called to the stranger. "Might Master Kitable be around?"

The man did not move from his place by the campfire nor stop stirring the pot propped on the cooking sconce.

Shimmer advanced. She stood beside him, but the man did not acknowledge her. "Pardon—"

"Colt is deaf," a voice interrupted from behind her.

She spun to see Master Kitable, his expression stern, in the open doorway of the vardo. His robes were a darker green than before, but the same green and silver pattern was obvious from his shoes up. He wore an assortment of enchanted items Shimmer knew would take her a quartercycle to fully decipher; she could feel the pulse of magic from every one. Oddly, the wizard held a white wolf skin in one hand.

In answer to the movement on the stairs, the man by the fire rose. Spotting Shimmer's shadow, he turned to face her with an embarrassed smile on his face.

"I didn't see you," he muttered.

Master Kitable descended the steps and extended a hand to the man. After fishing around in a pouch for a moment, Colt pulled out a spherical stone and placed it in his master's hand. The orb made Shimmer's hairs stand on end. As much as she wanted to activate Spell

Sight and explore the auras of the enchanted object, she pressed her lips together and said nothing. She was certain Master Kitable would not like her casting anything. That he had not immediately dispelled her surprised her.

"Thank you, Colt. I will take it from here," Kitable said.

The wizard gave back the stone, and Colt returned to the fire.

"You bound a permanent Sending to the stone…but only bound on one end." Shimmer pressed her lips as she thought it through. "Open ended? A contingency on the stone that—"

"I am not patient man," Master Kitable interrupted.

"So I have heard," she replied before she could stop herself.

His eyes narrowed. "If you have business here, Weaver—"

"Shimmer. My name is Shimmer."

Kitable scowled and compromised. "If you have business here, Miss Weaver, state it quickly or be on your way."

"I came to warn you."

His irritation was replaced by cautious curiosity, but he sobered his expression on the next breath as if he did not want her to know how interested he was.

"So, warn me," Kitable prompted when she did not continue.

Shimmer glanced at the man by the fire, shifting her feet. "It is a sensitive matter," she said, but it seemed useless. Although she would have traded every book she owned to get Kitable in his vardo alone, Shimmer doubted that would happen. She would try anyway. Surprises could be fun.

He followed her gaze to Colt then raised an eyebrow. "The advantage of having a deaf waggon driver is that he cannot eavesdrop. State your business, Miss Weaver, or be on your way."

"It is about the Celebrant Loni," Shimmer confessed.

Kitable rolled his eyes. "I know what she is."

"You know she is an untouchable?" Shimmer stuttered despite herself. There was a desire to shout the words, but she whispered them, desperate to keep the secret.

"Do you think I would be travelling with an untouchable and not be aware of it?" Like her, Kitable dropped his voice to a whisper.

She had to lean forward to better hear him, and her heart fluttered.

 # Chapter 9

"I figured if you knew she was an untouchable, you would not be travelling with her," she countered. "Does she know?"

"No, she is blissfully unaware, and I would like it to stay that way." The words were strengthened by the presence of a dozen spells in the air between them.

"Does Clarin know?" Shimmer asked next. The shadow of the waggon driver flickered by her feet as the campfire flared, fed by the ends of some kind of headboard Colt had disassembled for burning.

"It is not my duty to play nursemaid to Master Clarin," the master wizard informed her curtly in a voice that was gaining volume. "You can tell him if you want."

The absurdity of the suggestion made Shimmer lean back and laugh. "Not me! But I have a reason for that. What about you? You do not like him?"

"I like precious few people in the world."

"But what do you have against Master Clarin?" she pressed, feeling daring.

"Is there nothing else?"

"He's a wizard," Shimmer realized aloud. "No wonder you don't trust him! You've dealt with your share of wizards. How many have you killed anyway?"

"That is all, Miss Weaver. Good day." He pivoted away from her and left the square without looking back.

She was certain he was still within earshot when she finished, "That many, huh?"

Shimmer let the greatest wizard in the world stalk out of her sight without another word. She stood for a time longer at the base of his vardo stairs in a daze as she waited for her skipping heart to slow.

She had done it. She had spoken to him and even stood within his hovering spells!

Once Colt again became aware of her, Shimmer wandered back to Match and Mixer.

Within, her father sat with his feet on the table juggling three yarn balls. He sat up as soon as she walked through the sealed door. Instead of probing, Dust fixed tea and continued practicing. She had put aside her bag and was leaning against a wall by the time she managed to find her voice.

"How many wizards do you think Master Kitable has killed, Papa?" she asked.

Dust's eyes narrowed. "He threaten you?"

"No, no. He just seemed sad, Papa, like he was lonely."

"All unmarried men are lonely," her father philosophized with a toss of his yarn. He caught the three atop one another, freeing his other hand for pouring tea as he added, "So are most married men, come to think of it."

She accepted the tea and let him get back to his juggling. "More than that, Papa. It's that he doesn't ever expect *not* to be alone. He doesn't trust anyone, not even other wizards."

Dust caught the three balls and put them on the table carefully. "Shim, you remember the assembly he called when he decided to explain the Contingency, right? How about the years before that?" He paused, but Shimmer could only shrug. Her first memory of seeing Master Kitable was in Wayburn, but before that her days had been apothecary work and traveling with Match and Mixer. Before the day he explained the Contingency, Shimmer had not even heard of Master Kitable.

Dust's smile was sad as he sat down across from her. "Before that meeting, wizards from all over the world challenged him. For the sake of the secret he was keeping, Kitable could not let any of those who dueled him live. Dozens tried to beat him, Shim. Half of them wanted the secret, the rest just wanted to beat the best wizard in the world. Is it any wonder he feels he cannot trust other wizards?"

Shimmer raised her eyes from the tea with another sigh.

She would find a way to pull him from his shell, she decided. She would have him dancing.

"He deserves better," was all she told her father, but his knowing smile warned her he already knew the rest of her thoughts.

"Every man does," he said.

Chapter 10

Any of the protectors not on duty were assigned to dig. Prince Sol had gifted Tohmas a house in BellRoost as a command post, and Tohmas used that generosity to create a trap. He chose the protectors with mining experience to coordinate both ends of the tunnel, which they took on expertly. Prince Habal had selected his protectors with more than military prowess as criteria, and Tohmas was consistently impressed by the skills the bodyguards had.

The list from the Weavers arrived by noon on the first day, and after some consideration, Tohmas bought a selection of drugs and poisons. He rationed them to a dozen men, directing them to leave something poisoned behind should they have to leave BellRoost.

And Tohmas was certain they would shortly have to abandon BellRoost despite Sol's insistence to the opposite.

Once done with the Weavers, Tohmas sent for Kitable.

Inside the dim, dusty house, the wizard stared at the digging soldiers with a sour look on his face.

"Not more digging," he pleaded, and Tohmas chuckled.

"Can you move walls?" Tohmas asked.

"Yes," Kitable replied mildly, turning away digging protectors. "A better question is whether I am capable of doing so under the circumstances. How much time do I have, and how much am I moving? Are we discussing a house wall, a city wall, or a garden wall here?"

"You have until DoomDragon attacks, and I need a space through the city walls wide enough for a waggon, preferably several waggons."

The wizard cocked an eyebrow. "When is DoomDragon attacking?"

"If you figure that out, let me know. There is a fountain on the west side of the city surrounded by run-down stalls—leftovers from a farmer's market they haven't done in years. I want you there when DoomDragon shows his face."

The wizard snorted but bowed his head in concession. "I am going to be doing some more casting this evening. I will have your spell ready within a few candles. Tell DoomDragon to behave until then."

The rest of Tohmas' day was spent overseeing the excavations. As dusk deepened, Kitable returned to confirm he had created the spell and held it ready. He also confessed that he had created some detectors for Scrys, as relying on Carsh's limited ability to detect magic was unreliable. But when he made the stones that went red in the presence of a Scry, the results had been a surprise.

"I was being watched."

The realization seemed to worry the exhausted wizard as much as it impressed Tohmas. "If DoomDragon's casters can Scry without my noticing, then the undefended can be targeted directly." Kitable wearily rubbed his temples. There were new lines on his face.

"Targeted by what?" Tohmas asked.

The wizard took a moment to consider the reply, concentrating with effort. "Depends on the skill of the caster. It takes a certain degree of skill to cast through a Scry, and the stronger the spell, the harder that is. So far, I have only seen minor spells, and I think those were aimed without a Scry. I do not really know how bad this is. The two Northlander casters I met before were...erratic might be the best word. Lots of power, but not focused, not honed. Like a giant swinging a sword without taking time to aim." The rambling wizard pinched the bridge of his nose. "It's possible they lack the finesse for funneling a spell through a Scry, but maybe they just haven't tried yet. If it was me, anything less powerful than a Fire Blast would be possible. Not pretty, but possible."

Tohmas considered the news for a long moment. Unable to come up with any solutions, he let himself be distracted by the white pelt the wizard was holding.

Chapter 10

"Kit? Why are you carrying a wolf skin?"

For a moment Tohmas thought the wizard did not know the answer. He lifted the pelt and squinted as if he had forgotten about it in his fatigue.

"I went after the caster," he said slowly, lowering the wolf skin to his side. "I got the pelt instead. He was using it as some kind of shield. I'm not even sure how, but I'm hoping not having the damn thing will deter him from trying again for a bit. I don't know how many times he has spied on me."

"So now is a good time to be doing things we do not want observed."

Kitable nodded cautiously then handed Tohmas a black stone. "It will go red if you are being watched, unless the caster figures that out and manages to bypass it. They saw me use it. Only a matter of time until they work around it, but it's better than nothing."

"So, if it goes red, assume there is a Scry, but if it is black, assume there could be a Scry," Tohmas translated.

"Call for me if it goes red," was the last thing Kitable added before wandering off.

Three days dragged by as if weighed down by mountains. Darak came to see Tohmas' mostly-healed shoulder, but Tohmas hardly paid attention. As reports trickled in, he was again impressed by the creativity and speed of the Galanth men. A dozen strategic houses, as well as the fortifications the Galanth were currently manning, were rigged to collapse. The warning to be ready to move out was repeated among the camps of Fixer City at sundown every night.

On the third night, Tohmas woke to abject silence. The cool darkness lay heavily over the town, giving Tohmas no reason to be awake. Carsh was also rising from the chair where he had fallen asleep. Something was wrong.

The sons of Tamv drew their weapons as they came to their feet.

Through the window, the beginnings of light crept in from the east in a distantly cloudy sky. Behind him, Carsh's grass and bone bracelets rattled. Tohmas nodded at the warning.

Into the silence, a cry went up, distant and muffled. The clash of metal followed, and a scream of pain answered. Rising above the din came the alarm bells of the city, and Tohmas had his suspicions confirmed. BellRoost was under attack.

Celebrant

By the time a Soltan runner arrived to deliver the news, Tohmas had already readied his protectors in the streets. Any unnecessary horses, including Honest Justice, were led away, the streets too narrow for the steeds to offer much advantage. Carsh had to chase Bashuran down the road to make the stubborn stallion follow Honest Justice as he had been ordered to. In the end, the enormous horse trotted off, tossing his head and snorting with annoyance.

The Soltan runner needed encouragement to deliver the message that he seemed to think, because of the readied men, had already been given.

DoomDragon had come through the south gate and was already within the city. The Soltan defenders had been forced to fall back to the barricades a street back.

BellRoost was not large enough. They had little time.

"Far Crier, sound the alarm," Tohmas ordered. "Barmore's Fyrd, round up Fixer City. Arrow, Rest, and Lariton's Fyrd assemble on me. Everyone else is to get to the west assembly point."

Tohmas listened as the horns passed along the orders, knowing his men were abandoning the wall nearest the north gate. Holding the north wall was not part of his plan.

A moment after the orders were delivered, Tohmas heard an answering signal. Flystead's Fyrd gave warning that the Northlanders were at the north gate as well.

Both escape routes had been blocked.

Tohmas smiled at Carsh. His brother rolled his eyes, acknowledging that Tohmas had been right; DoomDragon had possessed the ability to break into BellRoost all along. Tohmas did not yet understand why, but the reprieve they had been granted had ended.

"Time to go," Tohmas called.

They already knew what was required of them. A horn from each of the fyrds, given in turn, signaled they were on the move.

"*Geddit*!" Tohmas commanded his protectors as he led the way into the streets, his sword and shield readied as they headed down the empty, dawn-touched roads.

Chapter 10

In the dim light of pre-dawn, the walls of BellRoost looked like ice cliffs. The builders had trimmed the planks well, leaving the invaders no purchase should they try to climb. Each board had been expertly aligned with its neighbors, running straight and true toward the fading starlight in defiance of the attackers. But, limited by the lumber of the north, the felled trees were too short, making the wall only half a dozen paces high. Further, the builders were accustomed to making houses, not defenses. The peak of the wall was nothing but a flat edge, not even sharpened. How easy it would have been to place a hooked ladder, Darknim thought as he and his men waited in the deepest shadows under the bridge.

But unnecessary. He and his men had crossed the river far downstream and made their way toward BellRoost hidden by the slope of the banks. Now he waited in the same cover for the first light of dawn and the signal it brought. His men were armed with axes, harpoons, and slings yet stalked as lightly as if hunting hares.

Dawn's light seeped from the horizon, a ray of ruddy red brightening the dark of the distant clouds. The clear blue sky was light as Darknim heard the creak of the gate above them.

His spies had succeeded in clearing enough of the defenders from the gate to gain access to the city. For a moment only, the defenders were unaware of the opening.

Leaving the safety of the river channel, Darknim padded onto the bridge and ducked through the open gate. With him came a hundred Hunters. They split quickly, spreading out to take the nearby wall. Darknim and his best dozen warriors took aim for the deeper streets, knowing his target was only now waking in his warm, quiet house near the city's center.

After only a dozen strides, the alarm bells sounded. Horns answered almost as quickly, blaring out commands and directions Darknim did not understand. But it worked to inform the rest of his forces that the Esparan knew of the attack. They charged in, unimpeded, and flowed through the opened gates with abandon.

The forces of Solta quickly rallied, presenting Darknim with, at long last, an opponent.

With dragon scale draped over him, he became the full embodiment of the DoomDragon of the North. Before the heavy swing of his dragon-wing ax, Soltan men fell. Sharp as glass but with the strength of petrified bone, the ax cleaved easily through the padded and chain armor of the defenders. The sheer weight of the ax lent itself to crashing into helmets, leaving shattered skulls in his wake. The depiction of the dragon along the haft seemed to fly on its extended wings.

After decades of living with his weapon as his closest ally, Darknim could just as easily have sliced the wings from a fly or perfectly removed only the tip of a man's ear. But fighting from street to street, the panicked Esparans receding before him like spring's thawing ice, did not require finesse. He was disappointed.

At first, only red-clad Esparans opposed him. They were uncoordinated, many of them young recruits too green to know how to plant their feet. Before the dragon-wing ax, they fled. Even the metal enforcements of theirs shields cracked when Darknim swung against them.

Hunters at his side, Darknim had just set the most recent file of Soltans running when he spotted a coordinated line of men bearing Prince Tohmas' green. They had positioned themselves two ranks deep at the road's access into a square, forcing the Northlanders to come in two at a time.

Darknim stalked forward, holding his ax in a lazy, one-handed position beside him. He felt the tension rise. Tohmas' men held together, cluttering their mismatched shields into a rough wall. The two men positioned behind lowered their spears toward him, the weapons little more than a sharpened stick. The forward ranks waited with their shields, braced for a charge.

Darknim lengthened his stride, and his Hunters allowed him to pull ahead. Once in range of the jab of a spear, he shifted himself sharply forward. He caught the spear and yanked it with enough force to take the wielder by surprise. A boy, probably little more than sixteen, stumbled. Before the neighbor behind the wall could flinch, Darknim swung the ax in an abbreviated chop, neatly severing his head.

As the first of the blood touched the cobblestones, he crashed his ax to his right, shattering a defender's shield. He heard a screech as the arm behind the shield shattered too, spattering blood and bone chips at the defender next in the line. Darknim chopped down and split the defender's thighbone.

Chapter 10

Following him in, the Hunters crashed into the gap Darknim created. The shorter axes took two or three chops to severe limbs, but his Hunters made the blows fall fast enough to be heard as a single strike. The dead crumpled to the ground, filling the cobblestones' cracks with thick blood.

The Galanth fled. Darknim managed to slice open a coward's spine but soon ran out of opponents as they scattered across the square. He paused to check a downed Hunter—someone had gotten a lucky blow under his rib cage. The wounded Hunter was sent back to camp. The lives of his Hunters were too valuable to waste on meaningless Esparans.

Darknim spotted a banner disappearing between the houses ahead. *Perhaps they will not all be meaningless.*

With a snarl, Darknim set his sights on the silver and green piece of fabric. His horn call brought any Northlander in range running, a force to dwarf any the Prince Tohmas may have mustered. It was high time one of the five sons of Zayban died. If Darknim could not have Habal, he would take his son.

He only got close enough to exchange blows with the occasional green-roped protector, though these proved themselves to be a match for the Hunters. Unlike the stragglers in the main forces, the protectors were accustomed to fighting alone. The longer reach of their swords made more than one Hunter regret their choice to attack.

Darknim felled two protectors quickly. From that moment on, no protector would meet Darknim in direct battle. Although he chased them down, the prince's best defenders would exchange only a handful of cautious blows before disengaging.

They were not cowards, Darknim was certain, but they seemed to know that crossing DoomDragon's path led to death.

Still, the Hunters fared well, and the group around the banner shrank with every retreating step. Darknim smiled as the Hunters successfully separated the prince from the majority of his forces, including many of the protectors who dodged away from Darknim. The Hunters flanked the pocket of defenders and cornered them in a small house.

Esparans were even weaker than he believed. After his experience with the soldier who had fallen off the wall, Darknim had expected the green and silver to fight him every step, but he was already hearing reports of Galanth forces scattering. Darknim and his Hunters would have to rout out the cowards once the prince was dead. Mice were difficult to drag from their dens.

The Hunters clattered into the door, armed with hewing axes. It did not take long for his men to render the door down to kindling.

As the Hunters pushed their way past the furniture barricade in the small house, Darknim was struck by how easy it had all been.

How many Galanth had been killed? How many had run? Why would the warriors who so fanatically followed their prince, as the soldier who had fallen from the wall proved, break and flee so readily? If the Esparans were not dead or fleeing, where were they?

The city was his. Darknim was no fool; he had some of his best warriors securing both gates. The Esparans could not be escaping.

Where have they gone?

He had a nagging feeling that he was overlooking something but—

The house before him collapsed.

Darknim stared for a moment, confused. There had been a building, a strong building. Now there was rubble filled with hacked beams, crushed roof tiles, and splintered panels. Thanks to the small size of the building, the damage was minimal as debris rained down on his Hunters, but the destruction was complete.

"A tunnel!" someone said, coughing into the dust. "I saw a tunnel within!"

Rigged, Darknim realized. They must have gutted the inside of the building then set a trap to collapse the remaining supports. It was an effective way to conceal their passage.

"Find the entrance!" DoomDragon commanded, but he knew it was futile. Even if the tunnel had only taken the prince and his defenders behind the next building, he would already have gained enough time. And Prince Tohmas, unlike Darknim, knew where he was heading.

The city was not that large. DoomDragon would find them, and when he did, he would destroy them. Of that, he was certain.

Beside the west walls of BellRoost, Kitable stood in the door to his vardo as people milled around him. His prince's commands kept him stationary despite how much he wanted to grab one of his waggon

Chapter 10

horses and go in search of Tohmas. He had his choice of steeds, for Honest Justice had been tethered next to Kitable's two older waggon horses. Seeing the warhorse without the rider seemed wrong, and it made Kitable worry more about the prince.

From the runners' reports, he knew the north end of the city had been lost to the Northlanders and that Prince Sol was unaccounted for, but he did not care. Clarin would have to keep Sol safe from the enemy's casters, and there had been no sign of that threat yet.

Then again, Kitable did not know what he would do if he spotted spells now. Tohmas had ordered him to wait by the west wall.

Clarin was on his own.

Time burned by agonizingly slowly as they waited. The guardians had set ranks, each fighter badgered until they stood perfectly at attention, not a boot out of place. Their duties done, the commanders hovered at the bottom of the steps of Kitable's vardo. He wasn't sure if they expected something of him. He could find Prince Tohmas if necessary. It just might be too late by the time he did.

Coming quickly out of the streets, three dozen protectors wove through the green and silver ranks toward his vardo, accompanied by the bloodied Prince of Galanth himself. Thankfully, all the blood seemed to be someone else's.

Prince Tohmas halted among the guardians. He cast a look around then, finding everything in order, nodded at Kitable. "Let's get this group moving. Master Kitable? An exit if you would?"

All eyes on him, Kitable dismounted from his vardo and faced the city walls.

His first whispered words activated a spell on the far side of the city that set off a series of small force and destruction spells. They were not visible to the naked eye, but Kitable knew his enemy watched with enchanted sight. The spells would light up like meteors to them and distract from the concealed spell about to be activated.

Kitable spoke the next word to, as his prince had requested, "move the wall."

His spell targeted an area for destruction. Experience had taught Kitable the danger of destabilizing large structures, so he simultaneously cast a series of smaller force spells to hold up the rest of the wall. An intricate shield kept the spell from being visible to divinations or alterations, such as Spell Sight, and hid it from the enemy's casters.

But spells were always more complicated than they appeared. To the Galanth forces, Kitable merely whispered a word, and the wall before them disappeared. At the command of the prince, the ranks marched through.

The black Rydan steed appeared among the warriors in answer to Carsh's whistle, and with Tohmas collecting Honest Justice from Kitable's waggon, both men mounted. Without a word, they watched the lines of Galanth men vanish into the fields beyond.

"You didn't say anything about putting the wall back, right?" Kitable asked as the ranks headed out.

Tohmas laughed. "No."

"Good. So where are we going, my Prince?"

"Away." Prince Tohmas glanced up, took in the streets, and explained, "Cities are only good as holding places if you expect something to change. I want open spaces for fighting. We go out to the plains."

"Prince Sol will not be happy," Kitable warned.

The prince shrugged. "I warned him BellRoost would not hold," he said as if to justify his indifference. He ran his eyes over the dispersing guardians and the lines of waggons joining the march. "Any sign of him?"

Shaking heads replied.

"A few Soltans came through," one guardian reported. "We sent them out with Boro's Fyrd to watch the front. No word of Prince Sol."

As they spoke, another small party of men in red tabards stumbled into their train, paused, and stared at the ongoing march. The bleeding group of six had clearly seen fighting. One was supported by his companions, unable to bear weight on his crushed leg.

The nearest Galanth men took the weight of the wounded man and, at an order from their warden, carried him to one of the Healing waggons.

"Prince Sol?" one of the remaining Soltan soldiers asked. "Has he made it? Have you seen..." The question trailed off as the man spotted the black rank band around Tohmas' arm.

The red-clad man considered the prince with intense concentration. It took him longer than expected to decide it was not *his* prince.

The man had a large dent in his helmet. *Probably matches a dent in his skull*, Kitable mused.

Chapter 10

"No," Tohmas replied, his voice soft. "No, Prince Sol is not here."

"I will have to go after him," the Soltan decided aloud. His sword dragged behind him as he staggered away.

"Someone carry that man to the Healing waggon," Tohmas interrupted. When the Soltan began to protest, Prince Tohmas moved Honest Justice into a position looming over him. "You are in no condition to rescue your prince. I will take care of it, warden. Go get your head looked at before you keel over."

The suggestion became a command when two Galanth companions scooped up the soldier and hauled him along the same path his friend had taken. The rest of the group followed.

"I could cast a Sending. I should be able to find Clarin," Kitable offered.

"Any chance the Northlanders will see that?" the prince replied, surprising Kitable with his level of forethought.

Kitable frowned. "I could disguise it."

Tohmas shook his head. "Too risky. We have no time." The prince nodded his head toward the march. "I want you with the celebrants, Kitable. Get going."

"I do not like leaving—"

"Now, Kitable," Tohmas firmly interrupted. "I want you with the celebrants because they travel in the center of the group and wear enough magic items to mask your presence. I expect DoomDragon will figure out this ruse and send his southern forces to cut us off. I want you close enough to discourage his casters while the fyrds fend him off. We are better set for a run, so they will not follow for long. I need you out there, Kitable. If his casters attack our main forces, this war is over."

Kitable stood at the bottom of his steps for a hesitant moment. In the end, he gritted his teeth and nodded. Tohmas was his patron, and that had been an order.

"I'll put a Tracker on you," Kitable said as he walked to the vardo door. "I will know if you are targeted by any spells. I will come to defend you if that happens."

Not waiting for the prince's response, the wizard put his hand on Colt's communication sphere and repeated the command. A short while later, the vardo began to move, Kitable stowed within.

Carsh brought Bashuran up beside Tohmas, raising his eyebrow. He had heard the promise to the Soltan. Others had as well. Carsh did not understand why they would do anything of the sort.

Tohmas had no intention of going after Prince Sol. Firstly, the prince had gotten himself into the mess by ignoring Tohmas' warning. Secondly, if the prince died, the remaining Soltan fighters would likely swear allegiance to Tohmas. He needed nothing from the Prince of Solta.

He did, however, want to make sure most of the forces were outside the city by the time he left, so he remained on Honest Justice and supervised the escape. No doubt the Soltan refugees that filtered into the ranks would quickly be incorporated into Fixer City. Maybe some would join the Galanth fyrds over time.

While his protectors continued to stare at him as if expecting action, a waggon pulled into the place Kitable's vardo had vacated. Tohmas heard a triumphant whoop.

"Let her through," he called as the protectors moved to intercept the intruder. The command was for the sake of the soldiers as much as for the woman herself.

It had been a while since he had seen Celebrant Loni, but she had not changed. Her painted, decorated face alight, she strode between his protectors with a spring in her step and a wide red grin. Tohmas was acutely pleased that Kitable had just left.

She knelt before him, her tangled hair tall upon her head. "A fine day for a battle, Champion. Are you done so soon?"

Carsh joined her grin. As far as the Rydan was concerned, their luck just improved.

"My sword has been bloodied," Tohmas replied. "This place is best left to the Northlanders."

Loni's expression fell, and he was not surprised. She often embodied the Warrior Queen aspect of Inac, who was known for being battle-hungry.

Her voice deepened as she rose. "You have a hole in your logic, my Prince. Your decision may be the wrong one because of that."

Although Tohmas believed her, he did not understand. Was it his decision to leave BellRoost that she was referring to, or his choice to leave Sol behind?

Chapter 10

"Your guidance is appreciated," he replied cautiously, "but my decision is made."

Her eyes narrowed. "Are you certain your heart agrees?"

The heart was the most important weapon a Rydan had in combat. Tohmas was expected, by tradition, to be guided by it. But his heart was still in the Outlands. He saw nothing in BellRoost of value. His Chief's honor was in victory, and Tohmas would fight for that where he was most likely to find it—on the plains. None of his Followers were in Espar, so he had no "heart" left to defend here. Carsh was with him. His family...

Family. Sol was his family. In light of the man's stupidity, Tohmas forgot that the Esparans considered the man his uncle.

His protectors expected him to do something. They didn't know how disinterested he was in fulfilling useless family obligations.

Since taking up the mantle of the Prince of Galanth, Tohmas had fought to hide his Rydan upbringing. Abandoning a family member would be at odds with the compassionate Esparan prince he had been masquerading as.

Loni did not expect a reply. She sauntered back down the corridor of protectors that had admitted her with a final warning: "If you leave now, Prince Tohmas, you will regret it."

He could not imagine the Goddess of War was asking him to simply stand by the exit doing nothing. Inac wanted him to fight.

The most obvious choice was to search for Sol.

Having Prince Sol indebted to him would be useful, Tohmas decided. Now that he had been proven correct about the risks in BellRoost, Tohmas thought it likely he could put aside his previous tactful approaches.

Tohmas dismounted, the horse too much of a hindrance in the tight streets.

He would need protectors with him, but not all of them. They would want a sign that fortune would stay with them. There were easy ways, according to the Esparans, to attract the gods' favor—four gods. Four, or even sixteen, men were too few. Sixty-four was the next lucky number.

"Sixty-four protectors with me. The rest hold this opening for us. See you in bit."

Celebrant

On foot, he headed into the streets. His protectors scampered to follow, more than one cursing as they drew their swords, set their shields, and tried to keep up.

Carsh gave a whoop of excitement as he leaped from Bashuran's back and matched Tohmas' stride into the city.

Ducking between buildings, they made their progress slowly toward the south gate.

As keen as he was to cut apart more Northlanders, Carsh did not understand why they were there. Sol was a liability and a nuisance. He should have been left to die, but Tohmas never did anything without reason. Carsh trusted his brother knew what he was doing.

It did not take long for Prince Sol's red and black banner to be spotted on a chimney, fluttering among a haze of smoke.

"Cud 'is leg rope an' run een circles," Carsh grumbled and Tohmas laughed at the image, as did the few protectors who understood enough Rydan. Indeed, Sol had hobbled himself nicely for the Northlanders; he was giving away his position!

Taking side streets and moving quickly through the surprised ranks of Northlanders, Tohmas and his protectors approached the surrounded house. The siege appeared to be a temporary arrangement. From the upper story, arrows occasionally threatened the attackers, but the Northlanders had taken shelter behind piles of debris, rendering the attacks inert. Carsh gauged their strength and decided the Northlanders had the numbers to crack the door even if every piece of furniture in the building had been pressed against it. If they wanted, they could have taken out a wall. Many carried axes, after all.

The Northlanders were not in the house yet because they chose not to be. They were waiting.

Carsh's knives danced around his wrists in readiness. They must be waiting for permission. They were waiting for their chief.

Carsh was looking forward to seeing DoomDragon again, if only to prove how good his aim was at long distances.

But Tohmas was unwilling to wait. Since the ground was held by Northlanders, the only way to go was up.

Chapter 10

Tohmas and Carsh snuck into a nearby building, found the stairs, and climbed to the upper loft. Then, to the amazement of the following protectors, Tohmas sheathed his sword, slung his shield over his back, opened the upper window, and squeezed out onto the roof.

Carsh heard the cries of the Northlanders who spotted him but did not heed them. Testing the roof, Tohmas tentatively found traction on the clay tiles and made his way to the ridge of the roof. Carsh followed him up, matching his brother's trot along the roof's peak, finding the angle not unlike the treacherous slopes of the DragonTail Mountains where they grew up.

With a short run, Tohmas leaped onto the lower roof next to Sol's banner. Although the tiles cracked, they held as he landed. Carsh skipped down lightly, landing on a different area. A pair of sling stones, one landing right after the other, narrowly missed his ankle. They ricocheted back toward the attackers.

Unslinging his shield, Tohmas bowed under its protection, low against the roof. Carsh ducked into his brother's shadows, annoyed. If he threw his knives, he'd never get them back. But the sling stones were making it hard to move safely.

Soon, the clip of stones against the strong carbiron shield ceased. Carsh checked the way he had come.

The protectors on the other roof were bombarding the Northlanders with roof tiles. Their ranged attack provided cover for a smaller group of protectors who made the leap onto the lower roof and quickly added their own shields to Tohmas'.

Defended, Tohmas knocked away the first of the shingles under him. When the next one caught, Tohmas pried it loose with his knife.

Once they had removed sufficient shingles to expose the trusses below, an arrow from within the house narrowly missed Tohmas' nose, forcing him back. Carsh snarled, irritated once more by stupid Esparans.

"Knock it off, you louts!" Tohmas shouted. "We're on your side!"

"Get Prince Sol," someone shouted.

Tohmas resumed his destruction of the roof. When the area looked weak enough, he put his boot on the crossbeam and pushed hard, snapping the wood. With the space wide enough, he jumped down.

Carsh, having the luxury of a view of the room, chose a more elegant descent. Swinging off the edge of the opening, he sprang off the rafter before landing next to Tohmas. Carsh stood with his brother as Sol arrived.

"Good gods! How did you get here?" the prince exclaimed as he rushed into the attic room.

Baffled by the prince's question, the sons of Tamv looked at each other then turned their stare to the hole in the ceiling.

Clearly, they had come in through the roof.

"*Sta*!" Carsh snapped at the protector who was about to climb in after them. "We be comin' up!" The protectors heeded the order and covered the hole with their shields. They returned the Northlanders' stones with shingles."

"We thought you may want a hand," Tohmas said. "These..." he jabbed toward the three men with bows, "seemed not to think so."

"We did not see your banner!" someone objected.

"Would you have me paint a bull's eye onto my forehead as well? I would rather DoomDragon *not* know where I am, thank you."

It took several breaths for the Prince of Soltan to find his voice.

"But where did you come from? How is the rest of the city? Where are your men?" he stammered.

Of the three, Tohmas only answered the last question. "Leaving. I had them ready since arriving. They are..."

Although Carsh made a point of listening to his brother most of the time, his attention was pulled from the conversation. A familiar creeping chill ran up the back of his neck, and he fell into a crouch in readiness.

There was magic nearby.

He lunged as soon as the magic walked through the door. Before even Tohmas could move, Carsh had caught the flyer by the throat and slammed him against the wall. A second slam sent the man to the floor.

It was then that he remembered the Prince of Solta had chosen a man of the wand as his prime protector.

"Oops," Carsh said belatedly. Although he anticipated an attack from the Soltan protectors, he turned to find only confused, aghast expressions.

"Your apology needs work," Tohmas scolded lightly, but his brother's eyes were alight with amusement. "Try to say it without grinning next time."

 # Chapter 10

Two hits, and he had completely disabled the wizard. For all their defenses, he had this flyer at his mercy.

"You knocked him out, Carsh. You carry him," Tohmas said, and Carsh frowned. Still, Tohmas was right.

Carsh threw the wizard over one shoulder.

"Wha—" was as far as the Prince of Solta got.

"Up," Tohmas told him. "We go along the roofs until we run out of roofs then climb down and head for the exit before DoomDragon arrives. Have these fools give you a leg up if you need it. Come on."

He did not wait for a reply. Being tall enough, Tohmas jumped, caught the rafter, and pulled himself up one handed. He was up and out of the hole before Sol had relayed any of the orders.

Fortunately, the Prime Protector of Solta was not heavy, and Carsh was able to pass him to his brother's outstretched hand. He was up on the roof next, sheltered by the protectors. A barrage of tiles covered their flight as they made their way to the next roof.

By the time they left the roof, the first of the Soltans were climbing out of the hole. Below, a group of Northlanders chased them, but the Galanth protectors discouraged them with more raining shingles and Carsh made his point with two deadly knives. The protectors broke from the main group slowly, taking advantage of easy places to further confound or distract the pursuit. Tohmas and Carsh, the prime protector still carrying the wizard, made their way down after a dozen houses. Sol and a handful of Soltans followed. The final group of Galanth protectors stayed behind to draw off the Northlanders.

For long moments, it was silent in the streets. Carsh felt the threat of attack distance itself.

"I owe you, Tohmas," Prince Sol said as he matched strides with Carsh's older brother along the deserted streets. "I did not think I was getting out of that one."

Tohmas shrugged lightly as if their risk had been nothing, but Carsh spotted the measured sigh his brother gave once they reached the western wall.

The remaining Soltan forces had been rounded up, and they greeted their prince with a shout. Prime Protector Severin was deposited in the Healing waggon as they rode away, and no one seemed to miss him.

 # CELEBRANT

Protectors joined them like a bow wave before the ship of Northlanders who followed them.

They were too late. The Galanth forces were already clear of the city.

Prince Sol and his men on their way, Carsh called for the protectors and their horses. Atop Bashuran, Carsh led the charge against the Northlanders who dared leave the city to chase the army. Both the Rydan and his horse were immensely pleased by the sound of squished Northlanders underfoot.

The enemy retreated to the walls, and Carsh begrudgingly called the protectors back. Tohmas had been clear on how far Carsh was allowed to go.

When they returned to the plains, Carsh gave a sigh of relief. He was free of the confining walls and back in his wilderness. Now they would wreak more havoc on the Northlanders.

They caught up with Kitable and the celebrants, and with permission from Tohmas, Kitable released the last of the magic he left behind.

The walls collapse around the city.

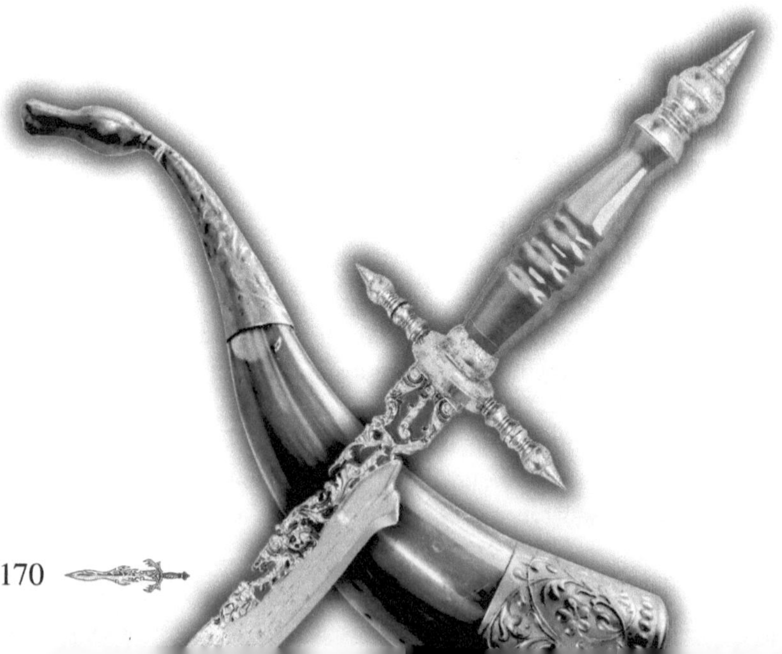

Chapter II

Tohmas had been right.

Sol kept his composure by force, taking to each task as it presented itself. Through it all, he kept hearing a voice in his mind repeating the simple fact: Tohmas had been right. Sol's inability to recognize that earlier had cost him thousands of lives.

For a short time, he blamed Tohmas for the fall of BellRoost since the Prince of Galanth had abandoned his posts on the wall. But a sizable force of traitorous Esparans had already been in BellRoost before DoomDragon's forces had entered the gates, making Tohmas' choice to withdraw his soldiers from the walls irrelevant. Sol could have posted three times as many fighters on the walls and the city would have still fallen.

He wanted to be angry with his nephew for failing to include him in his plans, but Tohmas had tried. It was Sol, not Tohmas, who was at fault.

The Prince of Galanth's quick decision to withdraw had saved more lives than it cost, as Soltan soldiers reported being guided out by Galanth soldiers. Sol had expected only the protectors who accompanied him in the retreat would survive but was surprised to learn that nearly a thousand of his fighters had managed to escape as well.

He reassigned them into two fyrds, finding some comfort in the monotony of such logistics.

Celebrant

For the first time since hearing the rumors, Sol began to believe that Tohmas did have the blessings of Inac. In a life where religion could be almost forgotten, Sol's faith was rekindled. Homage to the gods had fallen out of favor among the princes a generation before, their only ties to the gods the advising celebrants. Perhaps re-evaluation was needed.

Guilt gnawed at Sol as he visited the Temple waggons nightly and thanked the gods that the majority of BellRoost had been emptied at the beginning of the season. Only after homage and gratitude did he dare ask for guidance. The march was heading for Narsol, his capital city, and he was terrified. Being forced back to his capital meant desperation. Every refugee fleeing ahead of the Northlanders had made Narsol their new home. If Narsol fell, they had nowhere safe. It would be a final declaration of defeat.

While Sol directed his men from atop a newly acquired horse, he fought to keep his fear from showing. He ended up marching with Tohmas, providing guidance to his nephew as to the best route through the plains.

Tohmas was in a fantastic mood, which only improved the farther they got from BellRoost. Around their prince, the Galanth laughed about the traps they had set for the Northlanders. Master Kitable was given credit for the greatest upset, since his creation of an escape route had destabilized the west wall. Upon the release of his spell, the entire side fell in. They liked to think it flattened some Northlanders.

Sol watched, thinking he would find some indication of stress in his nephew if he just looked close enough but never did. Tohmas' soldiers sang boisterous songs as they marched, none of them worried in the slightest about being caught by their pursuers.

After all, Tohmas had been right.

And Tohmas continued to be right as they marched. Sol tentatively agreed when his nephew suggested having the fyrds march in parallel through the open fields, leaving the longest part of the train as the waggons, which had to use the road to keep moving at any reasonable pace. Soon, he saw the benefit. Doubling up the soldiers on foot brought the waggons farther forward, making it easier to access the resources, giving them more time to set camp, and making it easier to defend. Tohmas then instigated a flanking force on horseback, which he called wings, and assigned them to prevent the enemy from picking off the supply

 # Chapter 11

waggons. Although the enemy's main forces had not closed the gap, it was all too easy for the swift-footed Hunters to sneak ahead and lay in ambush for stragglers or the undefended Fixer City. It was much like the tactics of a herd of caribou that resented being the prey of a hunting wolf pack.

With the men marching in wide groups, they made good time. Sol once asked whether tramping the fields was a wise course, but Tohmas had laughed.

"Who is farming this land now?"

Sol understood.

After three days of marching, they reached the end of the fields. Tohmas and Sol were discussing the best route around the upcoming forest when a Gaidolon high guardsman, one of the few seen in Galanth's ranks, interrupted and reported, "Close to two hundred Esparans are waiting in the woods ahead. Prince Rairn request an audience."

Sol looked at Tohmas for the reply. Conferencing with another displaced prince was not worth losing their lead. If Tohmas believed stopping would delay them too much, Sol would easily agree.

But Tohmas considered the information and decided, "We had better meet with him." He called to his runners. "Have the fyrds halt at the woods. Send a rider to invite Prince Rairn to meet with us at the Temple waggons."

Prince Sol nodded in agreement, and the runner left with a token from each of the princes.

It took only a candle to reach the forest and for the sun to sink behind the trees, casting long, cool shadows over the fields beyond. A banner of white flew atop a tree, and a line of men, all dressed in white, stood outside the forest like ghosts in the twilight. The various waggons of the Galanth army took shelter in the shade of the long forest.

Sol took his place beside Tohmas, feeling uncommonly small. He squared himself up, making an effort to look like the type of prince his father had trained him to be. No matter how false it felt, he held the confident posture, his chin raised and his shoulder broad.

Inside, he remained shaken. He had never been a fighter. The sight of more armored men reminded him again how far he was from safety.

Prince Rairn, wearing white, heavily quilted armor, joined Tohmas and Sol in the clearing near the Temple waggons. He moved uncertainly.

Celebrant

His face looked like a skull, dark bags had formed under the man's sunken eyes, and his lips were perpetually curled back in snarl, exposing strangely perfect teeth. His age matched Sol's, but his worn face made him seem old enough to have grandchildren. His protectors, although Sol knew they were officially given a different title, formed a loose line a respectful pace away, looking as worn and uneasy as he felt. He hoped he was doing a better job of hiding his fading assurance.

Putting on a proud smile, Sol called, "Glad to see you are still about, Prince Rairn." They knocked knuckles in greeting. He had met Rairn only a handful of times in his life and wondered if the man would even recognize him.

Sure enough, Rairn's eyes flicked to his black armband. The Prince of Barlaby required the rank marker, matched to Sol's red and black colors, to know who he was.

"I would say the same for you, Prince Sol," the Prince of Barlaby replied, his voice coarse, "but since you are outside your city, I assume BellRoost has fallen."

"Fallen and occupied," Sol admitted with a sigh. Determined not to dwell on the topic, he quickly added, "We head for Narsol." Sol did not fear revealing the destination. No Prince of Espar would ally with the Northlanders, and it was obvious anyway—Sol had nowhere else to go.

Prince Rairn indicated the group behind him with a nod of his bearded head. "We could use your help here. The forest is—"

"We need to keep moving," Prince Tohmas interrupted.

The tired prince's eyes narrowed. At length, his stare found the black rope on Tohmas' shoulder. "Prince Tohmas, I presume." Prince Rairn glanced aside as he added, "I heard you were coming north, but I did not believe it to be true."

Tohmas stiffened. Nearby, Prime Protector Carsh had drawn a second knife, although Sol had not seen when. Both men stood like dogs with their hackles raised.

"I keep my word," Tohmas answered tersely. Had he interpreted Prince Rairn's disbelief as an insult to his integrity? Sol knew he should try to keep the peace between the two princes but could not find the words.

"Apparently," Prince Rairn coolly replied. "I wonder if you have come to regret it. The north is a harsh place."

Chapter 11

Tohmas shrugged and gave a sarcastic smile, goading Rairn openly. "Regret it? Regret cutting the throats of the Northlanders as they slept? Regret bloodying them in BellRoost then outmaneuvering them? We are merely moving to the next position to further the damage. You are wrong if you think this a retreat."

"And just how are you going to keep DoomDragon from milling you down before you get there?"

There was an unusual spark in Tohmas' eye when he answered, "I have some ideas. How are the winds here?"

He got silence for a flicker. Then, with his grey eyebrows furrowed so far they seemed to unite, the Prince of Barlaby asked, "What about the winds?"

"How do they blow? Which direction do they blow? How hard? How often? How are the winds?" he repeated.

"What care have I for winds?" Prince Rairn snarled. "Why would I want to know about the winds?"

Tohmas frowned so deeply Sol was glad that he had not asked the question. He had been about to. He did not understand Tohmas' interest in the wind any more than Rairn did.

"So you can know the range of your arrows." Tohmas' voice rose steadily. Sol's nerves tingled. Tohmas was generally hard to bother, but Rairn's disrespect was being returned. "So you can know the range of your enemy. So you know if their hounds can scent you. So you can tell if the storm will hit you or them first. So you can hide the smoke of your fires! Do you require more reasons?"

Prince Tohmas won a baffled, irate silence, filling Sol with familial pride and, to his surprise, relief. His budding confidence in Tohmas had been justified. Rairn was the elder and carried with him years of experience in surviving in the north, but Sol found himself more confident in Tohmas.

But the potential for repercussions worried Sol. He had survived among the princes by not creating enemies. The lands he owned had been gifted to him by his father and only defended in earnest by fighters from his father's generation. Interactions with the other princes were precious few and usually consisted of communications through one of Sol's strengths—the written word. Letters could be re-written until perfect. Speech could not be. He was no good at oration, yet felt he probably would have managed to mollify Prince Rairn better Tohmas had.

"The winds here are strong," Tohmas continued into the pause. "It would help to know if they are consistent. If you do not know, I will ask a Celebrant of Totho."

"Then ask a celebrant," Prince Rairn spat.

Tohmas shook his head as if disappointed in a young child. "We will keep moving, camp on the south side of the woods, out of the wind, then head south."

Sol nodded as the runners stepped up. Tohmas knew what he was doing. That was reason enough for Sol.

"You are a fool to let DoomDragon catch you in the open," Rairn objected, his eyes switching between Tohmas and Sol carefully as if seeing something out of the corner of his eye he could not place. "The forest—"

"Will provide no advantage," Tohmas finished for him.

The skull-faced man flushed. "The Northlanders are ill-accustomed to fighting in woods."

Tohmas' words were curt, no attempt made at courtesy. "As am I. What you suggest is a mutual disadvantage. I want open ground. These plains will do well for me."

"DoomDragon will catch you," Prince Rairn protested and, for a second time, looked at Sol as if expecting him to intervene.

Sol kept his mouth shut. He had learned his lesson in fire and rubble and death.

"I have ways of slowing him down. Galanth will march on."

In his desperation, Rairn addressed Sol, "Prince Sol, call back the forces of Galanth. The boy is mad if he—"

Before Sol could speak, Tohmas lunged forward, caught Rairn by the throat, and slammed him against the back of a waggon. One of the Barlabian defenders flinched as if to act but was stopped by Carsh's smooth movements. Carsh pitched the Barlabian off his feet and into the dirt instantly. The Rydan then positioned himself between the defenders and the princes.

The scene froze for a breath, Carsh crouched in readiness with a blade in each hand, Rairn pinned against the waggon, and Tohmas holding a jeweled dagger at Rairn's throat.

 # Chapter 11

"If you ever so much as think of suggesting one of my men disobey me again, I will put a knife through your spine," Tohmas hissed.

With that, Tohmas dropped the Prince of Barlaby. He and Carsh stepped away.

"We move," Tohmas reiterated. "Do what you want."

He was on Honest Justice by the time anyone could respond, and in answer to the horns, the Galanth forces were soon marching.

Sol paused, thinking he should say something but unsure what.

Princes did not kill princes. Even princes who warred on each other would never harm one another; their physical persons were sacred.

Yet Tohmas had threatened a prince.

Could Sol blame Tohmas' nerves? His inexperience? The stress of the march? Or did he need to accept the younger prince meant every word?

For a long while, there was silence between the two remaining princes as Tohmas rode away. Prince Rairn rubbed his throat, glaring with hatred, cold and certain, but said nothing.

Saying nothing because no one will listen. The Prince of Barlaby had been chased from his land. His remaining forces were threadbare. He still wore his marks of rank, but he could not force anyone to honor them. Like Sol, he had been defeated. Tohmas' partial victory brought that fact into sharp light.

Rairn had only two choices: be insulted or ignore the dealings. Being insulted would force him to stay behind, forfeit any alliance with the other displaced forces, and miss his best chance for survival. If he ignored the dealings, justifying them somehow, he could join the larger forces and benefit from their protection.

But ignoring the insult would require him to swallow his pride. Sol was not sure that was possible.

With a shake of his head, Sol mounted his horse. If he wanted to avoid ending up like Rairn, he knew what he had to do.

"That boy is crazy," Rairn declared. "You need to get a handle on him, Prince Sol. He is dangerous."

Sol chuckled. The idea was insane. "He is clever, not crazy, Prince Rairn. Get any thoughts of controlling him out of your head now. That 'boy,' as you called him, will not be handled by anyone. Thankfully, that may include DoomDragon."

Prince Rairn cocked his head. "You think he can stop the Northlanders?"

Sol thought he should consider his answer more, but the reply was obvious.

"I certainly think it is a possibility. He sees things in a way I never did. If any of us can stop them, it will be him."

"So, you will ride with him," the Prince of Barlaby concluded.

Sol nodded once more. "You would be wise to do the same," he advised gently. "I can ensure you are still welcomed."

The man paused. Sol sensed Prince Rairn's pride threatening to overrule his safety and the safety of his few remaining men, but Rairn surprised him.

"I will ride with you. Whatever my feelings about that ... about Prince Tohmas, my chances are better with you than alone."

The night was warm out of the wind.

Prince Rairn of Barlaby and his men were directed to set camp on the edge of the Galanth forces. The established pattern of Prince Tohmas' forces, completed by assembling barricades and digging trenches and latrines, was surprisingly efficient. It took less time than setting the camp for Rairn's few hundred.

For the first time in years, Rairn made use of other fortifications. His men did not have to be on watch.

He still did not sleep well.

In the morning, camp was struck smoothly, and the march began. Rairn made sure his men were close to the Soltan soldiers.

Rairn gathered rumors as best he could but had little time to sort through them for truths. He heard everything from stories of Prince Tohmas bargaining with dragons for passage down a road to claims that this new prince could hold fire in his hand thanks to the blessings of the Goddess Inac. It was too fantastical. Homage to the gods had never borne fruit for Rairn. He could not believe that the gods would so directly enter daily life.

The march paused at a river, which Prince Sol identified as MudCrow River, around noon the next day. While the army located a

Chapter 11

fjord, Prince Tohmas gathered his protectors and called for a celebrant. Rairn rode out to observe.

He was not the only one. Prince Sol sat on his horse at the edge of the gathering in silence with his protectors, including a scowling wizard prime protector. While the Prince of Solta seemed content to watch in silence, Rairn could not follow his example.

"What are you doing?" he demanded when Prince Tohmas was halfway through his commands.

"... a dozen torches," Prince Tohmas finished for his men. "And each of you should have an armful of timber. *Geddit*." The men dispersed. Rairn did not know the final word, but the protectors heeded it as a dismissal. "I am slowing DoomDragon down," Tohmas told Rairn. "The wind is with us here."

"Meaning what?"

"Meaning it blows down this valley and up the banks. It goes with the slant of the hill." As Tohmas spoke, a Celebrant of Inac arrived. The older man's bald head glistened with sweat from sprinting in his ruby red robes, but he resolutely held a lantern dangling from a golden chain. Tohmas acknowledged the celebrant with a nod. "I cannot be certain it will stay that way, but we have the blessing of Fire, so we can hope so."

"We will maintain a vigil for you," the celebrant agreed. "Inac is with you, my Prince."

"Fine, fine," Rairn dismissed the claims. He had not had a celebrant in his ranks in over three years, and he did not miss them. The smaller man in red did not instill him with confidence. People, unlike gods, could be held accountable if they failed him. "But what will this achieve?"

Prime Protector Carsh snickered with a wide, snarling grin and declared, "Laydee's Skirt!"

"It is called 'the Lady's Skirt,'" Prince Tohmas agreed, "and if you wait around, you will see why I prefer grasslands over forest."

They did not have to wait long. The first of the protectors returned with their wood and torches. Each protector paired up with another, and while one carried the timber, the other lit the torch with the Blessed Flame the celebrant cradled.

When the prince started assigning paces, Rairn finally understood what was going on.

"You cannot burn these lands!" he objected. "The fire will turn on you! Think of the damage to the farmlands! Think of—"

"The only person who will be using these farmlands right now is DoomDragon," Prince Tohmas interrupted, irking Rairn. "I will burn them, Prince Rairn, if it means giving my forces enough time to find another holding position."

"His casters will put it out," Rairn protested next.

"I have it on good authority that even powerful wizards cannot contend with a plains fire. With so many people to protect, he will be forced to turn wide. I might even catch some of those demons if the wind favors us long enough. We will spook him into giving us more time."

Rairn looked to Prince Sol, but the man was too afraid or too confused to protest. Rairn almost tried again but stopped himself.

The tone of Prince Tohmas' voice warned it was not up for discussion. While Rairn thought the plan foolhardy, he could not stop the young prince. As Prince Sol had shown, Rairn would be better off saving his breath.

He watched the line of fire start at the top of the banks on the north side of the river. Once at the rise, the crosswinds swept the flames up, driving them voraciously on. The fire leaped along the thin grasses like a sprinting wildcat. The smoke fled ahead of it, building into a thick fog.

Rairn followed the prince as he collected his protectors and crossed the river, dismissing Prince Sol to lead the march on. Once the other prince had gone, Prince Tohmas requested a spear and two pieces of cloth. He then drew his knife.

The sight of the prince dragging the jeweled dagger across a scar on his palm stopped Rairn's questions before they could leave his mouth. Without the slightest pause, Prince Tohmas smeared his blood over his hand and pressed it against the cloth. With the same hand, he drew a line across the palm of the handprint he had made.

The barbarism of the action stunned Rairn to silence, and he did not recover his wits fast enough to seek an explanation. He could only stare in amazement as the cloth was attached to the spear and the spear was stuck into the ground. Tohmas tied a horsehair braid to the dagger he had cleaned on the leg of his breeches and, without dismounting, attached the dagger to the standing spear.

Chapter 11

He tied the second cloth carelessly around his hand, using his teeth to finish the knot.

"*Geddit*!" he called, and no one stopped him. He was riding away before Rairn could find his voice.

Prince Tohmas had cut open his hand without flinching then written in blood like a savage.

How could this be a Prince of Espar? The princes had brought law and stability to the lands for two generations. Their newest member was tearing it apart. *Why does Prince Sol allow it?*

Rairn stared at the spear long after the rest of the forces had moved on. He wanted to confront the younger prince on his actions, but no one else had spoken a word yet and that made the Prince of Barlaby nervous. Why had the protectors not reacted to the injury the prince so casually inflicted on himself? Was the threat of that dagger enough to make them all keep silent?

Not Rairn. He would not be cowed by any boy. He wanted answers, and he would have them.

As Rairn turned to follow the army over the south bank of the river, he realized he was not alone in the river valley. Atop the bank opposite the place the fire had been started, dressed in white that whipped about in the gusts, the Celebrant of Totho sat regarding the fire with a blank expression.

Rairn could not tell whether there would be a vigil from the Gathering of Wind that night and, oddly, it seemed to matter.

The celebrant was the last to leave the smoky river valley, leaving a trail of embers in his wake.

Sedgan knelt, praying, in the Temple waggon as the army moved. As promised, he and his acolytes kept their vigil from the time the fires were lit until the sun set and camp was made. The fires did not turn on the Galanth forces, and at the end of his full day of prayer, Sedgan thanked the Goddess for that blessing.

He had only just kicked the kinks from his knees when there was commotion at the entrance to the Temple waggon. The acolytes moved out of the way with subtle lowering of their heads. Of the lot of them, only Acolyte Tamort, the eldest and most experienced of the acolytes, had the gall to smile in recognition of the woman in red.

Loni sauntered in. Typically, her smile was seductive, but this time she grinned like a child with a new toy.

Sedgan made a point of giving her a clear path to the altar, hoping she would just pray and leave. Disappointedly, Loni presented herself to Sedgan and calmly informed him, "You will want to speak to me shortly."

"Then you've not come to join the vigil for Fire's blessing?" he asked scathingly. "Shocking!"

Her smile, self-assured and calm, did not waver. "I will hold the vigil while you are occupied," Loni said, turned to the altar, and pulled up the hood of her cloak. Unlike her usual attire, which today was a bright combination of yellow and red that followed every curve of her body, the cloak was dark blue and billowed around her in a non-descript way. It looked almost modest.

"Occupied?" he wondered, but he did not have time to press her for answers.

This time, the acolytes scampered out of the way. Some leaped into corners or pressed themselves against the walls in order to get clear of the entrance, and Sedgan understood why.

Celebrant Barga was an imposing force at the best of times, but when she was angry, as seemed to be the case today, she was a landslide. The Temple waggon lurched on its axles, rocking with each stomping step she took. Her face a hue matching the rubies on the altar, Barga stormed past his startled acolytes and, like Loni had, stomped right up to Sedgan.

"You!" Barga cried as she wagged her finger at him, coming to a stop with the club-like finger nearly touching his nose. "You did this! I know it. You and your—"

Sedgan took a step back and regretted it at once. To the acolytes who were watching with wide eyes, it would seem as if he yielded because of some kind of guilt. Whatever the accusation, he was certain he was blameless, and he did not want them believing otherwise.

"By the Flame," Sedgan replied in a forcibly cool voice, "calm yourself, Barga. What is your claim?"

"Calm?" the Celebrant of Pari shouted back, throwing both brown-sleeved arms into the air. Sedgan was grateful the waggon had halted

Chapter 11

for the day; the tossing of Barga's substantial weight around would have upset the horses otherwise. "Calm down? After what you and your whore goddess have done? How dare you—"

Sedgan interrupted, feeling his face flush. "In the waggon of Fire, you would do well to mind how you speak of the Goddess, especially while such an important tribute is being kept that will keep even your gathering safe!"

Across the room, he met Tamort's eyes and, feeling the acolyte knew his thoughts, nodded for Tamort to fetch some of Prince Tohmas' soldiers. There was no saying if Tamort actually understood, but the eldest acolyte left the waggon quietly behind the raging Celebrant of Pari.

"I do not care!" Barga thundered on. "Your goddess is a whore, Sedgan. Lust, passion, and all that! As if no one can entertain those emotions without your consent! Is that what annoyed you? That we use all the things you preached without your permission? Is that why—?"

Two realizations struck Sedgan in succession. The first was that Barga was carrying on about her relationship with Celebrant Glorian, and the second was that it was not, and had never been, love.

Sedgan had known about the relationship between the two celebrants since its inception almost ten years ago and had always assumed, because Glorian was the Celebrant of Ocea, that the two celebrants had been in love. Now, however, he recognized all the signs of a slighted lover. He wondered how he missed it before.

"Enough, Barga!" Sedgan shouted, and Barga paused briefly. It could have been a natural pause for breath, but he hoped it was surprise at finally being dealt a harsh word. "I had nothing to do with Glorian's infidelity." By her intensified glare, he knew he had correctly reasoned the cause of her frenzy. "And if you insist on believing I did, consider this—I am neither an apothecary nor a wizard. If Glorian was led by Fire, it was divine power, in which case you can take your slight up with the Goddess herself!"

He gestured at the altar, having forgotten about the woman kneeling and feigning inattention in front of it. Loni was the only other person present beside the acolytes, and he cringed to think he had drawn Celebrant Barga's attention to her.

But Barga did not seem to see the woman.

Celebrant

Behind Barga, a green-clad soldier peeked into the waggon. Although he did not fully enter, Sedgan saw the rank rope was green.

A protector. Good. He needed someone to be the muscle against Barga. It had been a long time since Sedgan had used a sword, although he was trained in it.

"We are finished here. Get out," Sedgan said, feeling confident with the support of the soldier.

"How dare you!" Barga shouted. She surprised Sedgan by striking out at him.

To Sedgan's own amazement, he moved faster than the protector. With hands he thought had forgotten how, he caught the arm and twisted it. In locking her wrist, he brought himself against Barga. He no longer felt dwarfed by the other celebrant's size.

Barga cursed him creatively, but Sedgan did not care.

"You are a fool if you think you can get away with that in the presence of the Goddess of War, Earth," Sedgan hissed in her ear. Without releasing Barga's arm despite her struggling, he called to the protector. "She is not here to worship and so is unwelcome in this waggon. Remove her!" Three protectors entered at his call.

Between the three of them, they lifted her considerable bulk off the floor and moved for the exit.

"You will regret this, Sedgan!"

"I would regret it more if it was not done. Goodbye, Barga!"

Sedgan presumed the soldiers dragged her from the area as well as the waggon, for her screamed curses took a long while to fade. With her voice roaring in the distance, Sedgan faced the occupants of the waggon.

"Out. All of you. Now."

Loni stood and turned from the altar. Her confident smile seemed to put the concerned acolytes at ease as she waited for Sedgan to deal with her.

As soon as the door shut, leaving the two of them alone, Sedgan turned on her. "You had a hand in that, I take it?"

Loni shrugged. Her cloak lay open at the front, and her many necklaces glittered with her movement, drawing Sedgan's eye. "We merely provided an opportunity, Celebrant."

Sedgan re-established his focus, reviewing what he knew about the whore to figure out who "we" entailed.

Chapter 11

"Your girls. Seduction? You played a Celebrant of Ocea against—"

"He was a slave to Barga, Sedgan. We gave him the chance to be the master, and he found it so much to his liking he did not want to go back."

"A well-established relationship ruined by your meddling, Loni. You have caused turbulence in the Temples."

"We balanced the four," she corrected with another satisfied grin. "Now they all stand alone. There are again four sides, Sedgan, not three."

For a long moment, he was silent. He agreed. As much as he resented her and her methods, she was right. The alliance of Earth and Water was broken. Sedgan was grateful.

His silence served as her permission; Loni slid forward until her hips were pressed against his and arched her back lightly, her eyes raised. "She will not miss Glorian," Loni whispered. "She will only miss the power she had over him. That is Fire's realm, and she was trespassing."

Sedgan braced a hand against her stomach, feeling the need to maintain some distance between them. Although the waggon was not heated, he felt warm.

"Fine," Sedgan choked out. "I will not fault you this. The balance of the four is intact. You have done enough."

"Oh no," Loni cooed, tossing her head playfully as she drifted away from him. "I will do all that my Goddess requires."

Before, he would have argued that Loni had no way of knowing the workings of Inac, but her effectiveness made him doubt his convictions. Even the light on the altar seemed to glow brighter in her presence. As Prince Tohmas had said, Loni inspired people in ways Sedgan failed to. She, as she had proven, had her uses.

Sedgan called after her as she reached the closed door where he was certain a dozen acolytes were eavesdropping.

"Those pills you gave me ... where did you get them?" he asked.

Loni's face lit at his acknowledgement. "I have a cutter friend who likes to buy me drinks. I have to return the favor, of course, and ..."

Sedgan held up a hand, and Loni trailed off. "They were from a cutter's pouch then?" he asked.

"Yes," Loni replied with a nod of her head that sent her tangled hair bouncing. "Why? Did you find something, Celebrant?"

"Perhaps it is time I look into it."

She beamed, and her smile was more than he could tolerate.

Celebrant

"Now get out," Sedgan finished.

At sunset, Tohmas sighted the mouth of MudCrow River. Finally feeling hale enough to separate himself from the main forces for a short time, Tohmas agreed to spar with Carsh in the morning. He made his goal the lake that the river flowed into.

The delta of the river was wide, the waters shallow enough to allow the worn granite of the nearby hills to break the surface and create long, lazy currents. Inspired, the brothers sparred in the shallows, practicing how to compensate for the pull of water over their feet and using the drag to both strengthen their attacks and manipulate the speed of their opponent. Once Carsh had again reminded Tohmas of his wounded left shoulder by knocking him off the river stones and into the churning waters, he was declared the winner.

Tohmas turned his attention to the lake. He crossed the delta, trying to ignore the protectors who skipped across the stones to shadow him, and made his way up a long rise over the water.

From the top of the rise, Tohmas overlooked all of Bracken Lake. The waters lay still in the morning, the pristine surface reflecting dawn as a molten rainbow. The only break in the mirror of the water was the churning of MudCrow's mouth to Tohmas' right. A thick forest claimed the far bank. According to Sol's maps, the lake fed into another river somewhere between the trees on the north side which led down to Narsol. It was still a dozen days' journey on foot, and the river's multiple rapids would foil any attempt at using boats even if Tohmas took the time to build them.

The ground around the lake was broken as if a giant had thrown a tantrum and ripped out the earth. The hill Tohmas climbed ended abruptly in sheer bluffs. Two dozen paces below, the waters sat against the cliffs and wary swallows chirped threats up at him.

Tohmas turned around, facing the way he had come. The north side of the hill led up a slope that flattened at the top, overlooking the lake, and was backed by the precipitous drop. The grasses were tall, but the earth seemed too thin to support tree roots, leaving the hill otherwise barren. To his left, the winding route of MudCrow River made its

Chapter 11

way back to the north, a thick cover of trees following its every turn in the grasslands. To his right, the hill was still smooth, but the slope was steeper as it fed into a valley before rising in a much smaller hill backed by more forest.

The plains had ended, leaving Tohmas with the options of taking his march into the clustered, tangled woods or turning far west to continue following the road. Although the road travel permitted a swift pace, it followed the flattest route and left Tohmas no place to fortify should DoomDragon's men catch up.

And he knew they were not far from doing so.

"We stop," he decided aloud. He surprised his protectors by swiftly going back the way he had come, forcing them to leave the hill crest almost as soon as they reached it.

Once back at the camp, Tohmas announced his intention to the princes. He found Rairn and Sol breaking fast together and was smugly pleased to be disturbing their private conversation.

"Stop?" Sol repeated once Tohmas had explained. "Now? Narsol is a quartercycle away and—"

"Narsol is a trap," Tohmas cut in. "Once we put walls around us, we can do nothing but defend. I want space. The hill by the lake is ideal."

"A good city will be easy to defend," Rairn insisted.

"But that is all it can do. Yes, you could hold it, but to what end? Why would they let up the siege?"

"They run short of food," Rairn suggested. "They run short on patience. Enough quiet time will upset their fighters; they may get restless. Holding siege is difficult."

"How long did they remain outside of BellRoost, Sol?" Tohmas asked his uncle.

"Three years," Sol idly remarked, his eyes staring off toward the river as if imagining the lake and hill Tohmas described.

"Three years without any sign of weakness. They have an unending supply train and a patience for this war that evidently exceeds that of the Esparans. What are you waiting for, Prince Rairn? Why do you think this will end without someone forcing it to end?"

"Force it?" Rairn replied, skepticism heavy in his voice. "How are you going to fight back when you are cornering yourself?"

Celebrant

"The hill is backed by a lake with cliffs that can be defended easily yet still allow us access to a water source he cannot pollute and a supply of food he cannot deplete," Tohmas answered, uninterested.

"But to lose any escape—"

"I told you this was no retreat. Runner! Send the word out. Move the main waggons. The protectors know the way to our new camp." Tohmas turned away from Rairn. The conversation had ended whether the older prince wanted it to or not. "I need my guardians once more; this is going to get complicated. Lady's Skirt has bought us a few days, and I want to use them effectively." He turned to Sol. "How many of your men can swim?"

Dust was carefully counting out tablets onto the vardo's counter then sweeping them into a bottle when he spotted the man in red robes approaching. Despite instantly recognizing the celebrant, he did not pause counting until he reached ten and shoved the stopper into the bottle.

With a broad smile and a wave of his cap, he greeted the newcomer. "Welcome, Celebrant Sedgan! Welcome to Match and Mixer!"

The celebrant's eyes narrowed, and the wrinkled brow creased with his frown. "How do you know my name, peddler?"

If Dust was to be hired, it seemed only appropriate that he first prove himself well worth paying for.

"Easily, good Celebrant. You may not have visited us before, but you are wearing the robes of a full celebrant, and it being a small hill, there are no other Celebrants of Inac to be found but Celebrant Sedgan of Galanth. So, I bid you welcome, Celebrant Sedgan. I am Dust Weaver. How may I serve you?"

The celebrant held his silence, but Dust suspected it was more because of what the man was about to say rather than what had been said. At length, Celebrant Sedgan won, or lost, some argument with himself and held out his hand.

"I hear you are an apothecary."

 # Chapter 11

"None better to be found in Solta," Dust answered. As most of the other traders had already fled the besieged princedom, he could make the claim with relative impunity.

After another moment of hesitation, the celebrant opened his fist. "Can you tell me what these are?"

At the distance the celebrant insisted on keeping, Dust could barely make out the shape of three brown pills in the man's palm.

"From here, they look like pain pills."

The celebrant placed the pills on the counter of the waggon then put a silver shard beside it.

Dust's eyebrows rose at the glint of silver before he could check his surprise. He cleared his throat uneasily when he realized the celebrant had seen his interest.

"Am I permitted to destroy it?" he asked shyly. "If not, you should switch that coin for something more copper colored."

"You will do whatever you need to do in order to tell me exactly what is in these pills."

With the free rein, the smile returned to Dust's face. It was not often he got quite as much freedom in his work.

"Well then, I suggest you come into the back. This may take a little while, and I would rather you be comfortable." Before the celebrant could argue, Dust called, "Shim! Open the side door!" and disappeared behind the curtain.

Shimmer was standing in the opened doorway by the time Dust made his way inside. Celebrant Sedgan visibly tensed as he stepped past Shimmer and into the cluttered living space. With the many shelves of flasks, the rows of hanging herbs from the ceiling, and the innumerable bookcases along the walls, the back of the vardo was a small space for three people.

It smelled welcoming. Shimmer, Dust saw with an approving smile, had been mixing blends of perfumes.

While Dust went to sort through the bookcase against the far wall, the celebrant refused Shimmer's offer of tea.

"'Never drink tea with an apothecary,'" Celebrant Sedgan quoted.

Shimmer tossed her lovely head and laughed. "Old and sage advice," she confessed as she sat the man down on one of the two cushions beside the table at the center of their vardo. As the celebrant cautiously placed the pills on the rough surface in front of him, Shimmer admitted, "But it is just green powder tea, and I made it for myself. You can have my cup if you would rather."

The celebrant still refused politely.

"Shim, where's Markin's Lists?" Dust asked.

"Third shelf," Shimmer replied as she settled on the floor beside the table with her tea, leaving the second cushion for Dust. He knew she was listening with one ear for the bell that would ring if they had more customers. "Second book from the left, Papa." As always, her memory proved perfect. He found the gold-bound book exactly where she had said.

"A Decomposition?" she asked while mixing Dust a cup of tea. Once the brew was ready, she picked up a pill with her free hand. "Trade secrets?"

Dust laid the book on the table. It fell open to the spell he needed. The page, he noted sourly, had been stained by a variety of powders, leaves, and liquids over the years, which worked well as a bookmark. Thankfully, the words were still clearly etched on the fine vellum.

"Celebrant Barga may have some competition," he said with a laugh.

The celebrant's scowl intensified. "I am not interested in healers or Pari. I just want to know what those pills are made of."

Shimmer laughed again. "Doesn't matter to us, good Celebrant. You can do whatever you want with the information we provide." With a wink to her father, she added, "I'll watch the front. It might be early in camp set up, but I'd hate to be interrupted."

Dust winced. That lesson had been so well-learned, it never lost its potency. Interruptions at the wrong time during casting could be disastrous.

Shimmer disappeared through the curtains.

Dust cleared his throat with a sip of tea and settled cross-legged onto the cushion. It was a difficult spell but one he had done often enough to not be concerned about the words. The drawing of energy was like pulling stringy dough in Dust's mind; a soft touch was required to grasp as the magic energy, then gentle tension drew it from the source until it reached him and settled in his mind. Too fast, and the dough fell apart, and the spell failed.

Chapter 11

Although he could feel the build of power and the presence of the magic in his mind, there was no visual component to the process. As far as the celebrant would see, Dust was simply talking aloud. By raising and lowering his voice in great emphasis, he made the spell seem well worth the price Celebrant Sedgan paid. He was unsure how much of an effect it would have on the wary celebrant, but it was a habit Dust found no need to break.

With Celebrant Sedgan looking on in silence, Dust formed his dough into the spell he desired, enunciating each word with great care and poise.

Releasing the spell was anticlimactic. The magic slipped free of Dust's finger as he touched it down on the pill and methodically divided it into its components. Faint burning lingered in Dust's arm and finger. Despite all his practice, he had not perfected the amount of energy required for even that familiar spell. But the fire of the small additional magic would fade.

Dust opened his eyes and found himself staring at four small piles where the pill had been.

The first was a ball of wax for keeping the pill together, but he still sniffed it to make sure there were no surprises. It only smelled, and tasted, like beeswax, so he placed it aside.

The smallest of the piles was red flakes that a taste identified as sweet beet meant for making the pill more palatable. The next pile was green, ground powder that, Dust was surprised to realize, was nothing more than the tea his daughter had just made. Although the green powder was reputed to focus the mind and enhance reflexes, it was not what he expected to find in a pain pill. He sniffed his tea again to confirm but could not refute his conclusion. Since none of those would bring any kind of pain relief, he turned to the last pile.

It was, by far, the biggest portion of the pill, but when Dust smelled the familiar aroma, he had to scratch his head.

"What?" the celebrant demanded. Dust, having forgotten his audience, jumped.

He held up a hand, then called for Shimmer.

Shimmer came in from her place just inside the Wind Barrier. The celebrant lost his irritated stare and remained silent once she arrived.

Dust held out a sample of the leaves he had been identifying. "What is it, Shim?"

After a quick sniff, she chewed on the leaf and spat it out. Dust rubbed his beard to signal her to be truthful. He saw no reason to con the celebrant. Such boldness was reserved for times when movement out of the area was easy.

"Tastes like Willar's Weed," Shimmer replied.

"Can you think of any reason for Willar's Weed to be in pain pills?" Dust asked.

Shaking her head as she went, Shimmer moved to a bookcase and pulled another book to flip through. "Just an herb for seasoning," she confirmed to Dust's relief. He had been unable to come up with any medicinal purpose for Willar's Weed and had suddenly feared he was becoming senile. If Shimmer could not remember any either, he could trust his memory again.

She searched the book then, with a shake of her long, red hair, frowned. "Nothing. Filler?" she offered, and he joined her with his own frown.

He gestured to the table. "Everything in here is filler."

The celebrant crossed his arms. "Could it be something new?" Sedgan asked with a frown so deep Dust almost felt it darken the sunlight that lit the vardo. "Maybe Willar's Weed does something you do not—"

"We make our living off knowing the effects of herbs, Celebrant," Shimmer gently pointed out. "The weed can be toxic in high enough doses. It is no remedy."

"And green powder provides energy, not healing," Dust added. "Most pain pills contain things to make a person sleep, not wake them up and make them think they can go on despite their injury. All you have in here is the green powder, a sweetener, and the Willar's Weed. These are not good pills, Celebrant. I would recommend you cease using them immediately."

"Not mine," the celebrant corrected.

Dust could not decide if he believed the man. "Whatever you choose to do with them is up to you. I have given you a complete decomposition of that pill as you asked."

Chapter 11

The celebrant sat, despite the conclusion of their affairs, for a long moment at the table. At great length, the man sighed and took back the remaining pills.

The silver shard was gone already; Dust had passed it to Shimmer when she had handed him the tea. The celebrant did not seem to be considering the Weavers at all as he stood and moved for the doorway. Dust had to open the door for him, lest the man walk into the wood.

Dust watched the celebrant go and reaffirmed his decision to avoid prying. Something strange was going on with the celebrant, and for the first time, Dust did not want to know what.

I am too old for this, was his reasoning as he closed the door and cleaned the table of the mysterious pill contents.

Shimmer found him staring at the door when she returned for her tea.

"So?" she asked, shaking him from his thoughts. "Your tea is getting cold."

Dust made his way to the cushions around the table.

"He's angry about something but confused, like he knows what the problem is but doesn't know what to do about it."

"Is that so unusual?"

"For a celebrant, yes. By the time they get to wear those robes, they have served for at least twenty years, Shimmer. His faith should be all the answer he needs, yet he doubts. He feels—"

"Rule One?"

Dust dropped his sentence and laughed. He had taught her the two rules that had to be applied before they worried about something. The first rule was whether the problem was actually their problem. If not, then worrying about it made no sense.

Shimmer was right.

"It's not my problem," Dust agreed, "so I shan't worry about it."

"Always easier said than done, but it looks like we might be here a while. We might get to perform! I want to get dancing again, and now we have space and time. Think about other things, Papa, please. Don't get involved."

His mind had gone back to the puzzle of Celebrant Sedgan, but at her plea, Dust forced himself to think about other things. Too much

 # Celebrant

meddling had cost them various versions of Match and Mixer over the years. Their nomadic life was his fault.

But as he looked back at her, he noticed Shimmer shuffling the fortune cards with a mischievous smirk on her face. He chuckled.

As much as they knew better, some things could not be helped.

She dealt out the cards. "Let us see then…"

Chapter 12

The Circle of the Raven saw the fire long before any of the fighters did. Darknim moved his fighters north, allowing the fire to blow across their flank without casualty. It cost them time, far more time than he felt he had. It was another full quartercycle—ten days—before he finally felt he was closing in on his prey once more.

When they found MudCrow River, one of Darknim's Hunters brought him the spear that Prince Tohmas left behind. It came with a cloth bearing a bloody handprint and a jeweled dagger. Darknim saw no magic on the dagger, spear, or cloth, but Seria warned that Master Kitable might be able to track the items even if he had not bewitched them.

Darknim kept the three items, hoping she would be right. He was eager to deal with his opponents.

The Northlander forces crossed the river, camped on the far side, then continued their pursuit. The Circle located his enemy's camp on a hill backed by a lake a few more day's travel south. Upon the morning, Darknim had the Circle check again and discovered the prince had finally pushed his forces to their limit; they did not break camp. Instead, Darknim watched them build fortifications.

Using the Circle's ice pool to study the position Tohmas chose, Darknim was impressed. The Prince of Galanth had found a long cliff drop to cover his back, and the upper ground gave him an advantage in any charge or exchange of arrows or sling stones. Water was accessible, and the ground was stone to prevent undermining without magical aid, something outside the ability of Darknim's casters.

Still, the one thing the hill lacked was an escape route. It was a hefty oversight Darknim could exploit.

Tohmas remained atop the hill as Darknim marched his men along the plains, following the river. Still some leagues from their enemy, the army was met by a boggy section of the river which Darknim opted to move around.

He recognized his error when the ground edging the bog vanished under the weight of his fighters.

Rigged, he realized too late. They had dug pits, leaving the surface cover able to hold no more than a few people.

Unfortunately, the Esparans from Barlaby marching with Darknim reacted poorly when the ground gave away. It did not surprise Darknim. They were soldiers. They did what they were told, nothing further. In Darknim's opinion, paws, claws, fangs, and bears—the ranks they used—fought because they could not think. Darknim had long since started associating the number of black rank tattoos that streaked their faces with a progressively lower intelligence.

Instead of retreating the way they had come—a known safe route—the Barlabians nearest the collapse scrambled forward, piling onto each other in panic. The added weight was enough to collapse the next pit, which caused another scramble down the line.

Assuming there was more to this ploy than just pits, Darknim let those nearest deal with pulling the fools out—assuming they had survived the fall and whatever was in the hole—and instead gave the command to bring the fighters together with their spears.

Sure enough, the first line of Galanth riders charged from the river's tree line. How they had evaded his scouts, Darknim did not know.

The first attackers trampled into his men. There were a few screams from the horses as some Northlanders positioned their spears correctly, but the exchange largely favored the heavy horses. The commander of the charge held tight control of his men, leading them through the Northlanders swiftly and preventing much by way of retaliation. By the time Darknim's warriors positioned themselves to launch their sling bullets, the horses were almost back under the cover of the tree line.

Chapter 12

The volley of stones peppered the retreating horses into rearing or spooking but did little damage beyond that.

They were not yet at Tohmas' camp. Tohmas would have chosen this battlefield, Darknim reasoned. The riders had to be the protectors, for no other mass of horse-trained warriors was to be found in Tohmas' ranks. It explained the swiftly completed rush; the protectors were too valuable to have maintain an assault.

Although Darknim's Hunters hastened after the horses on foot, more than a match for a horse trying to navigate a forest, Darknim sounded a complete halt. His Hunters stopped.

He split his forces, surrounding the place the horses had retreated but entering the woods from a hundred paces up and downstream. He planned to pinch the protectors from either side, not chase them back down the route they had chosen for him.

The army spread itself into a wide arch like a wishbone. Darknim moved to the south to enter the woods around the river.

The northern rank found the Esparans first, and they were still fighting by the time Darknim and his fighters arrived to find the bare dozen remaining Galanth soldiers holding a rough line with their backs to the river. A glance at the banks showed a lack of horses.

As the thought entered his mind, a horse rose from the water on the far side of the river. Without a look back, the rider guided his steed to join the others who were waiting. Together, they disappeared into the trees.

There were men in the water. A raft was most of its way across the river, being pulled by men on the far side by a long rope. Wounded men lay on the raft, laughing with the recklessness of battle madness. The low wall on the edge of the raft protected the occupants from any assault originating on the bank.

Being farther upstream, the raft's wall did not obstruct Darknim's view.

"Spears," he called to his Hunters. He threw first, but they were quick to follow suit.

A dozen or more landed among the wounded. By the time Darknim had a new spear in his hand, the Galanth had arranged shields over the exposed side. He did not bother with a second throw as the raft reached the far bank and the men aboard scattered into the trees.

Celebrant

The last of the Galanth threw themselves into the water. Stones chased them, but none of his men could pursue.

Even after the last Galanth was dead or running, Darknim stood and watched them move in the water. His Hunters added their spears, but he was uncertain if any of them hit the shrinking targets. The men in the water seemed to disappear under, only to appear, unharmed, farther across the wide river.

He did not understand. Water was death. Darknim had seen men fall through ice and pull themselves out, but that struggle had been nothing like the calm, coordinated motions that somehow propelled the Galanth to the other bank. He had never known humans to move through water.

As the last of the Esparans climbed out of the water on the bank, Darknim's Esparan archers arrived and sent the enemy running for the trees. A few more injuries were inflicted, but the Galanth escaped, leaving Darknim staring at the river.

People did not move through water in the Northlands. Had Tohmas been counting on that? Had he even considered it?

By sunset, his Hunters reported the series of pits that had been laid between the river and where the horsemen had attacked. In the end, the bodies of Galanth and Northlander numbered about the same.

Considering his superior forces, Darknim considered that a victory of a sort.

For the first time, Glorian arrived early for the quartercycle meeting. Sedgan found it impossible to judge the boorish celebrant's mood as he entered the Fire waggon. Like a parrot, Glorian had always echoed Barga, but now, without Barga looming over him, the conversation was irregular and unpredictable. Glorian sat rigid in his ocean-blue robes, twitching irritably and constantly pushing back the spectacles over his fish-eyed stare. He wrinkled his nose at each repetition of the action like a bad smell was present, but he was too polite to comment on it. The expression deepened the wrinkles on the aging man's scalp and cast dark shadows over his glare.

 # Chapter 12

The conversation, however, still sounded like Barga. Glorian even called Inac a whore.

It did not take long for Sedgan to understand Glorian's bitterness; Glorian's lover had left him shortly after camp had been set on the hill. For the first time in years, Glorian was alone. In the conversation, Sedgan learned that, despite his status as Ocea's Celebrant, Glorian was not, and never would be, a family man. He did not want a wife, especially not since his experience with Barga, and he did not want a family.

The basic needs of his body were unfulfilled now.

All this made Glorian resent Sedgan and his Goddess, the Goddess of Lust, for making a man want pleasure. Streams of curses were as sporadic as the conversation. With one breath, Glorian cursed him, and with the next, he mourned the passing of the passion he craved.

Ironically, when the Wind Celebrant arrived, they both fell silent.

Calanor took his seat as if he did not see the crimson color of Water's face. Taking their cue from him, the other two celebrants found their chairs in time for Barga to finalize the group.

She entered with a flurry of robes to match her stomping steps. Her first glare was for Glorian. Her second was for Sedgan. The third, rather unprovoked, was for Calanor.

Sedgan did not even let her sit down, as she seemed to be avoiding the chair in an attempt to prolong her entrance. He tossed the two pain pills onto the table.

Her glare broke, and her eyes widened.

"I have a complaint to bring to the table," Sedgan announced.

"What are you doing with those? It is a crime to take pain pills from those needing them!" Barga snapped.

"They were given to me by a concerned member of my gathering. Apparently, they were losing confidence in Earth's healing skills."

"You dare? Your domain is not in healing! You have no control over—"

"Apparently," Sedgan interrupted, "you have taken the production of pain pills upon yourself, Barga."

"So what? It is not your place!"

"So, do you take full responsibility for everything in this pill, Barga?" he pressed.

Celebrant

Barga paused. If she confessed to being in charge of all the pills, then the responsibility of their falsehood fell to her.

"It is not your place, Fire," she repeated, and Sedgan had his answer.

"Not my place?" he demanded as he rose to his feet. "Followers of Inac make up the majority of the soldiers, and they are the ones wounded and dying under the care of your people! These pills are a problem."

"Are you skimming doses for yourself, Barga?" came Glorian's addition, and for once, Sedgan was happy to hear Water speak.

Barga's voice became a long hiss. "If you have a complaint against me, then bring it forward, Fire."

"I claim you are providing useless pain pills," Sedgan replied. "I claim you are buying filler herbs to stuff your pills so the money can go to your coffer. I claim you are killing followers of Inac through this lie."

There was a stunned silence until the Wind Celebrant cleared his throat and asked, "What proof have you?" The soft voice was still heard clearly through Calanor's scarf.

"Those pills," Sedgan answered. Although he wanted to call upon the word of the two apothecaries who had taken apart the pill for him, their testimony as outsiders would hurt his cause more than help it. "If the preparation of the pills is not transferred to the Healing Mothers immediately, I will take this complaint to the prince directly. Perhaps Master Kitable can tell what has gone into these pills and whether it would help the sick at all."

After only a moment of holding his stare, Barga stepped back. She knew well what Kitable would find if he was asked to look. He had her.

"If Fire feels spreading out the works of Earth may better serve his Gathering," she quietly said after another pause, "then Earth will accommodate his wish. Perhaps it will lessen my load." Barga spun on her heels and stormed off. She slammed the door shut behind her hard enough to make the light upon the altar flicker.

Sedgan thought it looked brighter once she was gone.

"You certainly can afford to lose some of your load," Glorian quipped after her maliciously.

Sedgan, for a long moment, had to wonder if he had won the confrontation at all.

 # CHAPTER 12

Tohmas watched for the protectors' return as the sun set. He worried a little about Carsh, not that he would ever tell his brother as much, and was silently relieved when the party entered the hill camp. They reported moderate success with the pits but that DoomDragon had predicted the trap. The river had worked well as a deterrent. In the warm weather, their steeds and clothing had dried by the time they reached home.

The wounded were swiftly treated and sent to rest to prepare for the arrival of the Northlanders at the hill.

In the dusk, Tohmas headed back to his tent, lost in thought.

He was disappointed that DoomDragon had not acted more rashly in pursuit of the protectors, but he accepted he had misjudged the Northlander. In their previous interaction, DoomDragon had retreated the moment the circumstances no longer favored him, and the escape from BellRoost had been surprisingly smooth. Tohmas assumed this meant the Northlander could not improvise and expected him to falter with the ambush. Instead, DoomDragon quickly adjusted to the threat.

In years before, the Esparans assumed they were fending off a mindless horde of barbarians seeking better lands, and it cost them many lives. DoomDragon had already demonstrated an ability to monitor Tohmas' forces at a great distance. He divided his forces—one at BellRoost and one confronting Tohmas in Barrow Hills—and handled both parts effectively. Tohmas knew Esparan princes who did not have that level of control over their armies.

Feeling partially excited and partially uneasy, Tohmas realized he would have to treat DoomDragon like a Rydan chief. This was no raiding party or a simple Leader. This was a full chief with authority, obedience, and patience. It was, for a moment, humbling.

As Tohmas approached his tent, Protector Nardon stopped him.

"We got a request from a companion of the Fyrd of Rest," Nardon explained. He glanced at a young man being detained behind him. Since no token had been presented, the lone man clearly was acting of his own accord and not on behalf of his superiors. "Do you want to hear it, or should we toss him out?"

No one generally challenged the perimeter the protectors maintained. Either the soldier was uncommonly bold, or he had something to say of some perceived importance.

Tohmas squinted at the companion as someone lifted their torch to illuminate the area. He immediately recognized Sabian.

Ciene's little brother had changed since Tohmas had last seen him, drugged and stupid, twelve days prior. The boy's shoulders were broader, and he held them without the slouch Tohmas expected from the youth. He wore his simple bloodstained and dirt-encrusted tabard but had acquired a baldric of blades to complement the throwing knives on his belt.

Guardian Faron had reported that the boy had recovered well from the incident on BellRoost's wall and had become a bit of a legend among the Fyrd of Rest. The companion's aim was impeccable with his knives, to the point of embarrassing even his elders.

It was possible Sabian still harbored anger for Tohmas' role in his brother's death, but the boy's stare was not accusatory. Instead, Sabian seemed calmly inquisitive.

"Sabian, what brings you to my door?"

The protectors straightened abruptly, and Nardon stepped aside to clear a path to the companion.

"Ciene always said that if I wanted to learn something, I should use my eyes," Sabian replied.

Although his statement baffled the protectors, Tohmas understood. Although he spoke to Tohmas, Sabian's eyes, filled with admiration, were on Carsh.

Sabian wanted to learn from Carsh. No one else was good enough.

Tohmas cocked his head to ask what his brother thought of the request.

Carsh took a moment, which surprised Tohmas. He had expected an immediate answer; to a Rydan, Sabian was an Esparan and thus worthless. Carsh had no reason to train the boy, let alone allow Sabian to follow him around like obsessed child.

After a long pause, Carsh nodded.

Tohmas studied Sabian again, trying to see what his brother had, but Sabian still looked like a youth. There was no subtly to his movements and little experience in his face. His eyes, however, were eager. Was Carsh seeing the enthusiasm and thinking it worthwhile? Or had he been impressed when they had first met and Sabian had nearly won the knife-throwing contest between them?

 # Chapter 12

"If you want to watch, then watch," Tohmas said. "I give you permission to follow us, Sabian. I will have your name removed from the Fyrd of Rest."

The protectors stepped away wordlessly. While Carsh and Tohmas retired to the tent, Sabian was allowed to set a personal campfire among the protectors outside.

Sedgan had only one private place—his tiny room at the back of the Temple waggon of Inac. After the other celebrants left, he retreated to his sacred space, only to find it had been invaded.

He slammed the door shut behind him.

"How, by the hells, did you get in here?" Sedgan demanded when he saw Loni sprawled across his slab bed. "How dare..." He let his sentence trail off. His ire seemed to have no effect on her.

One of the acolytes must have admitted her. He would find a way to repay them for their imprudence later.

She looked different in the lamplight that trickled out from his personal altar, but he could not figure out why. Once she adjusted her stretched form on the bed, he saw that she was, for the first time in her life, clean. She had been washed off all her typical filth. Even her hair, despite still being a fantastic tangle atop her head, looked redder than before.

"Your timing isn't bad," he said. "I'm still reeling from dealing with Barga, but my patience is unlikely to last, I warn you."

"I need to speak to you," Loni murmured, her voice unexpectedly sweet.

A subtle movement brought her long leg from under her skirt then extended it down the bed in the lamplight. One arm, heavy with bracelets and rings, lifted over her head and hung forgotten off the top of the bed, stretching her body almost out of the corset she was wearing. The red and gold embroidered piece was several sizes too small; the lacing on the front left large gaps, exposing the edges of her smooth breasts. Her waist was equally exposed by the short garment, and when she stretched, the space below the corset was wide enough to give him a view well below her navel.

Despite himself, Sedgan warmed.

The room was kept hot by the lamps on the altar, and he had just come from a much chillier room, he justified.

"Speak and be gone then," Sedgan insisted, but he had to turn his stare to speak with any authority. He was thankful for his anger. Only his annoyance kept his lust from fully surfacing. She was a beautiful woman, and tonight it seemed harder than ever to ignore that.

Lazily, and far too slowly for him to be satisfied, Loni lifted herself from the bed. As she sat, one long leg was still exposed through the slit in her crimson skirt.

"The four are broken. Water seeks lust when his goddess preaches love. Earth kills when her god commands healing. They are falling."

I need a drink. His mouth had gone dry in the arid air of the room. It did not help that he had started sweating.

Without looking at her, Sedgan located two cups and a jug atop a chest. It did not surprise him that she may have helped herself to his wine in his absence. He filled a cup.

"Barga threatens to extradite the followers of Fire from her waggons," Loni went on. "I cannot have that, Sedgan. What are you going to do?"

Once he had swallowed his wine, Sedgan shrugged. "What would you have me do? She is a celebrant and stands as an equal. The Healing waggons are her domain. I cannot interfere."

"Cannot? Or will not?" Loni's voice tightened, the force within it rising. "My people are dying in her care! I will not have it."

Beside him, the flame on the altar flickered. Sedgan slammed his cup onto the chest. He nearly put out the lamp, but after the breeze passed, the light seemed brighter.

When he turned, Loni stood between him and the bed. The smoke from incense—he did not remember lighting any—swirled around her arms.

"Are you still so incompetent?" she cried, throwing her arms into the air and stirring the smoke. "How could I have expected anything of you? I showed you their corruption, Celebrant, and you did nothing! I handed you their lies, and you did nothing! Now I tell you of their fall from grace, and still you do nothing! You have fallen, Sedgan! Just like them, no one can save you!"

The accusation brought his blood to a boil. "You dare?"

 # Chapter 12

"Yes, I dare," Loni shot back hotly. "And that is what terrifies you! While your acolytes cower before you, I alone dare! You are out of favor, Sedgan. The prime protector sees it, the prince sees it, and I see it too! Fire has turned from you! You have fallen!"

He struck her with the back of his hand, knocking her from her feet.

"I should have put a knife in your chest when you were lying on the road outside of Vait," Sedgan told her as she lay sprawled half on the bed and half on the floor, sneering up at him. "It would have saved us all so much trouble!"

"Then who would save you, Sedgan?" Loni hissed with vehemence. "You are outside of the Goddess' light. How will you find it now? You are the heretic here, not me! You. Are. Nothing!"

It was easy, with her positioned next to the bed, for him to push her back. With the nearly forgotten blade of Inac in his hand, he shoved her against the mattress and held her down with his knees. Everything moved with ease and precision. His muscles remembered every gesture. Rather than stabbing clumsily, he brought the knife to her throat for a quick, easy kill.

He paused.

The rage had vanished from her eyes. In place of the fear he expected, Loni was smiling.

Only then did he recognize what he had done. The hand holding the knife stung from when he had struck her. The handle of the knife was hot in his grip.

"I was beginning to fear you would never use your knife again," she said.

The blade, golden and ruby red, was indeed in his hand for the first time in over a decade. His hand, regardless of his rage, was steady as it held the knife against her throat. Although his chest heaved and his heart pounded, his body felt solid. He remembered well the Warrior Queen's teachings.

It took a dozen breaths before he pulled the blade back. Sedgan's hand shook at once.

"Welcome back, Sedgan," Loni whispered.

It should have turned his stomach, but the wrath that had taken him felt more like an impassioned kiss. He had been trained to harness rage. When had he forgotten to use it?

 # Celebrant

"Now," she said with a fire in her eyes that stopped his breath entirely, "prove to me you have truly found my light."

He had leaned away from her but was in easy reach for her scarred hand to grab the cloth belt of his robes and pull him down. The feel of her body against his was enough to light a new fire within him, and for the first time, he did not try to smother the flames. While his eager hands sought the bottom of her skirts, she expertly had his belt undone. Soon he was vividly recalling the teachings of the Lady of Lust.

Chapter 13

Sedgan awoke in agony. For a long while, he lay on the bed, feeling as if he had a tent piton stabbing into the ridge of his nose. His head must have been wrapped in cloth; his senses were muffled, and his eyes were bleary when he tried them.

He had never been more hungover yet could not remember drinking. The pain intensified, and he had to roll over.

Although he normally slept without clothing, he felt unusually exposed when he moved. His head, he realized as he slowly sat up on the bed, was not the only thing that ached. Every muscle in his body seemed to protest his movement, but he could not feel or see any injury. It was just a headache, albeit a profound one. Still, unexpected muscles were sore as if he had been through a forced march the night before.

Across his tiny room, the light of Inac was on its final drop of oil, and Sedgan remembered that he had not refilled it. That it had lasted this long was a miracle.

A sense of duty drove him to stand. Atop the chest next to the altar, Sedgan found a jug of wine and a single cup. He almost put away the wine, but the pounding of his head made him fill and drain the clean cup twice over, hoping to subdue the hammers in his skull. He then located the jug of oil.

Once the lamp was filled, Sedgan chanced a look through the shutters of his only window and found himself looking at the paling darkness of near-dawn. It was time, as a Celebrant of Inac, to start the day.

Celebrant

Memories stirred as he replaced the wine and cup. Loni had visited the night before. She must have let herself out the same way she had let herself in, for he saw no sign of her. That she had not stolen the wine was a shock.

So too was what he had done the night before. But, on searching, he felt no guilt or shame. Instead, he was sated. He had not felt as content in years.

Not bothering to send for warm water, Sedgan let the chill of the water that had been standing overnight in a basin wake him. He was in the process of washing his neck, still trying to dismiss the dwindling ache of his head, when a new pain made him stop.

His chest felt as if it was on fire. Atop his sternum, a razing heat scalded into his skin. He pressed the wet sponge against the place, but the feeling intensified until he was on his knees, clutching at his chest with tears in his eyes.

He had no idea how long he knelt beside the altar in agony. Just when he felt he could take it no longer, the pain subsided. It was another long moment before he could bring himself to pull the sponge from his chest.

Side by side, two undulating strips of roasted skin made the mark of his goddess in his flesh.

Sedgan could not move.

When he finally gained control of his body, he pulled out a mirror to better examine the burn. There was no denying the scar. He had been branded. How? And when? He had felt sore upon waking, but not there and not with this intensity. The burn was fresh, as if having just occurred. The skin around was still crimson in protest.

The light on the altar seemed brighter than ever as he pulled his abandoned robes from the floor and dressed himself. He gingerly tugged the robes over his chest, hiding the brand, and headed out to the main Temple waggon.

Most of the acolytes were outside eating breakfast, but one sat beside the waggon exit, facing the door to Sedgan's room. Tamort rose as soon as Sedgan entered the main room.

"Are you all right, Celebrant?" he asked.

Chapter 13

Sedgan wondered if he had cried out when his chest was set afire, but he did not remember. "Fine, acolyte," he replied, his voice forcibly even. "Why are you not with the others?"

"We decided someone had to wait for you, Celebrant," the near-celebrant explained with an apologetic shrug that blamed the boys outside. "We heard shouting last night. We thought you alone after meeting with the other celebrants. The younger ones feared you had harmed yourself."

"None of you saw anyone else?" Sedgan asked. Tamort shook his head. "Then why worry? Do you not have faith in me anymore, Tamort?"

Tamort took a step back. "I believe in Fire. You have no reason to question my faith, Celebrant; I swear!"

"Good. Then you can run the noon service today. I have errands that need doing immediately. I will return to see how you manage."

He explained nothing to the rest of the acolytes as he passed them and set his path to Fixer City. He asked the first young woman he found to take him to Loni's campfire.

Dozens of women sat huddled by the fire the young girl indicated, but none of them were the red-haired woman he needed. As soon as they spotted him, the crowd of women rose to their feet.

"Celebrant Sedgan," a tall, thin woman called. "We are honored! Thank you, Celebrant. Thank you for coming."

A little taken aback by the sincerity of the welcome, Sedgan hesitated slightly as he asked, "I... I seek your celebrant. Where is Loni?"

Confused glances were exchanged until all turned to the tall woman.

"Is that not why you have come, Celebrant? We have been without prayers for the Lady of Fire since Celebrant Loni fell ill three days ago. We would attend service, but without her—"

"Ill? She is unwell?"

Tear-filled eyes stared back at him.

"She collapsed by the fire three days ago," the woman told him. "We took her to Healing Mother Vera's waggon, and she has been—"

"Go to Acolyte Tamort if you need to worship," Sedgan interrupted. "Someone show me where that Healing waggon is."

A short-haired girl took him to the Healing waggon on the edge of Fixer City, where she left him staring at a room of wounded and sick. He spotted two raggedly dressed women in vigil against the far wall, a red-haired woman on the floor between them. The crimson hue caught the slight light of the candles and glimmered like a ruby.

The moment he stepped into the waggon, Healing Mother Vera, recognizable by the embroidered leaves on her collar, was at his side.

"Welcome, Celebrant. How may I serve you today?"

Sedgan's eyes remained on the sleeping woman on the far side of the room. "The woman there," Sedgan replied, pointing, "the one with red hair—do you know her?"

The older woman glanced over the room. "She arrived yesterday. Those with her said she had collapsed and struck her head. The head injury itself is relatively minor, but she had been starved. We believe that weakness was the cause for her fall. She is lucky to have hit her head and been brought to us. Much longer of starving herself and she may have died. The women care for her." Her voice was a strong whisper designed to not disturb others.

Sedgan could not speak. Healing Mother Vera interpreted his silence as expectancy. She continued, "She has been recovering well and may leave here in another day or so. There are always visitors for her. I only wish more of those in my care were as pleasant to treat."

"She was here last night?" Sedgan finally managed. "You are certain?"

"Yes, since yesterday afternoon. She lacked the strength to stand, Celebrant."

The burn on his chest throbbed.

One final, desperate thought entered his mind—*it had to be a dream*. But no, the night before had left bruises and burns on his skin. But if Loni had not been strong enough to stand, she was not the one who visited him.

All he could do was curse, his legs suddenly weak. *Now, prove to me you have truly found my light,* echoed in his memory. *My light...Oh Goddess...Oh my Goddess, how did I not see? Is it possible it was you?*

A Goddess had walked among them, and only Sedgan had seen her. Now he bore her brand on his chest.

He must have paled, for Healing Mother Vera called over a cutter to help hold Sedgan up.

A voice interrupted from behind. "You are not welcome here, heretic! Treachery and lies are what you are about! Be off with you!"

 # Chapter 13

The challenge brought strength to Sedgan's limbs as he recognized Barga's strident bellows. His rage steadied his heartbeat with surprising speed. Inac was with him. There was no doubt of that now.

When he turned, his knife was in his hand. "I will go where I will, Earth. Those are my people in there."

And they were indeed his; even the red-haired whore was a part of Inac's people.

"*Your* people," Barga snarled, striding out from the Fixer City waggons and positioning herself at the base of the step into the Healing waggon. Her long hair lay pleated expertly and woven with Pari's flowers in readiness for a service. "Your people? I thought you mistrusted Earth! Did you not say our healing was bringing your people death? What are you doing here?"

"He is merely inquiring after a member of his gathering, Celebrant," Healing Mother Vera interrupted gently from beside Sedgan. "I fail to—"

"That is not what he is doing!" Barga shouted. "He is spinning lies! He is seeking another knife to put in my side! I will not have you manipulating my people, Sedgan. You are not welcome here! None of your kind are welcome here! Any who bears the candle of Inac can find their care elsewhere. I shall close the Healing waggons to your people."

"You cannot!" Sedgan objected.

"I just did," she snapped and, with a lumbering swing of her robes, she spun on her heels and stormed off. Likely she was seeking someone who would be able to move him from his place in the doorway. His knife was still in his hand; she would be unable to do it herself.

"We will not allow that, Celebrant," came a soft, but firm, voice beside him. When he turned to Healing Mother Vera, her pale eyes were shooting daggers at Barga's back. "Our oath does not permit it. We are Facets of the Healing Spirit. Pari forbids us from turning away any who need our aid."

"Her oath forbids what she just did as well," he pointed out, but the old woman merely shrugged, her flower-patterned shawl drooping off her shoulders.

"Then one of us is right and the other is wrong. Now go see your friend before the celebrant returns with help."

Celebrant

With Vera urging him along, Sedgan found himself at Loni's side. The sad eyes of the other two women brightened upon his arrival. They lowered their heads in prayer as he knelt beside them.

Half-closed, emerald green eyes looked up at Sedgan from the floor. The burn on his chest throbbed, and he covered the wound with his hand reflexively.

Loni smiled weakly, her face drawn. She had lost weight since he had seen her last.

Seen her last, Sedgan thought. *Since last night.*

"You look different," Loni said. "Something about you has changed."

When first they had met, Loni had been lying across a bridge in the path of the marching army, claiming she would move only for one who bore "her mark." Her scarred hand, burned in the same double-flame pattern as Sedgan had seen on Prince Tohmas' foot, now matched the scar on Sedgan's chest.

"I bear your mark," Sedgan answered. Then, Prince Tohmas' confession had brought Loni to her feet. Sedgan hoped that the effect here would be the same.

Her eyes widened, and a smile bloomed on her face. A feeble laugh escaped her. "I knew you had not fallen too far!" she told him, placing her scarred hand on his arm, the flame mark prominent on the back of her hand. "I knew you would find the light once more! Our Lady is so strong. I knew she would bring you back!"

"Stand with me, Loni.," Sedgan said. "Barga has gone too far. We must stop the corruption of the others. Stand with me to bring Fire to them. Will you serve the Goddess now?"

With thin arms, she pushed herself up from the bed and, assisted, staggered to her feet. Although she teetered, she stood under her own power when Healing Mother Vera came over.

"Another day of rest would do her well," she lightly objected, but Sedgan could tell the old woman was not going to stop them. Barga was going to return with followers of her own shortly, which would endanger Vera's patients.

"I will see she gets rest and good food," Sedgan promised the grandmotherly woman.

"We have much to do." Loni explained. Each step seemed to give her strength as she made her way to the exit. They were outside under the

 # Chapter 13

sun when she stopped and whispered in his ear, "Fire will cleanse those who have fallen. It will be as the Goddess wills."

He saw no reason to disagree.

Despite the battles at Barrow Hills and BellRoost, Lance's fyrd of Gaidolons were still assigned watch with another fyrd. It could have been because they simply needed the additional people to ensure all watch points were covered, but Lance knew his people thought it was because of distrust.

They were Gaidolons and under the control of another prince. They could never be truly part of Tohmas' loyal Galanth fighters.

But the defense of Espar against foreign invaders was reason enough to be manning the wooden fortifications for long candles of time. They had a chance to shoot an arrow or two to discourage a sneaking Northlander scout early in the day, but as the sun sank on the horizon and their shift came to an end, that seemed to be the end of it.

"Keep to your post," Lance corrected a pair of restless members of the Fyrd of Arrow. The end of the shift was the worst for attentiveness. Their minds were probably already on dinner and a footbath. He'd heard some soldiers talking about an intrepid Fixer City worker who had single-handedly filled a barrel with fresh water from the lake and kept it warm with coals. More than one soldier was ready for the luxury and keen to be first in line.

The two younger soldiers straightened and stopped fidgeting, but they looked at Lance, not down the slope they were meant to be monitoring.

Understandable. Nothing had moved in the Northlander camp for some time. Although he rotated between the barricades and ridges to keep the fyrd on their toes, even he had no reason to think anyone would dare try the hill today. They Northlanders had been lightly bloodied three days earlier at the river ambush, which his fyrd got to hear about but not see themselves. The enemy had made good time marching to "corner" the Esparan forces on the hill but had arrived only the night before. They had been setting up their defenses all day.

Lance sighed, checking the sun's position as he joined Guardian Rusk. Most of the partnered Fyrd of Traiton were with their Guardian already, arranged behind a row of boulders the soldiers had dubbed "the Knuckles." It was an enviable position for the scattered members of Lance's fyrd who were lying or crouched farther down the slope.

"Eager to get back to some fires?" Lance asked the guardian, pointedly looking at the milling soldiers. Not one of them had an eye downhill. Rusk himself leaned against the middle knuckle of the row of boulders, his back to the hill entirely. The man sported a long strip of green—possibly a repurposed rank rope from a protector—over his right eye where he'd been injured at BellRoost. Although it was not swollen anymore, the man still smelled like crusted blood.

"Those antler-heads don't even have themselves organized yet," Rusk groused, then spat. "They won't be making any runs up here for days more."

It was true; the Northlanders had felled a section of trees on the next rise and were still turning them into logs and firewood. They had a low-lying location suited to trenching—a fine way to prevent horse charges—but had only started a shallow trench nearest the river. No new tents had been dug since the night before as far as Lance knew, and the campfire count hadn't changed either. Nothing had changed since midday. He could still smell their cooking fires, although the scent had ceased making his stomach growl.

But there was still a risk, and if the Northlanders surprised the fyrds on watch, the entire camp would be at risk. Lance could not find a way to point this out to Rusk without causing offense or undermining the man's position in front of his soldiers.

The smell of roasting meat against filtered through the cracks of the Knuckles, same as before.

Exactly as before.

Walking away from Guardian Rusk as the man started complaining about something irrelevant, Lance crouched at the pinky stone of the knuckles. He peered around it cautiously.

Nothing had changed. People milled belong, digging a trench that never got bigger, sawing logs that were never finished, and mounting barricades that never got bigger. And it still smelled like lunchtime.

"That ain't right," he muttered.

 # Chapter 13

Lance left Rusk and his fyrd and skirted to another post farther down the hill. Rushed, he did not take the path from cover to cover, but dashed across open ground where he had to. He ducked into the lowest post, having to crawl on his belly to stay below the rise.

Two Gaidolon guardsmen had volunteered for the post, knowing it was the most vital first-warning in the defense of the camp. Lance knew both well—Shinat and Carthy.

Both lay on their bellies, eyes on the hill, Carthy angled to the left and Shinat to the right. Lance came up between them.

The smell of cooking was less powerful here.

"Something's bugging me," he said.

Shinat grunted, his frown made longer by the droop of his long, blond moustache.

"Looks fine," Carthy replied, although he didn't take his eyes off the rocks and grasses he was on watch over. "All's quiet. I'm getting hungry. I thought you were retrieving us. Pretty dumb for a High Guardsman to do it himself. Wouldn't put it past you though."

Shinat grunted again.

"Doesn't look fine," Lance corrected, ignoring the jibe. He had known these two since his youth training as a guardsman, and they had been willing to disobey Prince Dorakon to continue serving Lance. He expected the attitude.

"No shift change," Lance pointed out. "In fact, very little change at all."

"And that's a problem?" Carthy asked. He edged over, trying to follow Lance's stare down to the Northlander camp. They were a hundred paces up the hill, close enough to see the color of the pelt tents, but not close enough to see any details about the people moving around them.

"Well it ain't normal," Lance grumbled.

"Let's check it out." Shinat's voice was as deep as a drum.

Lance nodded and sucked in a breath. If he was wrong, he would be putting himself and two friends in danger for no reason. He might get them all killed. He wondered what Guardian Rusk would tell Prince Tohmas if that happened. Crazy Gaidolons, taking risks and trying to make a name for themselves.

But it had to be done.

Lance pulled off his blue tabard, as did the other two, careful not to lift above the rise that hid them. Rolling through the dirt, they muddied their clothing to blend in a bit better with the hillside, although the sheep-grazed grasses would betray them. The light was low and would only improve their concealment.

It was going to be tricky to get back. But Carthy and Shinat did not hesitate. One by one, they snuck out of the cover and made their slow way down.

Much of the progress was made on their bellies, slithering like snakes between stones and shrubs. They moved slowly where they had to and kept to the shadows provided by the sunset and the slope of the hill.

When they were a dozen paces farther down the hill, everything changed.

Shadows of sunset were replaced by brilliant light. The lightly manned, half-built barricades on the edge of the quiet camp were suddenly complete and hidden behind a smoldering line of fire. Esparans and Northlanders fanned the fires until they blazed and rose, pushed by the increasing wind up toward the hill camp.

Shinat was a man of few words. He never used two words when one would do, as the expression went. But it was the big man's deep voice behind Lance cursing.

They had been tricked. Illusion or its ilk made the camp viewed from afar very different from the one Lance now saw. Most importantly, the fire was already underway, and the forces atop the hill were blissfully unaware.

Lance rolled onto his back and pulled his horn to his lips. He blasted a warning at full volume.

"Move it!" he called. There was no point in hiding. The fire would not care.

Breaking from the cover of the shrubs, Carthy, Shinat, and Lance ran back up, Lance blaring out the warning again and again between breaths. He had no idea what could be done about the wall of flames heading their way, but they had to try something. Their backs were to the lake cliffs. They had nowhere to go.

Horns answered his, confirming the forces were assembling and ready for attack. By the time Lance reached the brow of the hill, having

Chapter 13

called his fyrd away from the defenses to distance them from the fires, the illusion had been dropped. The raging fire climbed the hill in full view, the smell of cooking fires replaced by burning brush.

"Demons," Lance panted out, hands on his knees as he looked back the way he had come. His had not noticed how his legs burned from the sprint uphill until he stopped. The fire was already past the Knuckles vantage point and rising rapidly.

"Now what?" Carthy asked, having kept pace in the retreat. With his long strides, he could have left Lance behind, but guardsmen worked together, always.

Lance turned to search the rise where they had stopped, "Now, we hope we have someone with brains in charge. That, or we pray for a miracle." He did not see the princes or their allies. A wizard might help. Or at least…

Tohmas' booming voice rang out, the Prince of Galanth directing his protectors. He even had the Celebrant of Inac at his side.

Maybe we'll get both.

Lance left the rise to go help.

Chapter 14

When the sun rose over the tree lines and brought sparkles onto the lake below, Tohmas woke to find the enemy entrenched in the north slope of the hill.

The Northlanders had made good time over night, defeating the ambushes Tohmas set along their path. Looking none the worse for wear, the Northlanders and their allies now held the egress from the hill.

That much had been expected.

Tohmas spent the day watching the enemy. Mixed tents, combining cloth and pole with bone and pelts, dotted the lowlands to the north. The rise by the woods had been cleared of trees, the wood going to the barricades now separating them.

It was a day of inaction. He retired late as the wind picked up over the hill, carving long ripples across the lake.

Celebrant Loni met him at his tent. He had heard of her illness of late, although she looked hale now. She had been seen with Celebrant Sedgan more than once since they settled on the hill. He imagined Sedgan was the reason for her health and vigor now.

"This night is power," she said, standing among uneasy protectors under the moonlight. The moon was full enough to cast bright light across the camp, alleviating the need for torches, yet Loni still stood with a shielded lamp. It flickered dangerously low, making the gold on her crimson dance clothes look muted.

Chapter 14

"Have you words of wisdom for me, Celebrant of Fire?" he asked, unsure what she expected of him. Although he knew her mind was unstable at times, Tohmas needed Inac's favor, so he continued to heed Loni as a conduit of the Goddess.

High clouds passed over the moon, casting shadows. Her lamp flickered as a gust slipped between the cracks of the shielding.

"It will be as Fire dictates. Tonight, they all burn."

With nothing else forthcoming from the woman, Tohmas entered the tent, seeking the altar. A prayer seemed prudent.

As he settled onto his knees before the flame of Inac, a horn sounded an alarm. He rushed back out, his leather armor still on and his sword immediately in hand. He passed Celebrant Loni as he headed for a vantage point by the light of the moon, aware that she followed him but unconcerned by it.

Reaching a high point from which he could view the slopes facing the entrenched enemy, at first he saw nothing. The alarm sounded again, the Fyrd of Arrow identifying itself as the source. But the warning was only that an attack approached. Tohmas saw no threat.

But as he watched, embers became visible half way up the slope, blown up the hill by the evening wind. Following behind, fires appeared.

His heart sank. He had planned everything about the camp on the hill, knowing water would be available and how to get supplies into the camp. He needed only to buy time for other arrangements to be made. It had seemed perfect.

But with the wind rustling the grasses from north to south, he had accidentally given his enemy an opportunity.

The concealing magic released and the fire appeared in its entirety. Snakes of fire thickened as they climbed the hill he was on, dark smoke above.

Was this what Celebrant Loni meant? Was this Inac's support come manifest or a warning that he had lost her favor? He was torn.

But if his forces faced fire, he had to defend them. Thankfully, "Lady's Skirts" was Rydan in origin. Tohmas knew the counter.

"Same as last time," Tohmas shouted at the protectors. "Pairs with torches. Burn a line in front of the defenses and drive it downhill. Use coats, branches, blankets, anything. All of you, *geddit*!"

People scrambled to carry out the orders. Blessedly, torches were soon visible among the protectors, lit from the campfires within the camp. The protectors rushed along the brow of the hill, sharing the plan and getting into position.

Tohmas peered into the rising smoke, squinting. The grasses here were dry, but they were not kindling thanks to the rain the day before. Yet the fires caught readily and advanced as if flowing up the hill. It struck him as unnatural.

"Kit!" Tohmas called, turning in search.

"Here," Kitable's voice replied. The wizard stood in the trampled grasses Tohmas had checked just moments before, his long cloak flapping in the wind. "I didn't see it, my Prince. I am sorry. They hid it with illusions, and I did not see it."

Tohmas shrugged aside the apology. "Doesn't matter now. Can you slow it?"

Before Tohmas could finish the question, Kitable briskly moved away. It took Tohmas a moment to realize why; Celebrant Loni was still at Tohmas' back, her lamp providing a small glow as she wordlessly observed. A breeze passed, smelling of ocean spray.

Once he had distanced himself adequately, the wizard returned to business as if nothing was amiss.

"They're summoning wind to drive the flames," Kitable informed Tohmas, his voice curt. He lifted a hand and said a soft word. The fires fell back slightly and drifted along the slope like a trail avoiding the steepest sections. "I blocked it, but they'll try again. We need to set a wall up, or those fires will be atop you before you have enough room to burn a buffer."

The two other Princes of Espar arrived as Kitable began casting. The light of the torches they brought with them rendered Loni's lamp redundant.

Tohmas was grateful to see Prince Sol join him, for that meant Master Clarin attended as well. He had never expected to be grateful for the wizard.

When no one growled at his arrival, however, Tohmas realized Carsh was not with him. Where had the prime protector gone?

Unlike Kitable, Master Clarin stood oblivious beside the Untouchable celebrant and stared down at the fires.

 # Chapter 14

A line of fire, starting as a smolder in front of the defenses, began to advance against the wind with the help of the Galanth soldiers. Fighting against them, a gust of dry wind smelling of horses kicked up the hill.

Once his fire burned a strip along the brow of the hill, there would be nothing the Northlander's fire to burn. Halted by the lack of fuel, it would never reach the camp. The space needed to be wide enough to prevent the fire from skipping over it, but he did not think he had enough time.

Kitable spoke, and the wind died back down to the water-laden breeze that Tohmas assumed was natural.

Prince Rairn, his jaw set tight, growled like a bear from beside Tohmas. "I warned you about putting your back to the wall," he said, quiet enough to fall short of most of the onlookers.

"There is a counter," Tohmas replied, the words like curses. He did not have the time, or patience, to deal with Rairn's grousing.

"Force Wall?" Clarin asked, joining Kitable on Tohmas' other side. Loni joined the line of the wizards and princes at the brow of the hill.

Kitable nodded. "Only thing that'll hold it off entirely. We'll need extensions. Actually..." Tohmas found Kitable's stare upon him. "My Prince, could you call for the Weavers?"

He wanted to ask why Kitable did not do it himself, but they had little time. Not sure what Kitable was planning, Tohmas pulled a token from his belt and sent a runner into camp for the father and daughter pair. The runner left at a sprint.

Clarin's expression fell. "The apothecaries? What possible use are they?"

Kitable stiffened. "I told you not to underestimate them," he replied, glancing over at the Prime Protector of Solta.

The color drained from Kitable's face, and he took a step away so rapidly it had to be involuntary. Loni had stepped forward, a beseeching hand raised to him.

"A kiss for luck," she offered.

"Do not lay even a finger on me!" Kitable held his hands out, his calm lost.

Clarin responded with an amused, unimpressed snort. "You would jump at your own shadow," he asked with a scoff. The Celebrant of Inac, recognizing her opportunity, slid up to the Soltan. "I will happily accept the favor of—"

Before Tohmas could speak, Loni laid a kiss on Master Clarin's cheek. "*D'aems*," Tohmas cursed.

Clarin froze, shock flooding over his features in place of the smug grin he had worn. He looked down at his hands then peered at Kitable with his mouth agape. "What have—?"

Interrupting him, Shimmer Weaver crested the small hill. The moment she spotted Loni, she skittered away, her hands up as if warding off bad luck. She ran backward into her father as he tried to attend the summons as well, making him flounder and spin in place before retreating to join his colorfully clad daughter.

They, unlike Clarin, knew the danger the Untouchable represented. They would not make the same mistake.

Inac's blessings were mixed this evening. Was she seeking to help or hinder him?

Either way, he could not have his casters dispelled if he was to defend his camp.

"Celebrant," Tohmas intervened, gently guiding the woman to the side by the shoulder before she decided Shimmer and Dust needed her attention, "will you entreat to Inac on our behalf? We would appreciate any help you can give in calming the flames."

"Yes," Loni said, her eyes staring into the distance. Tohmas was not entirely certain she was speaking to him at all. "There is much to do this night. The fires will cleanse."

With strides made long by her self-importance, Loni marched down the hill toward Fixer City. Tohmas felt a spike of doubt, wondering if he had dismissed the one person who could truly assist him in knowing Inac's desires. *What did she mean?*

Clarin's voice cut through his thoughts. "You knew!" he accused Kitable now that Loni was gone. "That vile—"

"Any further comments," Kitable interrupted, his head snapping back to the fires as the blaze rose again under apparent magic influence, "will make her power all too obvious. Shut up, Clarin. If you do not have a Force Wall, cast a Transfer. I have four Force Walls."

"I have two," Shimmer Weaver offered shyly. She lowered her head and looked up through darkly painted eyelashes. "Just Anan's Force

Chapter 14

Wall, right?" For a woman Tohmas had seen dancing around fires after dark, it was odd to see her bashful.

Dust Weaver coughed nervously. "I, sadly, do not have that spell hovering. I also don't know it well enough to cast from memory."

Kitable addressed the three casters in a strong, artificial voice, reminding Tohmas of a Rydan's approach. Kitable did not want to be seen as weak before those who may challenge him.

"I will stand center. I want a Weaver on each side of me. Master Clarin, move to the end of the line after you cast the Transfer. Dust Weaver, can you cast a Transfer, or do I need to do it for you?"

"That one I know," the apothecary confirmed.

"Good. We hold as long as possible to give our fire a chance to make space. Start casting."

Feeling useless, Tohmas looked again for Carsh. Although he strained his senses, Tohmas was blind to the passage of power around him. He would have appreciated Carsh's perspective on the castings.

Shimmer Weaver cast her spells with single words, her hands outstretched. Kitable cast twice in rapid succession The other two casters waved their arms in a synchronized fashion. Each then took turns touching the Galanth wizard on the back of his neck before moving to their places. After only one final glance to confirm their positions, Kitable cast for a third time.

The four casters formed a line, a dozen paces between them each, their hands raised out as if pushing a wall. The magic itself was invisible and silent. Without Carsh to warn him, Tohmas could not tell where the magic was or even if the wizards had done anything but speak nonsense.

But the fire at the bottom of the hill stopped advancing, and the flames rose to the sky as if trying to climb a cliff.

What does Inac think of that?

The new line of fire slowly crept down the hill with the help of the desperate soldiers waving clothes and branches.

Tohmas searched again around him. *Where is Carsh?*

Celebrant

The air felt wrong.

Carsh crouched on the cliff overlooking the long drop to the dark waters of the lake, sniffing the wind. The chill warned of a season's change. In the night, the clouds above were nothing but darkness hiding the stars. They moved through rapidly on high, strong winds.

But down near the grass, it felt wrong.

Sabian had followed Carsh and crouched nearby against a waggon wheel. The only thing the Esparan boy fought now was sleep, his head bobbing low, then, with a jerk, righting itself. In between, he narrowed his eyes on Carsh, filled with questions but not bothering to ask, knowing Carsh would not answer. He had to learn by watching.

And for that, he would have to keep his drooping eyelids open.

A gust picked up, but unlike the brisk early breeze, it was warm.

It was as if there were two winds blowing. Something was wrong.

The alarm horns rang out, and Carsh stood up, peering into the distance. A glare of light was growing up the hill, and the breeze brought the scent of smoke. Fire. It was too far away to be within the camp but...

All thoughts cut off when Carsh sensed the flare of powerful magic nearby. He first thought of Kitable and, for a rare moment, hesitated.

But the person who appeared at the corner of the nearby command tent was smaller than Kitable and wore a long, black cloak over her clothing. Kitable would never be seen without his green and silver.

Carsh attacked. Only after throwing his first knife did he realize the woman was not alone. A handful of hulking shadows, likely burly Northlander warriors, accompanied her.

His knife stuck a magic defense and was slapped aside with a flash of blue light. The woman caster cursed as he dove after her.

It was the same flyer he had fought on the bridge outside BellRoost, the one who had burned him. This time, he would take her down.

The moonlight, briefly free of the high clouds, flashed off the sharp edge of an ax in Carsh's path. He slid under it, already armed with a knife in each hand. He raked low with his knives but caught only fur on the blades' edges, cutting into the thick pelt boots of his enemy instead of their flesh.

In the next heartbeat, the moon was enshrouded once more, casting the region into pure blackness. Carsh worked by his ears, following

  # Chapter 14

the rush of air and the grunt of the fighters as he planned his way to the caster.

Magic rolled toward him, heavy as an avalanche to his senses. He caught a large warrior around the middle, rotated behind him, and used him as a shield against the powers. The magic fell short, and Carsh used the moment to dig his knife into the side of the enemy. Feeling a presence at his back, he released the knife to dodge aside.

A glow rose on the horizon behind Carsh, and Carsh finally could see his enemies. The Northlanders surrounded their little caster with muscle and fur, giving him no access. He had driven them away from the command tent, cornering them between him and the cliff's edge.

And Sabian, Carsh abruptly remembered. The boy had positioned himself on the flank, and although Carsh could not see any injuries on his opponents, Sabian's knife was bloodied. At least one Northlander watched the boy warily as if surprised a colt had a strong kick.

In response to the dimming light, the caster spoke a word, and a light, like a handful of firebugs bound in a ring, rose above them. It hovered there, casting a red light over their gathering.

"Kill him," she commanded the fighters with her.

Carsh smiled. Her light had made it clear how outnumbered he was, but it also gave him a much better view for throwing his knives.

They charged him, three brutes with axes and rough swords. With a flick of his hands, he answered them with three well-placed knives.

The warriors fell, each pierced through the eye. Carsh skipped over them to launch himself at the caster.

Sabian joined him, attacking a Northlander and surprising the brute back. Ducking and swinging his feet—a move Carsh was proud to have taught him just that morning—Sabian caught the Northlander's legs. The opponent stumbled and put his weight on the edge of the cliff. The dry ground gave away. The enemy fell.

His scream made the caster turn, her long hair spinning behind her. Carsh grabbed her blond locks and yanked.

To his surprise, she pulled down and bent double. He saw her decadence—jewels and precious metals decorated her fine dress. They pulsed as magic to Carsh's senses.

Roaring as loud as the falling man had, she pivoted and slammed the heel of her hand into Carsh's side. He cut across the attack to stop her, but the blade rolled over her skin without contact, defeated by the magic surrounding her. Still, the impact of the strike pushed her blow off its course. Instead of slamming into his belly below his ribcage, it glanced off his hip.

Power shot through him, and a jolt like lightning sent him flying to the side. For a moment, all the darkness left, and Carsh saw only screaming white brightness.

The world spun as he opened his eyes. The ring of firebug lights hovering over the cliff flickered like a campfire. Four more Northlanders were between him and the cliff. He had a fistful of torn, blond hair in his grip. Through the pain of his aching muscles, he sensed magic moving away. She was heading for the command tent.

Tohmas would not be in the tent with the alarms sounding in the distance. But Carsh had to stop her anyway. First, he had to deal with the four Northlanders who had moved in to protect her.

He pushed himself up, amazed that he was allowed to stand without being attacked. When the swimming of his vision finally settled, he saw Sabian had taken up a place covering Carsh as he lay prone. The Northlanders held their axes up, using the blades as shields in case another knife sought their eye sockets. If ever they adjusted to strike, Sabian flicked his fingers in readiness, and they replaced their defenses, fearful of the throw that would end them.

It was a bluff, but an effective one. They had no way of knowing the boy had only begun his training with Carsh. His aim was good, but it would not be so perfect.

But, outnumbered as he was, Sabian's help was appreciated, especially as Carsh's right leg tingled still from the impact of the lightning.

Side by side, they faced the Northlanders.

Loni entered the Temple waggon circle at a brisk pace. The low campfire, kept burning overnight by acolytes of Inac, was down to embers as Sedgan sat beside it, a goblet of red wine in hand. The other celebrants were gone, the doors of their waggons closed for the night. Ocea's service had ended, and the altar to the midnight goddess was back in the waggon. The last of the worshipers, always few for the midnight service,

 # Chapter 14

had left for their homes. It was only her, the acolyte tending the fire, and Sedgan.

As she instructed, Sedgan awaited her return by the fire. *And to think he once had called me "heretic."* Now, he understood the truth.

She was the will of Inac.

She marched up to the Celebrant of Inac and commanded, "Now."

Sedgan swallowed the rest of the goblet of wine and rose. "Very well," he replied.

He left the fire.

Perfect. The goddess' will would be done now, with Loni as her right hand and Sedgan as her left. All the world would remember Inac's glory, and *only* her glory.

Chapter 15

The thick pelts guarded the Northlander from Sabian's short knives. He knew he was not as accurate as Carsh at a distance, and he had only two knives left, having broken one and lost the other already.

These Northlanders were something else—more powerful, more thickly muscled. He had expected enemies similar to the battle into BellRoost, but these were far more skilled than the masses Sabian had fought then. They used their axes as shield and sword in one. Sabian had failed to get through the defense. Hells, the only cut he scored was on his own knife when his blow had been knocked so far wide that he'd sliced the back of his opposite hand.

Hitting them was like striking a tree. He expected they'd bleed about as much.

It was insane to stand against four of them, yet he did. He had finally gotten Carsh to accept him as possibly worth effort. He was not willing to lose that opportunity because of some oaf in antlers, and he certainly could not let them gut Carsh while he was down.

Like the gambling games with Torbi at home, Sabian bluffed. He crouched as Carsh had, held his knives the same way, and threatened every one of the four with his knives if they let their guard down.

Finally, Carsh regained his feet.

"*Ohnennohn*," Carsh said, matching Sabian's stance at his side, his knives at the ready again.

Chapter 15

Rydans were nothing if not stubborn. There would be no retreat; Rydans did not surrender.

Carsh threw a knife and drew a fresh one in the same motion from his baldric. The blade, longer than Sabian's by a finger's breadth, caught in the leggings of the Northlander on the right. The man flinched and cried out but kept his feet despite how blood soon soaked through the furs.

Carsh threw another and caught a Northlander in the wrist below his enormous ax. The man ripped the knife aside and made to charge in, but he darted back when Sabian edged forward to strike from the side.

Both sides paused.

A cry went up from the command tent's entrance, and the woman—Sabian assumed she was a wizard by the way Carsh tried to kill her—came back into sight.

"Forget it!" she shouted. "To me!"

The four Northlanders stepped back, refusing to turn from the threat of Carsh and Sabian, and retreating, step by step. The moment they were within reach, the woman started speaking words Sabian did not understand.

Carsh roared in fury and launched a full handful of knives. Following up, he charged after the Northlanders, but it was too late; they vanished. The blades clattered to the grass and stones, passing through where the enemy had been. One blade skipped off a stone and fell from the cliff to be lost to the waters below.

With the caster gone, the fire ring light winked out, plunging them into a strange early-dawn sort of light.

No sun was rising. The firelight from the hill was intensifying.

Carsh cursed the escape of the wizard with variants on the usual words that Sabian had never heard. Growling under his breath, he retrieved the knives he could, even giving Sabian back one of his.

Sabian waited for his Leader, not sure what to do. The threat appeared to have passed, but there were still cries coming from the distance and smoke in the air. He wasn't sure he was allowed to ask what the next step was, but one thing could not go unsaid.

"There were nine."

Carsh cocked his head.

Celebrant

Three had died under Carsh's knives. One had fallen from the cliffs. Four had escaped. But there had been nine Northlanders with the caster.

"Nine," Sabian repeated, "plus the caster." Sensing Carsh did not understand, Sabian explained, "One did not go with her."

Carsh fell back into a fighting stance and sniffed the air. Sabian followed suit, but all he smelled was smoke.

They circled the tent, Carsh hovering around the entrance the longest. At length, he entered in, keeping low. He had a long sticking knife in one hand, his other still armed with a throwing knife.

When they passed by a pile of sleeping furs, Carsh lunged.

The furs rose up, a small Northlander suddenly coming to his feet. Unlike the larger ax-wielding companions, this Northlander was as short as the caster had been. But what he lacked in strength, he gained in speed. Before Sabian could blink, the Northlander struck Carsh twice.

The fight reminded Sabian of Carsh's spars with Prince Tohmas in the mornings—fast and furious, both parties familiar with their weapons. The thick furs protected the Northlander, catching Carsh's thrown knife. Keeping out of reach of Carsh's long knife, the Northlander returned the throw, forcing Carsh to dodge. When a second followed, Carsh caught it, replacing his lost knife.

The Northlander assassin retreated a step onto the bed of furs.

Sabian was certain getting involved would see him killed. He could not match this pace.

Instead, Sabian grabbed a large handful of the furs on the ground and pulled sharply. The sleeping furs shifted. The enemy stumbled.

Carsh was ready. His long knife slipped between the Northlander's ribs and into the heart of the assassin.

The man fell dead, blood seeping into the trampled grasses and dirt.

Carsh checked the body, confirming it would not rise. Satisfied, he snorted and wiped his knife on the dead Northlander. Then he met Sabian's eyes.

"*Gohd*," he said simply.

Sabian took a long breath. His hands were shaking now that it was done, and he clenched them, hiding the tremors from his Leader.

Questions filled Sabian's head as he followed Carsh out. Where had the protectors gone? Had the caster killed them? Didn't Kitable's magic protect Prince Tohmas' tent? Was that why the caster had come?

 # Chapter 15

But he voiced none of the questions. Instead, he accompanied Carsh to the great wall of fire nearing the camp.

At first, Kitable thought it would be enough. Although he had not been confident about calling on the Weavers, they proved themselves useful by holding the enemy's fire at bay as it grew. While the Force Wall required concentration to hold, both apothecaries handled it well.

He had expected the enemy caster would try to disrupt the Force Walls, either by attacking the casters or by disrupting the tether by binding a caster to an open spell, but nothing came of it. Instead, using a fraction of the magic that countering the Walls would, a series of Wind Creation spells drove the fires on. They were so brief, Kitable often failed to identify them before they vanished, leaving him no opportunity to dispel them.

It was a frustratingly effective strategy for his enemy to use. Most of the power facing the Force Wall was that of the fires themselves, goaded on occasionally by wind. Kitable's options were limited. Smothering the fires, summoning water to quench them, or trying to destroy them ... all his alternatives resulted in one thing—enervation. The affected area was massive, and so was the energy required to undo the damage. If Kitable expended himself, his enemy would be all too happy to attack him.

It took less energy to simply deal with the leading edge of the fire and keep it back.

For now.

As the fire continued to lash into the Force Walls, Kitable wondered if they would have enough time at all. The Weavers held, sweat showing on their faces, with their arms raised firmly. They would not last much longer.

Kitable turned his head to check on Clarin just in time to see a darting black cloud of magic strike Clarin across the brow. Clarin collapsed, taking his length of wall with him.

Attacking the casters it is then.

Clarin had been dispelled; his usual defenses were lacking. The Northlander casters had expended nearly no energy to land a powerful blow against Clarin.

Celebrant

Given sudden freedom, the fire flared up through the gap. A shout from the apothecary's daughter answered. A new Force Wall snapped into position, and the fire struck the smooth surface that glowed green under Kitable's enchanted sight.

Two spells, she had said. The Weaver had cast the second Force Wall with impressive speed and accuracy. As far as Kitable could tell, her new addition was perfectly angled to attach to the others while blocking the flames that had moved up the hill by a stride.

Holding both walls under the stress of the fire, however, was too much. The girl fell back a step and was soon kneeling with both her hands above her head, the tether between her and the walls pulsing with her channeled energy.

"Shim!" the father's voice called. Dust blindly rummaged through his pouch for something. The hand still raised to maintain the Force Wall twitched. "She will not hold. You take this part! I'll boost her." Without waiting for confirmation, Dust dropped his section of the Force Wall and sprinted to his daughter.

The fire flared through the opening Dust's departure created. Kitable activated his last Force Wall to block it.

The force almost knocked him over. He did not blame the girl for struggling. If he was having trouble, the effect on a mere dabbler would be infinitely worse.

But he held without failing and watched as the father placed gentle hands on his daughter's wrists and cast a Boost that would link their energies. Drawing new energy from her father, Shimmer Weaver stabilized.

None of them moved for what felt like an eternity. With his hands beginning to tremble, Kitable finally asked, "Do you have enough room yet, my Prince?"

"The bigger the gap, the better, Kit."

Kitable took that to mean "no."

He could push it longer if he had to, but what about the other two? An open spell was dangerous; if a caster pulled more magic than they could handle, the consequences would be disastrous. Casters, instead of falling unconscious or even dying on the spot, were known to simply vanish. As no one had ever returned from such a fate, they were assumed to be consumed by the magic powers they had sought to control.

 # Chapter 15

It seemed very likely that by the time Kitable reached that limit, the Weavers would have long since passed theirs.

They had not yet complained, nor had they dropped the spell. Were they willing to die to hold on? If Kitable held much longer, he would find out.

The ache of his muscles had started by the time the girl further slumped. It had to be good enough. Kitable was unwilling to be responsible for the death, or disappearance, of two people who were trying to help. And if he pushed himself much harder, he would be vulnerable to attack as well.

"Let it go," he called as he dropped the Force Wall. When he lowered his arms, his hands shook.

The girl fell instantly backward into her father's arms, and the older man slipped something into her mouth. From where he was, Kitable was uncertain how conscious the girl was.

The line of fire being driven down the hill was a dozen paces farther along, a stripe of burned, trampled land behind it. The fire at the base was significantly larger. Unleashed, it leaped forward like a mountain cat. The Galanth soldiers who had been driving the fires down fled to the camp, where they stood and watched.

The Northlander's fire blended into the Galanth's, and there, on the edge of the stretch of burnt land, it paused, having nothing to burn.

The Galanth army held its breath.

Magic flared nearby. Kitable ducked low to avoid it, but it adjusted its trajectory to follow as if guided visually. Instead of meeting his outermost defenses, the attack burrowed *through* the shield. As it passed through, another layer was revealed, another attack, that moved through the next shield. One by one, layers of the spell were revealed, each a destruction designed to bring down all his defenses. With his enchanted sight, the glittering arrow-like spell was as bright as a falling star.

Snapping a word of activation, Kitable threw a decoy into the path of the spell. It failed. He thought to try a dispel, but reading the auras proved the attack was defended against such a tactic. His chest clenched. The attack was meant to bind him. And if the enemy had an anchor, it would take only a thought for deadly magic to follow.

Celebrant

In desperation, Kitable grabbed an enchanted trinket from his belt, not caring which it was. He brought the pendant—it was one for amplifying distant things—into the path of the arrow of magic.

It crashed into the pendant and stopped, unable to destroy the alteration magic. Alteration was not the next layer meant to be present.

The final burst of magic fell from the attack, wasted and lost as it floundered against the final Molded Shield spell. His enemy had known his defenses thoroughly and planned for every every layer. Even some of his hidden spells had been known.

Kitable cast rapidly, not having what he needed in his hovering spells. He left the hole in his defenses, knowing only his Molded Shield protected him from a well-aimed shot.

The spell he formed coalesced and, ready, he waited.

A cluster of bushes in front of the defenses lit afire, the heat and sparks from the main fire reaching across the buffer they created. The delay with the Force Walls had not been enough. Kitable held his spell on the last word, leaving the small fires to the soldiers, knowing he could either extinguish it or defend himself. The magic swirled in his mind, needing a final command to consolidate it.

A new cascade of spell colors appeared to Kitable's enchanted sight—a fresh attack. It targeted the Molded Shield, and when it landed, if Kitable had read the auras correctly, it would destroy enough elements to kill him. Like the other spell, the new attack was defended well against destructions and could not be easily dispelled. But sure enough, the caster had not defended against alternation.

Kitable finished his spell and launched it. Instead of competing with the spell directly, the alteration wrapped the spell's targeting up, spun it around, and sent it right back at its owner.

The multicolored, flickering mass of magic disappeared through the fires, back down the hill.

Kitable cast again, holding another defense at the ready, but was satisfied by the answering silence.

Soldiers were batting at the flames near the defenses with blankets. They were losing the fight. New fires appeared, threatening the camp in the firelit night.

"*Inferrena*!"

 # Chapter 15

The shout made Kitable spin in place, the final word of his defense on his tongue, ready for activation as soon as he had a target. The word was commonly used by wizards to activate spells, but there should have been no one *behind* him able to cast spells. He expected to find the enemy casters somehow within the camp's defenses, attacking him with visual targeting.

Instead, Kitable found Celebrant Sedgan calmly standing at the head of a flock of acolytes. Every one of them, Kitable noticed dryly, had their mouths sagging open in shock.

He glanced over his shoulder. A section of the fires had gone out without so much as a snuff of smoke.

The celebrant spun to face the acolytes and shouted commands with an authority the wizard had not thought the man capable of.

"On your knees!" the celebrant cried, and the acolytes knelt immediately, as did a dozen other people who happened to be nearby. "The prayer of Inac! And I do not want you to stop until every last voice in this camp is hoarse!"

Through the smoke and ash, a chorus recited the prayer in a massive monotone.

Sedgan marched down the line, pointing a damning finger at the offending flames and repeating his earlier cry. The flames, one by one, winked out.

Tohmas edged his way to Kitable's side. On the third display of fire-snuffing powers, the prince was at Kitable's shoulder.

"It's not so amazing," Kitable said. "I made him that ring six years ago. Never could decide if a Fire Destruction spell was appropriate for a Celebrant of Inac or strangely blasphemous."

"So, it's magic," Tohmas whispered. "Good."

Kitable thought to ask if there was an alternative but decided against it. He rather feared what the prince would say.

"He does have a flair for the dramatic though," Kitable admitted. The drone of Inac's prayer gained volume with every fire Sedgan extinguished. More people joined in, and the main blaze still paced on the edge of the camp like a penned bear.

"How long can he keep this up?"

"I put over a hundred and fifty charges on that ring. Took me four days. I have no idea how many he used over the years. They're too small to be any use against the big fire."

The Prince of Galanth nodded, his lips pursed thoughtfully. "But useful here."

When the Prince of Galanth knelt and joined the prayer, bringing the rest of the onlookers with him, Kitable had to roll his eyes. Sedgan was not the only person with a flair for the dramatic. Even Prince Sol knelt into the firelight, joining the prayers like the goddess herself stood before them.

By the time Kitable decided his last defense had made the enemy rethink their approach, Shimmer Weaver had risen and joined her father in seeing to Clarin. She walked with fatigue in every step, but he was impressed that she was capable of standing so quickly after a collapse.

Dust Weaver woke a row of Esparan soldiers from their prayers. Soon, they carried Clarin away for his second visit to the healers.

At least, Kitable suddenly thought, *I hope so.* The man could be dead. It would not take much magic to kill an undefended wizard.

Perhaps seeing Kitable's curiosity, Dust targeted a Sending nearby and reported, *He seems well, except for being unconscious. A minor destruction, perhaps? A few hours of rest will see him on his feet faster than Shimmer. Good night, Master Kitable.*

Any of four minor destructions could knock a man out temporarily, and they were lucky that was all it had been. The caster must have spotted his target, taken stock of Clarin's vulnerability, and used only the smallest amount of energy needed to knock him out. The enemy was skilled at conserving their energy, that much was clear.

Taking his daughter's arm, Dust Weaver limped toward the distant waggons of Fixer City. It did not matter to them what happened next, and Kitable did not fault them. They had done their part.

After another candle, the fires had stopped sparking new flames on the camp side of the burned turf. Sedgan declared the need for a continuous prayer, assigning the soldiers and Prince Sol to maintain it. A line of soldiers watched, blankets in hand to beat back any fire that dared transgress.

At first Kitable thought the celebrant was merely trying to conserve the charges on his ring by delegating, but then the man left. He glanced

Chapter 15

back furtively as if expecting to be followed. Kitable wondered if he *should* follow to see what the man was up to, but the threat of the blaze was still his greatest concern.

Carsh joined them and reported chasing Seria away.

Kitable could not tell if they had entirely thwarted the casters or not. He was needed at the fire.

Timon was not quite asleep. Although the other Totho acolytes had extinguished the candles and bundled into their hammocks, Timon lay awake in the waggon of Wind. His father had once said that the whispers of dead spirits could be heard in the wind at night. As an acolyte of the god of the afterlife, Timon was content to lie and listen for those spirits when sleep refused to come.

It took him until after midnight—he heard the end of Ocea's prayers outside and enjoyed the deeper silence that followed—to realize he was not the only one awake. Celebrant Calanor was crouched at the center of the Temple waggon, apparently listening was well. Planted low on his heels under his long white robes and scarf, the celebrant swayed back and forth like a branch on a breeze, his eyes narrow in thought.

Abruptly, the celebrant leaped to his feet. Calanor's shout shocked Timon right out of his hammock. Timon had been an Acolyte of Wind since birth, and in all those nine years, he had never heard his celebrant speak in anything louder than a strong whisper.

"Out!" came the cry from the celebrant. "All of you! Up! Get out! The back door! Now!"

Timon was already on his feet as Calanor shouted among the hammocks, tipping them over.

"Run for Fixer City," the celebrant ordered. "Lose your robes! Hide your marks! Run, and do not return until I call for you! Go!"

By the time the celebrant was at the front of the waggon, no one was asleep, but no one had moved either. Then, with confusion plain on his face, the eldest acolyte rushed for the back. The rest scampered after him.

Timon could not move, and as he stood in the waggon baffled, he caught the stare of the man who had raised him. Overcast eyes that were only ever hidden and evasive gave him a loving look he had never seen before.

"Run, Timon," Celebrant Calanor said, and the command brought life to Timon's legs. Just as the smell of smoke reached Timon's nostrils, the Celebrant of Totho opened the front door.

Timon burst through the back at a run but had to skid to a stop behind the other acolytes. Over and around the white-clad shoulders, he saw a line people surrounding the waggon. Every second person carried a blazing torch in front of their concealed faces, forming a wall to keep the Wind-sworn boys from escaping. They seemed to hail from all walks of life—clothing and armor varied from rags to fine robes. Some were tall and proud with youth, others held themselves stooped with age. Square-shouldered men stood beside short, pudgy women. Every single one wore a cloth mask of red and the mark of Inac upon their clothes.

Despite the heat of the torches and the press of fire rising atop the waggon at his back, Timon felt as if he had fallen into an ice-covered river. He saw death in the flicking of the flames around him.

From the other side of the waggon, a second shout came from the Celebrant of Totho. "Here I am, you demons! It's me you're after!"

The masked faces turned toward the voice for only a flicker.

The acolytes scattered.

One acolyte shoulder-checked an attacker to make a path through the wall of torches. Trying to shove the boy back, the masked man struck the torch to the robes of the acolyte, quickly setting a blaze around the boy. The boy screamed in panic, his white-robed arms flailing. Timon drew back, repulsed.

To his surprise, the attackers also withdrew in unease, hastily exchanging glances like guilty children. For a moment, the other acolytes were free to flee.

Timon rushed back to the waggon, ducked underneath, and slipped out the side. He was practically under the hooves of his master's white stallion when the celebrant, trailing white robes, jumped from the stairs and onto the steed. A gathering of the masked people followed Calanor's movement, hands outstretched to seize the robes. Dodging them all, the celebrant slammed his bare heels into the sides of the horse, and with a scream of its own, the steed rushed forward. The circle of

Chapter 15

assailants surrounding the Temple waggon broke apart, unprepared to meet a charging horse. More than one person shouted directions, but for a moment, none of the masked people obeyed.

Timon ducked between two confused masked women but froze when faced with a blazing fire where, only that evening, the Temple waggon of Ocea had stood.

They had burned the entire waggon.

A man with a black mask shouted, "Catch the boy! We'll take the celebrant!"

Timon shook himself free of his shock. The screams of panic even louder than the cries of the boy who had caught fire.

He had never been a fast runner, but in his fear, he ran like a coursing hound. A prayer for speed crossed his mind, but he did not have the breath to speak it.

Leaving behind the circle of Temple waggons, where smoke and fire obscured the stars, Timon fled into the camp. He dodged between tents and other waggons then slid in the grasses and shrubs until the voices of the masked men and women fell away behind him. As he glanced behind him, his foot caught on the string of a tent and sent him tumbling.

The sight of a torch among the tents chilled Timon. The voices reached his ears once more.

Lose your robes! Hide your marks!

Hidden partially behind a tent, Timon tore off the robes he had worn all his life and kicked them away. He snatched a handful of dirt and rubbed off the mark of Totho from his forearm. It was then, with tears of terror, grief, and confusion burning his eyes, that he realized he had fallen into a campfire circle and was not alone.

A man sat by a low fire, looking tired enough to be crawling into a bedroll. He was dressed in common clothes but wore baldrics of knives across his chest and was in the process of wrapping his left hand, the bandage tinged with fresh blood.

The man's pale eyes narrowed on Timon, and for the second time that night, Timon froze.

If he ran, the stranger would easily catch him. If he did not move, the people chasing him would do the same. Either way, Timon was trapped.

Celebrant

"Oh, demon shit," the man muttered as he stood and pulled off his baldrics, then his tunic. The man slipped his tunic over Timon's head before the acolyte could decide on a course of action.

"They will suspect you," Timon said with a whimper.

The man pulled his belt off, tied the tunic down over Timon, and snorted dismissively. "I can deal with them. You can't." He slid the baldrics over his bare chest. "You just hold still and don't say anything." He dragged the acolyte to the campfire and sat him down. His free hand flung the white robes onto the fire. "Stay close to the fire, and don't worry. I'll not let them hurt you."

"Why not?" Timon whispered, but the appearance of the masked people prevented the stranger from answering.

Before the pursuers could put more than a single foot into the clearing, the stranger drew three of his blades and, to Timon's amazement, started to juggle.

Timon sat dumbfounded. At each catch, he expected the man to cut his hand. Was this the reason for the injury now bandaged?

For a moment, Timon almost forgot his peril, and in the heat of the fire, his tears dried.

One of the masked men, wearing the only red mask among black ones, stepped forward. "You!"

The stranger caught his knives and cocked his head in the direction of the intrusion. "Yah?" he called back calmly.

"You loyal to Fire?" the red-masked man demanded.

The stranger deftly drew a new weapon—a candle. He placed it on the log he had vacated.

Timon's heart dropped. The candle bore the double-flame pattern of Inac. The masks assailants also wore the mark of Inac. Now that he knew who Timon was running from, would the stranger forget the ruse and turn the acolyte over?

Timon could not move, his mind tangled. Their gods had always been allies. Totho and Inac were siblings! He tried to find a lesson where the two had come into such conflict, but none came to mind. Instead, the image of the burning waggon of Ocea filled his thoughts, and fear overwhelmed him. It was clear Inac's fury was burning hot tonight, and she meant to cremate anyone not loyal to her and her alone. The balance of the four was being torn apart. The Goddess of Fire considered justice

 # Chapter 15

and war to be her domains, but he could not see how those aspects were manifested in the raging fires that had trapped the followers of Ocea or those that had tried to burn Totho's acolytes.

"'The fire of my soul drives and sustains me,'" the stranger quoted from the holy writs, startling Timon to attention. "'By Fire, I live, and so by Fire, I would die.' What of it?" One knife gently rotated in the man's right hand as he stepped toward the masked crowd. There were a dozen people now. A line formed like the one that trapped the other acolytes. Torches blazed along the length, but the stranger did not seem concerned.

Timon remained seated by the fire, praying he would be ignored, for his legs seemed to have forgotten how to run.

"What about the boy?" the red-masked man asked. Timon cautiously lifted his gaze.

The stranger with the knives placed himself between the masked people and Timon. "That would be my kid brother, Ciene. Whatever you're looking for, you won't find it here."

There was a pause, and Timon wondered if the masked men would believe the lie. Although the stranger was armed better than the others, what could he do against so many?

Commotion interrupted. Just behind the line, a man in a green and silver tunic appeared at a run. Between the attackers, Timon saw the soldier slow then come to a hesitant stop.

"Stand aside," he commanded.

Timon's rescuer skipped atop a nearby rock to get a better look. "You idiots!" he shouted. "That's a protector! Obstruction of a protector is treason against the prince!"

Unlike Timon, the protector did not appear to be afraid of the line of people and their torches. Timon had never seen anyone look so calm when faced with danger.

"He serves the Champion," the man with the red mask shouted. "Let him pass!"

The protector waited as the gap widened. Once safe, the protector carried on at a run up the hill, where he disappeared into the largest tent Timon had ever seen.

Outside that tent, more protectors stood, weapons brandished, in a formation facing the masked people. The man in the red mask seemed to suddenly recognize the proximity of the protectors and stepped back sharply, searching for words.

The juggler spoke first. "I expect Prince Tohmas will not be pleased with you when he leaves that tent. I recommend you disappear before he does."

The men and women in black masks turned to their leader.

"Away!" he called, and the line broke up. With a narrowing of his barely-visible eyes, the masked man fixed Timon's savior with a dark glare. "We have done our duty."

They were soon gone into the shadows, and Timon was allowed to break into tears against the chest of the stranger.

Although he did not know how, Calanor knew the torchlight he saw through the latticed, star-patterned walls of Totho's Temple waggon was dangerous. Fires were coming. If the acolytes did not escape now, they never would.

He had been the last to go to sleep, having watched Totho's star light. The next time he saw the sky, the starts were hidden by the light of the torches and he was running for his life.

Lines of robed, masked men and women stared back at him, startled, when he burst through the door. Their group was still assembling, and several of them moved around the back of the waggon, trying to encircle him. Nearby, the waggon for Ocea was already surrounded and being lit afire.

He had to stop them from getting the acolytes, or Totho's work would be finished. The boys did not deserve to be caught in someone else's feud.

Although there were times when Totho's energy was that of gusts in a storm, Calanor usually tried to be more like his god's constant, easy presence. But the calm he had spent his life cultivating slipped his hold. In the light of the torches, he felt the touch of Inac's anger. He cursed them aloud.

Something cracked against the wood of the door behind him as he leaped from the stairs, trying to draw them away. Dimly, he realized the "something" had been a stone. Someone had thrown it.

 # Chapter 15

Enemies blocked his path. His robes, billowing like a cloud around him, took a dozen cuts as he wove between them before throwing himself onto his steed's back.

Stones and knives lashed out at him. There was no further doubt of their intentions.

The horse kicked, and a white-clad shape darted from under its hooves. Calanor's heart sank hard when he recognized the shape was Timon escaping from under the waggon. To Timon's fortune, the hoof hit a pursuer instead of the fleeing acolyte.

Upon the shout from his master, the horse bolted through the crowd. A stranger grabbed at the reins, but the horse dragged the masked man from his feet.

At first, Calanor was elated. The jumbled crowd of assailants scrambled, their plans upset. Behind him, the other Temple waggons burned, but now the coordinated attack was confused and scattered. Some masked people chased the horse as if expecting to catch it, while others turned and ran away themselves, as spooked as the stallion. Several more argued with each other, although Calanor could not hear why.

His elation faded when, cleared of the immediate area, Calanor attempted to slow his horse. Although the recent travel had accustomed him to riding, he had neither saddle nor bit to aid him now. He could not control the spooked stallion. Where the horse ran was where he went.

Calanor clung to the neck to keep his seat, knowing that to fall was death.

He vaguely recognized when they jumped the barricades of the Galanth camp and charged down the hill, kicking up ash and embers in their wake. Heat surrounded him like the warmth of a fireplace. *Is all the world burning tonight?*

On the horse's next jump, Calanor's grip failed.

He landed on his back and realized the knives of the masked attackers had not all caught his robes. His right leg was covered in blood, and his back ached sharply as he tried to rise.

Everything spun around him, and he wondered if he was dying. But instead of the uplifting touch of his god, the ground pulled him down. The wet places of blood went cold on his leg until he could not feel it anymore.

Celebrant

Finally, his vision cleared.

Bearded men and thick-haired women with bones and beads like jewelry looked down at him. Without a word, the Northlanders dragged him farther into their camp.

Chapter 16

Women dressed in seal pelts had tended Calanor's leg by the time he saw the morning light under the flap of the tent. Other than binding his wounds, they had tied his hands and left him. Harsh words had been exchanged between the various captors, but none of his enemies tried to speak to him directly.

At first light, a woman in cotton clothes made her way into the tent. She was small compared to the others and wore her long, blond hair in a perfect braid around her head like a basket from Polthian. Jeweled gold and silver trinkets decorated her neck and wrists, yet none of them sparkled as bright as her eyes when she met his stare.

Her eyes shone with every color of the rainbow, the light shifting like slow ripples through a pool. It was a spell Calanor had seen Master Kitable use, but he did not know its purpose.

She examined him from the doorway before finally approaching. "Nice piece," she said as she took the silver brooch from his cloak. "Master Kitable's work, I presume."

He had no reply.

"Alteration and creation woven together," she said, holding the jeweled trinket to her color-filled eyes. "You should be grateful for it. I suspect it saved your life."

The brooch had been Master Kitable's response to Prince Habal's insistence that his celebrants be protected. It would deflect anything meant to harm the wearer and explained why so few of the blades or stones hit their mark the night before.

When he still did not give her a reply, she stepped back and shouted out the entrance, calling in a new man.

He was as tall and broad as Prince Tohmas, with a long beard of grey and thick eyebrows to match. The biggest double-bladed ax Calanor had ever seen loomed on the man's back, the haft shaped like a dragon, the extended wings forming the blades. The metal was a dull black, but the detail in the carving made Calanor wonder if the smith had used a real dragon as model.

A strip of dragon scale looped over the pelts on his shoulder, but Calanor made out the rough iron pendant suspended from a hide thong around his neck.

The Northlander stood for a long moment, staring at Calanor.

Calanor met the stare placidly. He feared nothing. He needed nothing. He was spent.

The woman, looking like a child next to a giant, showed the Northlander the trinket in passing. Calanor was not surprised when the woman pocketed the item in answer to the man's shrug.

"Who are you?" the Northlander asked, shocking Calanor with his smooth Esparan.

"'I am a whisper and a spirit,'" Calanor replied. "'I am breath, but I am nothing.'"

One large eyebrow lifted. "'I am a sigh and a breeze,'" the Northlander continued the quote. "'I am the soul, and so I am everything.'"

For a moment longer, the icy eyes examined him. With a slight laugh and a shake of his head that made the tassels of his hair dance, the Northlander pulled a short bone knife. "You are a celebrant."

As the man advanced on Calanor with the knife, the Celebrant of Totho felt only disinterest. Sedgan had betrayed the balance of the four Gods. Barga was dead; Calanor had seen the burning waggon. Glorian? Calanor assumed him dead as well. The people of Espar had embraced Inac's Champion, leaving no room in their lives for the other three gods.

Totho had spared Calanor's life. What his god expected from here, Calanor did not know, but it was out of his control.

Chapter 16

"Anyone can quote writs! That does not make him a celebrant!" the woman at the entrance objected as the Northlander cut the ties on Calanor's hands.

The Northlander pulled Calanor's arm from his sleeve and turned his forearm to expose the waves of wind that had been drawn every morning since Calanor was ten. They were now a permanent stain on his skin.

"Fine, so maybe he is a celebrant," the woman demurred, "but that does not make him safe! He may still kill you!"

The large man snorted and lifted Calanor to his feet. He put away his knife and stared at the woman, his look sarcastic.

"Well, maybe not kill *you,* DoomDragon, although he may try. But he—"

"Our people," the Northlander interrupted, "believe that a slight against a celebrant is a slight against the gods. I will not have such a person mistreated in my camp."

"But—"

"Out, wizard," the Northlander commanded, and her mouth snapped closed. It opened then closed twice more, but she did not make another sound. When the Northlander put a hand on his ax, the woman left at a near-run. She shot a glare over her shoulder that was ignored.

"An empty threat," the Northlander confessed, releasing his ax shaft and turning back to Calanor. "Even if she only got the flat of my blade, she would shatter into a thousand pieces. Esparans are weak that way."

There was nothing for Calanor to do. He was deep in the Northlander camp and could not escape with an injured leg. Even if he could, there was nowhere to go. Returning to the Galanth camp was not an option, not with the mob of Inac's worshipers in power. The fortune of his god had saved him once already, but Calanor did not want to count on it for a second miracle.

"Do you have a name?" his captor inquired.

Calanor shook his head. "None I shall ever speak," he whispered.

His reply did not seem to surprise the Northlander. "Tothonar," DoomDragon decided. "To us, it means 'one who is near to Totho' which I can see is indeed the case. I am Darknim DoomDragon, and for your stay here, I am your host."

Calanor found himself speechless.

Celebrant

"You find it odd we share a religion, I imagine," the leader of the Northlanders said. "I found it strange myself when I discovered it! The four gods reach everywhere, do they not? This is the world of Ocea, Totho, Inac, and Pari. But you will find our observance of the gods different. We have no celebrants, for we have no gatherings or temples. We give our gifts to the gods in thanks when it is due, but we ask no favors of them unlike the Esparans. Still, we know they are there, watching and, we hope, being moved to sympathy by our thanks."

With a gesture, DoomDragon indicated they should leave the tent. Calanor followed the man out. His host quickly offered a sturdy arm as a crutch when Calanor limped.

"Totho is strong among my people, Tothonar. You will be very welcome among us. I fear the Esparans among my forces will not be as kind, so you would do well to keep to my company. I will have a bed made for you. When you are recovered, I would gladly have you speak with our elders. They will explain that which I fail to." He paused suddenly in thought. "I say all this without asking your own wants; I apologize. Why did you leave the Galanth camp? Do you wish to return?"

Calanor shook his head once more, both to refuse the first question and answer "no" to the second.

"Then welcome," Darknim went on. "Ask if you have need of anything. I am your humble servant."

In the dawn, Tohmas stood at the center of what had once been the circle of Temple waggons. He had not slept; almost as soon as he had cleared the body from his tent, Protector Larnin reported the fires in the Temple waggons. It had taken all of Flystead's Fyrd to keep the flames from spreading to the rest of the camp. Tohmas suspected the Weavers would have assisted, had they not been exhausted by the earlier defense of the camp. Kitable had arrived too late to save lives but aided in containing the damage.

Of the four, only the cedar walls of the waggon of Inac remained by morning. The other three Temple waggons had been reduced to piles of charred wood, fragments of cloth, and to everyone's dismay, bodies.

Chapter 16

Under the smell of wood smoke, the scent of charred flesh made Tohmas' nose wrinkle.

They began their search.

Thankfully, Celebrant Sedgan offered to hold a morning service, distracting the people and giving the worshipers something to do other than grieve for those who had died. It also kept them from paying too close attention to the prince and his soldiers as they sorted through the cinders.

Carsh hovered nearby, mostly worried about the Temple waggon of Totho. He had never considered Celebrant Barga or Celebrant Glorian valid representatives of the faith, but he recognized Celebrant Calanor. Tohmas could tell he was agitated by the idea that harm had come to a representative of a god.

So far, no living acolytes, besides those of Fire, had come forward.

Having considered the problem as Kitable rested, Tohmas was ready for the wizard's return.

"Any chance you can tell if we lost the celebrants?" Tohmas asked. Thus far, the searching had failed to identify the bodies. Knowing where the favor of the gods fell now would be helpful.

The wizard nodded miserably. It was not until the scintillating eyes looked up to him that Tohmas realized the wizard had pointedly been avoiding looking at the waggons.

Kitable turned once in a circle then pointed to the east where the waggon of Ocea had stood.

"Glorian?"

Kitable shrugged. "Unless he left his trinkets behind, which is unlikely. The celebrants wore their defenses at all times."

"Dinnae help," came Carsh's grumble, and the wizard nodded once more.

"There too." Kitable pointed to the west.

"Barga," Tohmas identified.

"No others," the wizard confirmed.

Tohmas took a deep breath to clear his thoughts, and the air tasted of smoke and burned hair. It was thicker than simple wood smoke, like a bonfire filled with plunder.

He had thought the night ended with one dead body in his tent, but dozens had died in these flames. Was DoomDragon responsible, or was he merely reaping the benefits?

He brought his thoughts to the task on hand.

"So, of the three, only Calanor may have escaped. Any idea where he may have gone?"

Kitable shook his head and stared at his feet.

"I have thirteen witnesses who claim they saw a ghost rider last night," Prime Guardian Vallant interrupted, striding in from the perimeter where he had been talking to onlookers. "Guardian Rusk's men claim a white horse rushed their fortifications just after the midnight candle. The last sighting they have is the horse heading toward DoomDragon's camp."

"A traitor?" Kitable said. He stared at the prime guardian as if the man had just claimed Rydans were friendly. "Calanor? I did not know him well, but I did not expect that!"

Tohmas caught Carsh's eye. The Rydan shook his head. Calanor had been the strongest of all the celebrants. Tohmas could not believe it either.

"Why else would he run to the Northlanders?" Vallant asked.

"To escape the fire," Tohmas replied. "If it was his sabotage, why did Sedgan not burn as well?"

Kitable's brow creased. "From a practical point of view, I happen to know the waggons of Inac are fireproofed. Maybe he tried."

"Maybe," was all Tohmas could give him. None of them believed it. Fortunately, Tohmas had another route of investigation to follow. "Sabian!"

Across the mess of charred wood, the boy cocked his head like an attentive hunting dog. He had, as he had been since Tohmas had given him permission, been hovering a dozen paces behind Carsh, but he ventured into the conversation when called. His left hand was bandaged from a minor cut during the skirmish with nine Northlanders overnight. Tohmas had already heard a truncated account of the events from Carsh. Although he had not specifically praised Sabian, Tohmas had the impression his brother had been impressed by the young Follower.

In the steamy morning, Sabian was missing his shirt and wore his baldrics over his bare chest.

 # Chapter 16

"Protector Larnin says he saw you talking to a group of people last night," Tohmas prompted.

"A dozen men and women wearing cloth over their faces," Sabian confirmed, volunteering nothing more.

While Sabian was watching Carsh to learn the knife, Tohmas never expected him to pick up the Rydan's speaking habits too. Like a proper Rydan, he answered only the question that had been asked.

"What did they want with you?" Tohmas pressed.

The boy shrugged his bare shoulders. "They asked if I was loyal to Fire."

"What did you do?"

"I quoted scripture. It worked."

"Any idea what they were after?"

"They were chasing a boy in white."

Opposite them, Vallant's eyebrows rose to hide under his helmet's brim.

"Did they catch him?" Tohmas inquired.

Sabian shook his head.

"Any chance we can find him?"

"I doubt very much any acolyte of Wind wants to be found right now," Sabian answered.

For a secsond time, Tohmas fell into thoughtful silence.

What now?

If they were to come across bad weather, and he had no Celebrant of Totho to provide suitable sacraments, what would the Esparans do? If the animals grew ill, and no Celebrant of Pari was available to fight it, would his soldiers think the forces cursed? Even if they held little purpose in day-to-day life for the Esparans, the celebrants were the voices of the gods when favors were needed. To be without would destroy morale. Who would believe he was fighting with the gods' favor now?

Prince Rairn had been without celebrants for years, a fact that was blamed for his sparsity of soldiers and the loss of his princedom. Prince Sol had lost his celebrants early in the war—two to desertion, one dead in battle, and one dead over the winter from a lung disease. Shortly after that winter, the war with the Northlanders turned against the Esparans.

People said the gods had abandoned the Esparans. They were counting on Tohmas to bring it back.

Celebrant

"Can we identify the masked people?" Vallant asked into the silence.

"By all accounts, there were a great number of them," Tohmas refused.

The prime guardian rubbed the back of his neck, making a face. "Ringleaders then? If you think this is a crime, we need to deal with the guilty people."

Tohmas lowered his voice. "If I do that, we lose the last divine favor we have. If I call this anything except the will of Inac, we lose this war."

Everyone fell silent. Whether this had or had not been Inac's doing, Tohmas had to pretend it was.

He assumed she would approve. She was also the Goddess of Victory. Faltering now meant losing.

"The will of Inac it is," said Kitable, and Carsh nodded. Tohmas ran his hand over his face.

"I will speak to the celebrant when he finishes his service," Tohmas promised. "Other than that, this was the will of the Goddess. The temples of Pari, Ocea, and Totho were corrupt and required purging. The Champion of Inac acts in the Goddess' name. That is all we need."

The group dispersed, leaving only Kitable and Carsh in the debris with Tohmas. Tohmas stood at attention, his eyes on the gathering nearby and the service Celebrant Sedgan directed.

"You have never called yourself Champion before," Kitable said quietly once the others had left. "Do you believe it too?" He eyed where Celebrant Sedgan led the people in another prayer and lit a symbolic piece of the wreckage. Instead of smoldering and turning to ash, the wood burst into brilliant white fire and was quickly consumed. Kitable sneered at the "miracle."

Tohmas thought for a long moment before answering. When he had first heard the title, he had disliked it. After a while, it became a tool—something to influence those who believed in the benevolence of gods more than he did. Now, he needed the title to keep the forces believing victory was possible.

Did Inac approve of the war? What about the next one Tohmas was already planning?

"I think I have to," Tohmas replied. Victory was the only choice he gave himself, whatever the cost. The Goddess knew that.

 # Chapter 16

In the uselessly large hall, far in the north where the weather was already chilling despite the late summer days, Darknim DoomDragon calmly took his place before his patron. To his right, dressed in ornate robes to show off his influence, Master Terant leaned on a staff. Although he had been protected during his confrontation with Kitable, Master Terant had lost the hair from one side of his head. No amount of trinkets could undo that damage.

"You failed me," Prince Marfaie boomed from his pelt-covered throne.

Darknim did not reply, unsure who the prince was addressing for a moment. Besides, the DoomDragon was not one for whimpering justifications.

"You assured me this attack would be the last we would hear of Prince Tohmas in Solta. I should be locking Prince Sol in his prison cell, but instead, I find myself without anything to show for the great effort exerted tonight. Why?"

Darknim stared ahead at the glittering prince, not bothering to speak. He knew where fault lay.

Finally, Prince Marfaie turned his gaze onto Master Terant directly. "Master Kitable lives. Was he not meant to fall? Did you not claim tonight would be his last?"

Unlike Darknim, who weathered the tempest of his patron, Master Terant bristled when confronted directly.

"We lost our anchor," he admitted. "An untouchable was present. And Kitable called for others from among their ranks. None of us expected these entertainers to fight the fire."

"So, Kitable was not enervated as you had hoped when you attacked from a distance."

"The fires were meant to wear him down." Master Terant turned an accusing stare to Darknim.

"The fires did the best they could," Darknim replied. "We were close, but not close enough. Even the assassin was detected prematurely."

"If your Circle had been available, I would not have been needed for the illusion to hide the flames in the first place!"

Prince Marfaie watched on without interrupting as if their discussion would decide who to blame. The fact spoke for themselves.

"Our Circle was broken," Darknim replied. "With Elder Tril's loss of his Aspect, there is no Linking. Their powers are divided and will remain so until a new Aspect is found."

Terant's glower deepened. "How long will that take? What good are casters who rely on spirits to strength them if the spirits cannot be summoned when required?"

Darknim shrugged heavily. "I do not know how long it will take. It has never been done before."

Terant scoffed openly. "Then we should consider them lost. Perhaps we ought to bring in other powers."

"I expect Elder Tril to succeed. It has been hundreds of years since the last Circle of the Raven was formed. This sort of constellation of powers does not happen lightly." Darknim paused in consideration. "Besides, if he fails or dies, the title of DoomDragon is void, and I lose sway over the tribes. We should all be hoping he succeeds"

Terant's expression went from disrespect to sudden shock as the scope of the problem settled in. Prince Marfaie's forces were not numerous enough to hold ground against the rest of the Esparans without Darknim's Northlanders. Marfaie's gambit would fail.

The prince's tattooed face remained impassive.

"How can we help his chances?" Terant asked, his voice choked.

Darknim shrugged again. "No elder has ever lost their Aspect as Tril has, but he is a young elder and has great strength. He has traveled north in search and will return once he finds a new spirit." He waited a dozen heartbeats, but the other two men had nothing to add. "If that matter is closed, I have additional information to share."

Without the Linking to give him the ice pool for powerful Scrys, Darknim had fallen back upon simple techniques—spies. He knew of *all* the fires that had burned that fated night.

He detailed the events at Prince Tohmas' Temple waggons but left Tothonar out of the account.

Prince Marfaie pensively leaned back in his throne. The silver-layered robes clinked loudly.

"What use is religion in this? We are fighting a war."

"The loss of the celebrants will hurt the cohesion of the forces," Darknim pointed out. "He builds his reputation as Inac's Champion.

 # Chapter 16

People are draw to that. But there is a reason we have four gods. One cannot stand alone."

The prince harrumphed.

"We will continue on, my Prince," Darknim said, bowing his head to the man on the throne, "if that is your desire."

"Eager to kill, DoomDragon?" Prince Marfaie asked.

"Eager to finish the task assigned to me."

Silence lingered between them like chastisement from a disgruntled parent. Darknim took comfort in the pause. Too often, his world was filled with wind, people, and weapons. Silence was a rarity to be treasured.

But Terant fidgeted beside him, feeling the impact of the empty air.

"So be it," Prince Marfaie said at length. "Before winter."

"If I do not manage to take Sol before the snows fall, the winter will weaken them for us."

"So long as they call for the others," Prince Marfaie reminded him, "it does not matter to me how you do it."

Good enough., Darknim thought. It would be difficult to root them out now that they were firmly entrenched atop the hill, but they had a few mooncycles to try. It was a tricky balancing act to maintain—bleeding without killing all.

But they had time.

In the days that followed, the two camps settled into their positions, both protected with walls and barricades manned by rotating soldiers. Although Tohmas was eager, he awaited an opportunity and would continue to do so until it manifested. The days had abruptly cooled upon the approach of the end of the Fourth Mooncycle. Autumn was not far.

Prince Sol made himself useful by coordinating the construction of pulleys and ropes to the water at the base of the cliffs. Carsh and Tohmas set the defenses at that approach as well, having the soldiers layer animal fat over the rocks at the egresses near the waterlines to make them even more treacherous. Construction of a boat was underway with the hope of being able to add fresh fish to their meals. It would never be enough to feed the entire forces, but every bit helped. With the access to the lake and river secured, provisions could be brought in.

Until the water freezes, Tohmas reminded himself. But until then, even if they could not reach Narsol by water, the enemy could not surround the entire lake. There were plenty of places to use as landings if need arose.

Unlike Sol, who had made himself useful, Rairn did nothing of note. Carsh asked about throwing the man in the lake, but Tohmas refused. It could not be done that way.

It was official now; they were trapped. But, as he told Rairn before, Tohmas would never corner himself unless he expected something to change. He had to make that change happen, and the timing was finally right.

There was one way off the hill—through DoomDragon. For that, it was time to bring in support. His Rydan allies would be keen to join this war. They simply needed to arrive before DoomDragon's forces broke through the Esparans' defenses.

But when might that be? In BellRoost, Tohmas had asked Sol a simple question. *Why has DoomDragon not yet won this war?* Despite a halfcycle of chasing and being chased by his enemy, Tohmas did not have the answer to that question. By what he had seen, DoomDragon *should* have overrun Sol's lands long before Tohmas' arrival. It felt like he was sparring with covered blades when he could have dug the dagger into his enemy's back long ago. The Northlander's forces were better than the Esparans in many ways, including numbers.

He was missing something. If he did not figure it out, he would suffer Sol's fate—defeat. How could he fulfill his purpose among the Esparan? He could not return to the Outlands defeated; his father would have every right to kill him. Rydans were not forgiving of weakness.

Victory was the only way.

That, or death.

THE END.

Sneak Peek of Northlander

Chapter 1

Atop the lake cliffs, the spectators lined the waggons and supply trunks. The crowd of observers, mostly Tohmas' trained protectors, seemed to get bigger every morning in the restricted space atop the hill. Since setting up the camp over the lake, it had been a long cycle of exchanging skirmishes with Northlanders, and the trapped men and women were glad for anything that would distract them. The occasional battle was interspersed with waiting, which favored the Northlanders and their access to outside resources. With the summer mooncycles ending, autumn loomed, threatening cooling weather and scarcer supplies.

Carsh, Tohmas' prime protector, sparred Rydan-style with his young tagalong, Sabian. Although Esparan, Sabian had taken to Carsh's weapons and style smoothly although he was no match for the Rydan Knife Dancer. But, knives bare, Sabian did his best. He was getting better steadily, Tohmas had to admit.

It was a miracle Carsh allowed the Esparan eighteen-year-old to shadow him in the first place. It took great skill and strength to win over a Rydan's prejudice.

Tohmas sat apart on a barrel, leaning against an entrenched shop waggon, wishing he could be in Sabian's place and exercise his bored muscles. Instead, all he could do was flip a Lourite coin over his fingers, working the dexterity of his scarred left hand. But he was a Prince of Espar, even if his heart remained Rydan, and he had other duties this day. He would have to take Carsh aside later for a proper match if he was to get a good challenge.

After, Tohmas reminded himself.

Once the spar was in full swing, Tohmas lowered his feet. "Protector Sanba, with me," he called.

The protector fell into step beside him, his tabard catching the wind. It had become stained by mud and blood, making it a mottled brown instead of green.

Tohmas moved away from the crowd to a place overlooking the cliff and the lake. Sanba joined him as Carsh kept the attention of the crowd off Tohmas by adding a flipping knife to his display. Sabian copied him, impressing the onlookers.

The other protectors followed him at a distance respectfully. Over the last year, Tohmas had come to know the protectors well, and they knew him equally well. So long as he stayed close, they were happy.

Sanba stood at his side, his blue eyes—an uncommonly bright shade like Tohmas'—scanned the lake then the cliffs. His stare lingered on the traps they had set along the sharp cliffs below to deter Northlander approach from the water. His posture tense, Sanba was ready to act should danger appear.

His steady resolve was one of the reasons Tohmas had picked him.

The wind picked up in the dawn and favored Tohmas with a gust down the slopes. The crash of the water against the cliff and the soft chirp of irate swallows kept his words from being overhead outside of the immediate company. Farther to the right, a group of soldiers worked the nearby winch and drew water for the camp.

"You went to the Outlands once before, Protector," Tohmas prompted the protector at his side. "You delivered a greeting to the south border of Polthian."

"Yeh," Sanba replied, his voice as curt as his nod and accented with Rydan slang, something the man must have picked up from Carsh, there being no other Rydans in the camp.

Tohmas smiled, feeling vindicated in his choice of protectors to approach with his request.

"I need you to do it again."

The older man narrowed his eyes, drawing his large eyebrows low enough to unite them over the bridge of his nose. He peered south

Chapter 1

across the lake to where another river began. The river there was treacherous and unpassable by boats. Still, it led toward the Outlands.

"Bit of a distance from here," the protector mused. "Three quarter-cycles? Maybe a full mooncycle to get there. Then I'd have to get back. Course you seem to be settling in, so maybe you'll still be here."

Tohmas followed the protector's gaze over the water and let his mind drift down the river to Solta's capital. From there, it was four princedoms to cross, including a rocky hillscape and a marsh. Most of it was forested. The fastest route would require navigation off the meandering roads.

"I can have you there tomorrow," Tohmas replied.

Sanba turned to him, a crooked smile cracking his dour expression. "Master Kitable, eh? I suppose that's why you princes spend so much damn money on keeping wizards around."

"He can get you down there, but he can't get you back. If the Rydans catch any scent of magic, they will kill you outright. So, no magic items, no enchantments, and no spells."

The older protector nodded in acceptance. "Take a message? Then come back?"

Tohmas envisioned the distant plains of the Outlands, seeing the tall grasses in enough detail to feel them swishing across his calves in memory. He could practically taste the moist earth as the rain peppered down on his stalking position and hear the wren warbling a warning. In his mind's eye, the land was still within his reach.

But the lands of his upbringing were not for him. He was needed here, as was Carsh. He had to send another. It was best they never know how much he longed for it.

"A message, yes. Pay close attention because mistakes get you killed," Tohmas warned.

It did not seem to faze the protector.

"When do I start?"

"Now," Tohmas replied, looking past the man. Lance Carraway, lacking his usual Gaidolon blue tabard, met his stare. "You need to be gone within the candle. It's going to get noisy later."

The protector frowned. "I'm going to miss out, eh?"

A cry went up from the crowd. At the cliff's edge, Sabian had launched himself at Carsh and stumbled. Thankfully, Carsh caught

261

Celebrant

Sabian's belt and held him, his feet still on land but his body out beyond the edge of the cliff.

A hush fell over the crowd. Lance nodded to Tohmas. Without looking back, the high guardsman vanished back among the waggons.

Carsh heaved Sabian back and tossed the boy onto the stones atop the cliffs. For a long moment, Sabian stared back the way he had fallen, no doubt reliving the long look down the rocks to the cold waters far below. All anger was gone from his expression, replace by white-faced fear.

The Rydan sheathed one knife and stood over his Follower. He extended a hand to help him up.

The lesson was complete.

Do not attack in anger. He could not rush in against DoomDragon. He was outnumbered and, for now, cornered. Fall was fast approaching. It was not time to be rash and end up dangling off the cliff.

"Pack a bag. There will be a lot of walking," he told Sanba.

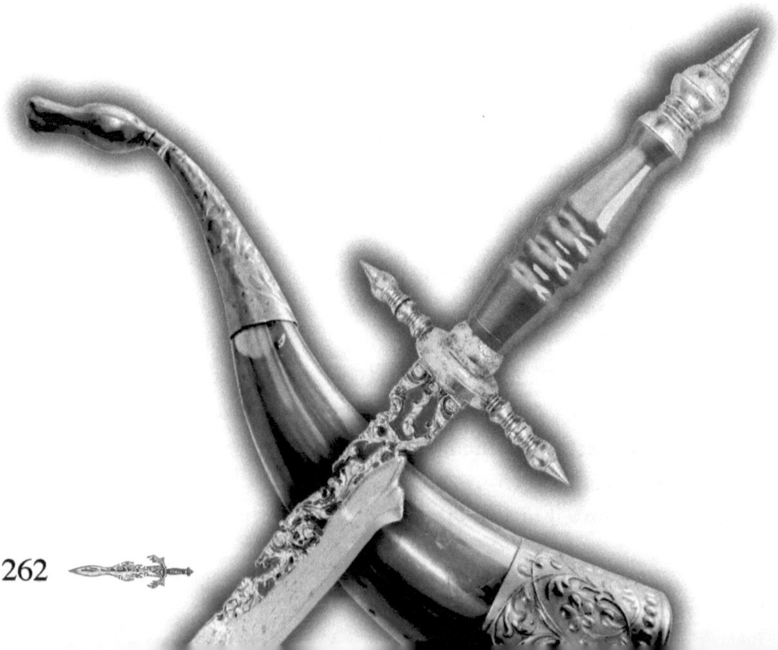

Glossary

Barlaby: Far north princedom of Espar. Overrun by Northlander
    CURRENT PRINCE: Prince Lorian Rairn.
    COLORS: White and White.
    CREST: None

Calendar: Universal calendar pre-dates the Demon Wars. Roughly based on the moon's phases:
    YEAR: Eight mooncycles of forty days, and one mooncycle (the ninth) of a variable length, thirty-five or thirty-six days.
    MOONCYCLE: forty days.
    HALFCYCLE: twenty days.
    QUARTERCYCLE: ten days.

Celebrant: Esparan priest, traditionally assigned to a single deity of the four. Overseeing a group of Acolytes.

Clandac: Central Esparan princedom.
    CURRENT PRINCE: Prince Dragal Galanth. Eldest son of Zayban.
    COLORS: Blue with Gold.
    CREST: Scythe

Companion (Black rank rope): Esparan Companions are not soldiers by profession. They become soldiers when they are required, but have other occupations.

Currency (Esparan)
    LEG: Wedge-shaped copper coin with a hole in it for threading on a string.
    TABLE: Eight legs strung together.
    SLIVER: Wedge-shaped silver coin with a hole in it for threading on a string.
    SLICE: Eight slivers strung together.
    SPOKE: Wedge-shaped gold coin with a hole in it for threading on a string.
    WHEEL: Eight spokes strung together.

Damoria: South west princedom of Espar, corner of DragonTail mountains and Outlands. Enemy of Galanth.
    CURRENT PRINCE: Prince Wevan Damoria.
    COLORS: Red with Yellow.
    CREST: Dragon

Espar: The overall region north of DragonTail mountains.

Esparan (race): People of Espar. Pale skinned and featured peoples. Religion of four elemental gods.

Forsinth: Princedom of Espar, known for pottery and claywork. Close ally to sons of Zayban
    CURRENT PRINCE: Prince Deiton Darvin-Galanth. (Widower of Elinea Galanth)
    COLORS: Brown with Silver.
    CREST: wine pitcher

Galanth: Southern Esparan princedom on borders with Outlands.
    CURRENT PRINCE: Prince Tohmas Galanth. (Son to Habal Galanth)
    COLORS: Green with Silver.
    CREST: Tree

GLOSSARY

Gaidol: Princedom of Espar with prolific trading routes. Borders contentiously with Trulin. Close ally to Nothor.
   CURRENT PRINCE: Prince Dorakon Lodaton
   COLORS: White with blue.
   CREST: Shark

Guardians (Red rank rope): Each Esparan city had a single Guardian named by the Prince. A Guardian may or may not have a Prime status, depending on the size of the city.

Inac: Esparan fire god. Female. Also known as the Bitch Goddess, Dame Justice, Lady of Lust, Warrior Queen.

Knock: An Esparan gesture of agreement. Originally from a time of blood-bonds, where the two people would press their fists together and cut across the two hands to bind their words and spirits. More recently, no cut is used, just the knock of fists.

Lour: Western princedom of Espar along the Crescent and DragonTail mountains. Deep iron mines. Finest metalsmiths in Espar
   CURRENT PRINCE: Prince Loritat Naygan.
   COLORS: Gold with Grey.
   CREST: Anvil

Meloch: Far north princedom of Espar, currently overrun by Northlanders
   CURRENT PRINCE: Prince Garit Carnilan. Deceased.
   COLORS: Black with Red.
   CREST: Raven

Northlander (race): Race of the far north; a hardy people organized into clans but united by a Circle of the Raven, which comprises of magic-users. When the circle is complete (7 members), they name a DoomDragon (all clan leader).

Celebrant

Nothor: Eastern coastal Esparan Princedom. Known for shipping and mechanical innovation. Close ally to Gaidol.
  Current prince: Prince Neillen Lodaton.
  Colors: Green with Gold
  Crest: Ship

Ocea: Esparan water god. Female. Also known as the Maiden, The Benevolent Mother, the Weeping Goddess.

Polthian: Esparan Princedom on southern border, close to Outlands.
  Current prince: Prince Emacen Polthian.
  Colors: Blue with red.
  Crest: Eagle

Pari: Esparan earth god. Male. Also known as the Mountain King, The Beast Lord, The Traveler, Healing Presence.

Prime (single strand of silver in a rank rope): A distinguishing rank above the main associated one in Esparan ranking. For example, a Prime Protector would be one step above a protector and command them.

Protectors (Green rank rope): Bodyguards of a Prince of Espar. Commanded by a prime protector.

Rabarch: Esparan Princedom.
  Current prince: Prince Barnon Galanth (youngest son of Zayban Galanth)
  Colors: white with red
  Crest: Dragon head

Rydan (race): Tribal people of the south Outlands, consisting of three clans (First, Second, Third), each ruled by a Chief. Primarily raiders and nomads, with a strong emphasis on horsemanship. Rydan horses are powerful warhorses, bound to a given master for life.

Glossary

Solta: Central princedom of Espar, currently under siege by Northlanders.
    CURRENT PRINCE: Prince Sol Galanth (Second youngest son of Zayban)
    COLORS: Red with back
    CREST: Shield

Tanble: Northern Princedom of Espar, currently overrun by Northlanders.
    CURRENT PRINCE: Prince Vornan Marfaie (believed deceased)
    COLORS: Black with grey.
    CREST: Sword

Totho: Esparan wind god. Male. Also known as the Tempest, The Gust, North Star.

Trulin: North East Espar Princedom. Breeders of powerful warhorses.
    CURRENT PRINCE: Prince Kelland Trulin.
    COLORS: White and Brown.
    CREST: Horse

Wardens (Blue rank rope): Under the Guardians, these are permanent Esparan soldiers who guard the city and maintain the peace. The number of Wardens answering to a Guardian depends on the size of the city. If a call comes from the Prince, the Wardens become responsible for a company of ~20 companions.

Wisavi: A wise-man and advisor to a Rydan Chief.

Author Bio

At a young age, Deborah's rampant imagination kept her up, lending great detail to all the terrible things lurking in the night. In desperation, her mother suggested she invent her own stories to distract her brain. She has been doing that since, channeling her ideas into sword and sorcery-style fantasy novels and shorts.

In her other life, Deborah is a veterinarian. She lives in Sooke, BC, Canada with her husband of 13+ years, their two sons, and three demanding felines.

WWW.DLAMBERTAUTHOR.COM

INSTAGRAM: @dlambertauthor
TWITTER/X: @dlambertauthor
FACEBOOK.COM/DLAMBERT42

Book Club Questions

1. What is the main theme of this book? How does it play out?

2. Which character do you most relate to? Why?

3. Who are you rooting for: Tohmas or Doomdragon? Why?

4. Which character changes the most over the story? For better or worse?

5. Shimmer is quickly infatuated with Master Kitable, though the affection is not reciprocated. How does Kitable handle it? What impact might this have on Shimmer?

6. Contrast Loni and Sedgan; how are they similar? How do they differ? Who would you put more faith in?

7. How did you feel when fires lit up the Temple waggons?

8. Magic takes a toll in this story, causing everything from pain to death. Does the ratio of power to consequence seem balanced? Why or why not?

 ## Celebrant

9. Have you come across stories with magical antithesis like the Untouchables here? Discuss which and how they differ.

10. Are you happy with Calanor's lot? Does he deserve what happens?

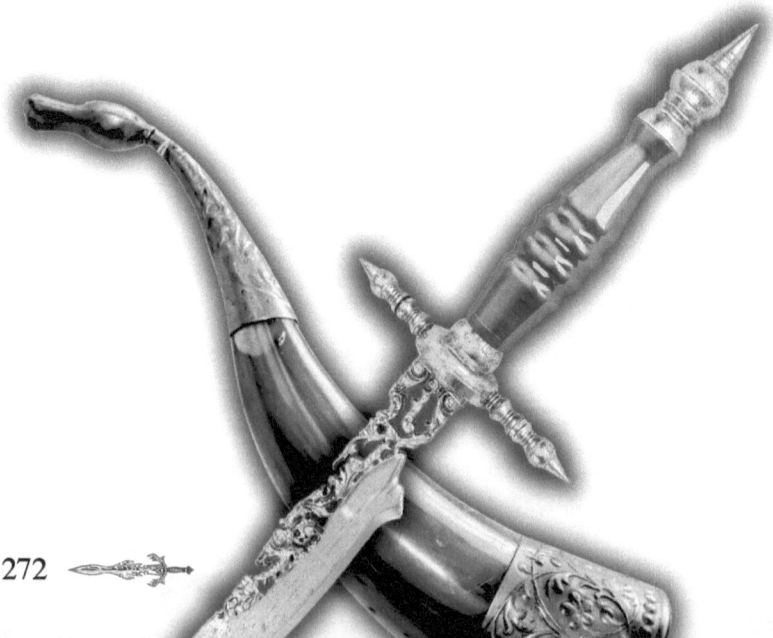

Discover more at
4HorsemenPublications.com

10% off using HORSEMEN10

www.ingramcontent.com/pod-product-compliance
Lightning Source LLC
LaVergne TN
LVHW041623060526
838200LV00040B/1412